Wind Riders

White Ghost

R. P. Wollbaum

ISBN: 978-1-989210-10-9 Ebook
ISBN: 978-1-989210-11-6 Book

Chapter One

Chapter Two
Chapter Three
Chapter Four
Chapter Five
Chapter Six
Chapter Seven
Chapter Eight
Chapter Nine
Chapter Ten
Chapter Eleven
Chapter Twelve
Chapter Thirteen
Chapter Fourteen
Chapter Fifteen
Chapter Sixteen
Chapter Seventeen
Chapter Eighteen
Chapter Nineteen
Chapter Twenty
Chapter Twenty-One
Chapter Twenty-Two

Guinevere,
Welsh, meaning, White Fay/Ghost

Chapter One

Gwen opened her eyes, stretched her arms over her head and, after a few moments, decided to get out of bed. If she didn't, her mom, or even worse, her dad, would come barging in all bubbly and cheerful and roust her.

While large for this vessel, her stateroom was, to her, small. Her closet at home was bigger than the room and bathroom combined. To make matters worse, her room was part of a small suite. Her parents had the adjoining stateroom.

Because next year she would have to spend a month of her two-month summer break on cadet field training, her parents had decided to pull her out of school a month early to go on a trip. She didn't know why she had to be a cadet – not only next summer, but during the school year. She was sure her parents could have gotten her out of it. But all the other kids in her peer group were in the program, so it might not be all that bad. Boring, but not bad. Lots of lining up and marching, followed by more lining up and doing exercises called PT by the instructors. Then more lining up and being sent home.

The good thing was, she didn't have to go to school Friday afternoons. The bad thing was, on the last Friday afternoon of the month she had to don her PT gear and, along with everyone else, regular army, reserve army and cadets, run. The cadets only had to run three kilometres, but it was hard on her nails and hairstyle.

Unlike her peers, all of whom attended private schools, she went to the public school. Her parents insisted she go to the school that all the normal kids went to. Which was not so bad, actually. Most of them were good people. In fact, there were a few kids like her, whose parents were wealthy and well-connected, yet insisted their children attend public schools. Most of those were her parents' friends.

Like her, almost all of the girls and a few of the boys could not see the point of being cadets, or of joining the army for five years after they turned eighteen. Gwen had decided that after basic training she would apply to be a hair stylist or office worker. Being a frontline soldier or supply technician held little appeal. Being stuck on some other god-forsaken backwoods planet for months on end held even less appeal.

But those were the rules and she, like everyone else, had no choice, especially if she wanted to keep all the perks her parents had. She well knew she would have to leave their planetary system if she violated the rules – and quite a few other planetary systems had rules just as onerous. And if that happened, she could not inherit any of her father's estates and only a small, minor one of her mother's on the planet Oaken. So, she would do the least required and get out of the army as fast as she could.

She didn't know why her parents bothered. They were no longer active in the army and were mostly figureheads. Occasionally, they would put on fancy dress uniforms and attend some parade, graduation ceremony or grand battalion ball. Sometimes they performed ceremonial duties as the official heads of state of their planetary system. They had no real power; that was all handled by elected officials. However, the populace not only respected her parents but seemed to love them.

She didn't know all that much about the army, but she knew the badges her parents wore on their uniforms indicated they were not of a high rank. They had some qualification badges she did not understand. Once in a while, they would put on black berets and her father would wear a Wind Riders patch on one shoulder and her mother a Zebra patch. Gwen knew that being a Wind Rider was special, and being a Zebra even more so. But she thought that was mostly because they were the honorary commanders of those units.

Like her aristocratic mother and father would actually serve time in either of those regiments! It was ludicrous to even think about it.

Their first trip had been a one-day affair in their high-speed yacht to Mountainview. This was the small planet in the centre of the Federation, which her father had been given to rule twenty-five years earlier. It was too small for anyone else to want it anyway. Mountainview was where the headquarters of her father's armies was located. It also served as the main supply depot, where all of the army's weapons, ammunition, vehicle upgrades and cyber divisions were stored.

Every recruit was sent to Mountainview for basic and advanced infantry training, and sometimes other specialty training modules. Only after that training was completed would recruits be sent for officer training, if they qualified. Then it was on to the branch of service they would be placed in, followed by one of the four divisions and finally, battalion, company, platoon and team assignments.

It was enough to make a girl's head spin, and Gwen vowed to do as little as possible for the shortest time possible and get out of the army at the first opportunity.

As a cadet, she was now allowed to stand beside her parents at the parade given at the annual recruit graduation ceremony. It was the first time she had ever worn the full-dress uniform. Pinned to the sash across her chest from left shoulder to right hip was her badge of office. She had a single private stripe on her shoulder, that of a cadet. Her parents were sporting a huge array of what they called *I-was-there* ribbons on one side of the upper chest, with another impressive row of award ribbons on the other. Both also sported five gold slash markings on one sleeve. Each slash denoted five years of service. They had a crossed rifle patch on the lower left sleeve with a maple leaf above it as well as three chevrons with the maple leaf on top that denoted Master Sergeant status. In addition, they each had a single gold maple leaf on their epaulettes that meant they were further classified as Master Warrant Officers.

Gwen's two parents had pilot wings. Her father's uniform sported a seldom-seen parachute patch with a red maple leaf in the centre, which meant he was a Pathfinder. They were the guys sent in before the other parachutists dropped, who, in turn, went in before the regular army.

She noticed her parents' uniforms were subtly different from those of the other Army units. Their epaulets were chain mail, not cloth. They had a black stripe running down the outside seam of their trouser legs. Only Wind Riders had those uniforms and wore the black berets.

Seeing all her parents' achievement decorations, including several wound decorations, Gwen suddenly came to the realization that perhaps her parents, at least in the past, had been a little more than just figureheads.

She was required to accompany her parents as they inspected the honour guard. Gwen followed their lead, stopping to speak with a few of the soldiers. To her shock, they called her Ma'am and, while the answers they gave to her minor questions were abrupt in the military manner and she could see their heads and stance go even higher and more rigid if possible, a few were struggling to keep their faces neutral.

She wondered why. She was just a 15-year-old kid with private stripes, cadet ones at that – and a girl.

Then the speeches and awards were handed out. Finally the parade, and then the overwhelmingly loud cheering as the recruits were dismissed for the last time. She was hustled off with her parents to a reception with the senior training officers and their spouses.

If her father weren't introducing her to some general or colonel, her mother was. Even these high-ranking people called her Ma'am, but, unlike the honour guard, beamed their pleasure at meeting her with large smiles and warm greetings.

Then to her embarrassment, came Aunty Megan, a Wind Rider major. Megan first held her at arm's length, taking in her uniform, then pulled her close and hugged her. That brought on the flood gates, as other high ranking Wind Riders came forward doing the same. Some she knew well; they were her parents' close friends. All were rich landowners and Gwen had assumed they were mere functionaries. Now, looking at their uniforms, she realized they were anything but.

Unlike the other high-ranking officers, they called her *squirt* or *kid* in the odd sounding Standard dialect they spoke among themselves. Barb had a tear in her eye as she hugged her; why, Gwen did not know, nor why she always did when they met. Nor did she understand why her father went to her right away after, as always.

Grownups, Gwen thought. *Always weird, grownups.*

They were driven to a large auditorium converted to a ballroom. She was seated in the centre of the head table alongside her parents and the heads of all the army divisions and their spouses. It was a full army dress ball. All the officers on the planet, from newly graduated second lieutenants to field marshals, were in attendance. Gwen noticed several of the officers wore Warrant Officer markings.

Following diner and speeches, the band started to play. After her parents began to dance, Gwen was approached by a young second lieutenant and she took the floor with him. She had been briefed on this. He was the top graduate of the year and had been chosen to dance the first dance with her. Gwen had been told it was a big honour for him and, as her mother had put it, "Don't screw it up!"

She mimicked what she had seen on the vids of high society affairs, holding her hand up daintily while he gingerly took it and escorted her to the dance floor. Then she held her head high and placed her hand gently on his shoulder as they began the formal waltz.

He stumbled slightly at one point and almost stepped on her foot. He apologized profusely.

"Shush," Gwen stage-whispered at him as she did the same thing, then she giggled. "You're making me screw this up. Mom is going to shoot me. This fancy stuff is hard, you know."

The lieutenant chuckled.

"Damn Master Warrant had me practicing this shit for a week," he said. "He'll probably kick my butt all the way back to barracks for this."

They both chuckled and, the ice now broken, relaxed, and tried to enjoy it.

"Girls have it easier, you know," Gwen said. "Well at least at normal ballroom stuff anyway. We just follow your lead and the long dresses don't show our knees trembling and our feet stomping on the guy's toes."

After the obligatory three dances were over, the lieutenant escorted her back to her table and she made an exaggerated curtsy to him and, with a twinkle in her eye, said, "Thank you, kind sir, for the gallant dance."

He gave her an equally exaggerated bow. "The pleasure was all mine, Ma'am," he said. Then Gwen stuck her tongue out at him and they both laughed. He hustled off to be harassed by his buddies.

"All right, daughter," her mother said. "You didn't totally embarrass us out there. Off you go then, enough fun for one night."

The next day she was flown to her grandmother's estates. As at home, there she had her own suite with bathroom and sitting room. She hadn't visited for a number of years and she was spoiled, not only by her grandmother but all the staff. She was used to the spoiling.

She went on long rides around the estate with her grandmother on one of her purebred horses. These were always fun times.

Her mother arrived a few days later and the three of them went riding together. Her mom was more relaxed than usual.

Then her father arrived and things, for Gwen, went downhill rapidly. At heart, her dad was a commoner and liked to act that way whenever he could get away with it. That her mother and grandmother not only went along but actually enjoyed it she could never understand.

The four of them drove over to her mother's estate, adjacent to her grandmother's. They saddled up four of her father's uncivilized large brute horses, placed packs on two other of the beasts and headed off into the wilds. Alone, with no staff at all!

The saddles, like the horses, were large and cumbersome. Not at all like the dainty saddles with the short stirrups she was used to. These stirrups were large and wooden. Everyone, including Gwen, was dressed in durable denim pants and shirts, not her usual riding attire. They wore hiking boots and ball caps – not high topped leather riding boots and helmets.

The halters were left on under the bridles and a long soft rope attached to the halters, which her mother showed her how to wrap around what she called a horn and the high cantle on the front of the saddle. A long oilskin jacket was rolled and tied behind the rear high cantle and an insulated denim jacket tied to the front.

There was, in addition to the main cinch holding the saddle to the horse, a rear cinch and a broad chest strap, but no strap running to the bridle to keep the horse's head down. The reins were very long, touching the ground, and untied.

Gwen rose to the saddle and, like normal, pulled the reins tight. The undisciplined horse immediately began to back up! Then got upset! Her father ran up and pulled the reins loose to drape alongside the horse's neck, while her mother and grandmother laughed.

"Keep a loose rein, kid," her father said. "Or you'll end up with your ass on the ground."

He mounted his animal, took the halter shank of one pack horse, her mother the other and, at the trot, they left the yard.

After a half hour, they stopped. The three elders dismounted and checked cinches and packs on the pack horses. Her mother looked at her and raised her eyebrows.

"Your saddle comes loose," she said. "We ain't stopping for you to fix it."

Her mother had reverted to her father's Standard dialect.

Gwen looked around for something to help her dismount.

"Oh, for God's sake, Marlene," her grandmother said in French. "Does she not even know how to dismount on her own?"

"That does appear to be the case, Mags," her father said in the same language, shocking Gwen some more. She didn't know her father spoke Parisian.

The three of them just stood there looking at her. Frustrated, Gwen flung herself off the horse and checked, then tightened, the loose cinch. To prove them wrong, she placed her left foot in the stirrup and after a couple of hops and a stretch, she forced her right foot over the rear cantle. As she sought out the right stirrup with her toe, the horse began to walk.

While she had been struggling to do that, the other three had mounted and began moving down the so-called trail. They walked for ten minutes and trotted for ten minutes. This went on for hours. Gwen's thighs and legs were screaming in pain when they finally stopped for the day.

Her mother and father first took the packs off the pack horses, then removed saddles from their own horses and began grooming the riding animals. Her grandmother finished first and started grooming one of the pack animals.

Her mother dug into one of Gwen's saddlebags and tossed a brush at her.

"Horse first, kid," she said. "Then us."

Gwen had not even dismounted yet.

With some struggling, and by mimicking the others, Gwen removed the saddle and blanket, then the bit and bridle, leaving the halter on and letting the shank drop to the ground. She began to brush down the animal, who, of course, tried to walk over to some better grass. Now she knew why her father had stepped on the halter shank when he groomed his horse, so she did the same. Once Gwen had completed the grooming, her grandmother handed her two halter shanks attached to two horses and pointed at the little stream next to their chosen camp spot. Taking three horses in hand, they walked together to let the horses have a drink.

"Always take the horses downstream, Gwen," her grandmother said. "We get our water from upstream. How are your legs?"

"Sore," Gwen said. Her grandmother smiled and patted her rear. She laughed as Gwen made a face.

"Come on," her grandmother said, and they led the horses back to the small clearing. The older woman showed the younger one how to twist a large screw-shaped peg into the ground and attach a horse's halter shank to it.

"This way, the horses can graze all night and not wander off," she said.

By the time they returned, her parents had made a small fire ring and a fire was merrily popping away. A coffee pot was warming at the edge of the fire.

"Next job," her mother said and beckoned Gwen to follow. Her mother showed her where to find dry, dead branches of the right size which, after her arms were loaded up, they brought back to the fire and stacked next to the fire pit, which now had a cast iron pot and pan on the edges. Her father was stirring something in the pot and four large chunks of meat were sizzling away in the frying pan.

Her mother was putting the finishing touches on a small tent she had set up and pointed at Gwen's pile of saddle and gear.

"Put them away properly," her mother said. "Or the blanket will not dry out overnight and your horse will be uncomfortable in the morning."

Again mimicking the others, Gwen awkwardly walked her saddle and gear over to where the others had their piles. She dumped the saddle on its front side, draped the blanket across the saddle, and the bridle and reins over that.

Her grandmother tossed her what turned out to be a rolled up sleeping bag and pointed to the tent. "Take the left side," she said.

Her grandmother had already put her sleeping bag inside and Gwen placed hers beside it.

Exiting the tent, she noticed her father was putting a chunk of meat in her grandmother's tin plate. He tossed a plate at her. She walked to him, she held it out, and he plunked a crispy steak on it. He motioned to the pot, inside of which were beans in a brown sauce. She spooned some into her plate and looked around. Her mother and grandmother were sitting on the ground cross-legged, their plates in their laps. Feeling a tap on her shoulder, she turned to see her father with a steaming tin cup of coffee in one hand and a large bun in the other. He handed her the cup and the bun, gathered his own food and, like the others, plunked down and began to eat.

Gwen sat beside him, placing the cup of hot coffee carefully on the ground beside her. She tried to figure out how she was supposed to eat this stuff. Her father reached over and pulled out the large, thick knife he had insisted she wear on her belt. He folded out the fork attached to the outside of it and handed it back to her. He pulled out the hunting knife she had also been forced to put on and handed that to her. He returned his focus to his meal. No one spoke, but they watched her as they munched away. Gwen figured out she was supposed to use the hunting knife to cut the meat and found, to her surprise, the meat to be dull pink on the inside and very tender. She also discovered how hungry she was.

The elders laughed and started talking. They made fun of her, which, while she would never admit it, she thought was kind of cool. She took a tentative sip of the coffee and found it not too hot, so took a deeper sip. It was sweet, with a little bit of an aftertaste, but nice. After almost the whole cup, she was feeling surprisingly relaxed and found herself blurting out remarks she would not normally say around her parents, who both laughed. Her grandmother did not look amused.

"Oh, come on, Mags," he said. "We are out in the woods and there's nobody around. I just gave her a wee taste."

Grandmother grabbed Gwen's cup, then sniffed and sipped.

"Gwen," she said. "There is hardly any rum in this at all." She shook her head, put more coffee in her own cup and made a hand-it-over gesture with her right hand. Father tossed a bottle of what looked to Gwen like water, and she poured a very generous portion into the cup, taking a sip.

"Now that's more like it," the grandmother said.

They sat around the fire after diner as the temperature dropped. The elders put on their lined denim jackets to ward off the chill and Gwen looked around for hers. Her mother pointed at her saddle and laughed.

"Flippin' rookie," her father said and smirked.

"I'll flippin' rookie you!" Gwen blurted out in Oaken and dove on her father. They wrestled around for a bit in the dirt. Then her father rolled away from her, put both hands out in front of him and said, "Okay, okay, I surrender." Once again, he shocked her. It was flawless classical Oaken. Her mother had never spoken Oaken that well and she had grown up there.

Gwen made her way to her saddle, wondering why she was so uncoordinated. She eventually retrieved her jacket and made her way back to the campfire. Then she started looking around somewhat frantically. Her mother tossed her a roll of toilet paper and pointed at the tree line.

"Try not to pee on your boots, luv," she said. Everyone laughed.

After returning from the trees, she found herself yawning. Her grandmother gathered her up.

"Okay," she said. "We're off to bed. Long day for us city folk."

Gwen took one last look at the campfire and saw her parents looking at her. They had an arm around each other, her mother's head on her father's shoulder, snuggled close. It looked like her mother had a tear running down a cheek, but it must have been the firelight. Her mother never cried; her nickname was the Ice Queen.

Just before she fell asleep, she thought she heard her father say.

"It's alright Mar, they all have to grow up sometime."

As she had so often heard in the past, she heard her mother's fist hit his shoulder and his grunt that followed.

"Damn men," she blurted out in Parisian. "What do you know?" It sure sounded like she was crying.

They spent a week traveling in the wilds. As the days went on, Gwen became more comfortable with her surroundings. She gradually fell into the camp routine, doing whatever task needed to be done without being asked. She also found that she was enjoying herself. She was giving back as much as she was receiving, within reason of course. Her father often taught her a new skill or showed her a new bird or animal.

Gwen had always loved her father, but now, it was different. She somehow felt closer to him. Her grandmother took her aside on what was to be their last night in the woods. They were close to home.

"This is your real father," she began. "Who he really is. Not who he has to be when he puts on that uniform or when he has to attend a meeting or a function. That is foreign to him. He had to learn how to be that man. When I first met him, I did not like him. He was always polite, but not like the aristocrat I was or those I associated with. There were other, personal reasons as well. Those are for another time.

"It was on my family's barony on Oaken. Our district had rebelled and was in open warfare with the rest of the planet. At that time, Oaken had a small army, just a police force really. They were not equipped or trained to face the mercenary army we had hired. We rapidly defeated those sent against us and were set to take complete control of our district, and even the planet as a whole.

"Your grandfather was one of the commanding generals of our army and your mother, an officer in the duke's personal guard.

"Then Oaken hired its own mercenaries. They were not from the Federation, or even the galaxy. They had armour that defeated our weapons and weapons far better than ours. They taught the people of Oaken how to fight us by using simple hunting and farming tools.

"There were only thirty of them but in less than a month they killed many of us. Your grandfather died in one of the earlier attacks. They lured us to a gathering of the Oaken forces, which were fortified. We attacked. It was hard fighting, but just as we sensed we might win, they hit us hard, like never before. None of our soldiers returned from that battle.

"Then the thirty, on their own, attacked our capitol city. They were unstoppable. Your mother's platoon was the last guard before the duke's chambers. She was the only one who got a shot off, but their leader hit her in the face with the butt of his weapon, giving her the scar you see on her face today.

"Oaken gave their leader our district as a reward. But he was never cruel or harsh. They asked your mother and those of the old Duke's Guard to join them. She, and they, did and she rose to be their commander.

"I had not seen your mother for two years. Then she called and said she was coming home for two weeks and could she bring a coworker along. It was your father.

"God, he was infuriating at times!

"He spoke flawless, high-class Oaken and a French I'd only heard my parents speak. His Standard was almost perfect, except for a slight inflection. Our old dog took to him right away and I should have known. At night, he would brew himself a coffee and sit on the porch of his guesthouse with his feet up on the railing and just look at the stars.

"Your mother asked him if he knew how to ride and he told her he had been on a horse a time or two. So, she saddled up one of our old cow ponies for him and she took him for a ride to a small pond we had. For sure he looked bad on that horse, but he carried on.

"The next day, she took him in the other direction to show him our fields and cattle. Again, he rode badly and the old horse plodded along sedately beside your mother. I caught the tail end of what happened next myself, as I also was riding down to see the cattle.

"Our herd had gotten out of the fence and into the barley field next to it. They would have gorged on the green barley and killed themselves. Your father exploded into action. He and the old cowpony were joined by our old cow dog. The three of them got that herd out of the barley and back into the pasture. In one fast motion, he was on the ground and, in less than five minutes, with a few twists of wire, had fixed the fence enough to keep the cattle in for a while. Then he gave me a scowl, pulled the saddle's cinch tight, vaulted into the saddle and galloped toward the house. We chased after him.

"The horse had not even slid to a stop and your father was out of the saddle and had the field hand foreman by the neck, lifting him so that only his toes touched the ground. He threatened to kill him if he ever saw him treating a horse like he had been treating the old cow pony again.

"I tried to discipline your father, saying it was not his place. He spit at my feet! Can you imagine? He called me a play farmer who didn't have a clue what she was doing. He said that, where he lived, he had over a thousand head of cattle and had forgotten more about farming than I would ever know. He was angry and I could hardly understand the Standard dialect he was speaking.

"He pointed at one of the servant's wives and told her what was wrong with the fence. To my surprise, most of the women hurried off and came back in trousers and work gloves, loaded up wire and fenceposts into wagons, and set out.

"See?" your father said. "They know what to do. Let them do it!"

"Then he unsaddled and brushed the old cow pony down, praising both the pony and the dog for their hard work. He scowled at me one more time and stalked off, muttering about spoiled rich people as he went.

"When your mother and I caught up with him after diner, he was once again sitting on the porch with his feet up on the railing and a half empty bottle of beer in his hand, his hat over his eyes down to his nose, our dog laying at his feet. As we walked up the steps, he pushed the cap back to look at us with that blank expression he always uses when he is not happy, and was once again prim, proper, and polite."

Her grandmother stopped talking and shook her head.

"Yes, I know," Gwen said. "He does that to me sometimes as well. I just want to scream at him."

"But you can't, because he is so very polite," her grandmother finished for her and she laughed. "All of them are like that. The thirty of them. You'll see."

They could hear horses approaching from the estate.

"So, before they arrive, I want to say this. The people do not love your father because he is their ruler. They love him because he was, and always will be, one of them."

And then the riders arrived, all original Wind Riders: Carol, Brett, Scott, Megan, and her mom Barb. To Gwen's surprise, her grandmother fit right in, looking over at her she winked.

"And your pop reminded me; I, too, am one of the people."

Amanda and Anne came riding in after getting roasted by the others for being slow.

"Ya," Amanda said with her head down, then she looked up and grinned ear to ear, holding up what looked like a large water bottle. "But we had all the booze, you dummies!"

A mock battle immediately broke out and most of the bottle ended up spilled on the ground. It was a good laugh. Anne had two more.

As the night went on, Gwen often observed her father. He was mostly quiet – took part in the ribbing when he felt the need but was content to sit and watch, especially her mother. His eyes never strayed far from her and her face shining in the firelight. Then her mother did something she did rarely: she swept her long hair on the right side of her face behind her ear. Gwen saw it for the first time in a long time...the ugly scar that started behind her ear and ended below her jaw.

Gwen sat and looked for a while, glanced over at her father and saw he had looked away, just briefly, then back once again to the others. She got up and moved behind her mother, sitting beside her and gently stroked the scar. All conversation stopped, some in mid-sentence.

"Did it hurt bad, Mom?" Gwen asked, her voice just over a whisper. Her mother did not answer and, when Gwen attempted to pull her hand away, her mother's hand kept it there.

"Yes," her mother said. "Yes it did. I almost died. Amanda saved me. Then, when the physical pain was almost gone, the mental anguish almost killed me. The Wind Riders saved me. Especially one stupid Master Sergeant who would never leave me alone."

She looked over at her father, but he was walking away into the darkness.

"Three times your father has saved me from myself," her mother continued, "And the Wind Riders twice."

"Ya, you can be a real bonehead sometimes," Barb said. She turned to Gwen. "Your mom gets a stick up her ass sometimes, kid, and we have to kick it out of her."

Her mom tackled Barb and they wrestled on the ground for a bit.

"To be honest," Amanda said, "We just did cleanup on the last one. Some boneheaded Zebras had done most of the work for us already."

"You were really a Zebra, Mom?" Gwen asked, astonishment in her voice.

"Only a Zebra?" Megan said. "Shit Gwen, your mom is THE Zebra. She started the damn bunch. Run, run run. Ha, ha ha. Zebra Zebra Zebra, hoo-rahh."

"And don't you bloody forget it," Gwen's mom said, tossing a piece of firewood at Megan that bounced off her head. Megan gave her the finger and they were back at it again, all except Carol, who had walked to the other edge of the camp, away from the direction Gwen's father had gone.

"Ut oh," Barb said. "This ain't good." She attempted to get up, but her mother pushed her down.

"Go to her, Gwen," her mother said. "She needs someone beside us tonight."

"It's time she learned how," she heard her grandmother whisper to Barb.

Gwen quietly walked up and stood beside Carol. She knew Carol had heard her coming. Nobody snuck up on a Wind Rider.

"You okay, Aunty Carol?" Gwen asked.

"You do know I am not your aunt, Gwen?" Carol said. "I think I might be a distant cousin to your dad, but I'm not your real aunt."

"You are to me," Gwen said as she put her head on Carol's shoulder and felt it quiver. She looked up and saw tears coming down her cheeks. This tough, don't-take-any-guff combat soldier, crying! "What's wrong Aunty?"

"I had a big family back home. I was the oldest," Carol said after a while. "Where we lived was a lot like here. Lots of trees, close to the mountains. My mom died in some godforsaken part of our world fighting in some small war that nobody really cared about, and my dad lost it. He drank too much. In fact, he drank away all our money. We lived off the charity of our community. Nobody ever said anything, but I was embarrassed by it all the time. I would see how well off everyone else was and I started to develop an attitude.

"Even when the Earl took a special interest in me and gave me a big important position in a new part of the army, I still resented all the rich people. My five years were up and I had many offers, good ones, from many countries, and I had made up my mind to leave our society. Then the team Amanda belonged to was compromised and Amanda was missing. My overlord, an earl, asked Duncan to take me with them on the search for her."

"I had been on missions similar to Wind Rider missions, but Duncan let me know in no uncertain terms that I was nowhere near as good as he and his people were. Then he reminded me of who he was and where he came from. You see, his mother was the earl's aunt and she had left that life behind, along with all the wealth and privilege she was entitled to. That their family had it hard, but they had prospered and, to take, in his own words, 'that chip off your shoulder and the stick out of your ass and get a grip on life.' His words to me.

"Then Barb told me of the time when my team and I had been in deep shit on one operation and that it had been the Wind Riders who had save our asses."

"So, Gwen, he saved my life twice. Once on that operation and again by taking me in. When I see him hurt like tonight, I hurt. Because I know he will not let me, or us, help him with it."

"Hey shit head!" Anne yelled out as she bounced a stone off Carol's back. "Quit hogging the kid's time. I want to hear all about that dreamy second louie she was dancing with at the officers' ball."

And just like that, Carol's demeanour changed and, dragging Gwen back to the fire, was one of the ring leaders of the harassment Gwen received.

Two days later, along with some additions, they were back on the yacht headed for Zarkos, the Capitol of the Federation.

Chapter Two

The additions had been her grandmother and four aides, who had recently graduated from officer candidate school. Each had been in the top ten of the class and they represented the four divisions of the army. Gwen's aide was from the PIG division. Like the Wind Riders, they were classed as light cavalry troops, but, whereas the Wind Riders were reconnaissance troops, the PIGs were infantry troops. The newly-minted second lieutenant, at 26 years of age, was older than the others and the ribbons on her uniform showed she had completed two tours of duty and was parachute qualified. That meant she had been promoted from the ranks.

Well, Gwen thought, *it was necessary from time to time to do those kinds of things to give the common people something to hope for.*

The woman was pretty, striking even, despite the limited makeup and modest hairstyle the military required. Gwen didn't know what she needed an aide for, but it would be nice to talk with someone other than her parents and grandmother. She seemed a nice enough sort, for a commoner, but a bit formal. Only to be expected. Gwen was, after all, an aristocrat.

The yacht landed to much fanfare. A band played and an honour guard awaited her father's inspection. They were then loaded into four separate vehicles and a motorcade, complete with armed guards and vehicles, swept them to their embassy, where all the staff and senior officials greeted them. Her father was escorted away for a meeting with the Zarkos ambassador and senior staff, while her mother was escorted to a small reception held by the supervisory staff. Gwen and her grandmother were herded to a larger room, the staff cafeteria, she thought. There, the rank-and-file members of the embassy staff awaited them. Her grandmother took her by the arm and, trailed by the two aides, circulated throughout the room, greeting people. Gwen noticed that her grandmother would stop at every third table, shake everyone's hands, and ask a few questions. With this as an example, Gwen did the same at the table to the right of the tables her grandmother worked.

She saw the looks of pleasure on the faces of those she spoke to and the sense of pride each person felt about the job they did. She also noted that their handlers, senior management types, kept them away from a group of people standing against the wall dressed in smocks and overalls. They also steered them away from the kitchen staff.

Oh, what the heck, Gwen thought, *they are our employees also.*

Trailed by the scrambling PIG aide, Gwen broke ranks from the hovering management team and walked up to those standing at the back wall. As she approached, instead of slouching and leaning against the wall, they all stood up straight. She went down the line, shaking each hand and stopping at every fourth person and talking to them. She asked them where they were from and what jobs they did. Most were locals. They were cleaning and maintenance staff; some were private contractors hired to maintain complex machinery. Finished with that line, she made her way through the tables to the kitchen staff lineup, and once again made her way down that line.

"Do you mind?" she said to one of the cafeteria workers. "They roused me out of bed early and I had no breakfast. We teenagers are always hungry, you know?"

"But, Ma'am," her handler protested. "We have a special meal planned for you elsewhere."

"Nonsense," Gwen said. "This food looks awesome. If it's good enough for the staff, surely it is good enough for me."

She winked at the cafeteria worker.

"Besides, everyone knows teenagers just love cafeteria food."

She made a show of taking a bite, smiled broadly to the cafeteria worker, then made her way to a table and asked if she could join the staff seated there. They all bunched over to give her room on the bench, and she tore in like any normal teenager. She soon had the table laughing at some lame joke she came out with at her own expense. She looked across the room and noticed her grandmother had done the same; she had her table laughing as she brushed away some breakfast she had dumped on her ample bosom.

"The benefits of being flat-chested," Gwen said to her table mates and they all howled. Finished brushing the crumbs off, Gwen's grandmother raised a fist at her and shook it, but she was laughing. Gwen stuck her tongue out in response, which had the whole room howling. Most of them had children of their own.

Later, in their suite of rooms in the embassy, her grandmother told the story and had her parents laughing so hard they were crying.

"You guys get all the fun," her father said. "I was stuck with a bunch of brown noses trying to impress me with boring speeches."

Of course, someone had smuggled in a vid camera and the scene in the cafeteria was all over the news that night.

The next day, they were taken to the opening ceremonies of the Federation Parliament. Her father, as head of state, was seated on the floor. The rest of the family was in a private box in the gallery overlooking the floor. While her father and, by extension, her mother, were forced to stay all day, Gwen and her grandmother were not. They were taken to a natural museum and spent the rest of the day viewing the exhibits, always with an ensemble of senior staff fawning on them. Once again, Gwen stopped and talked to a person working on an exhibit, asking them about themselves and what they were doing. Talking with the people working on the project at hand, she learned more than the answers provided by management staff.

She left behind her smiling faces, which was caught by the news cameras following at a respectful distance.

The following day, Gwen and her grandmother went to an art gallery. Gwen didn't find this as exciting as the museum, but all the same, she left many smiling faces behind her. That evening, it was off to the opera house to watch a ballet and she made sure she not only met the stars, but also the corps de ballet, the orchestra members, stagehands, ushers, ticket sellers and cleaning crew. It was much later than planned when they returned to the embassy and she dropped of exhaustion, asleep as soon as she hit the sheets.

The rest of the week was spent similarly squired around town, with increasing numbers of press following Gwen and her grandmother on their outings. Some rudely shouted questions as they were escorted into and out of the venues. More and more people lined up to see them and Gwen had to be constantly reminded of their schedule as she had the habit of stopping and talking with members of the crowd. But it was wearing on her.

"That's it, young lady," her grandmother said on Thursday evening. "You are clearly exhausted. Tomorrow, you take the day off and go shopping. And you, miss prim and proper army lady, wear some normal clothing for once and try not to draw too much attention, eh?"

The morning passed uneventfully. Gwen and her aide looked like sisters wandering the mall and looking at clothing, stopping at the food court and having a bite of food. Her aide had even loosened up, smiled and cracked the odd joke. They were both dressed in jeans and sneakers and casual blouses. No one recognized them.

They walked into a high-end boutique and her aide fingered some of the clothing with a dreamy look on her face.

"Like it?" Gwen asked.

"Shit," she said looking at the price tag. "This thing costs more than I make in a month."

"Try it on," Gwen said. "What will it hurt?"

The clerk, used to this, showed them to the changing room. It wasn't busy, and she thought the attractive woman and girl might draw some paying customers, seeing them trying things on. The clerk got into the swing of things and was soon giggling and laughing along with them as the older 'sister' tried on different outfits. What nobody noticed was that, after the aide had tried on something she really liked, Gwen would casually walk over to the cash register and place it on the growing pile of items stacked there. She also picked out a couple of casual outfits for herself.

Next it was off to the jewelry section of the store, where they laughed and giggled over the jewelry, some of which was added to the pile. The same for the makeup section.

"Right," Gwen said looking at her watch. "Time to go before Dad calls out the guard."

She led them to the sales counter and the pile of clothing there. She dug into her pocket and pulled out a small wallet. Inside was a platinum credit card, which she handed to the now shocked salesclerk.

"Please put it all on this card if you will?" Gwen said. "And if you would be so kind, can you deliver it to the New Germany Embassy, in care of Guinevere Kovaks? This is way too much to carry on the bus."

"Come on, Sis," Gwen said grabbing the aide's arm. "One more mall burger, fries and cola, eh?"

The aide was quiet as they made their way to the food court and the empty table they found in the middle of the now almost-full eating area.

"Look, Ma'am," the aide finally said. "You should not have bought all those things for me. This is my job, Ma'am. I am getting paid to follow you around."

"Ya, I know," Gwen said. "And I also know you had to put off your annual leave to take this job."

"Look, Eva," Gwen continued. "I never spend much of my allowance, so buying you those things will not kill me. You are a beautiful woman and deserve to look like it from time to time. Myself, I usually go to the discount stores where I can buy all this stuff for about a third of the price, but to each their own, eh?"

"Besides, I can't have my plus-one for my big surprise party looking shabby now, can I? I mean, I know you are going to make things tough for me with all the cute hotties that will be there all decked out, but hey, maybe I can snag some of your castoffs."

"As if," Eva said, blushing. "Hey, how did you find out about the party? I was threatened with a firing squad if I told you."

"Oh," Gwen said. "It was not all that hard. A slip of the tongue by a maid here or a cleaner there. It didn't take long for me to figure it all out."

"You brat!" Eva said and smacked Gwen on the wrist. "Okay then. Your penalty for bribing me to keep quiet about all this from your folks will be to outfit me for the party. A girl has to look good for all those hunks, you know."

"That's the spirit!" Gwen exclaimed and soon they were both back to laughing.

Suddenly, Eva's expression changed and she tapped the communicator in her ear.

"Get the car to the east loading dock. Now!" she said. "Alert mall security we are in the food court and will be heading for the service corridor leading to the dock....Yes, we have a problem! Get on it!"

"Come on, Ma'am, we have to go! Now!" Eva said standing and tugging Gwen to her feet. That's when Gwen saw the herd of press, some already snapping photos, rushing toward them, shouting questions as they came.

Eva took Gwen by the arm and pushed her toward the service corridor. But it was too late. The press had drawn attention and they were soon surrounded not only by the press, but also the public. As they threaded their way through the crowd, they came upon a young girl, maybe ten, who just stood and stared at Gwen with her mouth open. To Eva's dismay, Gwen stopped and crouched down to talk to the girl. Before she could speak, however, the little girl was knocked to the floor by an aggressive member of the press who had hit the girl first with his camera lens, then pushed her roughly. All the while he shouted questions about Gwen's body dimensions.

Gwen looked to the little girl who had blood coming from her nose and stood slowly. The look on her face made even Eva take a step back.

"I can handle jerks like you harassing me," she said softly. The room was deadly quiet now. She walked toward the newsman slowly, who tried to back up, but could not as he was blocked by all the people behind him. She came nose to nose with him, staring him right in the eye.

"I can even handle the rude questions you were asking me. I'm a big girl. But I draw the line at what you just did to that little girl just now."

Gwen took her communicator from her back pocket and grabbed the man's press credentials hanging around his neck on a garishly coloured cord. She took a picture of it with the communicator and one of the little girl, now sitting up, blood running down her face. Then a concerned woman pushed her way forward and to the girl. Now a gang of mall security, including two regular police officers, pushed their way forward and created space around the little group.

"I want that asshole arrested for assaulting a minor," Gwen said to the nearest officer. She pointed at the little girl, whose mother was trying to stop the nosebleed. "And I want some medical attention for her right now! Chop! Chop!"

Then she pressed another button on her communicator.

"This is Stripes One," she said. "Get ahold of Shelly and have her sue this asshole and the shit hole company he works for. Do it now! No, I don't need a goddamned security team here. If I had any more security people around me, I wouldn't be able to move at all!"

She knelt down beside the little girl and took her hand.

"How is my brave young lady doing?" she asked. The girl had tears running down her cheeks but had not wailed once.

"Are you really Duchess Guinevere?" she asked.

"Yes," Gwen whispered into the little girls ear. "But don't tell anyone. It will be our secret, yes? My friends call me Gwen. What's your name?"

"Samantha," she whispered back. "But my friends call me Sammy."

Now a couple of people in uniform arrived with a medical kit and took charge of the little girl for a moment. The pressman was being hustled away, none too gently, by the two police officers. He was in handcuffs. Gwen took the mother aside.

"I am so sorry for this," Gwen said. "I just came here to do a little shopping like I do at home. It never causes a big fuss like this."

"The little girl will be fine, Your Highness," one med tech said. "The nose is not broken and she does not have a concussion."

"Good, thank you. Please send the bill to me if you will? Eva there will give you the details."

"So, Sammy," Gwen said, lifting the girl to her feet. "The medics tell me my brave soldier will recover from her war wounds. But I do think my brave soldier deserves an ice cream for her bravery. If it is okay with your mom?" Gwen added, turning toward the woman.

"Can we? Please, Mommy," Sammy asked. Her mom nodded, clearly not knowing how to proceed. She nodded her head and curtsied to Gwen.

"All right, then!" Gwen said, taking the girl's hand in one hand and the mother's in another. "Off we go, my brave soldiers."

The cordon moved along with them until they came to the ice cream shop.

"Good day," Gwen said to the teenager at the shop. "I myself want a large chocolate dipped cone. And for my ladies?"

"Yes, please!" Sammy said.

"Very well, then," Gwen said. "Four large chocolate dipped cones, please."

Gwen handed the first one to Sammy, the next to her mother.

"Tell the car to meet us at the front entrance and that we will have two guests with us," Gwen said to Eva when she handed over her ice cream.

With an exaggerated flourish after she received her own cone, she was off, making the security people scramble to keep up.

"Well my ladies, off we go!" she said. "Our chariot awaits!"

Sammy's and her mother's eyes grew larger when they saw the size of the cars awaiting them. There were two big vehicles, the limo in front and an escort vehicle behind, along with eight large men standing beside the cars.

"Oh for god's sake," Gwen muttered. "A little overkill, don't you think?"

"Not my doing," Eva said.

"Ma'am," one of the guards said, holding the rear door of the limo open for her. "Baroness Isabel's orders, Ma'am."

Gwen motioned for Sammy to enter first, then her mother, and finally Eva before she entered.

"Please tell the driver your address, my lady," Gwen said rolling down the driver partition. "It is only fair that we transport our brave wounded soldiers home, right?"

Gwen rolled up the partition after Sammy had rattled off her home address, then took a bite of the cone.

"Oh, I have died and gone to heaven!" she said. "I haven't had one of these for over a month. The food they serve us at the embassy is ever so boring."

As they made their way through the streets to a quiet residential district, Gwen got the mother to loosen up a bit. As the little motorcade pulled up to a modest house they drew a crowd.

Gwen made a point of escorting Sammy to the door and making a bow to her before she once again entered the limo and they sprinted away to the embassy.

"Guinevere Magdalena!" her mother yelled at her once they entered their suite of rooms. "What the hell were you thinking! And you, Subby! I'll have you demoted to private and back in regiment before you can even turn your head."

"Yes, Ma'am!" Eva said at ridged attention. She snapped an even more rigid salute. "At your pleasure, Ma'am!" she held the salute.

"Okay," her father said, rising from his chair and returning the salute. "You are dismissed, Second Lieutenant, your displeasure has been noted."

"Yes Master Warrant, thank you Master Warrant!" Eva barked. She brought her right leg up to her chest, smashed it into the floor, spun around and marched out the door.

"Guinevere Magdalena...." her mother started in a fine fury now.

"Marlene Augusta Isabelle!" Grandmother said. "Get your head out of your ass! I told Gwen to go shopping and I told the Second Lieutenant to take the day off and go with her! They were there all day with no problems until someone spilled the beans to the press. You want someone to yell at? You yell at me and see how far you will get! Now Marlene Augusta, you *will* bring that young Second Lieutenant back in here and you *will* apologize for your behaviour!"

Marlene just stood there.

"Now, young lady, or I will yank your damn ear so hard I will pull it right off your big stupid head!"

Duncan pushed the intercom button.

"Please have the Duchess' aide return to the suite at her convenience, if you please," he said.

A few minutes later there was a knock on the door and Eva entered in her impeccable full uniform, her beret tucked under her left arm. All traces of makeup were gone and her hair pulled back off her collar. She raised her right knee, once again stomping it into the floor, and came to attention.

"Second Lieutenant Aslibach reporting as ordered, Master Warrant!"

"At ease, Lieutenant," Duncan said.

Then Marlene came to attention, marched two steps forward and, like Eva had done earlier, stomped her right foot onto the floor. Keeping at attention with her eyes above Eva's head, she said, "The Master Warrant apologizes for her behaviour and comments, Ma'am! No excuses, Ma'am!"

"Master Warrant Kovaks?" Eva said.

"Ya, stand her down Lieutenant," Duncan said. "Her mother threatened to yank her ear off, so that's good enough for now."

"Very well, Master Warrant Kovaks, I will not file a report of insubordination against Master Warrant Isabelle then. Apology accepted, Master Warrant Isabel. But you do that again and I will have you busted down to the ranks faster than you can make your head spin. As a chicken header! Zebra indeed! Dismissed!"

Once again Marlene smashed her right foot into the ground and then smiled.

"You little bitch," she said. "You would, too."

Marlene hugged Eva.

"I really am sorry Ev. I overreacted."

"Like always, Mar," Eva said. "Now, will you tell the brat to send back all the clothes she just bought me? It must have cost her my whole year's wages."

"Ya well, you're being promoted and receiving a raise," Duncan said. Turning to his wife, he said, "And it's coming out of your Zebra budget, not mine, Mar."

"Oh no you don't!" Marlene said. "You're not sticking me with no wet-behind-the-ears lieutenant. No way."

She was at the bureau with her back turned while she spoke.

"Well, there is no way I'm taking her," Duncan said. "I got enough wet-behind-the-ears lieutenants already. Nope, you're stuck with her."

When Marlene turned around, she had a black beret in one hand and a full bottle of vodka in the other. She began to twirl the beret around a finger and handed the bottle to Eva.

"What? Here, now in front of the brat?"

Marlene nodded.

"Ah fuck it!" Eva said. She spun the top off the bottle letting it fall to the floor, tilted the bottle up and drained it.

Marlene gently placed the black beret on her head and kissed both her cheeks.

"Welcome to the Wind Riders, Eva," Duncan said.

Then Marlene dug in her pocket and pulled a patch out of it, ripped the PIG badge off the Velcro holding it to Eva's uniform and gently attached the Zebra patch to it. She hauled off and hit her on the patch, hard.

"Now you are a Zebra," Marlene said before Eva could respond. "I was going to wait until after the cruise, but, like always, Duncan spilled the beans."

"But I haven't even done my qualifications yet," Eva protested.

Duncan came up and touched, first, her parachute wings, then the last I-was-there badge and the decoration ribbon. He pinned a wound stripe next to it then handed her a set of Pathfinder wings.

"Yes, you did, kid," he said, his eyes tearing up and his voice cracking. "Yes, you did." Then he walked out of the room.

"Goddamn men," Marlene said. "Always losing their shit. How the hell did your name get on the party list L-T?"

Eva pointed at Gwen.

"Guinevere Magellan! How the hell are the rest of us normal females going to grab any cute guys if this bombshell shows up? What the hell were you thinking?"

"That I could maybe snag onto one of her castoffs." Gwen said.

"Hey, good thinking, I never would have thought of that. Would you have, Mom?"

"No," Magdalene said. "But her father would have."

Gwen vowed to get ahold of Eva's service records as soon as she could. Something was not normal here.

Chapter Three

B irthday party day had arrived. It was to be a formal evening affair. Ambassadors, their families and several of the well-to-do and well-connected had all been invited.

The day was spent enduring a seemingly never-ending chorus of hair stylists, manicurists, makeup artists, and in Eva's case, seamstresses. Eva did not have a formal uniform – but if she did, it would have required changing to a Wind Rider one now. Women had the option of trousers and tunics or long gowns. Eva had chosen the long gown option, which was a simpler affair to make than the trousered version.

Gwen was now 16. Her grandmother had thought to celebrate in style and was technically the hostess of the affair. They were, after all big shots, even though they rarely acted the part. A girl only turns 16 once, she had said, and it should be special.

As the day's preparations progressed, her father, Duncan, wandered through to check on their status, or so he said. In fact, he spent most of the day soaking up the sun on the balcony attached to their suite. His deck chair was tilted back so he could put his feet up on the railing. He was wearing his normal off-duty attire: polo shirt, blue jeans, sneakers and a red ball cap with a white horse on the front.

Around 4:00 p.m., under the pretext of 'checking up on things,' Duncan made a beer run. This drew flak from her mother, who blasted him for not being ready yet. He just grinned, gave her a peck on the cheek, and went back to the deck.

By 6:30, things were in a fine frenzy. All attention was focused on Gwen. There were last minute touchups to makeup and hair, adjustments to the fit of her gown, and hands smoothing out last wrinkles – or imaginary ones. Her mother and grandmother carefully placed long diamond earrings on her ears and a beautiful diamond choker with matching diamond necklace around her neck. Diamond bracelets with gold filigree adorned her wrists. They stood back after some final adjustments and admired their handiwork.

"Oh, where is that damn man!" her mother exclaimed and spun around to chase father down, only to see him leaning against the doorway, his face expressionless.

Tonight, he was not decked out in his Master Warrant Officer dress uniform. Duncan wore a full general's uniform. Although more ornate than his usual one, he had chosen to display neither his I-was-there medals nor his decoration medals. Today, he had six five-years-of-service gold slashes. He still wore his parachute wings and Pathfinder wings, as well as the expert marksman badge on his sleeve. He also wore his large sash of office with a large brooch pined to it. His boots were highly polished and went to his calves. Duncan also sported highly polished brass-on-red tab rank insignia on his lapels and a highly polished eagle, wings outstretched, on his right collar. The uniform was impeccable, as was his hair.

Gwen had never seen him wear that eagle before. In fact, she could only recall ever hearing of five of them, all original off-world Wind Riders.

"Typical man!" her mother said. "You kept us waiting and now we will be late!"

"You two head down," he said softly. "I would like a moment alone with my daughter."

Gwen's mother, Marlene, was about to give him another blast, but the grandmother saw the look in Duncan's eyes, touched Marlene's arm to get her attention, and shook her head. Duncan's wife took another look at his face and saw it, too. She gave him a quick peck on the cheek, then, in a flurry of rustling silk, both women were off.

"You know," her father said. "You look a lot like my mother and her side of the family."

He approached her and, from behind his back, produced a sash of office similar to his. He gently draped it across her shoulder. He adjusted her hair to fall across the back of it and tweaked it so it fell on her hip properly.

"Today, everyone will be able to see what I see every day. A beautiful young woman, whom I love and adore with all my heart."

He held her at arm's length and his eyes welled up with moisture. Gwen knocked his arms away and rushed to him, crushing him into her chest. Then she kissed him tenderly on the neck, just above the eagle.

After a few moments, he gently pried her away from him. His eyes went wide and he frantically smoothed her dress and both their sashes.

"Your mother is going to kill me," he said. Then grinned. "But, as you outrank her, you can override the death sentence."

"Wh..What?" Gwen stammered.

"As of today, you are the Grand Duchess of New Germany and my heir," he said. The mischievous grin had returned to his face and reflected in his eyes. "Your mother is a mere Baroness."

Gwen caught on right away and grabbed his arm by the elbow.

"Quiet right you are, Your Highness," she said. "Shall we proceed before the riffraff become unruly?"

"But of course, Your Highness," he replied.

They were still laughing when they reached the end of the hallway where large dual closed doors led to the main reception.

Instead of the invective they had both been expecting, they received a smile from Marlene as they made their entrance.

"Oh my god," she said softly. "Look at the both of them. My oh-so-overly-handsome husband and my way-too-beautiful daughter."

The embassy official photographer was about to take a picture but was stopped as Marlene approached them first, drew a tissue from her small handbag, and wiped lipstick from her husband's neck.

"I leave you alone for five minutes," she said, "And you are off chasing other women."

"And I love this one dearly," he said looking in his wife' eyes. "Almost as much as I love her mother."

Then it was Mag's turn with the tissue. She lightly dabbed at her daughter's eyes so she would not smear the eye makeup.

Finally, the family was composed. The photographer shot a fast series of Gwen, the family, and a couple of Gwen with her dad.

The harried Master of Ceremonies barged in breathlessly.

"Right. Off we go then," Grandmother said. "Do pause at the head table, please, Your Highness."

The two women regally glided down the long center aisle toward the head table, nodding and smiling at those they knew. Gwen and her father stood to the side of the doorway out of view. Gwen's right foot began to nervously tap.

"Gwen!" her father said in a stage whisper. "Stop it. You're making me nervous. My goddamn knees are shaking so bad as it is, I am not sure I can make it to the table."

It was time. The Master of Ceremony nodded at them and they stepped to the centre of the doorway. Five buglers, one from each of the army divisions, blew a loud herald and all eyes of the assembly turned to the doorway.

"His Highness, Grand Duke Kovaks of New Germany and Her Highness, Grand Duchess Kovaks of New Germany!" the Master of Ceremonies belted out before another bugle flourish was blown. Gwen and her father made their way down the long aisle looking straight ahead, for all the world looking cool and calm, but Gwen could feel her father's arm shaking under her hand and he could feel her hand shaking on his arm.

The applause was loud and lasted during the long walk to the head table and until Gwen was seated. Then her father sat, followed by the rest of the head table. At last, all the guests were seated except one. She stood to Gwen's right, next to her grandmother. The woman raised a large glass in her right hand.

"His Highness, Grand Duke Kovaks!" she said, took a deep pull and put the glass down. She waited until the rest of the assembly had done the same. Some began to sit. Then she raised a glass of champagne high. Those who had sat, jumped to their feet.

"Her Highness, Grand Duchess Kovaks!" Once again, she drained her glass and thumped it back on the table. This time, Eva sat down, as did the assembly. The first course was served.

Even though she was famished, Gwen knew better than to wolf down the plate of food. She followed her grandmother's lead and daintily cut the pieces, then chewed quietly. Mother and Grandmother were busy chatting with others at the head table. Father was extremely quiet, not normal for him at all. One of the perks of being seated at the head table was being served first; on the other hand, Gwen had to wait while the others finished. The agenda said there was to be a short interval after desert, during which her father bolted as soon as he could.

"Well, ladies," Grandmother said, "We should take that as our cue to powder our noses."

The three of them rose and, trailed by Eva, made their way to the private washroom reserved for them.

Eva entered the room first to a "For chrissakes," from Marlene, then returned and stepped aside, holding the door, saying "all clear." She stayed by the washroom door the whole time, her hand in her handbag. Gwen didn't even notice. Nor had she noticed that underneath one of her overly large earrings, Eva wore a communicator.

After touching up their makeup, the ladies made their way back to their seats, talking gaily with others at the head table.

Duncan returned just before the proceedings were about to begin.

"Jaysus, Dunc," Gwen heard Barb say to her father. "You weren't that nervous facing down those Tallies way back."

"Had a gun and could shoot back," her father said. He hurried back to his seat and sat down.

The speeches began, culminating in an emotional one from her mother that left no eyes dry. Finally, it was her father's turn. He slowly stood and, glass in hand, made his way to the podium, which blocked his quivering pants legs. Duncan lowered his head and said nothing for a moment.

"There are few times when it is difficult for me to find something to say," he began. "This is one of them. I have agonized over this for weeks. I wrote speeches, then tossed them. My daughter deserves better than this. As she has shown this past week, she is funny, she is witty. Like any teenaged girl, she can be moody and bitchy and whiney and loving, sometimes all within an hour. Like any other over-indulged and spoiled young woman, she can be demanding and overbearing. But this week...this week, she began to show who she really is. A woman with a high capacity and desire to learn and experience new things. To have fun and to have compassion for those harmed. She has also showed her steel and determination. All of this on a public stage that no young woman should have to endure. But endure it she has."

He raised his glass and pointed it to Gwen.

"To my daughter Guinevere. The love of my life."

The room stood and toasted a now embarrassed Gwen.

Her father looked down at his empty glass, then Gwen saw the mischief grin.

"Somebody done drank all my booze!" he said. "Party's on!"

Scott had been waiting for that and tossed a bottle of beer up to her father, who cracked the top and took a deep pull. At that, Duncan nearly ran off the rostrum.

"He'll be back," Gwen's mother said, nodding at her father, who was now cavorting with his buddies. "I'm amazed he lasted this long. Come along, dear. Time to meet the riffraff."

She took Gwen's arm and began walking to the first table.

"Who you calling riffraff?" one large man at the table said. "Why, I remember..."

"Not in front of the children, Brock," her mother said.

"Shit, Dunc," Scott said. "I never seen you that scared. Not even on that first hill back in the day."

"Damn near pissed myself up there," her father said. "Easier in the bush. Not as bloody dangerous, either."

The family members made their way around all the dignitaries' tables. Duncan was more relaxed now – that is, until the first dance was announced, when he clammed up again.

He rose to the occasion and did his duty, dancing the first dance with Gwen and shaking the whole time. Surviving that, she was handed off to the ambassador. She danced her way through the other ambassadors before finally having a chance to sit and relax. She saw her mother and father sitting with their friends. Marlene had her head on Duncan's shoulder and he was stroking her arm.

There were few dancers on the floor when the band changed to more upbeat and trendy music. Gwen was spirited away by several young men her own age and the party, for her, really began. She was with a group her own age and social status and they were having a blast. One guy showed a lot of promise. He was eighteen, good looking, showed wit, knew what to say and when. He was the son of a Baron from Oaken and Gwen enjoyed his company.

Suddenly, without permission, he kissed her. Not just a kiss either; his hands and tongue both roamed. She pushed him away from her and slapped him so hard his head rocked to the side and he took a step back. Then Gwen turned and marched away.

He made to go after her, but was met by Eva, fire in her eyes and death in her manner.

"Got a fucking problem, buddy?" she growled.

The entire Wind Rider table had seen the ruckus and had stood. The boy knew he was in deep trouble and ran.

To her credit, even though she was seething, Gwen acted like it was no big deal and soon the party was back to normal. Until the next morning.

The next morning they boarded the luxury interplanetary ship, their home for the next month. As they exited the limo, more than the usual crowd of media was present and yelling questions at them. Gwen's head was pounding from the amount of champagne she had drunk the night before and couldn't hear what was being shouted. She learned later, after a three-hour nap, when she turned on the large vid player in her suite to find some music. There it was, on a news channel: in all her fury, they had caught her slapping the asshole at the party.

It cut to a news conference. A red-faced, imposing man stood in front of a microphone. The boy's father asked what right she, a bastard daughter of an unmarried man, had to strike his son and the heir to a long line of barons?

Just at that point her mother walked in.

"Oh," she said looking at the video. "I guess you have seen it, then."

Gwen bolted out of her suite to her father. She pummelled him as hard as she could on the shoulders and the chest.

"How could you!" she screamed. "You don't even have enough balls to marry my mother? I thought you were a man of honour!"

He grabbed her hand as she made a fist and aimed it at his head.

"Gwen! Enough!" Her mother yelled and pinned her arms to her side from behind, dragging her away from her father. He stood and walked out of the room.

Her mother turned her around and looked at her, sadness in her eyes, then pulled her into a hug as Gwen broke down.

It took Gwen ten minutes to calm down. She looked up at her mother and, seeing the tears there, started weeping again. Then Eva walked in and turned on the vid screen.

"Shit's about to happen," she said.

On the screen was her father, a coffee cup in his hand, smile on his face, sitting across from one of the most respected news spokeswomen in the galaxy.

"Grand Duke Kovaks, thank you for coming forward to address this issue," the woman said.

"Not at all," he said. "There really is not an issue, you know. Just an upset father overreacting."

"Well," she continued. "How do you respond to his accusation that you are not married to Baroness Isabelle and that your daughter was born out of wedlock?"

"It was a hasty comment made in the heat of the moment by an angry father."

"Well, our research shows that there is no record of marriage between you and Baroness Isabelle."

"Well," her father said, "Your research is faulty."

"The Baron is filing charges of assault on your daughter and has filed a suit against you personally, Your Highness. I hardly think he would do that if what he says is unfounded."

Her father's eyes narrowed hearing that and he leaned forward.

"Filed charges against my daughter for assault, did he?" he said softly. Anyone who knew her father would know, just by the sound of his voice, that he was extremely upset.

"Well then," he continued. "I am sure he will enjoy losing a lot of money when she is found not guilty for reasons of self-defence and his son is jailed for the sexual assault of a minor.

"As far as the other: Master Sergeant Duncan Kovaks and Colonel Marlene Isabelle were married 25 years ago by Queen Tanya of Oaken in front of about five thousand witnesses. Baroness Isabelle chose to keep her own last name. In addition, Queen Tanya is Baroness Isabelle's cousin, therefore she is my daughter's second cousin.

"In fact, I would be surprised if Baron Von Manschted is a baron by the time he returns home to Oaken and, by the time my lawyers are finished with him, he will be penniless. Like they say where I come from, payback is a bitch. Good day to you all."

"Shelly!" her father said as he walked back into the room where Marlene was wiping away Gwen's tears. Shelly's image came on the vid screen.

"Already on it, boss," shelly said. "Hey Mar, Gwen. Wow, nice right cross you have there, Gwen. Take after your mom. Okay, assault charges on Gwen were not even allowed to be filed and the kid is being arrested for sexual assault as we speak. I would like to take the credit, but the Federation was way ahead of me. Tanya is super pissed, has not only taken the barony away but also the name, is exiling the family and giving the title and the land to Gwen. I have filed a motion and all the family and personal finances have been put on lockdown. Even the hidden ones. CT works real fast when he is motivated. As a matter of fact, most of the funds in the hidden accounts are already in Gwen's name."

"Wow. Like always," her father said, "I owe you, Shelly."

"No you don't, Ghost, no you don't."

The screen went blank.

"Fucking asshole!" her father belted out. "I am so sorry, Gwen. Can you forgive me?"

"No, Dad," Gwen said. "It's me that's sorry. Sorry I ever doubted you. Did I hurt you?" she began rubbing his chest.

"Nah," he said grinning. "You mom hits way harder. Those were just love taps."

He walked to his wife and daughter and they had a three-way hug.

"You know," her father said. "Your mom turned me down. I asked her to marry me more than once."

"And I really disliked you, too," Grandmother said. She had been watching them. She then approached her daughter, brushed the hair from the right side of Marlene's face, and stroked the scar there.

"Because he had given her this," she whispered.

"What?" Gwen said, looking back and forth between her mother and father. Her father made to break away, but her mother held him there.

"No," she said. "Stay. It is time Gwen knew this."

"I was the commander of our ruler's personal guard," her mother continued. She was looking away, her eyes focused in the distance. "My station was with the last guards. We barricaded ourselves as best we could, but we were no match for them. I had a direct line of fire on the first one through the door, but the soldier behind him shoved him aside and took my blast square in the chest. The first soldier reversed his rifle and hit me across the head, then blew the door off the hinges and the rest of the team burst in and shot almost everyone. I heard him tell one of my young soldiers he had done well, had done his duty and there was no reason to die, no shame, he had done his best.

"Someone began to work on me. I heard Amanda say, 'Karen is dead, Ghost'. He stopped for a second. 'Can you save this one?' he asked. 'We are going to need brave ones like her.' Then he walked away, issuing orders. He could have killed me, Gwen. I would have killed him if the roles had been reversed. But he and his people are different. They can turn it on and off in a moment.

"Later, I was laying in the hospital, barely conscious. My head was fully bandaged. Only my eyes, nose and part of my mouth were unbandaged. He came by and checked on me, told the doctor to do everything possible to save me, that I was special, and he needed me.

"'Fucking guy,' the doctor said after he left. 'Be damned if I'd save the person who killed my wife and unborn child.'

"You see Gwen, Karen was your father's first wife and I had killed her and your unborn half brother or sister."

Her mother started to cry then.

"I am so sorry, Duncan," she wailed.

"Marlene, Marlene," her father said softly. He took her head in both his hands, looked into her eyes, then touched his forehead to hers. "It was over twenty-five years ago, Mar. Yes, I loved her; I still do. Yes, she was pregnant.

"She was supposed to be bringing up the rear, not up front. If she had told me she was pregnant, she would have been left in the LAV and not even been on the assault. Those were her choices. She was a soldier. That I did not need her help, had seen you already, well, it was her that saved your life, because she was in the way and I couldn't shoot you."

He took his head back and smiled.

"Then, instead of a nice scary scar, you would have an ugly third eye right here." He poked Marlene on the forehead and laughed.

"Asshole!" her mother said, then kissed him tenderly.

"Okay," her father said. "Like I said, long ago and far away. You, my beautiful daughter, whom I love more than life itself, are not a bastard; sometimes a bitch, but not a bastard. You have just increased your wealth substantially and added another title to your name. Bravo. For that, miss rich lady, you get to buy me a beer."

He moved off to the sitting room, beer in hand.

"Does he take nothing seriously?" Gwen asked. "Does she?" Her mom was chasing after him throwing a pillow at him.

"Yes," her grandmother, Mags, said. "Too much and too often. Sometimes I don't know how he does it. They make jokes, laugh about it. I think that helps a lot. He wasn't always a big shot, you know. He wasn't born to this. Not like your mother and I were."

The couple returned to the sitting room.

"He dragged us down to his level," Mags continued. "Kicking and screaming the whole way."

"And you loved every second of it," Duncan added, laughing.

Gwen's grandmother grabbed the nearest pillow, threw it at him and stuck her tongue out.

"You can be such an asshole sometimes, Duncan," she said, but she was smiling.

The rest of the month-long trip was uneventful. They stopped at many exotic places and experienced many new sights. Yes, the press was always around, but never intrusive. The events of the party were forgotten and the press moved off to more juicy stories, as nothing exciting was happening with their family.

To reach the last stop of their trip, they would have to take a combination freighter-passenger ship. The planet they were headed to was off the beaten track, but, Gwen had been told, was well worth the detour. The freighter would make other stops along the way, but just long enough to drop off cargo and passengers and load up more.

Her stateroom on the freighter was about the size of her closet at home, but comfortable. In fact, the family's whole suite was about as large as her bedroom. The atmosphere on board was casual and relaxed, not like the luxury liner's had been, where everything had been organized and regulated. Here, there were dining options: a more formal dining area or the buffet-style cafeteria. The cafeteria was always open; the restaurant was not. There was also a well-equipped gym, a nice lounge for the adults, and an arcade area, which she enjoyed and where she met other youth her age. Nobody knew who she was, so life was good.

The only fly in the ointment was a group of overbearing women. Unlike in most of the rest of the Federation where the sexes were equal, especially New Germany, these women came from a planet with a matriarchal society. Not only were the women in charge of everything, but it was a feudal society in which men had no rights at all.

These women were outright hostile to any man they ran across. The other passengers and crew had been warned and the men steered clear of them. Their planet was remote and exported unfinished logs and finished lumber but imported little. The ship would stop on the planet only long enough to unload the women and their baggage and be gone in just under two hours, not even taking time to refuel.

That would be in the morning. Tonight, the women were hosting a party. As her mother was a well-known warrior, she had been invited. Her father had not. He told Gwen he wanted some father-daughter time anyway and they ordered room service for supper.

Chapter Four

Father and daughter had finished supper and were now staring at a chessboard placed on the coffee table. Dinner plates and cutlery had been removed and returned to the wheeled trolley just inside the suite's door.

After Gwen had complained about little to do, there being no vid feeds on this vessel, her father had begun to teach her chess. At first, he had beaten her handily, but she had quickly picked up on the rules and improved. She found she enjoyed the matches. Now, she made her father work for it. He still beat her, but no longer so easily. In fact, she thought she might win this game. He had just fallen into her cleverly laid trap.

"Ah, shit!" he said after he removed his hand from the piece he had just moved and surveyed the board.

"Gotcha!!" Gwen said, taking his queen with her white bishop. "Checkmate...Woo hoo!"

She sprang up from her chair, both hands in the air, and began dancing around the room.

"Ya, ya," her father said. "Yak it up."

"I am the winner...and you are the loser..." Gwen began to chant.

Her father bolted out of his chair, put his head and shoulder down, caught her in the midriff with his shoulder, wrapped his arms around her, and lifted her in the air.

"Lemme go, lemme go, you big meany!" Gwen yelled out, punching him not-so-gently on the shoulders.

He kissed her on the forehead and put her feet back on the ground, but while his grip loosened, he still held her close. He couldn't put his chin on her head like he did with her mother; she was too tall for that, but he rested his cheek against hers.

Any retort she might have made was cut off by the sound of loud klaxons. She wasn't as concerned as she had been at hearing it the first time. Just another safety drill.

"This is the captain speaking. Passengers in their cabins are to remain there," came over the intercom. "Those in common areas, remain in place. Those in corridors, report to the nearest safety area. Crew, report to stations."

As they were in the stateroom already, they just collected up the chess pieces, stacked them and the board in the box, and stowed it away. What came next was disturbing. A faster, louder klaxon went off and she could feel the beat of the engine pick up.

"Action stations! Action stations!" came blaring over the intercom as the seals on the stateroom door clanged shut. Now Duncan, who, like Gwen, had been lazily putting things in order, sprang into high gear. He hit the button that activated all the magnetic feet to clamp furniture to the floor and rushed to his bedroom.

"Stash the food trolley into the closet, toss any loose cushions and other loose items in there as well, then shut the door and latch it," he said as he moved. They could feel the ship change direction, too fast for the artificial gravity to fully compensate for. Then they felt as much as heard a large bang, from someplace farther back on the ship.

Duncan came back in the room with two spacesuits under his arms and tossed one to her.

"Put it on!" he commanded. "Now!" He dumped his on the now cushion-less sofa, walked to the wall and hit a prominent red button there.

Four high-backed, high impact seats with seatbelts and shoulder straps slid out from the walls and locked into place. He confirmed Gwen had her suit on properly and locked her helmet in place. He escorted her to the nearest chair and buckled her in. He made a fast tour of the room, picked up a few minor loose things that Gwen had left and stuck them in his pockets, thinking them of no consequence, and expertly donned his own suit.

As the ship banked hard to the left it was hit again by something hard, this time closer to the top and midship. The blast made her father stumble, but just slightly. He rushed to Gwen's chair and pulled all the straps so tight she thought he might break her shoulders. Another blast and she could hear some sizzling as their ship fired lasers.

Then, in five rapid hard-felt jolts, the ship was hit hard and an explosion went off. Her father didn't hesitate or wait for an order. He hit a button on his chair and pulled all his straps tight.

They heard a series of small explosions in rapid succession, then a roar as all the air was sucked out of the room and into the vacuum of space. One more small explosion and their stateroom was expelled from the ship.

Less than a minute later, they were rocked by a massive shock wave, The guidance rockets attached to the escape pod their room had become fired for a few seconds and stopped. Her father hit another button and a small monitor popped out from his chair. He began typing on the screen.

Finished, he hit the button again and the monitor disappeared back into the chair. Now he hit his chest and the speakers in Gwen's helmet came alive.

Zulu Echo Bravo Romeo Alpha, Gulf Hotel Oscar Sierra Tango. Her father's voice came over her headphones.

Sierra Tango, Romeo Alpha, her mother's voice answered after several seconds.

Sit rep? her father said.

Romeo Alpha and ten in pod. Some W-I-A.

Copy. Senior and Junior five-by-five. Have sent comm to base. Have sent touchdown your comm.

Copy. Far side from you. Will link up with locals. Try and stay out of trouble.

She saw her father smile.

Recon is my name, stealth is my game. Gulf Hotel Oscar Sierra Tango out.

"Okay, Gwen," her father said. "Your mother is fine. She has ten people with her, some with wounds. She will touchdown on the far side of the planet we are headed for. Our vessel was attacked and presumably destroyed. Hopefully, we all escaped before they could detect our pods. I have disabled the tracking systems and have sent a distress call back to our base. It may take some time, but help will be coming."

"Can I loosen these straps now?" Gwen asked.

"No," he replied. "Pull them as tight as you can. The landing will be hard."

He was pulling down on his straps as hard as he could. Gwen imitated him.

An hour later, she heard the hull begin to pop and sizzle as the atmosphere heated it up. The rockets fired twice, then stopped. They hit, not the ground, but something that snapped loudly, over and over again. The pod began to tumble and bounce from side to side as they hit whatever it was hard, then again and again. The pod rolled and crashed, breaking something as it went, then came to a stop.

Because all her weight was on her shoulder straps, Gwen knew they were upside down. This was confirmed when her father tucked his head down to his chest, hit the belt release mechanism and crashed to the roof.

"Don't touch anything!" he instructed.

He moved to her chair, jammed his shoulder into her midriff, then hit her release button and grunted as she fell onto his shoulder.

"Gettin' a little chunky there, kiddo," he said and laughed as he lowered her to the ceiling. He took off his helmet and walked toward his bedroom, removing the suit as he did so.

Taking her cue from him, Gwen removed her helmet and, while looking around for a place to put it, surveyed the room. Much of the ornate and decorative fittings of the room had fallen off the walls, or threatened to do so, revealing the bare metal beneath them. Pieces of wall and furniture were scattered in heaps around the roof and some of the flooring was dangling by support wires. She started to remove the suit. That's when she found her right ankle was sore. She could put weight on it, but it hurt.

Her father emerged from his room. Instead of the casual business attire he had been wearing before, he now wore a pair of tough jeans, a long sleeve heavy cotton shirt, with a T-shirt under it, a pair of heavy hiking boots on his feet, and a dark green ball cap on his head. Over his right shoulder he had draped his heavily lined jean jacket; over the left a thick blanket with something rolled inside it.

He cleared a space on the ceiling-now-floor with his foot and dumped the blanket, then the jean jacket on top of it. He made his way to her room and Gwen heard him dumping contents from her dresser drawers, muttering. He returned holding an armful of her clothing, which he tossed at her. He also had her backpack and the large heavy canvas purse with the wide strap she had purchased on their last stop.

"Get out of the shit you are wearing," he said. "Then put this on. It's crappy stuff, but it will do for now."

"What do you mean crappy stuff?' Gwen said in a huff. "That is all designer, high-end clothing!"

"Ya, like I said, crappy stuff," he replied, then headed to the bathroom.

He came back loaded down with more things that he tossed on top of his small pile. Gwen squealed and crossed her arms across her chest. She had just put her pants on and was only in her bra and the pants fly and button were not done up yet.

"Oh for chrissake!" he said. "I've seen you naked before, you know. Get that dainty bra off and get the sports bra on. Then take those fancy underpants off."

He tossed a pair of his boxer shorts at her.

"Put those on," he said.

"Then go through that shit," he pointed at the toiletries on the floor. "Just the minimum, no makeup, no perfume, one brush and whatever feminine hygiene products you need. We will be moving a lot and fast, so make sure it's something that will be comfortable. We will most likely be out here for a while, so choose wisely. You carry what you bring."

Meanwhile, he was stuffing the first aid kit and emergency rations into his now unrolled blanket. He also placed there four full one-liter bottles of water, then carefully rolled it all up again. He used a spare boot lace at the top and bottom to hold them shut, and another in the middle. Then he placed it over his head and around his neck to hang on his right shoulder, across his chest and back. He adjusted the load a bit, then tied the two bottom ends together, before taking it off again and putting it on the floor.

"First lesson in survival training," he said to her. She was just pulling the T-shirt over her head. "You can take clothing off to get cool. But, if you want to get warm, you can't put on what you don't have."

Duncan walked to the closet by the door, stood to the side and flung the closet door open. Loose items crashed to the floor. He went through them quickly. Tossing most of the items to the side, he grabbed the large carving knife and matching long fork, three sets of cutlery, and two small metal serving plates. These he stuffed into her large purse. He returned to her bedroom and came back with two large heavy blankets, which he folded expertly and also stuffed into the purse. He placed it over his head and on his left shoulder, adjusting it so it sat on his rear.

Gwen had just finished dressing by then.

"Come on kid, hustle!" he exclaimed. "We have to get out of here. Fast! Point out the shit you want to carry. I'll pack it for you. Hurry!"

"But Dad," Gwen said. "They told us to stay put in the pod in case of emergency."

"Not this time, hun," he said. "That was a targeted attack. They will be looking for survivors all right, but not to save them. At best to kill them; at worst..."

He saw her wince as she tugged on her right hiking boot. He rushed over and took it from her, pulling the sock off. Then he began to probe her foot and ankle, looking at her face as he did so.

After a trip to the bathroom, he returned with a washcloth that he tore into strips and wrapped around the foot and ankle.

"Minor sprain," he said. "You'll be okay in a day or so. Put the boot on and lace it tight, right up to the top. It will be stiff at first, but as you move it will loosen up."

He put the blanket over his shoulder again, shifted it a bit, then stuffed his jean jacket into the purse and made his way to the door. He hit the button and the door blew out. Stepping out the door, he disappeared from sight.

Gwen had just finished packing the backpack and was closing it up when he returned. He approached and helped her put it on. He adjusted it so it sat high on her back, not low like she was used to. He buckled the belly strap she never used around her waist, then pulled all the straps tight and bounced the pack up and down. He grunted.

"That'll do for now," he said. He walked back out the door, waving her to follow.

They were in a thick forest. As she had surmised, the pod was upside down on the forest floor. The path it had made as they crashed was strewn with broken and shattered trees. The ground was clear in spots that indicated where the pod had first hit the ground and hit again on all the bounces after that.

The trees were tall and thick, almost blocking the sun. They were needled trees of some kind, with no branches near ground level. They could easily walk among the trunks unobstructed, and their steps were muffled as they walked on a carpet of discarded needles.

Fluttering of feathers and buzzing of wings betrayed the presence of birds and flying insects. The air was fresh and smelled of the trees, and the wind softly rustled through the treetops high above their heads like a distant stream. Other than that, there was no sound.

Her father pulled a small rectangular object from his rear pocket, turned it on briefly, then shut it off again and put it back. He pointed.

"We go this way," he announced and started off at a fast walk.

Gwen saw he was not walking normally. Each step was more like a slither. He put the weight of his foot first on the outside of his foot then rolled it to the toe. His head was in constant motion. He never made a sound, even when brushing against the odd low-hanging branch. Unlike her. She would occasionally tread on a fallen branch and it would snap, or she would stumble. And when she brushed against the same branch her father had just brushed against, the scraping of her clothing and backpack was loud.

Just as he had predicted, once she started walking her ankle had loosened up. It still hurt, but it was a dull throb now, not the sharp pain of earlier. Her calf muscles were getting sore and the weight on her shoulders from the pack were beginning to bother her, but he kept walking, so she did, too.

It was starting to get dark in the forest when he finally stopped by a fallen tree. Duncan removed the purse and the rolled blanket, hung them on a branch, and stretched.

"Too long behind a desk," she heard him mutter.

He once again pulled out the small device from his back pocket, turned it on briefly, glanced at it, and shut it off again.

"Five K," he said. "Not bad for the first day."

He picked up any obvious rocks and broken branches from an area near the fallen trunk and tossed them aside. Using first his right foot, then his hands, he piled the fallen needles into two rough bed shapes. Surveying his handiwork, he grunted and nodded.

Gwen had stood, watching him, catching her breath, and letting her heart-rate slow. She dropped the backpack at her feet and dug one of the water bottles from it. She took the top off, letting it fall to the ground, and took a deep drink, then she poured some in her right hand and wiped it across her face. She was just about to dump the rest of it over her head to cool herself down when her father took the bottle from her hand.

He took a mouthful of water, swirled it around his mouth, swallowed it, bent down, picked up the discarded cap and twisted it back on.

"We have four litres of water," he said. "It has to last until we can find some more. That could be many days."

He put the bottle back in her pack and hung the pack on another branch of the tree. He pulled the carving knife from the large purse and the sharpening tool that had come with the set. Sitting on the piled-up needles cross-legged, he started to run the sharpening tool slowly down the knife, spitting on the tool now and then.

"Dig out a packet of the rations," he said. "We'll split it. It tastes like crap and you will still feel hungry after, but it is food and it is healthy."

Gwen pulled one of the emergency ration packs from her backpack and stuffed it in her back pocket. Remembering something she had seen on a vid long ago, she began gathering twigs and small branches to make a fire.

"No fire tonight," her father said. "We are not far enough away from the pod. Maybe tomorrow."

She dropped her little armful of firewood on the ground and sat across from him. Then, remembering the ration in her back pocket, sprang back up again and pulled the pack out. It had not burst. Her dad laughed.

"That would be good," he said. "Watching you scrape all that goo from your pants."

He continued slowly sharpening the carving knife.

"That thing was sharp before, Dad," Gwen said.

"Ya, for cutting meat. Edge is too thin; will get dull fast. I'm redoing it."

"Sorry I was so noisy today," he continued. "I'm a little out of practice."

"What?" Gwen said. "Noisy? I didn't hear a thing."

"Ya, you were making enough noise to wake the dead," he said and chuckled. "When you walk, pick your feet up, don't drag them. For the first little while, watch the ground so you don't trip on anything, or step on any obvious branches. When you come to a low hanging branch, gently sweep it away and roll away from it. It will get easier as you practice. Tomorrow we will run for a bit. Nothing hard or fast or long. We need to put as much distance as we can between us and the pod."

Gwen fell asleep, exhausted, listening to him sharpening the knife.

When she awoke, Duncan was already moving around. He had found a large tree branch, as tall as he and as thick as her wrist, and was leaning it against the fallen tree trunk beside his gear. Another, slightly shorter one, was next to her backpack.

She stood and made her way to a large tree, went behind it, pulled down her pants and squatted. She cursed as her urine began to run toward her feet. She heard him laugh.

"Point your ass downhill next time," he said and chuckled some more.

Chapter Five

Gwen woke. They had been walking and running for several days. It took a moment to realize that, once again, she was sleeping, not in a comfortable bed, but on the ground beside a large tree trunk. That her father had been up for an hour was indicated by the fire crackling in the fire-pit they had built the night before. Her father was nowhere around, which, the last few days had shown, could mean almost anything.

Before her eyes, he was becoming a different person; somehow more feral. He looked like an animal on the hunt rather than a rich aristocrat, in fact, a ruler of a planetary system. He was almost silent as he moved through the forest, his feet gliding more than stepping. His head was always in motion, swivelling from side to side. He sometimes stopped, not moving for minutes, then ran again.

There didn't seem to be a pattern to their direction, although the sun was generally on their left. After several days of her father pointing out animal markings and signs, she had realized they were following game trails. Although seemingly random in nature, these trails had a pattern. They went to feeding areas and water.

Every day they ran faster and longer. Now they were running for ten minutes, walking for five, and the running pace had increased to almost what she ran in school meets. Now, she was the one who was breathless at the end of the day, not her father. He also had her doing the slow, rhythmic martial arts regime she first encountered her second week of cadet training. He had slowly increased the number of movements and the length of time they did them. They now practiced them up to an hour each morning. After supper, Duncan also had his daughter perfecting similar movements with the tree branch he had carved for her. In addition to the now very sharp kitchen knife, her father had a forearm-long branch he had shaved to a point on one end, then slowly rotated over their nightly fire. He said this would harden the point. He had shaved the shaft round so it fitted his hand.

He also worked every night on a tree branch like hers, but longer, up to his ear. He had made a similar point on one end. While he was rounding the shaft, he would stop, place the middle of the shaft on one hand, then start shaving it again. It was almost balanced. He had used it to kill some small animals for meat to supplement their rations.

She knew that the last two days they had been traveling parallel to a road. She knew because, from time to time, she could hear tire noise in the distance. They were within two hundred meters of it now. Occasionally, she could see it through the trees. Why her father did not flag down one of these vehicles, Gwen could not understand. They could use the help.

In fact, she could faintly hear tire noise in the distance coming their way. *Enough is enough,* Gwen thought, *If Dad will not ask for help, I will.* With him nowhere in sight, Gwen trotted to the road, climbed the small ditch bordering it and reached the centre of it just as the vehicle rounded the corner a hundred meters away. The vehicle braked to a stop as she waved both her arms over her head. That it was a military vehicle was clear, not only from its appearance, but also from the fact that two soldiers emerged from the front seat and two from the rear.

Her joy at being rescued turned rapidly to dismay when two of the soldiers drew blasters and pointed them at her, while the other two drew blasters and surveyed the area around the vehicle. One of the soldiers covering her tapped the communicator in his ear.

"Delta Base, Delta 82, we have the female in custody," he said in French. "No sight of the male target."

"Delta 82, wait one." The response came back, also in French.

"Delta 82, Delta command," a different voice said. "Eliminate the female. The male will not be far away; eliminate him also. Dispose of the bodies after taking vids of them. Copy?"

"Copy," the one called Delta 82 said. "Might as well have some fun with her first," he said.

"Hey, miss," he said in French-accented Standard. He and his buddy both holstered their blasters and advanced toward her. "You need some assistance?"

The two men scanning the perimeter similarly holstered their pistols and turned to watch. The first two men approached, then lunged at her. As they did, her father exploded from the far ditch, his sharpened pole raised above his head. Before the nearest soldier knew what was going on, Duncan thrust the pole into the man's back. Putting both hands on the pole, he leaned into it, shoving it right through the man's body to exit from his stomach. Then Duncan withdrew the shorter, arm-length stick from his belt and attacked the farther soldier, who was just turning to see what was going on.

At that point, the two soldiers approaching Gwen sprang at her. Gwen didn't understand it, but her body instantly reacted. Her right elbow caught the closest soldier under the jaw and she spun, lashing out with her left foot and catching the other soldier in the groin with it. Then she ran.

Gwen heard a loud scream and, looking back, saw her father removing the carving fork from the right eye socket of the soldier she had struck in the jaw. The one she had hit in the groin was writhing on the ground clutching his throat, his face turning blue. The second soldier by the vehicle had the arm-length stick rammed in his left ear, blood pooling on the ground.

.   Her dad looked up and waved her to him. Then he went to the vehicle and began rummaging around inside it.

Gwen vomited as she came to the vehicle and saw the damage her father had done to the soldiers. When she stood up, he tossed a rucksack at her.

"Put it on," he said. "Then head back in the bush and start running, the same way we were moving before. I'll catch up with you."

As she ran, she looked back and saw him removing the blasters from the dead soldiers, then remove the communicator from one of them. She turned and ran.

"Delta Command," Duncan said in Standard. "Delta 82."

"Go ahead Delta 82," was the response. "Is the mission accomplished?"

"Negative, Command," Duncan said. "I kind of lied. Delta 82 and his three buddies are dead. If this keeps up, I might have to think this is personal. I would recommend you send more people, Delta Command. You should also make sure you have a lot of body bags. You just gave me four blasters and a bunch of supplies. I did what I did with two sticks. What do you think I will do with some real weapons?

"The Ghost is in the wind, Delta Command, and he is coming for you."

Duncan threw the communicator from him and stuck the four blasters and their spare batteries in the second rucksack. Putting it on his back, he removed the two sticks impaled in the soldiers and ran.

The sun was beginning to set. As she had been taught, Gwen began to look for a secluded spot to camp for the night. She found a suitable one, removed her rucksack and began gathering firewood. It took about half an hour and, as she rose from starting the small fire, her father was…just there. One second she was alone, the next, he was standing in front of her.

He stripped off his rucksack, and after rummaging around in it for a minute, removed two packs of rations and tossed them at her. Then, he sat down and began sharpening his sticks again. At no time, while she cooked, or while they ate, did he speak to her. He didn't even look at her. When he was done with his meal, he tossed the empty ration container into the fire and resumed sharpening his two sticks.

"Dad, talk to me," Gwen finally said. "Can't you see how traumatizing this is for me?"

"Suck it up, Cadet," her dad said. He didn't even look up from what he was doing.

"What the hell is wrong with you?" Gwen blurted out.

"Suck it up, Cadet," he said again. "You think we are on a holiday excursion here?"

She pouted.

"ATTENTION, CADET!" he ordered. "You are in the field and under orders!"

Her body reacted automatically to hours and hours of training on the parade ground. She came to attention, her arms stiff at her side.

Now her father rose to his full height. She had never seen him like this. He appeared ten feet tall and his presence appeared all around her.

"Report, Cadet!" He said.

"Cadet Private Kovacks, Sir!" Gwen belted out.

"Do I look like a pussy officer, Cadet?" Duncan growled. "I work for a fucking living, Cadet! Not only that, but I am a frontline combat trooper, Cadet. Not some pussy teacher doubling as a Cadet trainer. I am a fucking Chief Master Warrant and you shall address me as such! Do you understand, Cadet Private?"

"Yes, Master Warrant Kovacks. The Cadet Private understands, Master Warrant!"

"Are you in the habit of disobeying orders, Cadet Private?" Duncan said. "That would explain why you are still a private, Cadet. Not even a private first class after your second year of training. Unlike the rest of your class. Just going through the motions are you, Cadet Kovacks?"

"No Master Warrant Kovacks!"

Duncan was right in front of her now. Her nose was almost touching his chin. His eyes held her like that for a moment, then stepped back.

"At ease, Cadet," he said. He waited until she assumed the position, her feet shoulder width apart, both hands clenched behind her back, eyes focused above his head.

"Until I determine otherwise," Duncan continued. "You are demoted to Cadet. You have lost the right to the rank of private. Understood, Cadet?"

"Understood, Master Warrant!"

"Now sit the fuck down, Gwen," Duncan said.

"What the hell did you think we do, Gwen?" Duncan said. "We fucking kill people, Gwen, and I am damn good at it. I have been since I was not much older than you. I killed four men today using two sticks and a carving fork. I can kill a person with my hands or my feet. Or from a kilometre away with a high-powered rifle.

"I am a Wind Rider, Gwen. In fact, I am one of the four original Wind Riders. Have you heard of the Ghost, Gwen?"

"Yes," Gwen said. "He is some kind of legendary super trooper."

"I am the Ghost, Gwen," Duncan said. "What you saw today is only a small part of what I am able to do. Your mother is The Zebra and she is almost as good as I am. Barb is the Voice. Scott, Brett and Bob are the other three original Wind Riders. Dianne, Amanda and Carol were next. Then CT, Anne and the rest of the Americans."

Gwen was stunned. All of these people were very rich and powerful. All were close friends of her parents. She'd had no idea.

"Today, you almost got yourself killed. You are damn lucky you were not. For whatever reason, these people have decided to kill us, Gwen. Not an issue for me. I was dead as soon as I put on my first uniform and have lived a pretty good life. Not so for you, girl. Your mother and I had hoped to shield you from all this, but apparently that's not possible."

Duncan became quiet for a time. He was looking at the fire, but Gwen could tell he wasn't seeing it. She had noticed him do similar things before. He would go quiet and look far away. Her mother had done it at times, too.

"Do you know what Guinevere means?" he asked, finally.

"She was a famous Queen from long ago," Gwen said.

"The Lakota call you White Ghost," Duncan said. "Because that is what your name means. It is from an ancient Home World language, not much used anymore, even on Home World. And, yes, she was a famous Queen in ancient times. Not only a Queen, but a warrior."

He went quiet again.

"You fucked up today, Gwen," Duncan said. "It was my fault. I should have told you why we were staying away from the road. But you also got it almost right. You didn't freeze, you struck out to defend yourself, then ran from a no-win situation. Only someone well-trained in survival could have tracked you here.

"You have possibilities, Gwen. I will teach you more. But not tonight. Tonight, you are my young, naive daughter."

He came over and sat beside her. Duncan put his arm around her like she had seen him do with her mother so many times. And she broke down.

Duncan waited an hour after she fell asleep. Then he moved away from their small camp, pulled a communicator from his back pocket and turned it on.

"Zebra One One, Gulf One One."

"Go ahead," Marlene said.

"Gulf One Two became a soldier today." Duncan said.

"Shit," Marlene replied after a minute. "Is she okay?"

"Ya, she'll be okay. She's starting to act like her namesake. How are you making out?"

"These fucking women are pigheaded stubborn," Marlene said. "They can't wrap their heads around men being soldiers."

"Stick with it, luv," Duncan said. "You should be good for a while. They'll be after us. Nothing I can't handle. Gotta go, luv."

Gwen slept badly. She kept replaying what she had witnessed that day. She didn't notice her father had not gone to sleep. All night he had watched her toss and turn, reminding him of others, including himself, who had suffered through that first awful sight of the newly killed.

Gwen awoke to see her father calmly shaving another stick. This one was half the length of his forearm. He had a cup of steaming liquid on the ground beside him and, from the smell, she knew it was coffee. Each ration pack had a packet of coffee in it. There was a pot of water warming on the fire and a pouch of the ration goo beside the rocks outside the fire. This would be placed into the pot of hot water, warmed, and eaten for breakfast. It tasted horrible, but it was edible and nutritious.

"Day off today, kid," Duncan said. "They will be checking all along the road for the next few days. They have no idea of how or how far we can travel. They travel by vehicle, wouldn't think of walking, much less running, as far as we do every day."

Duncan rose, plunked the pouch of goo in the pot of water to heat and sat back down again.

"Rough night, eh?" Her father reverted to his native Standard from time to time. "I'd like to say it gets easier over time, but I'd be lying. I'd like to give you wonderful words of wisdom to take your pain away, but I won't. Law of survival, kid. Kill them before they kill you."

"What..." Gwen said.

"Prey have choices, Gwen," Duncan said. "Run and maybe die. Freeze and die. Fight and maybe die. Kill and live. Have no doubt, Gwen: here, now, we are prey. Now we run and, so, live. You have enough training to fight, and maybe live. Now I teach you to kill, so you may live."

It began after their morning breakfast and exercise routine. He showed her how to use the moves they'd been practicing to attack; how to block a blow, redirect it and retaliate; where to hit to do the most damage.

"Most of your enemies will be men, Gwen," Duncan said. "We are bigger and stronger. While not impossible, it will be very difficult to use strength to deal with a man. You are faster and more agile, so use that. Speed, agility and skill. Then you learn stealth."

Every morning they worked on her unarmed combat. After supper, she was trained to use the knife or her smaller sharp pole.

As with the running, he sped up the training every day. And as with the running, his heavy sweating and breathlessness were soon gone. She was even able to land a blow now and then. Not often, but enough to make her try harder.

Then came the day. She was striking him more often now. The tables had turned and he was the one on the defensive. Then, she put him down on the ground. She had him and he knew it. He smiled up at her.

"Well done, kid," Duncan said. "You are good enough now to take down frontline soldiers with ease."

Then, to her astonishment, his right leg snaked around her head and she flew from him. In a flash she was up, but he was there first. In a move so fast his hands blurred, he hit her twice in the ribs, then swung his left leg and tossed her to the ground.

"But I am not just a frontline soldier, Cadet Private," Duncan said. He was smiling. "I am a rock'em sock'em recon trooper. I am a Wind Rider. I don't guard sheep. I kill wolves."

Then she noticed he wasn't sweating and sported no bruises from all her hits. He let her up and he had that twinkle in his eyes she had so often seen when he had pulled a fast one on her mother.

"Once in a while, Cadet Private," Duncan continued. "You will find a man as fast as you and as skilled as you. His strength will overpower you. Then you must use your agility and his strength against him."

They now ran every day for six hours, always with the sun at their backs. She learned a new skill daily. And she had begun to hunt. She learned how to hide, move quickly and silently, and where and how to set traps. First, she set traps for small animals, then larger, more deadly mantraps.

"We are only two, Cadet Private," Duncan said. "They are many."

He went on to explain that the two of them had the advantage. They knew that every soldier they came across was their enemy. Their enemy would be less sure. The two of them could infiltrate the enemies defences, do damage and leave while they rushed around trying to figure out what was going on.

"Tomorrow we turn toward the road, Gwen," Duncan said. Gwen had learned when he called her Cadet, they were working.

When he called her Gwen, they were not. "You have learned enough not to kill yourself. Now we start to fight back."

Days merged with days. Gwen could hear tire noise occasionally, if the wind was right. Her training now was in concealment and stalking. Her father was ruthless. Many nights she nursed bruised ribs and buttocks. A few times she thought she had him, only to find him hitting her from another direction. Whenever Gwen became upset or frustrated, he would do something dumb to make her laugh, like the time she sprang one of his traps and it threw her lunch right into her chest with a note attached that read, *You look hungry.*

They had made their small camp for the night, cooked and eaten dinner, and were gazing at the fire. This was usually lesson time for Gwen. Before this night's lesson began, Gwen asked a question.

"Everyone says you had a lot of land and cattle back on Home World, Dad," she began. "You didn't have mandatory military service like we do, yet you volunteered to join the army."

"We had something called the Reserve Army," Duncan said. "I saw a demonstration vehicle at our annual agricultural fair. It was an interesting vehicle, I got a brochure, went for an information night and found out I'd get paid to hang out in the bush and play soldier on the weekends. I was just barely eligible age-wise, had nothing better to do and, unlike you, wasn't all that interested in sports or the opposite sex."

"But you ended up being full time," Gwen said.

"Not at first. But the officers and senior noncommissioned officers saw I had a natural ability and started giving me more responsibility. I made corporal the soonest that could be allowed. The next summer I was sent for advanced noncommissioned officer training. I graduated in the top five. My folks were very happy and I got promoted right away to sergeant. Then mom died unexpectedly. Dad had been approached by my battalion commander about my going active duty. I was just shy of being eighteen, so my folks had to approve.

"After the funeral, with everyone gone, Dad brought out an old photo album. I knew my mom had been in the army; that's where they had met. But I thought she had just been an admin type. My dad was a radio operator. The front of the album was all Mom, about my age. She was dressed in the uniform of a very famous regiment back home and she had an eagle on her collar. That whole regiment was elite Gwen, but the Eagles? They were the elite of the elite.

"She spent almost twenty years in that regiment. Serving, in combat in some very nasty places. When she left, she was a colonel and had so many medals and I-was-there ribbons you could hardly see her chest."

Duncan stopped for a moment.

His father had told him that his mother was very proud of him and had arranged for him to attend Eagle training. This was something reserved for members of that particular country, or an invited elite super trooper from another country. His dad had highly recommended he take that training. If, when he had finished, he wanted to go active duty, good. If not, no big deal.

"That training was on a whole other level, Gwen," Duncan said. "First off, I was with kids my own age, who, like we do here, all started training at thirteen years old. They all knew each other. I knew some of them, but not all. And most of them made it very clear that my mom had left under some kind of controversy they held against me."

"Ya, peer pressure sucks," Gwen said. "I get the same shit, only different. Oh no! They didn't know you, right?"

Duncan had his goofy look. Again.

"Got that right, kid," he said. "Don't piss a Kovacks off. I got that damn Eagle, top five again. I started to take off and the general's wife grabs me. She was a colonel. She takes me up to their house. Imagine that. Dumb ass Kovacks at the General's house. General asks me to join their regiment."

"Ut oh," Gwen said. Duncan was smiling now.

"'No Sir,' says I. 'I am a Kings Own, Sir! I wouldn't want to drag the regiments name down because of my mother. Sir!' And I give him a hand salute, indoors. I figured, oh boy, that's the end of my short army career. The colonel, she laughs, 'Guess he told you, eh?' she says. The general flops his hand in the general direction of his forehead as a return salute. 'Sit the fuck down, idiot,' he says. The colonel sits down, undoes her tunic, so does the general and she slides a glass and a bottle of vodka over at me."

"Acts just like her, Paul, right?" the colonel says.

"'Ya, my aunt had a mouth on her, that's for sure,' the general says. 'What the hell are you talking about, your mom a disgrace? That's total bullshit!'

"'Your mother was one of our best, Duncan,' the colonel says. 'But after twenty years, she had had enough of the army and the colony. Her mom was Andrea Bekenbaum, Nicolas' daughter. So, Paul is your cousin. You are entitled, by birthright, to this training and that eagle and once you have finished your five years of service, full membership in the colony.'"

"What did that mean, Dad?" Gwen asked.

"That I am a direct descendant of the man who started that colony and that, because of my mom, I was an extremely wealthy seventeen-year-old. Just like someone else I know." And he tossed a piece of firewood at her.

"Early day tomorrow, kid," he said. Then he laid down and in seconds was asleep. Or so she thought.

In fact, it was a long time until he fell asleep, reliving that memory and memories of the stepmother Gwen had never known.

Chapter Six

T he next morning, it was clear her father was in no hurry. They did their usual exercise and weapons training routines, followed by breakfast. After eating their freeze-dried mush and cleaning up, Duncan poured himself another cup of coffee and sat down beside their small fire. He motioned her to sit, then began to speak, in what she was beginning to think of as his instructional voice.

He told her that while the Wind Riders were famous for their unconventional warfare tactics, their primary purpose was to obtain and provide information for the regular army troops. Much of their time was spent well ahead of the main trooper formations, concealed and silent, only fighting when they had absolutely no other choice. That is why they were called a *reconnaissance* group.

Gwen could hear noise approaching on the not-too-distant road. A short time later, a dust plume could be seen. It soon passed and began to diminish as it went down the road.

"So," Duncan said. "What have we learned the last week, traveling beside the road?"

"There is not much traffic on it," Gwen replied. "Usually, one vehicle travels from east to west in the morning and one from west to east in the afternoon. Yesterday, a large number of vehicles traveled from east to west and today, a smaller number returned."

"So," Duncan said. "Based on the size and construction of that road, would you not agree that more vehicles should be traveling on it each day?"

"Um..." Gwen said.

Her father smiled.

"That type of road is not designed for a lot of high-speed point-to-point travel," Duncan said.

He went on to explain that he did not know much about this planet. He did know they exported lumber. Trees were cut down, then transferred to a facility that sawed the trees into lumber, which was shipped to another facility for drying, and finally shipped to the spaceport. That meant that there should be a lot more traffic on this road each day than they had observed.

They had already discovered, of course, that armed men were traveling the road looking for them. This planet was ruled by women, so its armed forces should be female. That meant that some other foreign power had made landfall...*invaded*, more like.

"I assume that the invaders have a base to the east of us," Duncan said. "Each morning, a scout vehicle is sent out, probably to look for us, but scouting other things as well. In the afternoon, that scout vehicle returns to the base. By the lack of other traffic, I'm thinking the invader has taken control of the town that services this area. Yesterday, a convoy was sent to the west. It had five large armoured vehicles, two smaller ones and two large transport vehicles. Each one of those large armoured vehicles will have two crew members and ten troops. The small ones would have four. That makes fifty-eight troops in total. So I now think that, somewhere to the west of us, they are setting up a forward base. The vehicles we just heard were the empty transport trucks returning to the main base.

"So, what else does that tell us?"

Gwen just looked at him.

"The invader has complete control of this area," Duncan said. "They sent those two trucks back without an escort, which means they are not worried about anyone attacking them. Now I don't know about you, but I am getting a little tired of freeze-dried mush to eat and, while the rabbits and fish we have been obtaining are nice, we are running low on the freeze-dried mush. Also, your clothing is getting a bit ragged and you stink."

"Ya, like you don't," Gwen said as she tossed a large piece of firewood at him.

Unable to shave for the last month, Duncan's moustache and beard had filled out, mostly grey. A few times she had called him Santa Claus, because he was beginning to look like it.

"Armies everywhere operate the same way," Duncan continued. "So, based on the time they pass our position and the timing of their return, I would say we are about ten kilometres from the new base and twenty from the main one. For the next couple of days, we will just hang out here. It's a good spot. We will observe the amount of traffic on the road. Then? Well, we'll think of something."

It had been a boring month; the last week was the worst. At least on Oaken there had been some fight from the locals. On this planet, nothing. The women who ran the place were arrogant and had not the faintest idea of how to put up even a rudimentary defence.

Luck had seen him survive the debacle at Oaken. He had been wounded during one of the first attacks by the Off World mercenaries and had been back in New Paris hospital when it all ended.

He had refused to serve the new overlord. As a result, he had been sent into exile along with all the remaining supporters of the old regime. It had taken a long time, twenty-five years, in fact, to get to this point. Now, retribution was at hand.

Unfortunately, it seemed that Kovacks had escaped the attack on the transport ship, along with the traitor Isabelle and their daughter. Kovacks had been spotted in this sector with the girl. The traitor had not been located yet but it would only be a matter of time. They were slowly taking control of the whole planet and now had enough money and backing to escalate things further.

He could have taken one of the more comfortable transports, like most of the other officers. Instead, he chose to ride to his new command in a transport vehicle. His four-man protection detail was in the rear with the supplies; he was beside the driver.

The drive was not long, only three hours. The driver was one of the younger troopers born in exile. It had been a pleasant journey so far. They turned a sharp corner in the rough road and the driver slammed on the brakes, skidding to a stop and almost losing control of the vehicle.

In the centre of the road was one of their targets. The daughter. Her hair was unkempt, her clothing tattered and dirty. A stick as tall as her shoulder was in her right hand. She made no move to get out of the way; nor did she come forward. Her face showed no emotion, no fear, no elation.

The officer unlatched his door and climbed out. His protection detail piled out of the back and joined him.

"Grab the brat," the officer said. And his men moved forward.

Once his men were within a meter of her and about to grab her, she flipped up the stick and, one-handed, cracked the first one in the temple, downing him. Then she took the stick in both hands and jammed the blunt end into the throat of another. A beam of light from the left and another was down from a blaster strike. Then the driver screamed. The officer turned to the left and saw an aberration remove a large carving fork from the driver's ear. The last of his protection detail went down as the girl hit him across the temple with a hard two-handed swing of the stick.

The officer finally removed his blaster from its holster and frantically tried to get the safety off and line it up on the aberration, who simply walked toward him, in no hurry, a large carving knife in one hand, the long fork in the other. The officer fired, only to see the creature take a fast step to the right and turn sideways away from the blast. Before the weapon could recharge for another shot, the officer felt pain as the girl swung her stick across the back of both his knees, felling him instantly in withering pain. He felt more pain as she cracked him on the right wrist. She deftly plucked the blaster from his hand, took two steps away from him, and shot the last soldier she had hit with her stick in the forehead.

The officer was able to roll over and look up. The man approaching him was two meters tall. He wore a long grey beard and moustache, unkempt and now blood-stained. His greying blond hair was long, almost to his shoulders. Then he spoke and the officer knew he was doomed.

"Nice job, for a probie, kid," he said to the girl. Turning to him, he sneered, "Only made it to major after all these years? Good thing you didn't join us, then. Thanks for the truck and the weapons. Probie, see if any of those yahoos' boots will fit you, eh?"

"So," Duncan continued. "Now I know who is behind all this. It wasn't a problem for only thirty of us to wipe you out the last time. There will be a thousand or more here in a month or two."

"You think you know so much," the officer said. "You have no army any more. Without you, it was easy to stage a takeover. You and that traitor Isabelle are on your own. I will rejoice at your deaths."

"You people always were over-confident and mouthy," Duncan said. "Now I thank you for the information. If I know you people, you also have more information for me on your communicator. As far as rejoicing in my death? Well, I guess it will be from hell when I join you there."

Then Duncan leaned over and stabbed the major in the neck, severing the artery and slashing across to almost cut the head right off. As the man kicked his life out, feet drumming on the ground, Duncan wiped the blade on the man's tunic.

Duncan stood and looked at his daughter. She was white, almost as white as her namesake, but she was not shaking. That would come later. She was tugging a pair of boots off a dead trooper.

"Just hang them around your neck," Duncan said. "See if there is any grub or anything else we can use in the back of the truck."

As Gwen began rummaging in the truck, tossing cartons out, Duncan began dragging the bodies to the rear. He opened the fuel cap and, ripping a length of uniform from one of the dead, rolled it into a cylinder and stuffed it in the filler neck, leaving a long length hanging loose on the outside.

Gwen jumped out of the truck and began stuffing cartons into the two rucksacks she had found. With some effort, Duncan began throwing bodies into the back of the truck. He then reached across the dead driver's body, started the engine, put it into gear, then deftly jumped away as it slowly made its way toward the large drop-off at the edge of the tight curve. He lit the end of the rag in the fuel tank as the vehicle made its way past him. Then he and Gwen shouldered the packs and melted into the woods. They were too far away to see the explosion as the fuel tank caught fire and exploded. But they heard it.

Neither Gwen nor Duncan slept much that night; she, reliving what she had done, Duncan, holding and consoling her, his mind on far more troubling things.

The next morning, while Gwen was still asleep, Duncan turned on his comm unit for his customary weekly check. It beeped, telling him he had a message. It was encrypted, so he turned on his trusty old and battered laptop and sent the message to it.

After a short time, CT's image came on the screen.

"Hey boss," CT said. "Um...we have a bit of a situation here. Well, more than a little situation, actually. Some high fliers have taken control here, telling everyone you and the gang are dead. All of us were off-system on holiday like you guys, and we are now locked out of everything. All the company funds are sealed, as are our personal accounts. They think.

"We are working on a solution. Unfortunately, you are on your own for now. Gotta go, boss. Take care."

"Fucking hell!" Duncan blurted out. He quickly looked around and saw Gwen had gotten up and was looking over his shoulder.

"How fucked are we?" She asked, then raised an eyebrow as he was about to chastise her for her language.

"Not truly fucked, but close," Duncan said instead. "CT just confirmed what that blowhard said yesterday. Unfortunately for them, the Wind Riders were all on holiday like we were, and out of system. They think they have cut all our funding and access. But they have no idea what we are capable of. Help is still coming, luv. Just not as fast as we first thought."

"Shit!" Gwen said. Her nice comfortable life had just come crashing around her ears. "What about Mom?"

Duncan was already walking away, tapping his earpiece. He spoke a few words and then cringed. Gwen could almost make out the words her mother was yelling before the automatic volume control kicked in. After a few minutes of her father calming her mother down, her own earpiece kicked in.

"How the hell can you stay so goddamned calm?" her mother said. "Our world has just gone all to fucking hell!"

"And where have you been all this time, Mom?" Gwen asked. Her voice calm as well. Now she raised her voice. "Yesterday I killed four men and Dad, two. What the fuck were you doing? Having tea and crumpets with your lady buddies? These assholes plan on not only killing us but taking over this whole damn planet and there is nothing your pumped up female thugs can do about it."

Except for her mother's heavy breathing, nothing could be heard on the comm unit.

"Get off your ass and do what you have been trained to do," Gwen said. "You are Recon, you are Wind Rider, you are Zebra. Start acting like it. We have already figured out where the main base is in our sector and where the staging base most likely is. We have hit them twice in the last two weeks and inflicted ten K-I-A and two destroyed vehicles. Dad is already working on how to fuck them up more, now that we have more than two sticks, a carving knife, and carving fork. So, get to it, Master Warrant, get to it. White Ghost out!"

"You let her do what?" Marlene blurted out in a rage.

"I let her stand in the middle of the road with her walking stick to stop the truck," Duncan said. "I had it under control, but like another stubborn woman I know, she took matters into her own hands. She killed the first two before I even got out of the ditch.'

"Jesus!" Marlene said. "She's only sixteen. With no training."

"In the last two weeks, she has almost been raped. Had her nice comfortable life uprooted and been running for her life through some very tough bush. You had six weeks of basic training, another six weeks of advanced training and another four of special ops training. That was followed by almost twenty years of heavy combat operations.

"She's learning on the fly, Mar. She has to, or she and I will die. We haven't had the opportunity to meet any locals yet, but when we do, we will do what we did on Oaken. Train them to fight and win. She's right, get those stubborn broads to get their heads out of their asses or get the hell out of there and find someone willing to fight."

"Shit," Marlene said.

"Look," Duncan continued. "You took three wet-behind-the-ears raw recruits and made them the best damn recon team we have, Mar. if you could do that, I'm positive you can train some motivated locals to do the same."

"Whisky Romeo is coming, Mar," Duncan said after a moment of silence. "Or they will die trying. Let's get them some good intelligence to work with, eh?"

"Okay," Marlene said after a few seconds. "But what about the rest? We have lost everything."

"If they want it that bad let them have it," Duncan said. "We have enough knowledge, training, skills and money to completely disappear, Mar. Maybe it's time."

"Maybe you're right," Marlene said. She was calm now and he could picture her walking around her room.

"I bet you just swept your hair back behind your right ear, right?" he asked.

"Duncan, you can be such an asshole sometimes," she said, and he knew he was right.

"Now, tie your hair back, put on your stripes and show those pretend warriors what a real Amazon looks like, eh?" Duncan said.

"You are such an adorable asshole sometimes, too," she said. "Zebra out."

He looked over at Gwen, who was wiping the last of her tears from her eyes.

"What was that about the hair and the stripes?" Gwen asked.

"Your mom, when she is about to hit the real shit," Duncan said, "pulls her hair back in a tight braid and paints Zebras stripes on her face, making sure she highlights that scar I gave her. Sometimes she ties her shirt up over her navel just under her breasts, rolls up the sleeves and paints all of it Zebra stripes. All the Zebra do. PG even does it to her hair and makes it stand up like a Zebra main. Right intimidating it is."

"I'll bet," Gwen said. "How come she never let me see that scar except that one time with all your friends?"

"You can't always see all of our scars, Gwen," Duncan said, his voice just over a whisper. "Some are too deep to be seen." He walked away from her.

After an hour she tracked him down. He was sitting with his back against a tree overlooking a small clearing. He was looking up at the clouds between the tree canopy.

"Back home, I would find a place a lot like this, near a pond," he said, without looking around. "I would have a fishing pole with a line in the water. I wouldn't even have a hook on the line. That way I wouldn't have to explain why I was sitting under a tree looking at the clouds."

Gwen sat beside him, gave him a quick squeeze, then laid her head on his shoulder.

"Do you think of her often?" Gwen asked.

"Every day, sometimes too many times a day," Duncan said. "Your mom can be a major pain in the ass sometimes, but she loves me and I love her, dearly."

"I know that," Gwen said. "I was talking about your first wife."

She felt his shoulder quiver and looked up to see a tear run down and into his beard.

"Ya," he said finally. "Also almost every day. Her name was Karen, and she was just ten years older than you are now when she died. We had only been married for just over a year."

"And Mom really killed her?"

"Ya, but she was only doing her job, Gwen," Duncan said. "The blame is mine. I was in command, not only of that team but of our whole force. Karen was not really trained for that type of operation and I should never have let her leave the LAV. But damn, she was what we call a keener. She loved all the rah-rah shoot-'em-up shit. Both her mom and dad were career army officers. Her dad was a super trooper like I was back then. She wanted to prove not only to us, but to herself, she had what it takes. And, like a lot of keeners, she paid for it with her life."

Duncan looked down at his daughter. She was looking into his eyes and she reached up and wiped the tear from his eye. His face was neutral, but his eyes betrayed his sorrow.

"I have seen a lot of kids cut down," he said. "Some only a few years older than you. I have seen kids as young as ten or younger, cut down, just for being in the wrong place at the wrong time. It hurts every time, Gwen. But if I, and people like me, don't do something, or at least try to stop the assholes, they will keep on doing that shit. Small price to pay, I say."

"So," Gwen said. "You were not just a pretend figurehead soldier, then?"

"Nope," Duncan said. "Just a dumb farm kid who joined the reserve army for some fun. Like Karen, I jumped at the chance to go on active duty to prove to myself I could do it. The shit I saw over there? Well, I decided I needed to try and put an end to it. I was seventeen when I joined, and went active right after I turned eighteen. Been doing it ever since.

"Like I told your mom, maybe it's time to quit. Let somebody else be the boss and just go back to being a dumb farm boy."

"But what about all the people that need our help, Dad?" Gwen asked. "What about the people on this planet that need us?"

"Oh, I will help these folks out, if I can," Duncan said. "I really have no choice if you and I have any chance of survival."

"And what about our people?"

"Maybe they are better off without us, Gwen," Duncan said.

"No, Dad," she said softly. "They all love you and Mom. They know in their hearts how good they have it. I never knew why until that little girl got hurt and, when you calmly, on interplanetary news, put that pompous ass in his place, never raising your voice or making any threats. Then the swift and ruthless retribution, again with no boasting or bluster. I have also seen you pick up the spirits of the less fortunate just by making a stupid joke or asking them how they did something."

"Ya," Duncan said, and he smiled that mischievous grin of his. "Just like some over-indulged and pampered Daddy's girl did. Christ, I thought that reporter that knocked that little girl down was gonna shit his pants when you gave him the evil eye."

"Oh," Gwen said, she had her own grin on now. "Is that what that god-awful smell was?"

"You little shit!" Duncan said and he made to grab her, but she was too fast for him, spinning out of his grasp, standing and giving him the finger as she ran away, his laughter in her ears.

Chapter Seven

Over the next two weeks, Duncan and Gwen conducted three more ambushes on supply trucks. Each time, they chose a rough part of the road at a sharp corner or steep incline. However, in the last four days they had attacked no one, because they were too close to where her father felt the base was. When they located it, they skirted well away and out of sight of it. They searched for the perfect location to set up their own base.

Occasionally, they would spot a cloud of black smoke rise above the trees. In the dark of night, a red glow would sometimes light the horizon. Her father told Gwen it was most likely the invaders destroying some small settlement or logging camp.

They stumbled upon an area where the trees had recently been clear-cut. They didn't walk into it but kept just out of sight at its edge. Once, Duncan stopped and, after several minutes of scanning the surroundings, he dashed out into the clearing and returned with an axe head, a broken piece of the shaft still in it. The shaft had broken just under the axe head which rendered it useless, she thought.

That night, using a stone of the right size, Duncan slowly punched out the broken piece of wooden axe handle, then started to shape a new handle out of a sturdy tree branch. It took him almost a week to shape it into a handle using a knife lifted from one of the transport trucks they had ambushed. As the shape began to resemble what he was looking for, her father would carve a little, then test it in his hand, then began to swing it about. Once he was satisfied, he began to smooth the wood. Finally, he sharpened the axe head's cutting edge.

While the handle was much shorter than the original axe handle would have been, it was longer than a traditional hatchet. He could swing it about two-handed or one-handed as circumstances required. Gwen tried it one day. It was a little heavy, but not excessively so, and was balanced so it swung in her hands easily, the weight of it not a hinderance.

A few days later, they found another broken axe and a carpenter's hammer, both with broken shafts. The heads, although rusty, were still in good shape. Having seen the process once, Gwen took the axe and began to chip out the old wood using the axe already made and her knife. Her father, once again, used a rock and knife to work on the hammer's head.

Then they switched. Her father handed her a smaller tree branch and the hammer's head, while he worked on the axe head. He wanted her to make a smaller handle like the type normal for a hammer, but a little longer. Once the handles were to his liking, he had Gwen sharpen the hand axe while he worked on the claw end of the hammer. He put the claw in their nightly fire, banking the coals all around it, until it glowed orange. Then pulled it out and pried it a little, straightening it. It was slow work, as only a fraction would straighten at a time, but he worked on it nightly. Still, it had straightened a bit by the time they came upon the logging camp.

They saw ten men, ranging in age from a teen about Gwen's age to their middle thirties. There was also a girl about her age, who seemed to be in charge. Gwen and Duncan silently watched the camp for two days. They knew where each person lived, what time of day they woke, had breakfast, and where and what kind of work they did each day. They knew when they stopped for lunch and when they ceased work for the day. Each had a job to do and worked slowly and deliberately. It did not appear to be laziness, but a plan being executed – a plan to do things right the first time.

Gwen and Duncan noticed four horses in the camp, large workhorses paired up to drag logs back to the base. A system of pulleys was arranged to stack the logs as high as a tall man, using the horses to pull the ropes attached to the logs. These men were confident and knowledgeable. The girl would come by now and then and appeared to give instructions. The men would nod and change how they were doing things to suit her wishes. Once she was out of sight, they would shake their heads and resume doing things the way they had been before. Duncan chuckled the first time he saw that.

"Typical men," Gwen said. "A woman comes up with a better way to do things, the men nod their heads and, as soon as she walks away, do it their own stupid way."

Duncan just chuckled again.

"More like some smart ass teenager left in charge, who doesn't know shit about anything, telling guys who've done the job for years how to do their jobs," Duncan said. "Happens all the time. Used to get that from all the rookie officers fresh out of military college. All book knowledge, no practical knowledge."

"What?" Gwen said.

"Your mom has some really good ideas, Gwen," Duncan said. "Most of the time I do what she recommends. Other times? Well, not so much." He shrugged his shoulders and grinned.

"A smart husband just nods his head and says, 'Yes dear,'" Duncan said. "Then, when she goes away satisfied, hubby does it his way. Don't give me that look. Your mom does the same with me when I try to beak off about something I don't know much about and she does."

"Typical princess," Duncan said after watching the girl acting as camp leader for a few days. "An overprivileged and indulged one at that," he continued.

Each morning, after giving the men their orders for the day, the girl would go back into her much larger and better-built housing unit. She would walk out some time later dressed up in what Duncan said were 'pretend' hunter's clothing: tight-fitting boots that went almost to her knees, a bright green tunic over a tight pair of pants stuffed into the boots, a crossbow in her hands and a quiver with five arrows in it strapped to bang noisily at her right thigh.

From their observation post, father and daughter could see the deer and other ungulates scurry away well before the girl could catch sight of them. While both Gwen and Duncan were not in easy sight, they made no special efforts to remain undetected, unlike when they had been evading the invaders. They just sat behind some bushes or under a tree with low-hanging branches. The girl never noticed them – once even walking within a meter of their position.

"Ut oh," Duncan said one morning as he glassed with a pair of stolen binoculars. Routinely, each morning, they both scanned the road. Gwen shifted her binoculars to her father's sector and saw the dust cloud he had spotted. It was heading their way and moving fast.

Duncan picked up the hammer, and stuck it in his back under his belt, and took both axes in hand.

"Keep the damn princess out of my way," he said and in seconds was headed for the camp.

It wasn't hard for Gwen to keep track of the girl, who was very noisy as she walked through the woods. Still, it wasn't difficult to hear the two vehicles come bouncing into the logging camp at high speed and slide to a stop. They were the smaller scout vehicles with four soldiers in each.

To their credit, the loggers scattered, dropping whatever tools they had in hand and heading into the woods. The soldiers started yelling at them and firing their blasters at the running men. They hit one, but the range was long, so it was doubtful much damage was done to the stricken man.

The head girl started running to the camp. As she came to the edge of the trees bordering the camp, she fitted an arrow to the crossbow and sighted it at one of the soldiers. Gwen disarmed her by simply picking the arrow off the crossbow and tossing it aside. She then leg-looped the astonished girl to the ground. The girl looked up and saw Gwen above her with a finger to her lips.

"Don't be stupid," Gwen whispered. "Stay here and out of sight. I'll be right back."

What the girl saw was a girl about her age, dressed in dark clothing with many pockets on the pants, a pair of over-the-ankle boots, her hair in a braid that swung at her back as she silently ran toward the camp. A long, sharp pole was in her right hand and a large knife was strapped to her right thigh.

The 'princess' quickly learned how wrong her boots were for this type of thing when she tried to scramble to retrieve her crossbow bolt, then tried to place it back on the crossbow and sight a target while crouching low.

Then she saw an explosion of motion as a man erupted out of the woods, an axe in each hand, behind the two groups of four soldiers. He screamed a loud, high-pitched yell as he swung the axe in his right hand at the back of the head of the first soldier he came upon. The woodsman didn't even stop to see if he had killed the soldier as he swung the left-hand axe at the next one. He stopped screaming then, as the soldiers were doing the screaming now. Screaming in pain.

The first four were down before the others turned to see what was going on behind them. They hurriedly aimed their blasters at the man running full speed toward them, weaving as he ran, making it hard to get a sight on him.

Then the girl who had tripped her up and disarmed her, sprang at those four soldiers from the rear, screaming her war cry. The first solder she hit on his right temple. He dropped like a stone. She deftly swung the heavy pole like a toy baton and caught the next soldier in line across the front of his neck just above the Adam's apple. The third soldier turned around in time to receive the pointed end of the stick in his right eye. As the girl pulled the pole out of his eye, the man with the axes felled the last soldier.

Now the two surveyed the scene, both at the ready, the girl with her pole in both hands ready to strike, the man with his right axe raised to shoulder height, the left at belt height away from his side.

The girl saw movement as one soldier aimed his blaster at the man with the axes. A bolt from the crossbow whistled quickly out of the trees, hitting him in right ear.

Both the man and the girl turned in her direction. The man still had the right axe raised over his head, but the left was pointed in her direction. The girl had her pole raised above her head like a sword.

"It's all good, Pop," the girl said, bringing her pole down to the ground.

"Come on in!" the girl yelled at the crossbow-wielding lass. "It's all clear!"

The man went to each soldier. He kicked each body. Then he poked an axe handle into an eye. All the soldiers were dead. The man put one axe under his belt at the rear, keeping the other in his right hand.

All ten of the loggers slowly and cautiously crept out of the woods. All of them had an axe or a large stick in their hands as they did.

The leader girl saw the grey-bearded man say something to the strange girl in a low voice, who looked up at him. He nodded his head, then pointed his chin at where the ten loggers were cautiously standing, ready to bolt back into the woods.

"Come on in!" The girl said. "It's safe now."

The men walked quietly to within a meter of her and all of them went down on their knees in front of Gwen.

"Thank you, My Lady," one of the older men in the group said. "Thank you for taking pity on us My Lady and saving us, Ma'am."

"Yes, well..." Gwen stammered.

"If My Lady agrees," Duncan said. "Your servants will clean this mess up, Ma'am." His head and eyes were downcast as he spoke.

"Just so," Gwen said, catching on to what she should do. "Once you have given my instructions and set this in motion, you will return for further instructions. Now hop to it, man!"

Duncan soon had the ten men dragging bodies out of sight, then pickaxes and shovels were shouldered and the men went about burying the dead soldiers. By now the 'princess' had come into camp.

"I am sorry about the conditions, My Lady," the girl said. "This is but a primitive camp, Ma'am."

"Well," Gwen said. "It's going to look like a castle compared to what you are about to experience. We are leaving, and soon. Grab whatever you need and we go. No longer than an hour from now we must be gone."

The girl hurried off to her housing unit. A short time later Duncan and the ten men returned.

"Organize these men for travel," Gwen said. "We must be gone within the hour."

"Yes, Ma'am," Duncan said. "May we use the horses for transport, Ma'am?"

"See to it," Gwen said. "Quickly now! There is no time to lose."

Duncan backed away from her a few feet eyes down, then turned and got the ten men into motion.

"What now?" Gwen asked quietly while looking around her unconcernedly.

"You're doing perfect," Duncan said the same way. His eyes were downcast as he spoke. "We should move about 10 klicks or so before we stop. To the west, deeper into the bush.

"Ah for fucks sake!"

He had seen the loggers' leader dragged out two large, heavy suitcases from her house.

"Clue that dumb shit in, will you?" Duncan said, then he moved off toward where the men were loading packs to put on the horses' backs.

"Just what exactly do you think you are doing?" Gwen said as she came up to the girl who was looking around for some help with her baggage.

"Sorry, My Lady," the girl said. "I will have some of the men arrange my baggage transport, My Lady."

"Do you see what I am wearing and carrying?" Gwen said. "This and another pack of belongings is all that I have. If you can cart those two bags all by yourself, while you run, for the next ten kilometres, fine by me. Those men and those horses will only be carrying what we need to live for the next few weeks, not all your bloody beauty products. You need two complete sets of heavy durable clothing, a good pair of rugged heavy duty work boots, your crossbow and some food. That is all. If you don't have a suitable backpack, there most likely will be one in those vehicles there. That's where I got mine. Hop to it now! Or I will leave you here on your own!"

Duncan was smashing the radios in the first vehicle and as he saw the girl tossing things out of the suitcases, he reached into the transport and tossed a rucksack to her. Then he made his way to the next vehicle and began working on its radios.

Gwen walked over, picked up the rucksack and tossed it at the girl's feet.

"If it can fit in this and you can carry it, you can keep it," Gwen said.

By the time the girl had figured all that out and was trying, with limited success, to don the rucksack and adjust it, the men and horses were ready to go. Duncan confirmed each man had an axe and or a hatchet and a hammer. Two large, two-man crosscut saws and two bow saws had been strapped to the packs of the horses. The men had clearly done this type of thing before. The packs were well placed on their backs and Gwen could tell the packs were full and heavy.

"Right!" she said, "Off we go. Lead the way, Dunc."

Duncan took the lead, followed by Gwen and the 'princess', then the men and four horses. The first stop was at their own primitive camp, which Duncan and the men quickly dismantled and spread around to make it look like no one had been there. One of the loggers attempted to take Gwen's pack and put it on one of the horses.

"Nonsense," Gwen said as she took the heavy pack from the astonished man and deftly adjusted it on her back. "Those horses have enough to carry. Dunc, carry on."

With Duncan in the lead, they made their way into the woods. The farther they went, the more open under the trees it became and soon the horses had little trouble negotiating the terrain. After several hours, they could hear air vehicles flitting about looking for them, but never close. The loggers and horses were having little difficulty, but the girl Duncan had nicknamed the 'princess' was a different story. They had to stop every ten minutes or so to let her catch her breath. After the second stop, Gwen took the crossbow and quiver from her, attaching the crossbow to the top and across her pack, and the quiver to the back of it.

The sun was beginning to descend behind the treetops before they found a suitable spot to stop for the night. There was a small running stream beside a small clearing. The ten men quickly set up camp. They demonstrated considerable expertise, each doing what needed doing, alongside Duncan and Gwen. The 'princess' just dropped her pack and collapsed.

Soon there was a small fire going. Food was sizzling in a frying pan and water was boiling in a kettle and a pot. Horses had been watered and Duncan had shown the men how to stake the horses down so they wouldn't disappear on them, yet still be able to move around and graze or lay down.

The men had rigged up the canvas that covered the horses' packs into two tents, one for themselves.

"My Lady," the older logger, clearly their leader, said. "This tent is for you and our young lady, Ma'am."

"Thank you," Gwen said. The man looked at her with an astonished look on his face. He was clearly unused to being spoken to in that manner.

"For myself," Gwen continued. "It is not raining, so I will just set up my spot over there by the fire. The young lady may require the tent, however. But do make it smaller for just her and take the rest of the canvas to make yours bigger. Dunc will not require a tent."

Gwen had to boot the girl's feet to wake her up. Then Gwen handed her a tin plate with a chunk of meat and some potatoes and beans. The girl looked around her as she took it, saw Gwen walk back to the fire, cross her legs and sit down on the ground beside it as the men gathered around. She made her way over and sat beside but slightly behind Gwen, then dug hungrily into the plate of food.

Once again, Gwen astonished the men around the campfire by taking up the tin plates and walking them down to the stream, where she began to give them a rough cleaning. She was soon joined by the youngest man who had gathered up all the other plates and pots and began to clean them also. He squatted away from her and never even glanced at her. As Gwen gathered her plates, he spoke softly.

"If it please My Lady," he said. "I will take those, Ma'am."

"Humph!" Gwen said. "Nonsense! I am not a cripple."

When she returned to the fire ring, she handed her pile of plates to one of the men and asked him if he would pack them away. Then she looked at the young girl who was looking at her with a disapproving look on her face.

"You," Gwen said pointing at the girl.

"Take my pack and put it there beside Dunc's."

The girl quickly stood, did a fast curtsy, and hurried to do Gwen's bidding. Then she grunted as she tried to lift what she thought would be a light pack. With it barely off the ground and carrying it in both hands, she waddled over to where Gwen had told her to put it and tried to gently lay it down on the ground. She almost succeeded. Duncan, who was setting up his sleeping pad, could not hold back the snigger. The girl exploded into anger.

"Who the hell do you think you are!" The girl yelled. "No man can laugh at a woman!"

As Duncan stood, she slapped him hard across the face. Duncan stood at attention with his eyes focused above the girl's head. She hit him again.

"Lower your gaze when I speak to you!" She yelled and hit him again. Duncan did not move.

She made to hit him again and her hand was held away by a very strong hand on her wrist.

"If you fucking hit my father again, I will kick your ass until you can't sit down for a week!" Gwen said into her ear.

"But My Lady..."

"Get your fucking ass over to your tent. I will deal with you shortly!" Gwen said. The girl hurried away, almost tripping in her haste. She had looked into the murder in Gwen's eyes.

"You okay, Pop?" She said.

"She hits like a girl," Duncan said, rubbing his nose. "Hits hard for a girl, though. I'll live."

"Go easy on her," he said to Gwen's back as she walked to the girl's tent. "She don't know any better."

"Sit down and shut the fuck up!" Gwen said as the girl made to stand up. "You don't know shit! That man has seen and experienced more than you ever will! He could have killed all eight of those men without any help from me at all. He just indulges me to teach me my job. He could kill you with one flick of his wrist. Who the hell are you, some overprivileged rich kid? What the fuck do you know? Fuck all!"

"S-S-Sorry, My Lady," the girl said barely over a whisper.

Gwen looked over at her. She was down on her knees and trembling.

"Oh, for fuck's sake!" Gwen said. "Stand the fuck up!"

The girl stood, shoulders slumped and eyes downcast. Gwen took her large knife out of its scabbard and hit the girl lightly across the back with the flat of the blade.

"Back straight!" Gwen ordered then hit her on both shoulders. "Shoulders up, arms alongside your legs tight! Butt in! Stomach tight! Head up!"

Each order was emphasized by a tap from the knife on the offending body part.

"Eyes focused!" Then Gwen placed the knife under the girl's chin and raised it until it was at the proper height.

"This is how you will address me from now on, just like Duncan was when you accosted him!" Gwen continued.

"Unless you are given permission, you will not speak. When you address my father you will address him as Master Warrant Officer Kovacks or Mr. Kovacks. You will stand as you are right now when addressing him or me, is that clear?"

"Yes, My Lady," the girl said.

"Now, we are going to go to Master Warrant Officer Kovacks and we are going to apologize. You will follow my lead and do as I do. Understood?"

"Yes, My Lady!" The girl said just over a whisper.

"What was that?" Gwen said. "Is something wrong with my ears?"

"Yes, My Lady," the girl said louder.

"Are you whispering or are my ears going bad?" Gwen said.

"Yes, my Lady!" The girl said, much louder.

"That will do for now. Follow me and walk like I do, as best you can," Gwen said.

Gwen marched toward Duncan in the way she had been taught on the parade ground, her back straight, arms swinging to almost shoulder height. Duncan saw her coming and how she was coming, quickly ducked his head to hide the smirk, then stood, assumed the position of at ease with both hands tucked into the small of his back and his feet shoulder-width apart.

Gwen came to a crashing halt a meter away from him, brought her right foot up to her belt and smashed it into the ground, assumed attention with her eyes focused above his head, brought her right hand sharply to her forehead, and held it there. The girl attempted to do the same. Duncan struggled hard not to laugh. He came to attention and returned the salute. Gwen, and belatedly the girl, smartly returned her hand to her side and came to attention. Duncan resumed the at-ease position.

"What can I do for the Lieutenant, Ma'am?" Duncan said.

"Master Warrant!" Gwen said. "The Lieutenant would apologize for her recruit's actions, Master Warrant! No excuses, Master Warrant!"

Duncan saw Gwen quickly nudge the girl with her left foot.

"I would like to apologize for my actions, Master Warrant Kovacks," the girl said.

Duncan moved up until he was almost nose to nose with the girl. She looked him in the eyes and he could tell she was scared, but defiant.

"Are you looking at me, Recruit!" Duncan said. He allowed his spittle to spray onto her face as he yelled. "Did I give you fucking permission to look at me, Recruit!"

The girl quickly lowered her eyes.

"What the fuck are you teaching this recruit, Lieutenant!" Duncan said, now nose-to-nose with Gwen. "Give me ten, rookie! Now!"

Gwen quickly dropped and did ten pushups. Finished, she stood to attention again.

Now Duncan moved back in front of the girl, who, taking her cue from Gwen, was standing as straight as she could and looking above Duncan's head.

"Now," Duncan said. "What was that youngster trying to whisper to me?"

"Master Warrant Kovacks!" She belted out. "I am sorry for hitting you, Sir!"

"Better," Duncan said. "Almost! First, you have not yet earned the right to use my name, Recruit. Second, I work for a living, unlike the Lieutenant here. I am not an officer and a gentleman. I am just an officer. You will address me as Master Warrant, is that clear!"

"I apologize, Master Warrant!" The girl belted out.

"There is no I in the army, Recruit!" Duncan said. He remained nose-to-nose with her. "You address yourself as Recruit for now. Understood?"

"Yes, Master Warrant, the Recruit apologizes, Master Warrant!"

Duncan moved back to Gwen, addressing her nose-to-nose.

"Normally I would give the recruit punishment," he said. "Unfortunately, in her condition, the recruit would most likely die from a heart attack. Instead, the Lieutenant will do her twenty pushups."

Gwen quickly dropped, punched out the twenty pushups, then came to attention once again.

"Very well, Lieutenant," Duncan said. "If the Warrant would suggest, Ma'am? Perhaps we should muster the other recruits and the Master Warrant, with your permission, Ma'am, would clue the clueless bastards into what is about to befall them, Ma'am?"

"As you will, Mr. Kovacks," Gwen said. "The recruit and I will join you shortly."

"Thank you, Ma'am," Duncan said.

He came to attention and saluted. Gwen returned his salute, then, taking the girl under the elbow, turned and marched to the girl's tent. Now Duncan did laugh, but quietly.

"Look," Gwen said to the girl when they came back to her tent. "Where we come from, men and women are equal. Not like here. Whoever has the most skill or experience is in charge, man or woman. My father is very skilled and very experienced. He is normally in charge. Everyone defers to him. Do you understand?"

"Yes," the girl said. "My mothers have told me men run the rest of the Federation."

"Not our part," Gwen said. "My father does, but he does not want to. There is no one else who can, though. He is training me to take his place and I don't like it too much either. I was a lot like you not so long ago."

"Look, my father and I have been running 20 to 30 kilometres a day, depending on the ground we are covering – hefting that pack I asked you to move that you could barely lift. We have to, or those invaders will kill us if they can find us. All of us, and I do mean all of us, are going to have to work together or we will die.

"Did you see those men when they came out of the woods after the fight? They all had their axes with them. They were ready to fight to save their lives. It is in their genetic code. They were historically bred to hunt, to kill, to fight. Their historic role was to protect the family; this was perverted over the ages so that men ran everything. But not really. A woman was always in the background.

"Men are physically stronger than we are and their minds are adapted in ways ours are not, to fight and to kill. But we are faster and nimbler. We, too, can fight and kill. My mother is one of our best soldiers, and there are other strong female soldiers in my family. Your people have, like many others, forgotten your history. My people have not.

"Now come. My father is about to tell the men what I have just told you."

Gwen, with the girl beside her, marched up to Duncan, came to attention, and saluted. Duncan returned the salute and motioned for them to sit. He had stoked the fire, which was now large and burning hotly. He had also motioned the men to join them and sit. Duncan stood.

"Listen up," he began. "Gwen is my daughter. She will oversee your day-to-day requirements. I am in charge overall. Yes you heard me correctly, a man is in charge. Where we come from position is earned by merit, not on gender or who you are related to. There is no way someone with many years of experience should be under the command of someone who doesn't have a clue as to what they are doing."

He let the men think on that for a moment.

"All of you men kept your axes or hammers with you when the invaders attacked," Duncan continued. "That was not by accident.

Men are programmed to fight and protect. You are only lacking experience."

Duncan looked around him and saw some of the men had questions.

"Please," he said, "ask a question if you want an explanation."

"But, sir," one of the men said. "Women are always in charge. Men are too stupid to make decisions."

"And in many places in the Federation of Planets," Duncan said. "Men say the same things about women. Not where I come from. The majority of professional soldiers are men. That is what we have been bred for over the ages: to hunt, to protect our families and our people, while the women stay home and raise the children and, in times of war, tend the fields. In ancient times, women were also trained to fight and hunt, as I am training my daughter."

"But we are dumb and slow and cumbersome," another man said. "It is only right that women be in charge."

"They are faster and nimbler than we are," Duncan said. "Their minds work differently than ours do, but only slightly. We are stronger and have more endurance than they do. We can hunt better because of that speed and endurance. Sometimes our minds can solve problems more quickly, but not always. The big difference is the nurturing. A woman must look after her children at a young age. Men cannot, since our bodies cannot give the milk that babies need to survive. Women do."

The men looked from one to another. Duncan could tell they were thinking hard on what he had just said. He also saw the girl look at Gwen, questions in her eyes.

"Gwen and I have been running between 20 and 30 kilometres per day for the last three months. Running, not walking," Duncan said. "In the last three weeks, we have killed around thirty of the invaders, at first only using a kitchen knife and some sticks. We had no choice, as they were hunting us. And they will kill all of us if they get the chance.

"Gwen was just like that young woman over there when we first started out. She was a spoiled and overindulged daddy's girl. She had been given everything she asked for, whenever she asked for it. She had servants do her every bidding. She didn't even know how to make her own bed. God forbid if she had to clean her own dishes or make her own food."

More than a few of the men chuckled; the rest smiled.

"But she knew how to run," Duncan said. "she did it for sport in school and she was good at it. She also grew up with two parents who were soldiers, very good soldiers. Also, in our society, everyone, man and woman, must serve in the army for a minimum of five years once they reach eighteen years of age, and enter cadet training at age fifteen. So, Gwen has had a year's worth of learning how to stand correctly and walk correctly."

Now he looked over at Gwen and smiled.

"She was not good at any of it but the running," he continued. "Gets that from her mother, she does. Run run, rah rah, go go. All the time."

Gwen tossed a piece of firewood at him. He stuck his tongue out at her and laughed.

"Damn kids nowadays," Duncan said. "No respect anymore."

There were some nervous laughs this time.

"I have been fighting and killing my people's enemies since I was not much older than my daughter," Duncan said. "I am a highly trained and experienced killer. I also know how to train others how to fight and kill. I have met these invaders before. With just twenty-nine of my comrades, I defeated over ten thousand of them once before. Not by ourselves, of course. While not impossible, very improbable. No, we trained the local people, much like yourselves, how to fight them. Using simple tools, just like you have. Knives, axes, hammers.

"I will give you tonight and tonight only, to make a choice. You can join my daughter and me and join the fight to kill these invaders. Or you can leave us and go your own way. If you stay, my daughter and I will train you to fight and drive these invaders away. If you choose to leave, well, I wish you the best. You leave with what you can carry on your back. That goes for you too, princess.

"One last thing. Each of you men go over and heft Gwen's pack. She has been running with that weight for almost three months now. Now, I'm off to bed. The morning starts before daybreak."

Duncan moved over to his camp spot. As a group, after some thought, each man came over and hefted Gwen's pack, then looked first over to Gwen, who was talking with their girl, then back at Duncan.

"Now you know," Duncan said to them. "This is no joke, and she is still learning. I carry more weight than she does. I can still go twenty kilometres in a day and fight at the end of it.

Good night, gentlemen."

"Look," Gwen said to the girl. "My dad is not only the head of our army, he is our head of state. These invaders arrived here to kill us. But then, we believe, they saw how weak your planet was and decided to take it over. My mother was a member of their army at one time. They were trying to take over another planet and my father and his twenty-nine friends defeated them. They had better weapon systems than the invaders and better training. They were still only thirty, though. My father and his friends trained the local people how to fight. They did the hard work. The locals stood and held the invaders. They might have beaten them without my father's help, but it would have cost them many dead and wounded. My father and his friends joined in, attacking from the rear and that was that.

"My mother was the commander of the enemy ruler's elite personal guard. When my father and his friends attacked the palace, they did so alone against two hundred troops. My father was at the head of the group that attacked the ruler's personal apartments. My mother had a direct line on him and fired. Another woman shoved my father out of the way and took the blast herself. She died on the spot. My father hit my mother across the head, felling her, then shot his way into the residence. He and four of his friends killed the ruler, his whole family and most of the guards stationed inside the residence. One of his friends had stayed behind to try and save the woman – who was my father's wife at the time – and once she saw she could not, began to save the enemy guard who later became my mother. Meanwhile, my father talked the remaining guards into a ceasefire. They would all have died if they had chosen to keep fighting.

"This is the other thing my father will teach us: when to stop fighting. I still don't know when to do that. I want to kill them all."

"My father was not kidding," she continued after a pause. "If you want to go, you can. We will not stop you from leaving. For tonight only. If you choose to stay, you choose to stay and fight, and maybe die. I am staying."

Gwen stood and made her way over to where her pack was, leaving the girl to her thoughts. Duncan looked at her and raised his eyebrows.

"She doesn't know it yet," Gwen said. "But she will be coming with us."

"Good job, kid," Duncan said. "So, point of order then. Unless you are pissed for some good, and I do mean good, reason, we don't salute when in the field, Lieutenant."

"Thank you for pointing that out, Master Warrant," Gwen said. "Technically we were not in the field, but in base."

"Very astute observation, Ma'am," Duncan said. "If the Master Warrant should point out, the Lieutenant does not salute the Master Warrant, Ma'am, the Master Warrant salutes the Lieutenant."

"Well, the Lieutenant was unaware she had been promoted from Cadet Corporal to Lieutenant, Master Warrant," Gwen said.

"My apologies, Lieutenant," Duncan said, his eyes were laughing. "The Master Warrant has no excuses, Ma'am, and ensures the exalted Lieutenant that this behaviour will not be repeated, Ma'am."

"Very well Master Warrant, see that it does not," Gwen said. Her eyes were also smiling.

Duncan continued. "There is a reason for not saluting in the field, Gwen. Combatants are trained to pick off officers first, then anyone else who looks to be in charge. Next, when reporting to a superior officer, only the ranking trooper salutes. Under arms, the rest will perform the rifle salute. Otherwise, they will stand at attention."

"Shit," Gwen said. "Still lots to learn. Why the promotion? I still don't know shit."

"Language, Ma'am, language," Duncan said, then laughed. "Early days yet, luv. Clue the kid in, Gwen. We need her. In their heads, the men know what I am saying is correct. But they still need a woman in charge. For now that is you, but you need to clue that dumb ass in, and fast. If she doesn't get up to speed and quick, we leave her behind. Clear? Otherwise, she will get us all killed."

Chapter Eight

The ten men and one girl woke up to see father and daughter, pants rolled up to their calves, barefoot, shirts open in the front, sleeves rolled up over elbows, doing a slow motion, what looked like a fighting routine, or dance. They were unsure which it was. As slow as it was, Gwen had sweat running down her face and her chest, and Duncan had moisture on his face. Duncan spoke quietly to Gwen. They then backed away and faced each other. Both made a fist with their left hands, covered it with their right hands, and bowed to each other. Then they took fighting stances and Gwen attacked Duncan.

They moved quickly, so fast their movements were blurry. They did this for almost five minutes. When they stopped, they once again bowed to each other. Gwen went to the stream and wet herself down. Duncan approached the ten men and one girl who had gathered to watch. Everyone stood somewhat in line and in attention.

"All who are staying with us, take one step forward," Duncan said.

The men looked over at the girl then at each other, then raggedly took one step forward, the girl with them, just a shade later.

"Very well," Duncan said. "Each morning, before mess, we will do that exercise. We will add more movements and complexity each day. The Lieutenant will explain the movements and the reasons for them this evening. For now, we need morning mess. The horses need feeding and watering. We must be on the move within an hour and half. Move it people!"

They made fifteen kilometres that day. They stopped only because it was clear the girl could go no further.

"She's a keeper," Duncan said to Gwen as they went about setting up their camp. "She didn't complain once all day. She would have kept going if we had let her."

"Ya, I noticed that," Gwen said.

"What?" She asked at her father's raised eyebrows. "I am young and dumb, but I can see someone trying, same as you can."

Gwen stalked off in a huff, Duncan quietly chuckling at her back as she went. His communicator beeped in his ear.

"You got me, go," he said.

"Well, well," Marlene said. "You are in a good mood today."

"Our daughter just defended a young and dumb raw recruit," Duncan said.

"Oh?" Marlene said.

"Ya, we now have ten men and one princess with us," Duncan said. "Oh ya, and four horses. Bonus."

"Gwen is defending the princess, I take it?"

"Ya," Duncan said. "But not without reason. The kid has potential. How's it going on your end?"

"Most of these fucking women are a bunch of bullheaded idiots!" Marlene blurted out. "Bunch of idiots they are. I finally found some more accommodating, regular-type-people women. They and their men are understanding what I am saying. We are taking off today. We are about forty in total."

"It's a start." Duncan said. "More than my eleven. The bad guys are actively taking over this part of the planet, luv. They are killing everyone they find and burning their stuff down. Best get out of Dodge as fast as you can. The men are willing, just downtrodden. Up to you to clue them in. Should be a little easier for you. They are used to women being in charge and you for sure know what it means to be the wrong gender."

"Ya, I guess so," Marlene said. "How are you going to handle that?"

"I have Gwen," Duncan said. "I just promoted her to lieutenant. So, she is in charge. But she has clued everyone in as to what is what. No biggy. The princess is about her age and she is trying hard. She has a lot of potential, just like another young and dumb keener I once met."

"Ya, laugh it up, asshole," Marlene said. "I still love you anyway. Horses. I didn't think of that."

"Ya, these are draft horses," Duncan said. "Some kind of Clydesdale mix by the look of them. As you know, they were originally bred to be heavy cavalry horses and are mean and nasty."

"Oh ya," Marlene said. "I learned that the hard way more than once."

"Ya, well," Duncan said. "We still need to find some of my type of ponies for most of what we need to be doing."

"Ya, I get it," Marlene said. "Low tech; they won't be looking for that."

"The men are not as dumb as they pretend to be," Duncan said. "They do most of the work around here. Touch base with them. They will clue you in to where you need to be once they understand what needs to be done."

"Just like you showed the women on my mother's estate way back when," Marlene said. "I get it. Okay, we better break this down. Give Gwen a hug and congratulations from me, luv?"

"You got it," Duncan said. "See ya when I see ya."

"Thanks, Mom," both of them heard. "Keep your head down. Please?"

"No problem there, daughter," Marlene said. "Zebra, Zebra, Zebra. Watch your asses, wolf hounds. We are on our way."

Gwen walked up to her father. He was standing by a pine tree. His hand against the trunk and his head low. She put her arm around his waist and her head on his shoulder.

"I miss her too, Dad," she said quietly.

"Probably more than me," Duncan said. He put his left arm around her and gave her a quick squeeze. "Now back to work, kid. We gotta get the hell out of here."

A few nights later, after his customary nightly class, Duncan had the map found in one of the transport trucks they had liberated spread out in front of him. He turned on his liberated GPS unit and was comparing it to the map.

"Master Warrant," the oldest of the ten men said, standing beside him. "If the recruit could be of assistance. The recruit has knowledge of the area, Master Warrant."

"Very well, recruit," Duncan said. "We are looking for a suitable place to make a base. It needs to be as undetectable as possible, yet suitable for ourselves and our horses to rest for a time. Speak freely, recruit. I only have these maps to guide me and no practical knowledge of the planet."

"Yes, Master Warrant," the man said. "You have been doing very well so far, with no knowledge of the area. If I may, Master Warrant?"

The man gestured to the map. Duncan handed it to him. The man looked at the map for a moment. Then stood and did a circle around himself, looking at and over the trees, then squatted back down and looked at the map again.

"I think we are about here," he said, pointing a finger at a point at the map. "These things are good, but not perfect. There is a good spot just here. At the rate we're traveling, a day's movement from where we are now. We will have to go this way, though. There is a big cliff and a ravine that the paper does not show. We will have to skirt around it."

Duncan checked the GPS unit and saw the man was completely accurate with where they were.

"Very well, Recruit," Duncan said. "Tomorrow you take point. I need a break anyway. Good job, Recruit. Your name is?"

"Alvin, Master Warrant." Alvin said.

"Good job, Alvin," Duncan said. "Keep up the good work. You may get promoted from dumb recruit yet if you don't pay attention."

If anything, Alvin came to a more rigid attention than he had been before, raised his right knee to his belt and stomped it hard into the ground, then marched away to his buddies. There he babbled to them for a while. They looked over to Duncan before they all started to pound Alvin on the back.

"What's all that about?" Gwen asked as she came up.

"Alvin knows the area and showed me a good spot to set up base camp," Duncan said. "He's taking point tomorrow."

"Okay," Gwen said.

"Now go and give them shit," Duncan said. "Alvin is a good man and has a good head on his shoulders. Just let them know you're still in charge, Gwen. But don't get too crazy."

"Gotcha," Gwen said. She walked over to where the men were.

"What the hell is going on here, Recruits?" She yelled out. "You think this is some kind of party? Recruit Alvin, drop and give me ten, now!"

The other nine men were all in line and at attention, mostly, as Alvin dropped and started his pushups. Gwen made her way down the line of men looking each one in the eye and up and down their bodies. Finished, Alvin stood, joined the line, and came to attention.

"Right," Gwen said. "Recruit Alvin will be taking point tomorrow and guiding us to our next location. Do make sure you don't fuck it up tomorrow, Recruit Alvin, or you will find my boot so far up your ass you will not be able to sit down for a week."

As she turned to walk away, she saw the girl standing and smirking at the men. Gwen marched her way toward the girl, who now knew she was in trouble and came to a rigid attention.

"What the hell are you laughing at, Recruit Princess!" Gwen said, now nose-to-nose, with the girl. "Drop and give me ten!"

Gwen waited until she was once again at attention.

"You have been pampered long enough, Recruit Princess," Gwen said. "Tomorrow you are on point with Recruit Alvin. Starting tomorrow night, you will bunk with the other recruits. Is that clear, Recruit Princess?"

"Yes Ma'am, clear, Ma'am," the girl said.

"Very well," Gwen said. "Do make sure you and Alvin don't fuck it up tomorrow, Recruit Princess, or you will do Recruit Alvin's twenty pushups after he does his. Dismissed."

Gwen held her laughter until she reached Duncan, ten meters from the rest of the group. Then the both of them had a fast and quiet laugh.

"Seriously," Duncan said, wiping the tears from eyes. "Good job. Give them praise, but not enough to make their heads too big at this point. I chose to recognize Alvin's name. He is doing very well and came up with a great idea. I think he will make a good leader, but time will tell. You chose to give the princess an acknowledgement. Not her name just yet, but more than just *Recruit*. All this has an impact on the others.

"We are making a team here, Gwen. Right now, their reward for doing a good job is that we acknowledge them by knowing their names. But it has to be earned, not just given to them. Keep at the girl, she has a lot of potential. So does the young boy. That first night, when he approached you at the stream washing the dishes – he risked a lot speaking to you like he did."

"Shit," Gwen said. "I didn't think of that. Ya, coming from his society, he took a major big chance talking to me like that."

"Right," Duncan said. "Both of them are young enough, but old enough. We train the young ones, they train others. If anything, the girl will have it tougher than the boy. He has nothing to lose. She does. Keep at it."

"I kind of feel sorry for her," Gwen said. "We are taking everything, including her name from her."

"You think your being my daughter would have made a difference to your drill instructor at boot camp?" Duncan said. "If anything, that would have made it worse for you. In the field, if we all don't work as a team, we all die. We are only as strong as our weakest link, Gwen. This is not high school. There, if you are not popular you, at most, get humiliated once in a while. Here, you die. Not only you but your whole team. When the shit hits the fan, Gwen, we don't fight for our leaders or our country, we fight to keep each other alive."

Chapter Nine

The camp gained a homey feeling. The original canvas dwellings had become, first, simple lean-tos made from branches, then, as the days went on, more elaborate structures. There was little else to do in the afternoons.

In the mornings before morning mess, they did their tai chi exercises, followed by more rigorous cardio workouts. Each day they went on longer and longer runs. Each day, more weight would be added to their packs. But they had the afternoons to themselves. They looked after the horses, or themselves; they made alterations to their dwellings, or relaxed and did nothing.

In the hour before evening mess the loggers were instructed on combat techniques. At first, they practiced without weapons, then, slowly they started with sticks and poles. Later, axes and hammers were added to the mix. After cleanup from the evening mess, Duncan would instruct them around the fire pit on tactics and the reasons behind them. Then the men had time to themselves, when they usually chatted, sometimes about what they had just learned and sometimes about their hopes and dreams for the future.

The girl Duncan had nicknamed Princess had started out tentative and quiet, but one by one the men had drawn her out. Now she was one of them. If anything, her punishments were more severe than theirs when she made a mistake. Sometimes she was singled out for no apparent reason and punished.

One night, while still gathered around the fire pit, the youngest man stood and came to attention.

"The Recruit asks permission to speak, Master Warrant," he said.

"Not up to me, Recruit," Duncan said he looked over at Gwen.

"The Recruit wishes to speak, Ma'am," Duncan said.

"Very well, Master Warrant," Gwen said. They had been expecting this.

"The Recruit may speak freely," Duncan said.

"Master Warrant," the young man said. "This recruit feels that Recruit Princess has been unjustly singled out for punishment, Master Warrant. Many times, Recruit Princess has done nothing to deserve punishment, Master Warrant."

"Is Recruit Manfred questioning the Lieutenant's judgment, Recruit Manfred?" Duncan said.

"Yes, Master Warrant," Manfred said. "This recruit feels that Recruit Princess is being unjustly punished for things she has not done, Master Warrant."

"Drop and give me ten, Recruit Manfred," Duncan said. "Recruit Princess, attention!"

The girl jumped to her feet and came to attention. Duncan came nose-to-nose with her.

"Does Recruit Princess also think she is being unjustly punished?" Duncan asked. His voice was firm, but not unkind.

"No, Master Warrant," she said. "This recruit has much to learn and her punishments are justified, Master Warrant."

Now Duncan turned and faced Gwen.

"Lieutenant!" he said. "Are you unjustly singling out Recruit Princess for extra punishment?"

Gwen stood and came to attention.

"It is the Lieutenant's opinion that Recruit Princess requires extra instruction from time to time, Master Warrant." Gwen said.

"You other recruits," Duncan said, as Manfred completed his pushups and came to attention. "Do you feel Recruit Princess is being unjustly punished?"

"Well, speak up!" he demanded. No one said anything.

"Very well then," Duncan said. "Recruit Manfred, ten laps around the camp with full pack. Now!"

"Excuse me, Master Warrant," another man said. "This recruit wishes to speak, Master Warrant."

"Go ahead, Recruit," Duncan said.

"Master Warrant, this recruit also thinks Recruit Princess is bringing unjustly punished, Master Warrant."

All the other men stood and came in line with the two men.

"I take it you all agree then," Duncan said. He turned and looked at Gwen.

"Well, Lieutenant, it seems your troops, except for Recruit Princess, are all in agreement," Duncan said. "What do you have to say for yourself, Lieutenant? Either all ten of my recruits are mistaken, or you and Recruit Princess are, Lieutenant. Which is it?"

"I may have been somewhat over exuberant in my duties, Master Warrant," Gwen said. "I do have an explanation, Master Warrant."

"No excuses, Lieutenant!" Duncan said. "If the Master Warrant wanted his wet-behind-the-ears Lieutenant to give extra punishment to his recruits, he would have asked the Lieutenant to give them. The Lieutenant will join all her recruits and will run, not jog, around the camp ten times with full packs. That includes you, Recruit Princess. Now! Move it! Move it!"

Duncan stoked up the fire while the twelve others gathered their packs, then ran around the camp ten times. Exhausted, they put away their gear. He motioned for them all to sit around the fire again.

"Discipline has a purpose," he said after they were all seated. "You all must learn to act as a team. Recruit Alvin was the first to see this.

Now Recruit Manfred. I apologize for not noticing the Lieutenant was singling out Recruit Princess for extra punishment.

"That said, we all need to learn to work together as a team. We are only as strong as our weakest member. Right now, that is Recruit Princess. She is a fast learner, though, so you other recruits better pay attention, or she will soon be better than you are."

Duncan waited for the group to catch their breath some more before continuing.

"It is important to know each other well," he said. "That includes our strengths and weaknesses. Once we engage the invaders, we will have no time to figure all that out. We must all know or we will all die. I have to know you will be there to cover my back when I need you.

"The lieutenant already has proven herself to me. She has much to learn, but she has proven she will not do something dumb enough to kill me. That is what she and I are trying to teach you. You must learn enough to stay alive yourselves and to keep your teammates alive as well. Think on that the next few days. Think about what you saw at your logging camp that day. How the Lieutenant and I worked as a team. Yes, I most likely would have killed all eight of those soldiers. I also would most likely have been badly wounded, if not killed, if the Lieutenant had not done her job."

Duncan stood then.

"Recruit Princess, a moment of your time if you please," he said and walked away from the fire ring.

He waited for her ten meters away from the fire ring. The light was dim but he was visible, just. The girl found him in the wan light.

"Very good," Duncan said as the girl came to attention behind him. "You passed that test; you found me. You may be saveable yet. Question is, do you want to be saved, Recruit?"

"Master Warrant, Recruit Princess does not understand the question, Master Warrant," she said.

"At ease, Recruit," Duncan said in his normal voice. "Here." He handed her his water bottle, the girl took it, and took a deep draught. She had not had a chance to have a drink after the run. Then she started to cough. Duncan laughed.

"The Lieutenant did the same thing when I did that to her," he said and he took the water bottle back from her.

"I like you, kid," he said. "I see things in you that you don't see yourself. You were willing to take that gang down with your crossbow all by yourself that day. They would have killed your ass. No mistake on that. Right now, you would be dead, dead, dead. But I admire your heart."

He took another pull at the water bottle and handed it to her. She shook her head. Duncan shrugged his shoulders and put the bottle in his back pocket.

"I can teach you skills," he said and turned to face her. He poked her between her breasts.

"But I can't give you this," he said. "You have the heart for it. I can't teach that. When you killed that soldier with your crossbow that day, what were you thinking?"

"He was aiming his blaster at you," she said. "He was going to kill you."

Duncan smiled.

"He would have tried," Duncan said. "But you instinctively did what you thought you needed to do. How did you, how do you, feel about killing that soldier?"

"I threw up right after," she said. "It still bothers me."

"Good. It should," Duncan said. "I still remember my first kill. I don't remember them all, it would have driven me mad if I did, there have been so many. I may not show it, but they all affect me. If you would have told me you hadn't felt a thing at killing that soldier, I would have walked back to camp alone, because I would have killed you right here. A person like that will kill me sooner or later."

Duncan turned away from her then. He first looked up to the sky then down at the ground.

"I have been in many fights, kid," he said. "Each time, I was not thinking of myself. I was thinking of my friends to the left of me and to the right of me. I could not let them down; they were counting on me to do my job or they, and I, would die. We have to learn this, kid. If we all don't do our job, no matter how minor that job is, the whole country or planet will fall. That is why Gwen and I are so hard on you.

"Each of those men proved today to me they are willing to die for you. Question is, are you willing to do the same for them?"

"I,...I don't know Master Warrant," she stammered out.

"Right answer, kid," Duncan said. "You don't know, yet. Tell me, why did you try to take the pressure off Manfred when he stood up for you?"

"It was not right for him to be punished for me, Master Warrant," she said.

Duncan said nothing, just nodded his head. He was smiling but she could not see it in the dim light.

"Okay, Recruit," he said. "We call all of you *recruit* for a reason, Recruit Princess. That we have chosen to call you Recruit Princess instead of just Recruit means you have done something to impress us."

He looked over at her. She was still standing tall, but her head was down and she was looking at the ground.

"You do have a first name, Recruit Princess?" Duncan asked. "Calling you Recruit Princess is demeaning, not only to you but to Gwen and me as we don't know your name and we should. We know everyone else's name."

"This recruit's name is Christine, Master Warrant," she said.

"Recruit Christine, are you willing to serve alongside these men as equals?"

"Yes, Master Warrant."

"Are you willing to do whatever is necessary to help these men, Recruit Christine?"

"Yes, Master Warrant."

"Are you willing to die for your teammates, Recruit Christine?"

"I can't hear you, Recruit Christine!"

"Yes, Master Warrant!" She belted out.

"Yes, what?" Duncan also belted out.

"Recruit Christine is willing to die for her teammates, Master Warrant!"

"Good job, Christine," Duncan said. He clapped her on the shoulder.

"And I will die for you. Just keep that to yourself, eh? Welcome to the brotherhood, or, in your case, the sisterhood. I am still gonna kick your ass when you need it, Christine."

"Yes, Master Warrant. I understand, Master Warrant." Christine said.

"Okay, get your ass back to your team, kid."

Duncan turned and looked at the stars as Christine jogged back to the fire ring and her comrades. They gathered around and she hugged each one of them in turn.

Gwen found him still looking up at the stars.

"Is it always this hard?" she asked softly.

"Ya," Duncan said. "Especially with the special ones like her. My first wife was one, Dianne another, and then your mom. Each special in their own way. I have lost others who were special, Gwen. That is what happens sometimes. I watched one of my teams get wiped out one day. The last of them went down swinging his empty rifle like a bat at the ones coming for him after he had run out of ammunition. Because he did that, Amanda did not die that day. And others, most of whom will never know he had saved their lives, lived."

"You are another special person, Gwen," he said. His voice was quivering. "You do things instinctively that I have to try hard to do or simply cannot do. And, goddamn it, I am going to do all I can to make sure you don't get fucking killed doing what you do."

Then he took off. Gwen knew she would never find him. He was not called the Ghost for no reason. She made her way back to the campfire, waited until she drew Christine's eyes, then beckoned her and moved away.

"You okay, Christine?" Gwen asked.

"Yes, Lieutenant, Recruit Christine is fine, Lieutenant."

Gwen smiled.

"When I say your first name without rank, we are woman to woman," Gwen said. "When I say Recruit Christine, I am the officer and you are the recruit. Understand, Christine?"

"Yes, Ma'am," Christine said.

"So," Gwen said. "Tell me about yourself. Who are you? What is your station in life?"

"I am sixteen years old, Ma'am," Christine said. "My mother owns four thousand acres of timber and two thousand acres of planted ground. She has a minor position in the ruling class, Ma'am."

"My mother is what we call a Baroness," Gwen replied. "She owns ten thousand acres on a planet called Oaken. Her cousin is the ruler of that planet. My grandmother owns five thousand acres and is also a Baroness. That is more than just a minor position of nobility, Christine. I am my grandmother's heir and my mother's. I also have two baronies of my own. My father is called a Grand Duke. Essentially, he is the ruler of four planets. Put together, those planets have around sixty million people on them. I am his heir and am called Grand Duchess. I have enough wealth to buy this planet ten times over. Think about that."

"And you know what?" she asked. "None of that means shit right now. My dad and I are out here all on our own. My mother is on the other side of the planet stuck with a bunch of dumb, stubborn, bullheaded women who can't see what is happening around them.

"All I have is my dad, and now you eleven. If all of us don't pull together, we are going to die, Christine. Four of these invader assholes tried to rape me. My dad killed them all, by himself, with nothing more than a carving knife.

"I was, if anything, less equipped for this life than you, Christine. I didn't have to do anything. Everything was done for me. These last months I have had to grow up fast. Your men have shown they have the balls to stand up for you, Christine. They didn't have to, you know. They could have stayed quiet and let us keep doing what we were doing. This was not only a learning experience for them but for you. Do you see that?"

"Yes, Lieutenant, I see that," Christine said. "Those men could have said nothing and let it all continue. I can't say as I would blame them. They have been treated horribly."

"Okay," Gwen said and, like her father had done earlier, clapped Christine on the shoulder. "Now get your ass back to your teammates. Just don't forget, we girls have to stick together; there are only two of us."

As Christine made her way back to her teammates, Gwen began to see what her father had been trying to teach her for the last five years. By helping others, she was helping herself.

Chapter Ten

As the days turned into weeks, the recruits learned more and more. They were no longer loggers; they were becoming soldiers. One by one, each earned the right to be addressed by their name. Gwen found herself doing less and less as the recruits learned more. Now, they were all training with weapons and tactics. Her father would teach them a skill, then have them practice it, then have them set up a situation and attack him or his daughter. Sometimes the lessons were painful. Duncan rarely held back. Each of them knew they would have died had it been real.

To his credit, while he did make them feel foolish, Duncan never belittled them. After each failed attempt, he would explain what they had done wrong and show them what they should've done.

What they didn't know was that it was becoming harder for Duncan to surprise them with each attack he made. They had finally reached the point where he felt they were ready to do something for real.

"Recruits," he said one night at their campfire. "I don't know about you, but I can sure use some new clothing and some new food. The lieutenant and I had found the invaders' forward base before we found you folks. It is probably still there. This is the final test. If you don't all die, I will no longer call you *recruits*. Lieutenant, I would recommend the Lieutenant provide the Recruits with the intel on the base if it please you, Ma'am."

"Very well Master Warrant," Gwen said. "Carry on. I believe I have this in hand."

She should, Gwen thought. Her father had been drilling the plan into her head for days now.

Unexpected by the recruits, but not to Gwen, Duncan disappeared that night. This left all the planning of the raid up to Gwen. After two days, she was sure they were as ready as they ever would be.

They set off on the fifty kilometre journey to the base. They took the four horses, lightly laden. They would need them on the return journey.

It took two days to reach the enemy base and two more days to observe and make a plan of attack. On the morning of the attack, one of their horses was missing. The attack had to go that morning so the plan was modified.

Thirty men inhabited the camp. They knew that ten were cooks or clerks, which left twenty soldiers to handle. The plan was to attack just as the sun broke the horizon. That was the time the cooks awoke to prepare breakfast. The others would still be asleep. It took all night for eleven of their group to creep up silently on the base camp. Five would attack from the west. The other five, with Gwen, would attack from the south. Two had other plans.

When Gwen saw the first cook leave his bunkhouse, she stood and screamed her war cry as loud as she could. Pole raised above her head, she charged the camp along with her five troops. The troops from the west also rose and charged, each screaming loudly as they ran. In a short time, they were among the disoriented soldiers running from their bunkhouses. Sprays of blood were flying everywhere a hammer or hand axe found its mark. The screams were now coming from the soldiers, not the attackers.

Just as they thought it was all over, a thunder of hooves was heard. Soon a horse broke into the camp. Duncan, an axe in his right hand, charged into the camp at a full gallop. Five soldiers armed with long-barrelled blasters turned around too late. Duncan was suddenly

among them, flailing his axe left and right as the horse bit or kicked
soldiers that got in its way, either with fore hooves or hind legs. It was
soon over. The five soldiers lay dead. Two more soldiers soon were as
the horse stomped on them.

Duncan moved the horse over to the communications building,
jumped off, flung open the door and charged inside. A loud scream
was briefly heard, then crashing and smashing of equipment.
Duncan emerged with paper in one hand.

"Come on!" He yelled. "Get your heads out of your asses! Grab
what we need and let's get the hell out of here! Three of you yahoos
go grab the horses. Chop chop, people!"

He made his way to the dead soldiers with the long blasters and
stripped them of their weapons. In less than an hour, they were on
their way back to their own camp, horses and people loaded with as
many supplies as they could carry. They were running, not walking.

"Good job, troopers," Duncan said that night after they'd stashed
the supplies they had grabbed.

"Nobody died or got hurt this time. Now which one of you
dumb asses didn't spot the forward listening post? Never mind; I
handled it for you," Duncan finished, without waiting for a reply.
"Every plan is a good plan until the attack. Then shit happens. We
can plan everything except for last minute changes our enemy makes
or how hard they will fight us. "

The piece of paper Duncan had retrieved from the enemy camp
proved to be a map. It detailed where other logging camps were,
where future enemy forward posts might be situated, and the
location of the main base itself. Duncan told Gwen that the numbers
at the bottom of the map indicated radio frequencies the enemy was
using.

Gwen and Duncan began an intermittent radio monitoring
schedule. They were the only ones who understood the Parisian
language the invaders used, although Gwen was not fluent.

Duncan sent men to the other logging camps and, within a week, their little band had grown by thirty men and fifty horses. There were more horses than men because the invaders had generally killed all the inhabitants in a camp but left the horses. Gwen and Christine remained the only women.

Gulf Alpha One, Gulf Charley Tango, Copy? Gwen heard in her earpiece one evening. This was her father's friend CT calling Duncan.

"Charley Tango, ya got me, go."

"Alpha One, sit rep?"

"Three zero Gulf India, five zero cav transport, two Foxtrot Oscar."

"Copy Alpha One, break, wait one...."

"K Ghost, all scrambled now. Working on getting some bodies for you guys. Many volunteers, little transport. Working on it. I can get you four Cherokee and twelve ponies, special transport, but only once, for now. Interested?"

"Outstanding, CT. Can you include some decent comms and do you have my coordinates?"

"Yes to both. You want some decent firepower?"

"Not yet, CT. We have plenty of axes and hammers; a few crossbows. Good enough for now."

"Okay boss, I'll try for one hundred meters to the south of you in about two hours, okay?"

"Ya good and...CT? Make sure those Cherokee are all single and young, eh?"

"No problem, boss. LB said about the same. Gotta go, boss."

Gwen walked up to her father and raised her eyebrows.

"I just told him we now have forty um...General Infantry troops. Well, they will be soon at least...and fifty horses, plus two female officers," Duncan said. "They are working on getting help to us, lots of volunteers, but we need transport. We will be getting some help in about an hour.

"You remember your trip to the ranch last year?"

"Ya, some of it was a lot of fun," Gwen said. "Especially meeting the Cherokee kids."

"Four of them and twelve horses are coming," Duncan said. "CT asked if I wanted some firearms and I told him not now. Two reasons. First, we are doing alright using what we have and will be getting better all the time. Second, using firearms would be a direct giveaway as to who we are and draw way too much attention."

"But won't the incoming transport ship do the same thing?" Gwen asked.

Duncan smiled.

"Need-to-know basis, kid, and you don't need to know," he said. "Now, you just keep everyone over here and away from those trees to the north, eh? I got some shit to do."

Almost in the centre of the little clearing in the trees north of camp and, almost on time, the light shimmered and four young Cherokee men on their horses appeared. They quickly moved to Duncan's location. Another shimmer and to the edge of the clearing came several boxes, followed by twelve horses, half of them with loaded pack saddles.

The four warriors quickly got control of the twelve loose horses, then looked to Duncan.

Duncan had been watching them. The oldest appeared to be eighteen or nineteen, the youngest he knew was sixteen, and all wore hatchets at their waists. Their horses each had two quivers of ten arrows on one side and a recurve bow on the other.

"Daddy couldn't come so he sent you, eh?" Duncan said to the youngest.

The other three men laughed while the youngest ducked his head.

"The kid is not going to sit down for a month once his pop finds out," the older man said.

Duncan laughed, mostly because it was true.

"Right," Duncan said. "Leave the boxes there, I'll have the grunts bring them in."

Duncan motioned them to follow and the group moved off toward the camp. As they came into view, there was a scramble for weapons and the men assembled in a tight line. Those with shields came to the front and crashed their shields together to make a small wall. Christine was shoving the slower and newer men into their places in the line while Gwen looked on, more inquisitive than alarmed.

For their part, the Cherokee barely acknowledged the line of men assembled before them armed, for them, to the teeth. Duncan chatted away between the first two riders. He motioned for the riders to stop, then walked up to Gwen and saluted.

"Our cavalry detachment has arrived, Ma'am," Duncan said after he had received his return salute from Gwen. "I will show them where to set up Ma'am, if you choose. Also, Ma'am, I would recommend detailing a section of the troops to retrieve our new supplies, Ma'am."

"Very well, Master Warrant," Gwen said. "You may show the cavalry where to make camp. Sub-lieutenant! Take a section of men to the clearing where the cavalry just came from and retrieve the supplies!"

"Yes, Ma'am!" Christine said. Not one man moved from the line.

"Sub-lieutenant!" Gwen said, just as Duncan was going to make a 'recommendation'. "Stand the men down first! Where were you when they issued brains, Sub-lieutenant? Out getting your hair and nails done?"

Duncan turned quickly so his smile couldn't be seen. One of the Cherokee snorted as he tried to contain his laughter.

"Master Warrant!" Gwen yelled at their backs. "That better not have been one of my cavalry troopers snorting, Master Warrant!"

"Why no, Lieutenant, Ma'am," Duncan said. "Was one of the horses got a fly in its nose, Ma'am, so it was."

Now Duncan's snorts joined the other four men's.

"Give a probie a little authority and it goes right to their heads," he said so only they could hear.

"Damn flies is bad over here, Ma'am!" he said. He looked over at Gwen who turned so the others couldn't see her back, put her right hand behind it and gave him the finger.

As the four troopers quickly set up a picket line for their horses and began unloading, Duncan surveyed horses, men and equipment. The horses were in great shape; clearly the best had been sent. The men, even the young one, were also. The three men all had braided hair with an eagle feather woven in it. The young one had braided hair but no feather.

Duncan looked over at the camp and saw dinner was ready. He motioned the Cherokee to follow and headed that way. Once there, all of the local troops, including Christine, were looking the four over. Duncan let them stand there, the men with their arms crossed on their chests and looking right back, zero expression on their faces.

"These men and their horses have come to help us," Duncan said. "They are trained hunters and trackers, and three of them are experienced warriors. I have worked with their people before. They are good at what they do. Watch them, learn from them. I witnessed the oldest kill a beast twice the size of his horse, both at the full gallop, with one arrow. They can all do that, or they would not be here. Each of them volunteered to come here and help you. The list of volunteers was long, so, I assure you, these are the best of the best. Almost. But even the young need to learn, eh? No better way to learn but by doing it. Just like all of you."

Duncan motioned the Cherokee to grab some food, did so himself, then headed back to their part of the camp with them. As soon as he sat down, he cracked a joke at the expense of the young one, Little Bear's son. The poor kid didn't have a chance as his older brethren tied into him. The meal finished, their dishes were tossed to the youngest, who had no choice but to take them to the stream and wash, to more laughter and jibes.

Seeing movement at the edge of his vision, Duncan turned and saw an agitated Gwen approaching them.

"Ut oh," Duncan said and jerked his chin Gwen's way. "The looie looks pissed, boys."

"Ya," one of the warriors said. "Them green lueys tend to do that from time to time."

When Gwen was within a meter of them, all four men stood, came to attention and Duncan saluted.

"Why are you men singling out that trooper?" Gwen said, not bothering to return the salute.

All four men stayed at attention, Duncan still saluting. The young man came running back, dropping the dishes on the ground, joined the line and came to attention as well.

Gwen perplexed, suddenly remembered her lessons, came to attention and returned the salute.

"Cavalry troop all present and accounted for, Ma'am!" Duncan said. "I would like to remind the Lieutenant, Ma-am, that disciplinary matters among the enlisted personnel are my responsibility, Ma'am! This will be handled and a report made to the Lieutenant as soon as possible, Ma'am!"

Gwen, not knowing what else to do, nodded her head.

"Now stand there and shut the hell up," Duncan said. "You too, Little Bear. Rest of you yahoos, I sure hope you have some beer. Been a while."

"So, daughter of mine," Duncan said after a beer was fetched for him. "What real soldiers do in the field is a whole lot different than what happens in the base or in training. All of these guys but the young pup have passed into warrior status, been there and done that."

"You, junior," Duncan said seeing the youngster's defiant look. "You are only a Cadet Corporal if I remember correctly. You should not be here and not only disobeyed orders to be here, but deprived myself and my trainees of an experienced warrior. That should make me pissed, very pissed.

"Now, see that female standing there? She is my daughter. I know you know that, just like I know the two of you spent a lot of time together last year. What you don't know is that she was a Cadet Private back home. In her time here, she has stolen ten horses on her own, killed twelve enemy soldiers and counted coup on eight with that big stick of hers, then killed them after.

"Question, lover boy, seems like she is more qualified to protect you than you are to protect her. When both of you grow up some more, then maybe I will let you chastise me. Don't count on it, though.

"Junior, you got our plates dirty again, go clean them, again. Lieutenant, back to your own side of the camp if you please."

Duncan saluted again. Before Gwen had a chance to return it, Duncan dropped it and sat down. She heard the four men laughing as she walked away.

Gwen stomped her way over to the small campfire she and Christine shared, angrily tossed a piece of firewood into it and crashed to sit on the ground.

"Anything I can help the Lieutenant with, Ma'am?" Christine asked.

"Damned fathers can be such pain in the ass sometimes," Gwen said. "Is yours just as bad?"

"Don't know, Gwen," Christine said. "Never met him. Mothers though, oh yes, they can be a pain in the ass."

Gwen looked over at Christine, then laughed.

"Ya," Gwen said. "My mom is worse than my dad sometimes. You've never met your dad? Your mom and dad didn't get along so split up?"

"No," Christine said. "I don't even know who he is. Men just are sperm donors here. They have no role at all otherwise."

"Oh," Gwen said. "Well...I can see how that could be an advantage at times, but still..."

"We are allowed to pick among the approved men," Christine said. "Not all men are deemed suitable for breeding purposes."

"Oh..." Gwen said. *I'm starting to sound like a broken record* she thought. "Different where I come from."

She left it at that.

Over the next two weeks, training intensified as the four newcomers taught the former loggers new skills and refined the ones they had learned. In many ways, the training was harder for Gwen than that she had received from her father and she began to suspect her father may have been holding back on her. This appeared especially true in the hand-to-hand fighting. All four of the Cherokee worked on her and worked hard, even Junior, as everyone began to call him.

She was able to hold her own, however, even with the most experienced of them. One day, the warrior she had been training with backed her up. She was holding back, not wanting to hurt any of them. Suddenly, her right foot made contact with a stone on a fire ring. She lost balance briefly and the warrior made contact, dropping her to the ground. He quickly pulled a long stick from his belt and hit her on the shoulder with it.

As she lay there, she saw a huge smile come on his face. He raised both hands in the air, shrieked a long undulating cry, jumped and ran shrieking to his comrades, all of whom began to dance around him, chanting in their own language and dancing their high-knee step dance.

"What's all that about?" Gwen asked her father as he came over, reached down a hand, and helped her up.

"He just counted coup on you," Duncan said. "For a warrior it is more important to count coup than to kill an opponent. Especially one as skilled as you are. It is cause for great celebration. That'll teach you for holding back on them."

"Really?" Gwen said. "Is that so?"

She walked to the small camp she shared with Christine, reached into their tent, came back with two arm's-length sticks and started walking toward the celebrating warriors.

"Gather the troops, kid," Duncan said to Christine. "You are about to witness an ass kicking."

Gwen walked up to the dancing men and tossed a stone to bounce off the one who had hit her. Once she had his attention, she stood straight, clasped her hands together and bowed at him. Then she stood straight, put her right arm behind her head, stick upraised and her left pointing at the warrior with the other.

"Like to play with sticks, eh?" Gwen asked. She jerked the stick in the left hand in a come-and-get-it gesture.

To his credit, knowing he was about to get a severe lesson, the warrior approached and circled around her, seeking an opening to attack. Gwen rotated in place keeping her stance sideways to him, then attacked. It was fast, violent, and soon over. Then she beckoned to the other warriors.

"Come on, then," she said. "Four big tough men against little old me. Come on, how hard could it be?"

The three took coup sticks from belts and joined their comrade, forming a circle around Gwen. She didn't wait for them to figure out what they were going to do. At times, her hands were so fast they blurred. The only way the onlookers knew she had connected was when a meaty smack was heard and a warrior went down, holding some body part or another.

Once they were all down, Gwen went from man to man and touched them lightly on the shoulder with one of her sticks. Then she stood straight, clasped her hands together and bowed at them. With a mischievous grin on her face, she stood straight again.

"You boys should have known better," she said, almost laughing now. "White Ghost was trained by her father, Ghost. White Ghost did not wish to make her cavalry troopers look bad to her other troops. You have counted one coup today. I have counted four."

Then she yelled as high-pitched a scream as a woman can and held it, flicking her tongue as she did. It sounded like her namesake as she let it trail to a low moaning sound. Out of breath, she stopped, took a gulp of air, yelled again, this time jumping as high as she could, then pranced over to her little camp.

"Guess she showed us, eh?" the one who had counted coup on her said.

"Well," Duncan said, helping him up. "That was just with the little sticks. You should see her with that big one of hers."

The next morning they all did, as she and her father worked together with their long poles. Duncan was holding back and she knew it. He was also working his ass off to make sure Gwen didn't hurt him.

Getting too old for this shit, Duncan thought.

Soon, they all saw what she could do for real. This time she had a different pole. It was the same length overall but the shaft had been shortened to accommodate a long, sharp blade that had been attached. Now, as she sliced across an enemy's throat, she would cut it, sometimes right to the backbone. With each eye poke, the blade went in deep, then was twisted and withdrawn.

Over the coming weeks, ambushes were made on single patrols. So devastating were the attacks that the invaders seldom went out in less than four-vehicle patrols. And still the invaders lost men and vehicles.

The little band was slowly growing as word spread. Still only men. They did not always win. Twice the invaders sprang traps on them; not that it went all the invaders' way, as the trappers suffered badly both times. Still, eight of their men had died from blaster wounds. The bodies were taken away, so the invaders never knew.

Duncan never chastised anyone for the ambushes. He gathered the recruits around and asked questions, not only about what had happened, but also on how things could have been done differently. He then accompanied the section involved on the next few raids.

The invaders tried the same trick once on a raid Duncan was leading. It was not a total failure for the invaders; they scored a few hits, but nowhere near as severe as the first two.

Returning to camp that night, word went around camp about how the Master Warrant had been everywhere during the attack, seemingly all at the same time. Several times he saved a trooper from being killed. Once again, he gathered his section around him and asked questions. Then he nodded his head.

"Very good," he said once they were finished. "This is how we learn. We ask questions: what happened, how could we have done something better. We need to do this all the time, not just after we get handed our asses. Also when we are successful. We can learn from both success and loss."

Duncan rose and made his way to his own little camp. Gwen knew something was wrong because his stride was off. She watched him cringe as he ducked under the tent flap and entered it. Gwen casually made her way over to his tent and ducked in, then gasped.

"Shut the flap and don't say a fucking thing!" Duncan hollered.

He had his shirt off. Two large blaster burns had raked across his chest and one across his back. Gwen quickly grabbed his first aid kit and began to work on the burns.

"Nobody hears about this," he said through his teeth as the salve Gwen gingerly applied began to sting. "They feel bad about not seeing that attack as it is."

"Ya, I know, Dad," Gwen said. She raised her tunic and shirt to show a healing blaster scar on her belly.

"Fuck!" Duncan said. "Why didn't you come to me for help?"

"Because you would have made a big fuss and not let me out of your sight, that's why," Gwen said. "I have a job to do, Dad, just like you do."

"I know, kid," Duncan said, his pain now forgotten and tears riming his eyes.

"I just want to get you home safe," he continued, stroking her cheek. "I just want the old Gwen back."

"Oh, not to worry, Pop," Gwen said. She wore her mischievous grin now. "I'll be back to spending all your money on useless knickknacks ten minutes after we get home," she said.

Duncan laughed, then gasped as she hit a tender spot on a burn.

"Do try and make it a little less painful than what you're doing to me now, eh?" he grunted.

"What kind of fun would that be, Pop?" Gwen said. "Daughters are always supposed to be pains in the butt for their dads."

They laughed together softly and each stroked or patted the other softly as they spoke. Caught up in the moment, they were unaware that Christine had seen and heard it all when she had become concerned and stood just outside the tent. She quietly backed away and went to her own tent. She didn't know why, but she began to cry.

Gwen found her like that. Sitting on her bed, knees up, arms around knees, head on her arms, crying softly.

"Hey!" Gwen said. She came quickly to Christine, lifted her chin, and wiped some tears away.

"Was it that damn Junior?" Gwen asked. "I'll kick his ass, I will!"

Junior had been doing what boys did at his age when around girls. Well, boys from anywhere but here.

"No," Christine said. "He knows better."

She looked away from Gwen then.

"I saw you and your father," Christine said after a short while. "The love you have for each other, how he lets you experience things, yet always knows, is always there for you when you need him – and you for him."

"Ya," Gwen said. "It must be tough for you to see that. It's all new for you."

"My mother, our mothers," Christine said. "Don't even show that much devotion to us. We are more status symbols than children for them."

"Hey," Gwen said. "My mom is like that a lot of the time. We call her the Ice Queen. But she has a kind and soft heart, especially around Dad and me. Well, most times anyway. Rarely in public, though."

"Not so with our mothers," Christine said. "They are like that all the time."

Then Christine softly lifted Gwen's shirt and ran her hand gently across the blaster scar there.

Gwen looked her in the eyes, then gently pulled her hand away.

"You're a nice girl and all," Gwen said. "But I like boys, Chris."

"What?" Christine said, then caught the look on Gwen's face and where her hand had been.

"N-n-n-o-o, My Lady," she stammered. "I, I like boys too, I think..."

"I was just concerned, My Lady," she said quickly. "You should have told me, My Lady. I would have helped. You would do the same for me. I saw you with your dad just now."

Gwen put a hand on each side of Christine's head and looked into her eyes.

"You can't say anything Chris. Please?" Gwen said. "All of you look up to us as examples. It is hard, but we, my dad and I, have to make it look like we are invincible. Do you understand?"

"I...I think so," Christine said. "Something like how we cart off our dead. The invader thinks they cause us no harm."

"Ya, something like that," Gwen said. "That's what my dad says, anyway. What the hell do I know? I'm just a dumb over-indulged and pampered rich girl."

"Just like me," Christine said and they both laughed, jumped up and made poses like the pampered aristocrats they had grown up around.

"That Junior," Gwen said. "Oh, what a hunk of man-flesh he is."

"Perhaps," Christine said. "I believe Curtis is ever so much more handsome."

"Chris!" Gwen said and hit Christine on the arm.

"What?" Christine said. "Just because my mom is a bitch doesn't mean I have to be."

"Ah, we're both too young anyway," Gwen said and she dejectedly sat down on her bed. "My pop won't let either one of us near any guys."

"Really?" Christine said. "He would do that for me? Look out for me?"

She started to cry again. Gwen quickly went to her side again and put her arm around her.

Fuck, Gwen thought, softly rocking Christine as she cried. *The women on this planet have really screwed the pooch.*

Chapter Eleven

Over the months, the number in the camp had grown too large to stay together as one group. They were now four hundred strong and had split up into four separate companies. Leaders had been promoted from among the first group to lead the new ones. Duncan primarily stayed in camp now, coordinating each of the four groups, assessing information and assigning tasks. Other men had been trained to assist him and he now always had a group of ten around him. This did not give any of the ten who served him privileges; they trained everyday like everyone else and participated in missions equally.

The cavalry had grown to fifty active troopers and fifty more in training. Suitable horses continued to 'show up,' although more fast, nimble horses were still needed to balance out the draft horses. The Clydesdales were more than capable and appeared to enjoy the work and the training. Some of the more experienced troopers were being trained on effectively operating with the large animals and were making up a new cavalry division now.

The light cavalry had been divided into sections of ten troops each, with one assigned to each of the four companies. However, the company Duncan called his own had two light cavalry sections.

Gwen, Christine, Junior, Curtis and six other underage troopers, including another female, were the members of this section. Most of the time they scouted new camp locations or suspected invader areas. Occasionally, they were assigned to conduct a raid. Initially, one of the older Cherokee or Duncan accompanied them. However, they now primarily operated on their own.

They were quickly gaining a reputation and a nickname. The invaders called all the light cavalry Ghost Riders. On one raid, for a laugh, Gwen had covered herself in ashes from their fire before they attacked. Her whole section liked the look and began to do the same. The invaders referred to them as the White Ghosts. Gwen made the most of it, always letting one invader live after each attack to report who had attacked them.

The ten youth were becoming close friends. They did almost everything together. They were all seventeen years old now, some soon to turn eighteen. After one successful raid, and having cleaned up as usual, all in the stream together, Duncan came to their camp, a bottle of clear fire in each hand. He sat them down and passed the bottles around.

"You are all doing well," Duncan said. "You are beginning to impress me. In fact, if I were put under interrogation, I might let it slip that I might be pleased with all of you."

They laughed and sat a little taller. Getting any sort of acknowledgment from the Master Warrant beyond a grunt and a nod was rare, and he had just said he was proud of them.

"All of you know the rules of conduct," Duncan continued. "All except a couple. Junior already knows, but you local boys, well...this is new for you and the local girls. Gwen, well, Gwen should know...." He shrugged his shoulders and grinned.

"At your age, at times, girls and boys will be attracted to each other," Duncan said. "Rule number one: if a girl, or a boy, says no, that means no. If the girl, or boy keeps it up, if the offended party doesn't do something about it, their troop mates better, or my people and I will. It has to be consensual. That includes boys attracted to boys, or girls to girls. Doesn't matter. If I catch even a hint of any sexual wrongdoing by anyone against another trooper's wishes, I will personally kill them. Clear?"

He looked all ten of them in the eye one by one. He was not smiling now.

"Second," Duncan said. "If a girl becomes pregnant, she and the young man she bedded will stay in camp until the child stops nursing and a childcare provider can be found. If it takes two years, so be it. No more raids or missions for either parent. Clear?"

Again, he looked each of them in the eye one by one. He still did not crack a smile.

He stared at the fire for a while. Beckoning for a bottle, Duncan took a deep pull from it and handed it to the trooper next to him. He grinned.

"Party's on!" he announced as he stood and walked away into the darkness.

Gwen found him where she thought he would be: sitting under a tree with his back against the trunk. He had a bottle beside him and at first she thought he was talking to himself.

"Fuck, I miss you," he said. "Especially now. She could really use you or Magdalene with her, Mar. I try, but what the hell do I know? I'm her fucking dad. I'm a guy. Shit!"

Gwen tapped the communicator she had on her ear.

"You should see her, Mar," Duncan said. "She is so goddamned beautiful. What the hell do I say to her? There are only two other girls here and they are her age. The men, shit, they don't know squat, even less than I do."

Gwen heard a sniffle on the other end and, when her mother spoke, her voice was quivering.

"I miss her so, Dunc," Marlene said. "you at least have been with her these last two years. I have not even seen her, just heard from her now and then, usually when she is pissed at us."

Gwen silently stood by her father, then tapped her ear again and placed the communicator on the ground facing up at her. She heard her mother gasp as the communicator cast her hologram at her mother.

"Oh my god, Duncan!" Marlene gasped out. "She is fully grown! Her hair. Her eyes, they are so like yours. How can you be so cruel to show me this, Duncan?"

"No Mom, it's me," Gwen said. "He didn't even know I was here. I miss you too, Mom."

"She moves and fights like you do, Mar," Duncan said. "The bad guys call her and her gang the White Ghosts."

"That's you, Gwen?" Marlene said. "I should have known. How'd you get that name?"

"She always leaves one alive after an attack, Mar," Duncan said. "Show them what that survivor sees, Gwen."

Gwen turned her back, brought a little bag from her belt and began to rub her face. Then she turned around. Her mother didn't say anything at first. What she saw was a grey face with streaks at the side of the mouth to make it look frowning and fierce. Then she laughed.

"Shit," Marlene said. "That's better than mine!"

Then Gwen took her shirt off to rub the ash off her face. Her mother gasped again.

"Duncan!" Marlene said. "How the hell did she get that? You're letting her go on raids?"

"Yes, Mom," Gwen said. "I go on raids. I plan most of them, too."

She grabbed Duncan and made him stand, then ripped open his shirt exposing his scars as well.

"So does he," Gwen said. "Somebody has to show these people, Mom, or these invader assholes are going to kill them all."

"I know, Gwen, I know," Marlene said. "Duncan, can Gwen and I have some time, please?"

"Oh, thank god," Duncan said. "I'm off the hook. See ya, Mar."

He made a hasty withdrawal.

"You can be such an asshole sometimes, Duncan," Marlene said to his receding back.

Marlene could just make out the middle finger as he disappeared. She laughed as her hologram image came alive in front of Gwen. Like Duncan had been, she was sitting under a tree in the dark by herself. Like Gwen and her dad, she wore a combat uniform she had looted from the invaders. Gwen could see the large knife strapped to her right leg and a hatchet holstered on her left. A handle for some kind of weapon peeked over her left shoulder. Her hair, as normal, flowed down her right side. Now she pushed it behind her ear and stood.

She opened the front of her shirt and pulled it down off her shoulders. She had healing blaster marks on both shoulders and one between her breasts. It had been a long time since Gwen had seen the older, life-threatening scars from edged weapons and bullets.

"We are doing our bit, Gwen," Marlene said. "Not as well as you are yet, but we are getting there. At least you don't have these pigheaded women with you. Shit, they are worse than men! Don't you dare tell your father I said that."

"Lips are sealed, Mom," Gwen said. "Not all that easy here either, though. The guys fight great. It's just....well, they are still learning to be men. You know what I mean?"

"I think so," Marlene said. "It's hard to get them to open up."

"That's because you are a woman and have women with you," Gwen said. "We have Dad and the Cherokee. They help a lot."

"I hear you have two other girls your age with you?" Marlene said.

"Ya," Gwen said. "One is kinda new and still learning how men should be. Christine is my bestie. Well, as good as can be in the army anyway, I outrank her a little. Not much, she's a subby and I'm 'dumb ass luey.'"

Her mom laughed as she buttoned up her shirt. It was good to see her laugh.

"Only thing better than a dumb ass green luey is no luey at all," Marlene said.

"I feel sorry for her, Mom," Gwen said. "She has never met her dad. She sees how Dad and I are like when we are alone, and I come back to the tent and find her crying. She's getting better, because dad has kind of adopted her. Still...."

"Your dad always was a sucker for a damsel in distress, kid," Marlene said. "Surely her mother loves her?"

"No, Mom," Gwen said. "She says kids are a status symbol for them. Heirs, nothing more."

"Ya, I have seen it," Marlene said. "And it happened all the time on Oaken. Arranged marriages. A lot of the time husband and wife disliked each other. Many times, men like my father couldn't care less about their kids, especially daughters, until it was time to marry them off to someone like themselves. Sometimes the wife's dislike of the husband carried over to the kids. The only times they would be all together would be for formal functions. Shitty all the way around. At least your grandmother loved me and showed it."

"Look Gwen, sometimes you need a woman to talk to. Unfortunately, I'm the only one around for the next while. You need to talk, give me a heads up and I'll sneak off like tonight and we'll talk. Okay?"

"You got it, Mom," Gwen said. "Dad tries...Shit, he laid down the law tonight. Guess it was time. Would have been nice if it was father-daughter though, and not the whole group."

"Mission comes first, luv," Marlene said quietly. "First, last and always. The mission comes first. Otherwise, many of our troopers die, Gwen. At your age, hormones start raging. If you were back home, a female drill instructor would have clued you in. And the boys? Well, a not-so-nice version of your father would have not-so-nicely clued them in, believe me. I've seen your dad do it. I had to clue Brock in, too. That was right at the beginning of our having women serve alongside men, Gwen. It's different now."

"Same with us ten, Mom," Gwen said. "Well, the rookie is learning. We do everything together, almost."

"Good. Maybe, just maybe, those two girls will let other girls know," Marlene said. "What's been going on here is not natural, kid. Ya, we have girls that like girls and boys that like boys in our world too, but not to this extent. They actually toss women that prefer to be with men in jail here, Gwen and outright kill the men.

"Okay, gotta go or some dumb ass woman will be plotting to take over," Marlene said. "Love you, Gwen. Stay safe."

"You too, Mom," Gwen said as her mother's image winked out.

Gwen came back to camp. Her father was waiting at its dark edge for her.

"You okay, kid?' he asked.

"Ya, I'm fine," Gwen replied.

"You kind of shook your mom up, Gwen. She hasn't seen you for almost two years. Not like me, in your face every day."

"Most of the time I love it, too," Gwen said hugging him. "Most of the time. Some of the time you are a pain in the butt."

Duncan squeezed her back.

"I told your mom about that new bunch of red uniformed troops we have been running into," Duncan said. "They haven't seen them over there yet, but the invaders are thicker than normal. She also said their interrogation of prisoners has revealed that some nasty and well-equipped people are headed our way. And that they are coming against us. You guys be careful out there, eh?"

Chapter Twelve

All along the front, they were pushing the invader and pushing them hard. The invader was now on the defensive and consolidating to conserve resources. Nevertheless, Gwen's sector had gone quiet. Duncan had decided to extend her group so that some of the busier teams could be rotated out more frequently.

Gwen's sector was on the extreme outside edge of the front. That did not mean the sector was unimportant. If the invader decided to pull a fast one, it would be right here. But the resulting constant vigilance had begun to take its toll. Gwen's team started making mistakes and began to argue about things that normally went unnoticed. Never big mistakes or arguments, but signs it was time to rotate out for some R&R. Command had agreed and tomorrow another team would replace them. They would meet the new team after dark, brief them, then mount the horses the new team had brought in and head back to base.

Just after the sun reached its zenith, those eager for R&R slowly began to gather their personal gear. Not that they had all that much. Their uniforms consisted of pieces leftover from those made for other personnel. Unusable fabric scraps had become bindings for worn boots.

"Hey, G," Don called from his watch position. "Got movement on the ridge." He referred to the ridge on the other side of the valley.

"Probably just a deer," Chelsea said.

"Nope," Don said. "It's a vehicle of some sort."

Gwen grabbed her battered pair of binoculars and crawled up to the concealed observation point.

"Never seen anything like that thing," Don said. "Looks like some kind of small SUV."

"Nope, well, ya, sort of," Gwen said.

Passengers emerged from the right side of the vehicle, advanced a few meters and lay down. Another appeared in the roof hatch, holding a weapon. Finally, the driver exited the vehicle, laid a weapon across the hood and began scanning their position on the opposite ridge with a large pair of binoculars. As soon as that happened, the two soldiers laying down stood, hung their long weapons on their chests and moved to the back of the vehicle. They removed a pair of objects from the rear and moved ten meters to each side and in front of the vehicle, opened the tripods attached to them, and returned to the vehicle.

Pretty soon, those same two soldiers had a small stove going and were boiling water in it.

"Keep an eye on them," Gwen said and she started slithering back downhill.

"What the hell do they think they are going to hit with those weapons from there?" Don said. "Waste of time."

Gwen picked up their radio and turned it on. As she pushed the button to transmit, it quit.

"Shit!" She said. This was their backup set of batteries and now they were shot.

"Chelsea, Little Bear," she said. "Head back and contact our reliefs. Do it now! Stay low but move fast once you get on the bottom of the hill. Tell them to stop and hold until dark. And radio base right away and tell them I said, Black Shirts on our front. Remember that, Black Shirts on our front. Also tell them I verified it."

"You sure, G?" Little Bear asked.

"Ya, no doubt," Gwen answered. "G-Wagon, crew weapon on the roof, driver is the designated rifleman."

"Fuck!" Little Bear said. "You think they are here for us?"

"Ya," Gwen said. "But we stay focused. We should have heard from the Wind Riders before the Black Shirts turned up. It should be PIGs up there, not Black Shirts."

As Chelsea and Little Bear made their way cautiously down the hill, Gwen slithered back up beside Don.

"They can hit us with every one of their weapons, Don," Gwen said. "Easily. Those little boxes they deployed on each side of the vehicle? They can detect movement up to a kilometre away. There will likely be three more of them and a much bigger and better-armed one somewhere around here."

An hour later, the driver moved to his door, removed a longer weapon from the front of the vehicle and lay it on the roof. One of the others brought a spotting scope out of the rear of the vehicle, set it up on the hood and began looking through it.

Gwen rolled on her back and glassed to their rear.

"Shit'" she whispered.

Chelsea and Little Bear were still in the dry creek bed and out of sight of the G-Wagon, but the four relief riders with the four trailing horses were in full view.

Gwen heard the crack of the shot just as it hit the rear rider, then the next and the next and, just as the front rider discovered what was going on, he was blown off his horse. Little Bear had dragged Chelsea to the ground as he heard the shots. The spooked horses moved off a short distance, then after a few nervous minutes, started to graze.

"Don't move a muscle," Gwen said. "Or we are both fucking dead."

The driver removed the clip from his weapon, reloaded it and placed it back in the vehicle. The spotter reached into the vehicle, grabbed a microphone, and made a report. Ten minutes later, a light drone passed over their position, hovered over the dead troopers for a minute, buzzed around the area for ten minutes, then disappeared out of sight again.

It was after dark when Chelsea and Little Bear made it back to the position. Don moved down and Little Bear took his place.

"What you think?" Little Bear asked.

"Time for the Black Shirts to be reminded what a Wind Rider does," Gwen said quietly. She looked to the rear. "Wait an hour," she said. "Then head toward the rally point. We will meet you there. Come on, LB, time to earn our pay."

It was after midnight before Gwen and Little Bear made it close enough to strike. Like her father had predicted, these troops were over-reliant on their technology to warn them of intruders. All four were sleeping. Withdrawing their hatchets, the two sprang on the sleeping men.

The last one to die was the driver. Gwen hit him in the right wrist with her razor sharp hatchet first, then the left, then the right knee. She took the flashlight from the man's vest, turned it on and shined it on her now blood-streaked face.

"You forgot one thing, asshole," she said. "My father is the Ghost, my mother is the Zebra and I am the White Ghost. Zebras kick Wind Rider butts, asshole. What the fuck did you think we were going to do to you?"

She raised the hatched high and drove it deep in the man's forehead.

"Any of their boots small enough for me?" she asked. She started walking toward one of the remotes and Little Bear turned on another flashlight and began looking at feet.

"Nope," he said. "But I get a pair."

Gwen dropped the remote unit in the back of the vehicle and headed for the other one.

"Strip them of weapons, ammo, and anything else we can use," she said.

"Wanna have some fun?" Gwen said as she tossed the other remote in the back and slammed the door shut.

"Ya, I'm a little bored," Little Bear said.

"Know how to use one of those?" She asked, gesturing at the automatic weapon mounted on the roof.

"Oh ya," he replied. He had a big grin on his face.

"Up you go then," Gwen said. She shut the left rear door and took the driver's seat, starting the engine. "Oh, I've missed that sound."

Looking around the vehicle, she found the night vision goggles, put them on, adjusted them, put the vehicle into gear and drove toward the next G-Wagon's position. They knew that, once they got into position to attack the next vehicle, they would be out of range of the powerful 20mm cannon on the command vehicle and the sensors deployed by their target would be focused away from them. At least, they hoped.

She stopped well in range for Little Bear.

They scanned the target. As at the first location they attacked, these troopers were all sleeping; no one on guard.

"Anytime, LB," Gwen said.

The words were barely out of her mouth when the silence and darkness erupted into gunfire and light from tracers and flames from the barrel above her head. Red ribbons from the tracers made a line that moved up and down the laid-out row of sleeping bags. After thirty seconds the firing stopped.

"If you fucked up my new bus, I'm gonna be pissed," Gwen said.

She grabbed the weapon from the clip that held it onto the dash, made sure a round was in the chamber and the safety was off. Putting it to her shoulder, she aimed it at the bodies and moved toward them.

"Grab the sensor on your side, LB; I'll grab the other one." Gwen said. "Just toss it into your new vehicle and take off. I'm pretty sure we woke those other yahoos up."

She ran to the other sensor and ran back, tossing it through the open rear window of her vehicle. Making her way to the bodies, she quickly went over them, grabbed the weapons and their harnesses, also tossing them through the rear windows. Quickly moving around the vehicle, she slammed all the doors shut and, climbing into the driver's seat, fired up the engine, put it into gear, and took off. That's when she noticed the radio was making noises. She turned it up and heard repeated call signs and requests for response. She grabbed the microphone clipped to the dash and waited for a break in the transmissions.

"Well these idiots got one thing right, they had the radio turned down low," she said.

"What's your call sign, trooper?" she heard.

"Hmm...lemme think." Gwen said. "Oh ya, Whiskey Romeo Gulf One Two Oscar. Shithead, sir."

"Yo, Two Bravo, what are we born doing?"

"Running," Little Bear said over his radio.

"What are we bred to do?" Gwen asked.

"Kill lions," was the response.

"What do we love to do?"

"Kill Black Shirt ass. Zebra, Zebra, Zebra!" Little Bear yelled into the mike.

"Thanks for the wheels and the weapons, Shithead Sir," Gwen said. "We took out the first vehicle with just hatchets, buddy. I'll be sure to tell Ghost of your generosity. He misses his long gun. Night, night, sleep tight. Tach 3 LB."

"LB up," she heard.

"Tach 5," she said and switched to their base frequency, waited a few seconds, hit some buttons and waited.

"LB up," came seconds later.

"G up," Gwen said.

"Woo hoo," Little Bear said. "Back in the saddle again."

"Ya ok, yak it up," Gwen said. "I only had one month of pop gun training and some hand blaster stuff. I know where the trigger and the safety is on the one I had, but that's about it."

"Same as shooting the pop gun, but louder and the kick is harder."

"Crappy radio discipline, Two Oscar," she heard her father say.

"One Alpha, Two Oscar," Gwen said. She was serious now. "Team three engaged by long shooter. Four KIA. Eight Tango KIA, two Gulf Whiskey Twos repatriated with full weapons, ammo, and comms. One Lima Alpha Victor and two Gulf Whiskey Twos still in place. Tangos are Bravo Sierra, I repeat, Tangos are Bravo Sierra, confirmed. Position, one klick west and two east of our pos. Two Bravo and Tango will repatriate our KIA. Two Oscar and Foxtrot will reposition to alternate. Copy?"

"Copy. All Two team RTB; copy?"

"Copy."

"Good work Zebra, Ghost out."

"Who the hell you calling a Zebra?" Her mother's voice came over the radio.

"Tach One, Zebra Alpha," her father said, and the radio went silent.

"Good news, bad news," Duncan said, once he had changed frequencies.

"Hit me," Marlene replied.

"Good news," Duncan said. "Black Shirts are here. Bad news, they're working for the invaders. They just wiped out one of my recon teams with their designated rifleman. Good news, Zebra Two just took out two Black Shirt recon teams."

"Shit," Marlene said. "Who's Zebra Two?"

"White Ghost and her team," Duncan said. "She and LB took out the first GW Two team with hatchets, and the second with the crew gun from the first. Now we have two GW Twos, all their weapons, ammo, and toys. You tell your people this is a whole new ballgame, Mar."

"Wait one," Marlene said.

Several minutes later she was back.

"You sure those were Black Shirts?" Marlene said. "All their units just reported in. Situation normal. Nobody missing."

"That's what White Ghost reported, Zebra," Duncan said. "But then again...I'll get back to you. Remember to let your people know to stay under the radar."

They both signed off and Duncan set out to find Little Bear.

"You sure those were Black Shirts, LB?" Duncan asked.

"Hell if I know," Little Bear answered. "Only Wind Riders I have ever seen are you and Colonel Carol. We were all trained by PIGs. You guys all use the same vehicles, gear and uniforms, so if there are no unit patches it's hard to tell what unit it is. And these guys weren't wearing unit patches."

"Well, let's have a look at those vehicles for a bit," Duncan said, and headed toward them.

Little Bear smiled. He knew that, once in a while, Duncan would slip back into his Home World Standard language, which he had just done with the 'have a look' comment.

Seconds after opening the rear door leading to the cargo area, Duncan stood and looked at Little Bear.

"Grab my computer bag for me, will you?" He said. "Then grab your team and get back here. Oh ya, grab Gwen too. Hubba hubba, LB."

Duncan found what he was looking for and swore. Then he looked into the other vehicle and confirmed what he had found in the first. He had the tailgate down on the first vehicle and was stripping an assault rifle on it when Little Bear and his seven troopers returned with Gwen in tow.

"Sergeant," Duncan said. "Pick three of your people to join me, with you. You others, demonstrate the capabilities of these vehicles and weapons systems. Any of you qualified as a designated rifleman?"

"That would be me, Warrant," Little Bear said.

"Okay, pick one of those long rifles and make sure it's satisfactory," Duncan said. "The other one is mine. The rest of you, pick an assault rifle, strip it, clean it. The four coming with me, take four full clips each. Crew weapon trooper, go over the weapons and ammo on this vehicle. We are out of here in half an hour. Somebody show Corporal Kovacks how to strip one of these weapons. Then make sure she is at least familiar with how each weapon works and has some preliminary training on the assault rifle. Get at it, gang."

Duncan had not stopped what he was doing while he was talking. He had finished inspecting the taken-down weapon, quickly reassembled it, pulled the bolt back and dry fired it twice, then grunted. Next, he did the same with an automatic pistol and, finally, the long gun.

"Those guys were Wind Riders, Sergeant, not Black Shirts," Duncan said. "Minor detail, but important. I know what to look for, you don't, so don't sweat it. Just realize how lucky you two were. We are going to take out the rest of that team, Sergeant. I have a few tricks up my sleeve that will help us, but remember, these guys are good."

Now he took his computer bag to the front passenger seat and pulled out his battered laptop. He found his vehicle charging cord, plugged one end into the laptop and the other into the socket on the vehicle's dash. After a few seconds he nodded as the charging light began to blink indicating it was charging his long-dead battery.

Looking around, he found a suitable piece of firewood, grabbed it, and marched away from the vehicle two hundred meters, put it on the ground with the flat face toward the vehicle and walked back. Picking up the assault weapon he had cleaned, he put in a full clip, went to one knee, pulled back the bolt and fired a shot. Then another. He adjusted the rear sight slightly, then fired twice more. Stood and fired five shots. Grunting, he adjusted the sling and slung it around his chest so it hung barrel down.

Next, he walked to within fifty meters of the firewood, loaded a clip into the automatic pistol, and slowly fired five rounds. He grunted again, pulled the clip out of the weapon, ejected the round in the chamber and put it back into the clip. Walking back to the vehicle, he placed the pistol on the tailgate, picked up the long gun, loaded a clip into it and started walking away from the vehicle. Seeing what was going on, Little Bear did the same with his long rifle and, grabbing the spotting scope, jogged to join Duncan.

"You first," Duncan said, taking the spotting scope from Little Bear. He set it up on its small tripod and laid down behind it.

Little Bear jacked a round into the chamber and laid down beside and slightly ahead of Duncan.

"Target acquired," he said.

"Range 805, crosswind left to right, one meter per second," Duncan said.

"On the way," and the long gun boomed.

"Left three," Duncan said. He heard a click as Little Bear adjusted the sight.

"Target acquired, on the way." Boom!

"Right half."

"On the way," Boom!

"Zeroed," Duncan said. Then five more booms.

"Not bad for a rookie," Duncan said and he shifted the spotting scope over to Little Bear and put his rifle to his shoulder.

"Target acquired, on the way," Duncan said then fired. Without waiting to be told where the round had hit, he adjusted the scope, sighted again and shot. Then fired five rapid shots out of the semiautomatic long rifle.

"Close enough for the girls I go out with," Duncan said. "No time to dial it all the way in. These are new weapons and will take more than a few rounds to get broken in properly. Go sight-in the rest of your weapons and make sure you put two rounds through the grenade launcher. I got some other shit to do."

The clearing became crazy-loud as all the other weapons were fired and adjusted, including the grenade launchers and the squad machine guns. The whole camp, except the personnel on guard duty, gathered around to watch. Those on guard witnessed the fun from their positions.

While that was going on, Duncan had fired up his laptop and was attacking the keyboard with a vengeance. He was done by the time the sighting process was completed.

"Okay, people," Duncan announced, coming out of the vehicle to address the Cherokee and Gwen. "The three coming with me, gear up. The rest of you, collect your gear and get some sleep. Going to be some long days ahead."

He tossed the used pistol and assault rifle clips into the back of the other vehicle, loaded both weapons with full new clips, then grabbed a box of ammunition and reloaded the long rifle's clip. He selected a weapon harness, put it on and adjusted it. He confirmed all the pouches for ammo clips were full and the clips in them were full.

"Who's driving?" Duncan asked. "I sure ain't."

Gwen stuck her hand up.

"Not this time, kid," Duncan said. "Maybe next time. Little Bear, you drove this thing here, you just volunteered. We only have four hours till dawn; let's go!"

With that, he jammed his long rifle into the corner near the passenger's dash, pulled the assault rifle from his chest, sat in the front passenger seat and slammed the door shut. Rolling down the window, he laid the rifle on the door, the barrel sticking out of the window. Duncan looked at Gwen and smiled.

The other three loaded in, slamming doors. Little Bear fired the vehicle up and waited.

"Onward, Smithers," Duncan said. "Tally Ho! The hunt's afoot!"

Little Bear put the vehicle in gear and roared off, dirt spraying behind them.

"Uh...Where we goin' boss," he said.

"Oops; silly me," Duncan said. He hit a few buttons on a box mounted on the dash. The lights of a heads-up display came alive on the windshield in front of Little Bear.

"Just follow the little blinking light, Smithers," Duncan said. "Try not to bust an axle or some shit, eh? Lights off, night goggles on, everyone."

"Okay, boys and girls," Duncan continued. "You are seeing a few more details in your goggles than you are used to. You have IFF info. All of us are green. The bad dudes will be red. You will also be given approximate distance to targets or friendlies. I haven't had time to rig up comms for us yet, so just use our regular hand signals this time around. My little gizmo tells us we are half an hour from our assault point. We will dismount there. Little Bear will stay with the vehicle and man the squad gun in case we need it. We will be five hundred meters from the target. At that time, we should be able to see what we are facing. At worse, we blow those guys away, grab the vehicle, and head back to camp. But I'm hoping we can do what the sergeant and corporal did earlier, so be ready with your knives or whatever."

When they stopped a half-hour later, they were exactly five hundred meters to the rear and the outside of the target. As Little Bear manned the squad gun mounted on the roof, Duncan and the other two Cherokee headed toward the dark position. A short time later, Duncan waved Little Bear forward, they all piled into the vehicle and made their way to the next position, taking it out the same way.

"If everybody is asleep in the next one," Duncan said as they moved toward the last position, "Somebody has really screwed the pooch."

Everyone in the vehicle smiled. They had been with Duncan long enough to know what his colloquialisms meant.

"Not to worry," he continued. "Let me do the talking if somebody says something. We will show up as friendlies on their IFF if we show at all. I did, after all, design all these systems. We all go in on this one. That squad gun is no match for their armour anyway. If I don't get the officer first, I need that person alive, okay? Everyone else is fair game."

The vehicle was parked sideways just to the rear and below the summit of a small hill. Nobody was manning the weapon mounted on the turret and four of the targets were wrapped in sleeping bags on the ground behind the vehicle. The rear door was down and a dull light was coming out of it. Duncan motioned that he would take out the soldier in the vehicle and the other four spread out and, rifles at the ready, made their way toward the sleeping figures.

Duncan let the weapon drop to his chest, drew out his blood-stained knife, and quietly crept behind the figure dozing behind the monitors mounted on the wall of the vehicle. It was a female lieutenant. He grabbed her in a chokehold from the rear using the seat back for leverage as the struggling woman awoke and tried desperately to free herself. In seconds, she was unconscious. Duncan grabbed her by the belt at the rear and none-too-gently dragged her on her back and dumped her on the ground beside the rear door.

When she came to, she saw four pairs of combat boots with camo pants stuffed into them surrounding her.

"What the fuck!" she said. "This is the front line in a shooting war, not a training mission!"

She began to stand but a boot roughly shoved her back on the ground on her back.

"You should have remembered that before all you so-called 'Wind Riders' went to sleep," Duncan said.

The lieutenant looked around her and her eyes went wide. All four of the troopers had dark red stains on their chests, arms and faces. The one who had spoken had a long red-stained grey beard.

"So," Duncan continued. "What are my Wind Riders doing out here? And who sent a green, barely-trained crew to do it?"

"Whaaat???"

"I am called Ghost," Duncan said. "I am, or was, your commanding officer, although it's been a while since I've been back home. Looks like things have changed some. I'll make you a deal. You tell me what I want to know and I'll let you live. You don't, you die. It won't take me long to find out anyway using all the toys I designed in that LAV. Your choice."

Duncan withdrew his pistol, armed it, and pointed it at her forehead. He waited.

"The Duke, Duchess and Baroness Isabelle were shot down and believed to have been killed by the people on this planet," she rapidly stammered out. "A group of colonels took power and ordered us here to retaliate."

"How many and who?" Duncan asked.

"A full battalion of Black Shirts and us. I mean my troop."

"A little overkill for an underpopulated backward planet, but okay, I can see that," Duncan said. He put the gun on safe, holstered it, and held his hand out to help the woman stand. She grabbed it and he pulled her up, then to him as he quickly disarmed her and yanked her communicator from her head. Then he turned her loose and pointed to the rear.

"Your base is about twenty clicks that way," he said. "Pretty sad when three half-trained kids and an old man take out a whole Wind Rider squad."

"Four and half trained kids, Warrant," Little Bear said.

"White Ghost don't count," Duncan said. "She is, after all, only a cadet corporal."

The four of them further shocked the young lieutenant by laughing.

"Just don't tell the Countess I said that, eh?" Duncan said. "She might take my after-dinner pudding away from me or something. So, L-T, the story about my and the duchess' deaths is not exactly true. Now, when you get back to base, you let your C-O know that the Ghost is in the wind and he is coming for him. Thank you for the vehicles and weapons systems, L-T; we will be sure to put them to good use. If you guys don't surrender, we will kill you all. And, L-T? I really would have killed you – and I will if I ever catch you again. Now git!"

"Grab the remotes somebody and the weapons and ammo from those four turkeys," Duncan said as the young lieutenant hurried away into the dark. "Somebody better know how to drive this pig. I got other shit to do."

Duncan placed himself in the chair the luckless lieutenant had been sitting on, fired up more monitors, and retracted the surveillance mast. Nobody bothered him while he worked. Soon everything was loaded up and they were headed to pick up the other two vehicles. Once they had reached the first vehicle they had assaulted, Duncan gathered his group around him.

"Little Bear," Duncan said, "Select two of your people to take those two vehicles back to camp. Then you and me are going hunting, eh."

"What's up, Warrant?" Little Bear asked as the two vehicles took off.

"I want another LAV," Duncan said. "There is a Black Shirt observation post five klicks to the east. Head straight for it. I've patched the coordinates directly to your driver's pod. It will be a whole lot easier this time."

Then he was back in his chair in the rear of the vehicle, punching keys on the keyboard.

It was full daylight when they blew by the young lieutenant walking to her base. Little Bear had his head and shoulders out of the driver's compartment and waved a bloodstained hand at her. An hour later, they approached the LAV that served as the Black Shirt command vehicle from the rear. Duncan climbed up to the turret and, arming the machine gun, waited while they came into the small camp and stopped. The hatch was already open. All five of the troopers assigned to the vehicle were gathered around the camp stove waiting for their breakfast. Their officer had just opened his mouth to say something when Duncan depressed the trigger and almost blew him half, then moved his way to the four other troopers. They had not even moved.

"Man the other turret, Sergeant," Duncan said. "You don't hurry up, I'll blow all four of the G-W Twos away myself."

He dropped inside the turret and rapidly armed the firing system on the 20mm auto cannon. He targeted the nearest G-Wagon on the right, waited for the arming system to acquire the target, and let loose first on the vehicle, then the troopers standing around it. He shifted the targeting system to the farther G-Wagon and did the same. Then, targeting the nearest vehicle on the left, he swung the turret to a new position, firing as it came to bear. By the time he shifted to the far G-Wagon it exploded from Little Bear's effort, followed by three more high explosive rounds hitting the troopers.

"Very good. Enough fun for the day, Sergeant," Duncan said. "Time to take our new toys home."

"Ya, who's gonna drive yours, Warrant?" Little Bear said.

"Oh, I know how to drive," Duncan said. "But why should I when I have all you young eager beavers chomping at the bit to do it?"

"Oh, look at this," Little Bear said as he dropped back into the main compartment of his LAV. "I don't even have to police up their weapons. Everything is stacked neat and tidy in the back."

"Outstanding," Duncan said as he moved to the driver's position and adjusted it. The vehicle was still running, so he put it into gear, spun it around, and floored it.

"You snooze you lose, kid," he said and laughed. "Now you get to eat my dust all the way back to camp. Good job today, LB."

"Like some gray-haired old guy can beat me," Little Bear said as he fired his LAV up and, in a large cloud of black diesel smoke and dust flying from the tires, he took off after Duncan.

"Oh my," Duncan said. "No respect from the kids around here. Ghost might get pissed if people start calling him Old Guy instead of Ghost. You earned it, LB."

After a few seconds of no reply from the radio, Duncan switched it a couple of positions and waited.

"Anything new to report?" Marlene asked after a couple of minutes.

"Five Whiskey Romeo vehicles repatriated. Twenty Whiskey Romeo KIA. One Bravo Sierra Heavy vehicle repatriated; five Bravo Sierra confirmed KIA. Four Bravo Sierra light vehicle destroyed. Sixteen Bravo Sierra suspected KIA or severely WIA. One Whiskey Romeo on foot headed RTB. Copy?"

"What's our bill?" Marlene asked with dread. They had just taken out almost fifty heavily armed and well-trained troopers.

"Thirty rounds of 7.62. Ten rounds of 20mm HE. Four new uniforms maybe, and Gulf One has some kind of ringing in his ears."

"What the hell are you doing on a raid?" Marlene exploded.

"Doing what I am trained to do," Duncan said. "By the way, the three of us have been reported dead and some colonels have taken control of everything back home. One Bravo Sierra full Bravo in place and used to be one Whiskey Romeo team in place. I'll let you know what else I find out now that I have some decent comms."

"Just your whole gang did all that?"

"No, your daughter and LB took out the first eight. Me, LB and two others all the rest. These Cherokee kids are good, Mar. Too good to be PIGs. Ut oh, I gotta go, call you later."

Duncan hit another button and waited a second.

"That better be you Charley Tango, or I'm gonna be more pissed than I already am," Duncan said.

"Ya, it's me," CT said.

"What the fuck is going on?" Duncan said.

"When word got out you were shot down and killed, four colonels took control," CT said. "The speed it happened tells me it was all planned. Remember that I told you, most of us were off-planet on long holidays while you were? Anybody that didn't go along with the new gang was tossed in jail or killed. The old gang are not allowed back to the system and all our funds stolen, they think. Once I received your distress beacon, I was able to arrange a zap transfer of those four Cherokee kids. But they shut down all the machines right after that.

"What with the stuff we had stashed at Marlene's place and our own resources, we are on the way, boss. There will only be two hundred of us, but we are fully equipped, loaded for bear and extremely pissed."

"ETA?" Duncan asked.

"About a week," CT answered.

"OK, we have a full battalion of Black Shirts at my location," Duncan said. "I just relieved them of one of their LAVs. There was also one team of Wind Riders. They were kind enough to let us have their G-Wagons, their LAV, all their weapons and ammo and uniforms. I let their L-T live. Needed someone to report they are in big doo-doo now. I have a good crew here. These locals fight hard and the Cherokee you sent are excellent. You don't hurry up, there will be nothing for you to do."

"What about the invaders?" CT asked.

"Our old French friends from Oaken," Duncan said. "We are taking big chunks out of them. Shouldn't be much of a problem. Get ahold of Mar when you can. She is with the local army on the other side of the planet. She's had better comms and intel capabilities than I have had, until now anyway. I'll let her know to expect your call. It shouldn't be long. I still have my aerials tied down and am on the move."

"Okay, boss," CT said. "Can I let the gang know you guys are still alive?"

"Ya, why not?" Duncan said. "I let that LT know and she will report it. Just don't bug me, okay? I'm a little busy."

"Will do, boss. Some very anxious folks here."

"I'll bet," Duncan said. "Gulf One out."

He hit another button and waited.

"Zulu One, Gulf One. Copy?"

"Gulf One, Zulu One."

"Okay Mar, Charley Tango and two hundred on the way, ETA about a week." Duncan said.

"Only two hundred?" Marlene said. "Shit, you've got about two thousand against you now. I have about eight."

"Nibble nibble, Mar," Duncan said. "These guys are not high quality troops. I would say they are right out of boot camp. They are gonna fall apart once the real fun begins. I have my antenna still tied down and got excellent reception, Mar. CT should be getting ahold

of you soon. You take all of your people and the two hundred and
get rid of the Frenchies. That should pull a lot of the Black Shirts to
you. This shouldn't take long. After? Different story. Gotta go, hun.
No way I'm letting LB pass me."

Half an hour later, the two LAVs came screaming into camp and
slid to a stop, Duncan ahead of Little Bear – just.

Chapter Thirteen

G ood morning, my brothers and sisters of the Black Shirt
Brigade," a cheerful voice said over every comm unit, whether
personal or vehicle, in the base camp. "Wakey wakey, Black Shirts. I
am called Master Warrant by those who know me."

A hologram of a tall man with greying-blond hair and a grey
beard appeared. He wore dark blue, nearly-black combat fatigues
and a tactical vest. The vest held full magazines and four hand
grenades. He carried an assault rifle, and an automatic pistol was
mounted high on his left side. In addition, a sling was across his
chest and the barrel of a long gun could be seen peeking over his left
shoulder.

"Now, I know all of you must be a little groggy, being woken
up like this," the man continued. "I am sure you were all sleeping
soundly thinking your scouts and forward operating posts were
keeping you informed and safe. Oh yes, the Wind Rider section.
Nobody could possibly get past the mighty Wind Riders and then
your scouts and FOPs, right?

"Wrong, people! We are here, we are ready. Are you? I think not.
Wind Riders are here – the *real* Wind Riders – but we are not here
to save you. Heck, even Zebra is here. Right, Master Warrant?"

Another hologram came alive. This person had friends standing
nearby. All were dressed in the same manner, except they had black
and white stripes on their faces and bare midriffs and arms. One of
them had jelled her hair to stand upright and had colored it like a
Zebra mane.

"Of course, Master Warrant," she said. "Zebra is always at your service, Master Warrant."

Another hologram came alive. This one showed a teen perched behind a machine gun mounted on the cupola of an LAV in motion. Her hair was pulled back tight and trailed behind her. Her face was painted white except for streaks at the edges of her mouth that made her look fierce.

"Heck," the man said. "Even White Ghost has decided to come along for the fun.

"You have until the sun clears the horizon, Black Shirts. Anyone not in formation in front of their tents by then will be killed. You all know how well you did trying against the Wind Riders. Well, now you are going to be facing the people who trained the trainers who trained them. And this will not be pretend war, people. This time little beeps will not go off in your ears to tell you you are dead. This time you really will be dead.

"Think about it, Black Shirts. Think hard and long. Did your new commanders really tell you the truth. Are we all dead?"

The holograms winked out, leaving confusion behind them.

Noncommissioned officers went to their officers for orders. The junior officers went to their senior officers and so it went, all through the base that morning.

The colonel ordered a stand-to-arms. Older officers and noncommissioned officers did not allow their troopers to gather arms and staff positions.

As the bottom of the sun began to clear the horizon the comms came alive again and, as the words were spoken, those who had lined up in formation in front of their quarters were told by their officers or noncommissioned officers to drop to the ground once the shooting started. The colonel hoped like hell he had enough firepower to survive.

I am the Ghost in the wind, bringer of justice

You have been tried and convicted
Prepare to die.

The last words were barely spoken as the far horizon lit up. Soon heavy shells rained down on every manned position, followed by mortar shells and LAV cannon fire. Their own LAVs, artillery and mortar positions were engulfed and torn to pieces by incoming artillery and antitank rockets.

Officers and noncomms were flung off their feet one-by-one as the long-range rifles took their toll. A third of the camp was destroyed before they had even acquired targets. All of their targeting systems had gone offline or were scrambled. Then the drones, their own drones, began to fire on them. Any LAV that did get a hasty shot off was soon destroyed by multiple hits.

They had trouble seeing the attackers who either came from the darkness or from right in front of the now blazing sun. Soon, automatic squad weapons and, right after that, assault weapons began to fire as the dismounts joined in the attack.

"Had enough yet, Colonel? How many more of your young troops have to die because of you, Colonel?"

"Stand down, stand down!" The colonel yelled into his comms unit. "All troops to disengage, stand down and disarm!"

"Very good, Colonel," Duncan said. "Gulf Alpha One to all Charley, stand down, ceasefire in effect. Permission to return fire if fired upon."

"I say, my good man," Duncan said to Little Bear, standing and replacing the clip in his long gun. "To the club, Jeeves."

"Oh, I'm Jeeves now, not Smithers?" Little Bear said.

"Why no, my good man," Duncan replied. "Smithers may be good enough for the country bumpkins, but Jeeves needs to be driving for the upper class."

Addressing the enemy, Duncan said, "Assemble whatever is left of your people in the parade square, Colonel. Any walking-wounded as well. We'll handle any of your other wounded after, if they are still alive. Some of my troops don't like invading Off Worlders much."

The troops making their way to the parade square saw a number of their fellow soldiers lying dead, with arrows sticking in them, or with slashed necks, smashed in skulls or other gruesome wounds that had nothing to do with firearms. Soon their path was lined with blood-smeared soldiers carrying bows, crossbows, hatchets, spears, and blasters. Horsemen came into view, some on light horses with bow, arrows nocked in; other soldiers rode large horses and carried long blood-stained spears or wicked-looking flails with spiked balls on the ends of chains.

Once the remaining Black Shirts were in formation in the parade square, a line of LAVs and G-Wagons encircled them. Thirty legends lined up in front of the Black Shirts. At the centre, three figures stood in the at-ease position: a grey-bearded man flanked by the attractive teen in whiteface and an older woman. The woman's hair was similarly pulled back into a tight ponytail that fell across her back. Her face, bare midriff and arms were painted black and white. Each stripe emphasized a battle scar. These three figures had been dead, they had been told – dead for the last two years.

"I go by many names," the grey bearded man said. "Today, I was Ghost. Sometimes I am called Master Warrant. Beside me is my wife; today, she is Zebra, sometimes she is called Master Warrant. On my other side is my daughter. Today, she is White Ghost. Sometimes she is called Grand Duchess.

"To be perfectly clear, I am Grand Duke Kovacks, this is my daughter, Grand Duchess Kovacks and my wife, Baroness Isabelle. We are very much alive. We are also very pissed off.

"Colonel! Front and center!"

To his credit, the colonel marched up smartly, came to attention, and saluted. Duncan waved his hand in the general direction of his forehead in response.

"Any reason you can think of to keep me from shooting you right here in front of your troops, Colonel?" Duncan said.

"No, Your Highness. No excuses, Your Highness," the colonel said.

"Grand Duchess? Baroness? Your thoughts?"

"Whatever Your Highness wishes," Gwen said. She cocked her assault weapon and pointed it at the colonel.

"Not so hasty, my dear," Marlene said. "However justified we may feel right now, we are bound by law to treat prisoners justly and to hold them for a trial. Or has the Grand Duke forgotten the laws he has been harping on for so long?"

"Of course, Baroness," Duncan said, with that look in his eyes that told her he had been playing. "It is good someone around here remembers what they have been taught.

"Very well, Colonel. You and your senior officers are to be held under house arrest. You may inform your junior officers they are to report to the people behind me for their orders. Have your senior noncommissioned officer report to me. Right now!"

A grey-haired veteran with Master Sergeant stripes marched smartly forward, raised his right knee to his chest and slammed the foot into the ground.

"Master Warrant, Sir!" the master sergeant said.

"Got that wrong today, Master Sergeant," Duncan said.

"Sorry, General," the master sergeant replied. "My apologies, Sir!"

"I confuse myself some days, Master Sergeant." Duncan said. "If you would, Master Sergeant, have your troops fall out and return to barracks. Then report back here to me. Not to worry, I'll still be here. I don't know where to bunk in yet."

"Very well, General, Sir!"

Once again raising and stomping his right foot, the Master Sergeant spun around and marched to his troops.

"A-ten-hut!" He yelled. "All troops are to march to barracks and hold in place until further notice. All junior officers to report to the senior officers at the front of the formation! All senior officers to join the colonel in the senior officers' mess! Dismissed!"

The noncommissioned officers took charge of their companies, platoons, and sections and marched their people to their barracks. The junior officers formed up in front of the thirty legends, the senior officers made their way to their mess, and the master sergeant once again reported, in his foot-stomping manor, back to Duncan.

"So, who did you piss off to get demoted, Master Sergeant?" Duncan asked.

"Questioned the previous colonel, General," he replied.

"What happened to the Color Sergeant then?" Duncan asked.

"Not sure, Sir. I was cowering on the ground with my company, Sir. But I hear he was shot right at the beginning, Sir. Tragic it was, Sir."

"7.62 to the back of the head, Master Sergeant?"

"I wouldn't know, Sir," the Master Sergeant said. "As I said, I was on the deck at the time, Sir."

"That's your story and you're sticking to it," Duncan said. "I get it, Sarge. Okay, apart from any other vipers you know of, Sarge, what about the kids?"

"Just dumb kids, Sir," he replied. "Most of them just out of training. They were just trying to do their jobs, Sir."

"Ya, I get it," Duncan said. "Shitty hard lesson they learned today, though. Okay, Sarge, get at it, eh? Then find out where the hell I am going to be and report. And, Color Sergeant? Do make sure all of the malcontents make it to lockup? The fighting is over."

"SAR!" the newly promoted sergeant said. He saluted properly and Duncan came to attention and returned the salute.

"Always was a good man, that one," Marlene said. She was undoing her ponytail as she spoke. She bent her head and shook it to free up the hair and brushed the left side behind her ear, leaving the right long.

"Ah, do you have to?" Duncan said as she rolled her shirt down to cover her stomach and did up all the buttons.

"All in good time, lover boy," she said and slapped him gently on the check.

"Oh, get a room already, you two," Dianne said, coming up to them. She gave Duncan a hug. "Missed you, boss."

"Hey hands off, you floozy," Marlene said turning Diane away from Duncan, then she hugged her too. "Thanks for coming, Dianne."

"What? And miss the big show? Are you kidding me?" Dianne said. Then she broke away and moved to Gwen, who, having removed the ashes from her face, was now beginning to unbraid her hair. Dianne softly moved her hands away and began doing it for her.

"Good job today, kiddo," Dianne said.

"Thanks Aunty Dianne," Gwen said. "Just doing my job."

"Ya, just like the rest of us, kid," Dianne said. Finished with the braid, she turned Gwen so she could look at her. She hugged her close.

"Duncan's baby girl be all growed up now," she whispered. Then she turned Gwen loose and quickly moved away before Gwen could see the tears in her eyes.

Barb didn't care; hers were streaming down her face as she came and hugged Gwen.

All thirty of her father's friends came and hugged her. The last was Carol.

"So, kid," Carol said. "Any good-looking hunks with your gang or what?"

"Aunty Carol!" Gwen said. "Hands off my guys. You know how hard it is for a girl to get a guy around here? Shit. With all you hotties around, I don't stand a chance."

"That's my girl," Carol said and she hugged her again. Gwen could feel her tears on her own cheeks as she did. She pushed away from Carol and almost ran to her parents.

"They all love you, Gwen," Marlene said. "They have been with you your whole life. You never knew who they really were. Now you do. Go now, be with your friends. You can bring them by to join us. Just wait an hour or so first, eh?"

"Ah shit, Mom," Gwen said. "Now I can really tell you have been hanging around with them again. Eh?"

"Oh shut up," Marlene said. "I did not!"

"Oh no, eh? Like, show up in an hour, eh? Like, we wanna get pissed without the kiddies around first, eh?" Gwen said.

"Oh you!" Marlene said. "Get lost!"

Mother and daughter looked at each other for a second and then in unison, said "Eh!" Laughing, Marlene jogged off to join the others.

An hour later, as Gwen and her nine friends approached the Wind Rider bash, they saw her mom and the other Zebras and Black Shirts harassing the group of her father's friends.

"Like, get lost, eh?" Marlene was saying.

"No," Brock said. "Like, you get lost, eh. Hoser, eh?"

"Like, who you calling a hoser eh, hoser?" Shandra said. "You is about as much a hoser as a hose can be, eh?"

"What's all that about?" Christine said.

"Well," Gwen replied. "My father's people talk a little different Standard than the rest of us do. Most of the time it's the same as ours, but once in a while, like now when they are all together. they kind of slip up. Five of them also speak a little differently. Watch, it's coming.

They have been patient and taking their medicine so far. Oh, here it comes!"

Gwen was grinning ear to ear now. Anne had just joined in on the fun. Now Gwen stepped forward.

"Ya, like, y'all southern Cali folks are the only one that speak proper 'merican, ya? Like, really. Y'all can't come up with sompin' better than that?"

And so it began. Soon everyone was making fun of everyone else's accents or argot. Her mom got a lot of it. Sometimes her Parisian accent would get the better of her when she got flustered, and all her friends tied into her. She was laughing right along with them and suddenly she swept the hair on her right side behind an ear and the party really got going.

"Does your mom do that all the time?" Chelsey, the new girl, asked.

"What, joke around?" Gwen said. "No, not all the time."

"No, I mean what she is doing with your father."

Duncan had his arm around Marlene like normal and Marlene had her head on his shoulder, also like normal. She was running her hand up and down his back and he was rubbing his hand on her arm.

"Oh that," Gwen said. "No not all the time. Just enough to piss me off. Ah shit, now they are going to kiss, watch."

And they did.

Gwen picked up a pebble and tossed it at them, catching her dad in the back of the head.

"Get a room already, you two!" Gwen yelled at them.

"Oh we plan to," Marlene said. "Very soon."

"Hey!" Duncan said. "What's that we say about green lueys, gang?"

"Only thing better than a green luey is no luey at all!" the whole bunch yelled out.

"Shit," Gwen said. "I should have known better." She gave her parents the finger. They both laughed.

"Love you too, Gwen," Marlene said.

"My mom only does that with my dad when she is positive nobody is around to see it," Chelsey said. "The same with me."

"You know your dad?" Christine said. "I don't."

"Yes," Chelsey said. "One day mom will get caught and they will kill my dad and toss mom in jail. They will send me to be reeducated."

"No, they won't," a male voice said behind them.

A man and woman in combat fatigues were standing behind them. They had their arms around each other's waists.

"Mom! Dad!" Chelsey said. She sprang up and jumped into her father's arms.

"What the hell are you two doing hanging out with the kiddies?" Marlene said as she and Duncan came up.

"These are Chelsey's parents, Dunc," Marlene said. "Nice to finally meet you, Chelsey. Your parents have been worried about you. I let them know Duncan was very impressed with you and I told them everything the Master Warrant said about you."

"Thank you, My Lord, Lady," Chelsey said and did a little curtsy.

Duncan and Marlene looked around them.

"Somebody let some stupid lord in here?" Duncan said.

"Oh, they let all kinds of riffraff in here, Dunc," Marlene said. "Someone told me a Grand Duchess was lurking around here somewhere. Can you imagine?"

"Come on you two," Duncan said pointing at Chelsey's parents. "Help us root out this riffraff and toss them out on their ears. Lords and Ladies. My goodness. Hey gang, there are lords and ladies lurking about around here."

"Oh my," Shandra said. She was well into it now and beginning to slur her words. "Bad enough having all these brass hats around here."

"Hey!" Amanda said. "I'll have you know I work for a damn loving."

"What? Brock said. "You work for loving?"

"Wha?" Amanda said. Then she giggled. "Aw, shut the heel up, eh?"

"That's a new one," Anne said. "What's a heel, eh?"

"They'll do that all night," Gwen said. "Come on, grab a couple of bottles and let's go hang out someplace else."

"What? Too good for us, eh?" Carol yelled at them as they moved away.

"Na," Little Bear said. "More like we want to get away from all you randy old timers before you try and take advantage of us young innocent kids."

"Why, you little shit!" Carol said. She raised a fist at him, but she was smiling.

The ten of them looked at each other. Gwen smiled and nodded her head.

"Like, ya, eh?" They all yelled, then ran for their lives as all kinds of cups and bottles were thrown in their direction.

Chapter Fourteen

Early the next morning, Gwen and the other irregular troops assembled and were briefly inspected by ten of the 'Old Timers'. Dianne and PG, being officers, kept Gwen and the other officers in their groups behind. The other eight, being senior noncommissioned officers, gathered up the irregular noncommissioned officers, dismissing the troopers.

Dianne had Gwen and the other officers sit down. Pacing back and forth, Dianne stated what was now expected of them. First, they were to concentrate on whatever mercenary forces were still in play; next, they were to eliminate the invaders; lastly, their mandate was to upgrade and maintain this planet's government and infrastructure. She indicated that some of the original Wind Riders would be helping them out.

Gwen was told to stay behind once the other officers were sent on their way.

"You have a competent 2-I-C?" Dianne asked.

"Huh?" Gwen said.

"2-I-C," Dianne said. "Second in command."

"Ya, Christine," Gwen said.

"Nope, not her, Dianne said. "Not any of your section or fire team. Anybody else?"

"Doubtful," PG said. Today the upright black-and-white hair scheme was replaced with a mauve color, down on her right side.

"Ya, you're right," Dianne said. "I'll ask Ghost."

"Probie," Dianne continued. "You are needed in the command tent. After they are finished with you, hunt us down for further instructions."

"Yes Major," Gwen said. "Um...Major? Where is the command tent?"

"Hell if I know, Probie," Dianne said. "That's what I have green Lieutenants for. Now get!"

Gwen moved off. She knew the command tent should be somewhere in or near the centre of the camp. It only made sense, as that would make it convenient for all companies and platoons to be distributed around it. This proved to be a correct assumption, because, as she reached the camp's middle, she saw a large tent with several local troops guarding it. These must have been from her mother's contingent, as Gwen did not know any of them. Their style of dress and weapons were different from her contingent's.

"Help you out, kid?" one of the guards asked as she came up.

"I have been ordered to report here," Gwen said.

Both the men looked at her, clearly expecting something else. She didn't elaborate further.

"And just who the hell are you to be so important?" the other guard asked.

"Please inform someone inside that the lieutenant is reporting as ordered, if you please," Gwen said quietly.

"Lieutenant," said the first guard. "Ya right. You better be or MY Lady will kick your butt for you."

The guard disappeared inside, returning a few minutes later.

"Wait here," he said and resumed his post on the left side of the tent entrance.

Five minutes later, another guard came out of the tent.

"If the Lieutenant would follow me, Ma'am?" this one said as he opened the entrance and beckoned her to follow.

Inside, at rows of desks, people delved through stacks of files. Gwen was taken past these to an area sectioned off by a canvas wall and told to wait. After another five-minute wait, the guard signalled her to enter. He left and closed the canvas "door" behind him.

Gwen had just started to march forward to report, when her mother rushed forward and, pulling her close, hugged her. Then she pushed her away to arm's length, released her, and took three steps back.

"Oh my god," Marlene said. "You have grown. And your hair is truly blonde, not from a bottle like I had thought."

Before Gwen could say anything, she was spun around and Barb was hugging her. Once released, she saw Barb was holding back tears. Another set of hands pulled her in for a hug, this one long and tender. Once again, she was released and the hugger looked her up and down. The hugger's eyes went far away for a moment and a tear almost started to form.

"Jesus, Kovacks," Carol said. "She looks just like one of them."

Gwen looked at her dad in confusion. He just shrugged his shoulders.

"Ya," Barb said. "Looks a lot like her Grandma, not as tall, though, and with better muscle tone."

When Gwen stood next to her father, the top of her head came to the tip of his ear. Carol was standing next to Duncan's other side now and came to the bottom of his ear. Carol was considered very tall for a woman in the Federation. Marlene and Barb were considered slightly taller than normal women here. Both came to his chin. Diane topped out at his shoulder height, which was normal. Then again, her father was taller than most men in the Federation.

Blonde hair and blue eyes were also rare. Gwen had both, as did her father and Carol.

"No," Duncan said. "Now that I see her, she is a little taller than Mom. Didn't really notice before."

"Okay," Duncan continued. "We can chitchat later. Time to work. Gwen, we will be entering the next room shortly. In that room will be a table and chairs. You will sit on my right. The others already know the drill. Inside will be a colonel and two majors. Our job is to hear what they have to say, then determine if they are telling us the truth. Understood?"

"Um...okay," Gwen said.

"For the next little while you are the Grand Duchess Gwen," Duncan said. "Not the wet-behind-the-ears probie looie."

"Very well, Your Highness," Gwen said.

Duncan turned and they entered the next canvas-walled room. Gwen sat on Duncan's right, her mother at his left, Barb next to her, and Carol beside Gwen. In front of them, a colonel with a major on each side of him stood at attention. Duncan growled 'at ease' at them. All three came to the at-ease position.

"You have one chance and one chance only to tell me your stories," Duncan said. "What you say and how you say it will determine what course of action I order."

"Your Highness," the Colonel said. "My majors, other officers and men, followed my orders, Sir, as they have been trained to do. I issued no unlawful orders, Sir. No orders were ever given to commit atrocities or crimes, Sir. Until yesterday morning, Sir, to my knowledge none of the troops under my care committed any crimes or atrocities, Sir."

"You call the killing of four primitively armed people at long range normal, Colonel?" Gwen said with malice in her voice.

"I apologize for the Grand Duchess' outburst, Colonel," Duncan said. "The four people killed were under her command."

"I am sorry for your loss, Ma'am," the Colonel said. "In my troops' defence, Ma'am, they were operating under well-established rules of engagement, Ma'am."

"This was justified as per contract, Colonel?" Barb asked.

"Yes, General," the Colonel replied. "It was our standard contract agreement, Ma'am."

"As far as the takeover of New Germany, Colonel," Duncan said. "What was your role in that?"

"I was off planet at the time, Your Highness, on another contract. I was not notified until after the contract was completed and we returned to New Germany, Your Highness. Nor was I included in the planning of it, Sir."

"Is this true, Major?" Carol asked the major on the right.

"As far as I know, Ma'am," the major replied.

"If I may, Your Highness?" the other major said.

"Sir, the Colonel was not and is not involved in that matter in any way, other than to follow lawfully given orders, Sir," he continued. "In fact, Sir, the Colonel refused an order issued to quell a peaceful demonstration by the people in our barrack's town, Sir. He was dropped a grade as a result, Sir. He, and we, were given this green battalion and this assignment as punishment, Sir."

"Thank you, Major," Duncan said. "I will take your comments under consideration. Very well, gentlemen, you may return to your commands now. Please have the remnants of your battalion assemble in the square before evening mess. I will pronounce my judgment at that time. Dismissed."

All three men came to attention, gave the high foot-stomping salute, smartly spun on their heels, and marched off.

"Working on it, boss," Gwen heard CT say in her communicator.

"Is he always working?" Gwen asked.

"Not always," Barb said. "Just most of the time."

"Dianne will put her foot down soon," Carol said. "Right now we need him doing what he does."

"Or your father will be doing it," Marlene said nodding at Duncan who was pounding away on his battered old laptop.

Marlene tossed a beer at a surprised Gwen.

"What?" Marlene said. "I was swilling beer with my comrades at your age. Of course, they were not Baronesses and Generals."

The three older women each had a beer in hand. Carol had two; she gave one to Duncan who waved it at her, took a pull from the bottle and went back to pounding his keyboard.

"So," Carol said as the four women sat down. "Any truth behind this White Ghost shit?"

Gwen shrugged her shoulders.

"Don't know what you have heard." Gwen said. "Just did my job. Only difference between us and the other sections was that we always let one live to tell the tale. They probably embellished it a lot."

"Ya, like the one about taking out a fire team of highly trained, equipped and motivated Wind Riders on your own with primitive weapons?" Marlene said.

"Wasn't on my own," Gwen replied, a little defensively.

"Oh, excuse me," Marlene said. "Your boyfriend Junior was along."

"Didn't leave one alive that time," Carol said.

"Assholes didn't deserve it," Gwen said. "Killed my buddies at 800 meters with a long gun. They didn't even know anyone was around, let alone hear the shots that killed them."

"And that is what I get paid to do, hun," Marlene said quietly.

"Your mom can make a kill shot up to a kilometre away with that big gun of hers," Carol said. "Saved my ass a time or two. Same with your pop."

"You will learn all this soon, Gwen," Barb said. "I kill from much further away most times. Other times I am on the radio giving instructions. In many ways, I kill more people than your mom, Carol and your dad put together. You, though – yours have been up front and personal. Different ballgame."

"Bring your section to see us tomorrow morning, Gwen," Marlene said. "You are to be trained for a new mission. Now that you have swilled down that beer, take off and leave us old ladies to wallow in self-pity at our lost youth."

"Ya," Carol said. "Take off, eh?"

"Hoser," Barb said.

"Eh," all four women said.

Gwen left to the howling of their laughter.

"You get shit for something?" Junior asked Gwen when she returned to her section.

"Na, just had to attend some stupid meeting," Gwen replied. "We have to assemble on the parade square before evening mess. We also have to report for special training for some hush-hush mission tomorrow morning. So, don't let anybody get too pissed tonight, okay?"

"Here we go again," Junior said. "Always us for the special missions. Shit."

"Well maybe if you acted more like a soldier," Christine said, "We wouldn't get all the shit details as punishment all the time."

"Ya, like you act like the proper officer all the time," Junior came back.

"Play nice now, children," Dianne said as she and PG walked up to them.

The four young folks came to a crashing attention, Gwen saluting.

"Ah, give the kids a break, Major," PG said as Dianne returned the salute and told them to relax.

"They've not been given proper training, Major," PG said.

"Yes, you are very correct, Captain," Dianne said. "Then again, neither have you. Or I."

The two of them laughed. PG held out a case of 24 beers.

"Remember, though, kiddies," PG said. "If you're going to drink like real soldiers tonight, you are going to have to work like real soldiers tomorrow."

"To the club I think, Captain?" Diane said as they began to walk away.

"Oh, I am rather bored with the club, Major," PG said. "I do believe I shall go to the polo grounds. I hear they have some good-looking ponies there."

"I believe you are correct, Captain," Dianne said. "And they wear those wonderful tight pants."

"What the fuck?" Chelsey said.

"Off worlders," Gwen said. "They get weird sometimes."

Gwen had been nursing her beer and had just decided to grab a second one. They had previously been informed to put rank insignia on the best uniforms they had for the morning's formation. They only had two uniforms each, both well-worn and patched. Somehow, they would make do and look as good as they could.

Two hours before they were to assemble, a messenger from headquarters showed up and informed Gwen she was to report to headquarters and that Christine was to take over command temporarily.

When Gwen arrived, she was immediately granted entrance by the guards. Those inside were dressed in immaculate uniforms. Gwen was ushered into the inner sanctum. The ten Wind Riders there were also in full uniform, including chests loaded with medals.

"Oh, you ain't seen nothing yet, kid," Carol said. Gwen noticed Carol had a brass eagle on her right collar. Barb and Megan had one as well. No one else did.

Carol, Barb, and Megan motioned Gwen to follow and entered a cordoned area. This turned out to be an office-bedroom combination. A full uniform hung on the door.

"Strip, kid," Carol said. "Can't have the Grand Duchess looking all shabby now, eh?"

With the three women helping, Gwen was soon dressed in a full uniform. Her hair was bound in a tight bun, like the other women. Her sash of office was draped across her chest from shoulder to hip with her badge of office pinned to it. She turned around to survey herself in the mirror.

Instead of her previous cadet's uniform, she now wore a Wind Riders uniform—minus the beret and chainmail epaulets. Her epaulets sported lieutenant bars. Her name tag read Kovacks. She wore one ribbon denoting two wounds, and another four, each showing180 days in theatre. Her uniform was adorned with cavalry and recon medals and sported rifleman insignia on her sleeves.

"Cleans up nice, don't she, Mar?" Carol said.

Gwen turned around to see her mother decked out in all her finery. She was inspecting Gwen from top to bottom, no expression on her face, just as any master warrant would to any junior officer before an important parade. She walked behind Gwen, tucking down the belt a bit at the back to make it straight. Moving again to her front, Marlene ran her thumb quickly across the two wound stripes, then became all business again.

"She'll not embarrass me," Marlene said.

"You and the kid are missing something," Duncan said walking in with two swords in his hands.

He tossed one to Marlene and the other to Gwen who almost dropped it. Gwen noticed the hilt of another poking over his left shoulder.

"Help the rookie out, would you, General? Can't have a Cossack showing up defenceless now, can we?" Duncan said.

Carol took the sword from Gwen's hands, draped it so it hung on her back like her father's and adjusted it to fit. Then she quickly, without looking, placed her own the same way. By then, Megan and Barb had already put theirs in place.

"Right," Duncan said. He handed Gwen a peaked cap with officer's braid on the brim. He showed her how to hold it under her left arm.

"Make sure she has it squared away when we walk out, eh?" He said and headed for the door.

Megan quickly opened it. Gwen knew the drill now. Duncan walked out first, then she, followed by her mother, Carol, Barb, and finally Megan. The personnel in the outer room were in line and snapped to attention as they walked in.

They were quickly joined by two lines of five Wind Riders on each side, dressed in full combat uniform, weapons in hand. Their heads swivelled as they moved toward the parade ground, rifles ready to fire.

The square was full. Fully uniformed Black Shirts stood to one side, the local troops on the other. Armed Wind Riders were stationed all around the square. Her father, or more likely her mother, was taking no chances.

As they mounted the raised platform, five of their guards placed themselves across the front of the podium, five more joining them.

Duncan waited until the formation was at parade-rest, then moved to the microphone.

"Colonel Jefferson, front and centre!" He ordered. "Colonel, you disappoint me. Not only did you deploy a green battalion to an active war zone, you also did not properly train this battalion for their mission. You are fined one month's pay and three months at reduced pay grade. Rejoin your troops."

"This whole battalion disappoints me," Duncan continued. He was not speaking loudly. "All members of this battalion are fined one month's pay. All officers are to receive the punishment of one rank reduction in pay for three months and all noncommissioned officers receive the same punishment. Further, all enlisted personnel with more than two years' experience receive the same punishment."

"As good as we are," Duncan continued after giving them a few seconds to think about what he had just said, "there is no way one thousand troops armed primitively and two hundred Wind Riders should have won the battle. Yes, you would have experienced casualties, but our casualties should have been 90 to 100 percent. You should have wiped us out!

"Totally unacceptable, people!"

He paced back and forth twice.

"We have a responsibility to the people of this planet to remove these invaders," Duncan said. "You officers and senior noncommissioned officers! You had better get your troopers doing their jobs properly and fast! We start an offensive operation in five days!"

"To the local volunteers, you have done well. You suffered minimal casualties in this operation. Do not expect that to happen again. You will now be conducting operations as an army force, not as guerrillas. No more hit-and-run attacks. Now we hit hard! We fight as whole units, not in individual fights."

He called them to attention. Carol stepped forward and began to order individuals to come forward. She did so alphabetically. There were fifty; ten were Black Shirts. All received awards recognizing acts of valour.

Each member of Gwen's section was also given awards, which she handed out herself.

"Trooper known as White Ghost!" Her father belted out. "Front and Center!"

No one moved.

"Right now, Lieutenant!"

Gwen marched forward, turned to face her father, came to attention and saluted.

"Lieutenant Kovacks, on her own, assaulted a Wind Rider position with only an axe and a large knife," her father said. "Before Sergeant Little Bear could come to her assistance, Lieutenant Kovacks killed or incapacitated three Wind Riders.

"The quick and decisive actions by Lieutenant Kovacks was instrumental in our victory. For this and for her other brave examples of the last two years, we award her with a Distinguished Service Award."

He pinned a medal on her chest, shook her hand, took two steps backward and saluted. Then he had her turn around to face the parade.

"This is the real White Ghost, people," Duncan said. "A girl, not yet eighteen. She has fought, sometimes for her very life, many times for two years. We grand warriors think it is a big deal to be in a conflict area for a hundred and eighty days. Heck, we even get awards for it. We often bitch like hell if we have to be in combat operations for longer than ten days.

"This girl has been fighting, almost continuously, for two years! With her section for a year and a half! They are all kids and they all make us look like pussies!

"Ghost Section is awarded a unit citation! Ghost Section has participated in hundreds of raids – always outnumbered, always outgunned, yet suffering few casualties. They are an example for the rest of us.

"Lieutenant Kovacks, return to your section!"

Once again Gwen saluted, then quickly marched to her comrades, the only green uniform among the faded and disheveled black ones.

"Enough of this shit," Duncan said. "This uniform is uncomfortable and hot. Colonel, dismiss your troops and report with your senior officers to me, if you please."

The colonel brought all the troops to attention, saluted, and dismissed them as Duncan and the rest of his command group walked back toward the command tent, once again surrounded by their guard of ten.

By the time the colonel and his two majors arrived, Duncan and the others were once again dressed in tan combat uniforms, all hint of officialdom gone except for rank badges Velcrode to chests.

"On behalf of my troops, I would like to thank Your Highness for the awards, Sir," the colonel said. "It was unexpected, Sir."

"Why not?" Duncan said. "Technically they are still my troops and under my command. Sorry I can't give you one, Colonel. Your people did okay, but okay is not enough. I'm not kidding; we go on the offensive in less than a week. Get your people as ready as you can, Colonel, or a lot of them are going to die."

After Duncan jerked his head at the three officers, Megan tossed them each a beer.

"Are you sure this is legal, Duncan?" the colonel asked. "The Federation could come down on us hard."

"As I said, technically you are still my troops," Duncan said. "I have not authorized any operations on this planet. Therefore, I am not breaching any agreements. So, no, I am not worried about the Federation."

"What about the usurpers?" the colonel asked.

"One thing at a time, Colonel," Duncan said. "We are working on it. I don't think it will be a problem. I am still the head of state, even though I never exercise my authority. My barons and baronesses also still have authority under the constitution and could assume control should it be necessary. Time will tell."

Chapter Fifteen

S hit, Gwen," Christine said. "Your pop really put you in the spotlight."

"Comes with the territory," Gwen said. "It sucks, but it is what it is."

Gwen had changed and was again dressed like the rest of her section, in her much-patched and repaired black combat uniform. An aide from headquarters had retrieved her dress uniform and sword and taken it back to headquarters.

"You really are the Grand Duchess, then," Chelsey said.

"Just like I really am the White Ghost," Gwen said. "Doesn't mean shit in the middle of a fire fight. I bleed like the rest of you. My shit stinks and my blood runs red."

Gwen had her head down and was absently tossing small twigs into their fire pit.

"You guys giving my bud Gwen a hard time?" a male voice said.

Gwen looked up to see Brock and Shandra standing there. Other than the pistols they had on their combat vests, they were unarmed. They had a bottle of clear fire in each hand.

"Mind if we join you?" Shandra asked. She didn't wait for them to reply, just sat down beside Gwen, spun the top off the bottle, took a swig, and handed it to Gwen.

"She's right, you know," Shandra said. "Her shit definitely stinks. I changed enough of her diapers when she was a kid to know that."

"Look, guys," Brock said handing out the other two bottles. "We serve alongside her mother. If anything, her mother is tougher than

we are. She fights harder and longer than we do. Gwen doesn't have
to do shit. She could just go through the motions. She doesn't
though, does she? Ever wonder why?"

"I asked the Baroness why once," Shandra said. "After she kicked
my ass for me for asking, she told me.

"'How can I ask my troops to do something I will not do?' she
said. 'How can I live with myself if one of my teammates gets killed
or injured?'"

"Think about that, kids," Brock said. "I don't fight for some piece
of paper, or a flag, or some politician. When the shit hits the fan,
I am fighting to keep Shandra and especially the Baroness safe. It
doesn't matter if I get killed or wounded. My teammates are my
family; they are all I have."

Brock took a deep pull on a bottle, passed it to the next person
and looked off into the distance.

"Our job as Zebras is to go in first," Shandra said quietly. "We
find out where the enemy is. Then we support the troops coming
in. If we don't do our jobs, a lot of people get killed. The same job
Ghost Section has been doing. Did you think you were getting all
the shit-hard details because you were being punished? I did when
the Zebras first started. No, you are given those assignments because
you are the best at what you do."

"The Baroness is the best officer at this type of work," Brock said.
"Well, almost. Duncan is better. Gwen here? She's better in some
ways than both her mom and dad. In other ways, not so much. One
thing she shares with them, though: Gwen cares about all of you.
That thing she did with that Wind Rider listening post? I would have
had a hard time doing that with the weapons I have. She did it with
a hatchet and a knife. The same with Junior."

No one spoke. The section members were thinking about times
Gwen had been there for them. She seemed to be everywhere, all at

the same time. Any time any of them needed help, she was not far away. If not Gwen, other members of her fire team.

"All of you know she doesn't have to be here," Shandra said. "Especially now with a whole battalion of her people here. Yet here she is, in a dirty, smelly uniform, sitting on the ground, swilling crappy booze out of the same bottle as nine other people.

"It's the same with Junior," Brock said. "His dad is the head of his people and," she said as she turned toward him, "I know for a fact you're gonna get your ass kicked when you get home, kid. He and Gwen could both be partying it up in luxury at headquarters."

"The two of you did a good job on that listening post," Shandra said, addressing both Junior and Gwen. "Brock wasn't kidding. The Zebras could probably have done the same thing, but not as cleanly."

"Ya, well..." Junior said. "Gwen had it pretty much under control by the time I got there. But I did one thing she didn't."

"Ya what?" Gwen said. She was still absently tossing twigs into the fire-pit.

"I counted coup and you didn't!" Junior said. He pulled his coup stick out of his belt, jumped up and screamed before dancing around the fire.

"You did, too, you asshole," Gwen said as she jumped up and chased him around the fire pit. He stayed just out of her reach.

"Our work here is done," Brock said quietly to a laughing Shandra. "Time to go."

They quietly stood and moved off.

"Thanks, guys," Junior said breathlessly as he caught up with them.

"I was having a hard time trying to figure out how to get her out of it. Everyone else didn't know, or was too scared to say anything."

"No problem, Sarge," Brock said. "Least we could do. We owe her mom a lot."

His voice was quivering and he almost ran away from them.

"He wasn't lying," Shandra said. "He will die for the Master Warrant. We all will. The whole fucking army."

She too ran off before Junior could see her cry.

"Right!" Amanda said as she finished her inspection of the ten oh-so-young soldiers before her. "First things first. Get in that building and get kitted out. Now, Recruits, now!"

They exited with arms full of uniforms and boots.

Amanda pointed at a tent.

"That's yours," Amanda said. "Stack your gear. Then get your asses over to the showers. I refuse to work with stinky people! Move it, Recruits, move it!"

An hour later, the Black Shirt colour sergeant approached Amanda as she observed ten troopers run through an obstacle course. She held a clipboard with paper and a stopwatch clipped to it.

"Jammy duty you got there, Master Sergeant," he said.

"Ya, right," Amanda said. "I should be getting my hair and nails done with a nice soothing massage after. But nooo. Check these troopers out, they say. So here I am with a bunch of clueless recruits instead."

"Move your asses, Recruits!" Amanda yelled as the ten ran by. "My ninety-year-old grandma can run faster than you idiots! Ya, that means you, Kovacks; get your ass in gear before I ram my boot up it!"

"What's this all about?" the colour sergeant asked.

"Dunno for sure," Amanda said. "Don't tell us sergeants much any time, Sarge; even less this time."

The next week was brutal. Amanda woke them before dawn, yelling. They ran five miles, each day with heavier loads and equipment. They were allowed a quick breakfast, during which they received instruction. The past two days they had learned how to take apart, clean, and put back together firearms of different types. They went to bed after the sun set, only to start the next day before dawn.

The recruits were taught to operate various weapons and allowed to shoot five rounds from each. Over the next three days they fired more and more bullets. Cleaning and oiling the weapons was added to their duties before Amanda abruptly shut off the lights.

Always, they were yelled at. Punishments were given for anything, no matter how minor, by a shouting Amanda.

The next day the routine was changed.

They were marched to the firing range and were in position and firing as soon as it was barely light enough to see their targets. After firing five clips of ammunition with the weapon of the day they returned to their tent to clean, oil and stack the firearms. By then it was too late for breakfast and too early for lunch. Instead, they were put through the obstacle course with full combat loads, minus weapons. Only after returning their equipment to the barracks were they allowed to go to lunch. They just barely made it time; the cooks were ready to close up shop.

After lining up in front of the mess hall and being yelled at for five minutes for taking so long to finish lunch and making Amanda look bad, they quick-marched to a rough rectangle of flattened ground. Other troops were sitting around the perimeter and the recruits were told how lucky they were to be able to sit on their lazy asses.

They watched troop sections practice close-contact, unarmed combat. They were from a Black Shirt company, and their officers practiced with them. Each section of ten was instructed by a Wind Rider. When finished, the section would join the others watching as the next section trained.

Now Amanda yelled at the recruits to enter the rectangle. She paired them off and told them to start. As they practiced she paced the edges, watching everything. At times she would come to a pair and demonstrate an improvement; other times she just yelled at the offending person.

Gwen had never received any special treatment, good or bad, from Amanda. She was punished when required or left alone, just like the others in the section. This now changed.

"Kovacks!" Amanda yelled out. "What the hell do you think you are doing? You trying to get one of my recruits killed?"

"No Sergeant!" Gwen said coming to attention. Amanda was quickly in her face.

"Yes, you fucking are, Recruit! You are trying to get one of my recruits killed. Everybody but Kovacks get the hell over there and sit the hell down!"

"Well, Kovacks, show me what you've got, eh? Now!"

Amanda turned sideways, bent her knees, and readied her fists. Gwen came at her and they sparred for a short time before Amanda shoved Gwen away from her and walked around the perimeter of the rectangle.

"Do you see?" Amanda said. "Do you see how this stupid recruit is trying to kill my recruits?"

Then she walked back into the centre of the rectangle and assumed her fighting stance again.

"You keep holding back on me Kovacks and I am gonna kill your ass!"

Without warning, Amanda attacked and Gwen was forced to step back, blocking and defending. Amanda was not holding out; she was going for it, going hard. Finally, Amanda got through Gwen's defences and landed a solid right foot hit on her ribcage. As she tried to spin away, Gwen felt, next, a solid punch to her stomach, then she was thrown to the ground, hard.

Amanda walked away and allowed Gwen to stand.

"You better get better fast, Kovacks. I'm gonna break something you might need this time!"

Amanda attacked again. This time faster, using more deadly attacks. Gwen had no choice now. If she wanted to survive, she had to fight back.

"That's more like it, Kovacks," Amanda said, prone on the ground.

She held her right hand up, Gwen grabbed it pulled her up. They bowed to each other.

"If we do not train like it's for real, in a real fight, we will die or be badly wounded. Then we are no good to the rest of our team and the whole damn attack can fail. Recruit Kovacks was holding back on her training partner.

"How the hell is your teammate going to learn anything if you hold back, Kovacks? All you are doing is teaching them how to die! Kovacks has more talent in her pinky finger than most of you have in your whole bodies! She should be teaching this damn class, not me! Now, full combat loads, recruits! We haven't made our daily sightseeing tour yet today. Move it! Move it!"

"Jesus!" Amanda said after she and the other Wind Riders were the only ones left at the rectangle. "She was still holding back on me – and fucking near killed me a couple of times."

"I think they all were, Sarge," Megan said. Megan was the officer in overall charge of the training. "They don't have anything to prove to themselves. They've done this shit for real."

"Fucking hell," Amanda said as she stretched a bit. "Ribs are gonna be sore for a week."

She wasn't the only one hurting.

"Owe! Watch it, asshole!" Gwen said as Junior accidentally hit her with his pack as he donned it. "Shit, the Sarge can hit hard."

"You gonna be okay for the run?" Christine asked.

"Ya, I'll live," Gwen said grimacing as she placed the pack on. "Barely."

Amanda was her usual abusive self, running around their little formation as they struggled under their loads, running backwards at times while yelling at someone. They returned to camp and lined up at attention, while Amanda walked down the line scrutinizing each of them individually. They were breathing heavily, but no one let on how much they were suffering.

"Okay, dismissed," Amanda said, and she moved off.

Hands went to knees and huge gulps of air were drawn in. Some recruits collapsed to the ground, Gwen among them.

"You gonna be okay, kid?' a quiet voice asked. A gentle hand started removing equipment.

"Ya, I'll live," Gwen said. "I think." She looked up into Megan's eyes.

"Officer on deck!" Gwen yelled. The section rose to attention, some with packs half off.

As the ranking officer, Gwen saluted. Megan saw the wince in her eyes as she did so.

"At ease," Megan said softly. "Drop those packs before you break something I might need later."

She waited until they were all standing at ease again.

"I know and you know that all of you were holding back today," Megan said. "Next time, don't. You don't have to try and kill each other like the Sarge and Kovacks here did, but fight. None of those Black Shirts have half the training you guys do in hand-to-hand. They need to know what it really looks like. Right, carry on. Kovacks, a word?"

Megan took them around the corner of their tent and pointed. Amanda was hunched over taking big gulps of air, one forearm on a knee, the other hand holding her ribcage.

"Amanda is good at hand-to-hand, kid," Megan said. "You hurt her pretty bad. And you were still holding back. She'll never tell you this, but she is very impressed. With all of you. You keep that to yourself. Hear? Not a word of what you just saw and heard. Got it? Now get back to your section."

"Fucking kid is just like her mom," Amanda said. "Runs like a demon."

"Fights like her old man, though," Megan said. "You gonna be okay?"

"Ya it's all good," Amanda said. "I'll survive, after a month or so of hot baths."

They walked away together chuckling, Amanda groaning every time she laughed too hard, hurting her rib, making Megan laugh harder.

The next day, the recruits were handed weapons they would be using from then on. Gwen's assault rifle was long-barrelled, with a grenade launcher under the barrel.

"Great!" Gwen said. "Now I get to lug around an extra ten pounds of grenades."

"I'll trade ya," Junior said. In addition to a long barrelled assault rifle, he had a long-range sniper rifle. "I gotta lug this ten-pound long rifle and twenty rounds for it."

"All right, can it!" Amanda said. "Normally Gwen would be your designated rifleman. She has the best scores. She is your officer, though, and needs to be doing other shit.

"One more little training jaunt and then we will see what we will see."

Amanda motioned them to gather around. She spread out a map on their squad table.

"Somewhere in this area, a platoon of Black Shirts is hiding out," Amanda said. "Don't ask me; I don't know where they are. Your task is to find and eliminate them. You have three days to do that, so draw sufficient rations. Your weapons will fire blank rounds and have laser designators, but otherwise will function normally. If you are hit, you will hear a loud noise in your ears and your laser designator will no longer function. At that point you are out of the fight. Good luck, Recruits."

Amanda left the map on the table and headed for the door.

"You not coming, Sarge?" Christine asked.

"Hell no!" Amanda replied. "I need a holiday from you yahoos."

"That shows all of them?" Gwen said two days later.

Everyone agreed. Gwen was about to outline her plan when Jessy spoke up.

"Not all of them, L-T," he said. "Got five more over here." He jabbed a finger at a point on the map just outside the perimeter of the enemy camp site.

"They are all cammoed up; looks like an ambush of some kind, L-T."

He found a stick and drew the layout of these new positions.

"Yup," Gwen said. "Ambush for sure.

"Chelsey, take your fire team and ambush the ambushers. Once you're done, try and help us out."

"Sure, L-T," Chelsey said.

"You guys head out an hour before we do," Gwen continued. "Hit them after we start our attack."

"Got it, L-T," Christine said. Jessie was a member of her fire team and they clustered around him as he further elaborated on the enemy positions.

"Not gonna be the same piece of cake," Gwen said. "Just a bigger portion for us. No fucking around, Junior. No time. They out-number us two-to-one until Chelsey's section can come help us."

"Got it, Gwen," Junior said.

They began their personal preparations for battle. Each had their own routine. What Amanda had not noticed was that they all had their hand axes with them.

Gwen looked to her left and right. Junior was one hundred meters behind. She nodded, then pointed her rifle in the air and let fly a grenade. As soon as she did, her little line opened up with everything they had, lighting up the night with the muzzle flashes. Shrieks arose from the camp as designators registered hits all through the enemy compound. From the left, another fire team engaged its targets.

The firing stopped as resistance was eliminated. Just then, an attempted ambush attacked at the rear of Gwen's location – except her fire team was no longer there. As soon as return fire from the enemy camp had stopped, Gwen and her team had moved ten meters to the left. All the attackers were doing was marking their own positions.

Each of the ambushers quickly received a sharp hit on their back or head. Then the whooping started. The ambushers looked up to see five figures draped in all kinds of foliage prancing around them whooping.

"You is all dead, dead, dead!" Gwen yelled as she resumed her high knee prancing and whooping. All five of them brandished their coup sticks in the air.

"Fuck!" Amanda said.

Then two more flashes lit up the night and all five of the whoopers hit sensors went off.

"What?" Marlene said. "Not whooping and dancing anymore?" She jumped up and down and started a hip-rolling dance around Gwen's fire team. Duncan changed his partially empty clip for a full one. Going to a knee and sighting through his scope, he fired five quick shots into the distance, setting off five more designators. He stood and danced with Marlene.

"You is all dead, dead, dead," he said in a singsong voice.

"So are you, Ghost," came over their earpieces. Duncan and Marlene's designators went off as a drone flew by at high speed.

"Ah, come on, Voice," Duncan said. "That's cheating and you know it."

"Too bad, so sad," Barb said. "Voice needs her practice, too. Night night, kiddies."

"I told you guys these kids were good," Duncan said. "Did you believe me? Nooo. No way some green-ass kids are gonna kick our asses."

A rush of air split the night as an air transport dropped down.

"Okay, kiddies," Duncan said. "See you back at camp. Exercise is over."

The Wind Riders jumped in the air transport and with a roar of blasted air, they were gone.

"Ya, they're ready," Amanda said.

"I'll say," Marlene said. "Got a hot casing down my neck from Junior. He fucking near sat down on top of me."

"Never even saw where they were until they opened up," Megan said. "You didn't see them, Mom?"

"Hell no," Barb said. "Too much ground interference. They blended right in. Didn't even show up on infrared."

"Good enough for me," Duncan said. "Mar?"

"Ya, they're good enough." Marlene said. "They better be."

The members of Gwen's section were still in high spirits when they returned to their tent – even after the ten-mile hike with nearly full loads. They had barely dropped their packs when Amanda ordered them all outside.

Aligned in front of the tent were the thirty original Wind Riders. Ten of them had one hand behind a back and a bottle in the other.

The ten walked forward and, spinning the top off a bottle, handed it to a member of Gwen's section. Then, both hands placed a beret on a head.

"Don't kill the whole bottle," Amanda said. "And don't keep the beret."

"You playing with us, Sarge?" Gwen asked. "No way are we good enough to be Wind Riders."

"Ya, you are kid," Amanda said. "Now drink up before you make me look bad in front of the Master Warrant."

Looking at her little line, Gwen shrugged her shoulders, tilted the bottle and killed it. Her whole line did.

"As far as we are concerned, you are Wind Riders," Duncan announced. "The Army? Not so much. You have to finish a couple of other things first. Not to worry. though. They will come later. Two days from now, you will be trained for a special mission. It should only take a couple of days. Tonight, you relax. You're going to need tomorrow to recover.

"Who's got all the damn booze?"

"Where the hell were you two, Mom?" Gwen asked an hour or so later. She had a pretty good buzz on by that time.

"You guys are pretty good," Marlene said, "We didn't spot you until you moved out to deploy. Junior damn near sat on me."

"What?" Gwen said.

"Hey Junior!" Marlene yelled. "What's that you have in your back pocket?"

Junior reached into his back pocket and removed a playing card. It had a zebra imprinted on the back of the Ace of spades on it.

"Ah sheeit!" Junior said. He passed the card around.

"This look familiar?" Marlene asked, holding up a spent cartridge casing. "It's not one of mine. Went down my neck. it did."

"Our job was not to stop you from completing your mission," Duncan said. "Our job was to ambush you after. Good job on spotting Megan's fire team. Dianne should have got you, but we didn't count on your changing positions like you did. Yes, Marlene could have killed Junior easily. But that was not her mission at that time. By the time it was her mission, Junior was gone.

"Sorry guys, I had not been on a mission with these guys for about six months. They were not using that tactic before. Gwen, you need to have a talk with Voice soon. We have to know why we couldn't see you with her drone."

"We learn when we win," Marlene said. "We learn when we lose. That's the point of these training exercises. We will be discussing what happened with the Black Shirts tomorrow. Us? Well, we pretty much know how we screwed up already. Now, I'm out of here and if my hubby doesn't come along right quick-like I'm gonna cut him off for a month."

"Ya like you would last a month, Mar," Shandra said. "We all know better, Ice Queen."

"Shove it, Shandra," Marlene said, smiling.

Nobody but Marlene noticed Duncan was already gone.

"Fucking Ghost," CT said when he finally noticed Duncan's absence. "Always disappears when it's his turn to buy."

"Somebody else is gone, too," Amanda said, nodding toward where Gwen had been sitting.

"Hey, Mom, Dad," Gwen said as she came upon them. "Mind if I join you?"

They were sitting as they often did: his arm around her shoulders, her head on his.

"I have the admission," Gwen said holding out a bottle she had swiped before she left.

"Ya, come on in, kid," Duncan said.

Gwen sat down on the other side of her father.

Megan and Barb were making their way back to camp when they spotted the trio. Gwen had her head on Duncan's other shoulder now. Barb tried, but she couldn't fully hold in her choke.

"Get in here, Barb," Marlene said without looking back. "Bring the kid with you."

Barb sat beside Marlene, who pulled her head to her shoulder. Megan sat next to Gwen and Gwen sat up straight. She looked over, saw Barb's shoulders shaking as her head stayed buried in Marlene's chest. Marlene was gently stroking Barb's head.

Duncan stood and walked away. Megan quietly stood and motioned Gwen to follow her.

"Why does your mom cry all the time like that?" Gwen asked softly once they were far enough not to be heard.

"Dad died about five years ago," Megan said. "She still misses him. It's not so bad now, though."

"Oh ya," Gwen said. "Sorry, Megan, I forgot."

"You were pretty young then, Gwen; no big deal," Megan said. "What bothers Mom the most is seeing the three of you like you just were."

"What? Why?" Gwen asked.

Megan stopped and looked at the ground. Then she looked up at the sky, something Gwen saw the original Wind Riders do a lot.

"I have two brothers, Gwen," Megan said softly. "They are still back home, alone."

Gwen moved so she could see Megan's face. Tears streamed down her cheeks. She pulled Megan to her and hugged her. "I miss them terribly," Megan was able to blurt out before she completely lost it.

"It's not just you four is it?" Gwen said after Megan had cried herself out. They were sitting on the bank of a small stream now.

"No," Megan said. "But all of us left someone behind. Except for Duncan. His folks were already dead."

A quick shudder went through Megan again and she looked over at Gwen.

"I know about Karen," Gwen said. "And I know about what happened with my mom and dad, and that Mom killed Karen and Dad almost killed Mom."

Megan nodded.

"Did you know her?" Gwen asked.

"Ya, I did," Megan said. "I was about your age when I met her. She was almost the exact opposite of your mom. She was one of those touchy-feely types, you know?"

Gwen nodded her head.

"Everyone loved her," Megan continued. "She was like my big sister. Can't tell everything to our moms, eh?"

Gwen chuckled along with Megan.

"Your mom is different," Megan said. "She holds her feelings in. She has paid a big price for it, a couple of times. She does have it in her, Gwen. You don't notice it because it is normal for you. She always lets you know she loves you Gwen, always."

"Ya, I know," Gwen said.

"Good," Megan said. "Because I love your mom and I didn't want to have to kick your ass."

"As if," Gwen said.

"When we get out of this shit," Gwen said after a while. "Do you think you could teach me to fly?"

"Sure, why not?' Megan said. "It's not all that hard. Your dad learned. We just don't tell him until after? Don't need him kicking my ass, eh?"

Dawn was breaking when they gave each other a last hug and went to bed.

"Good, the kid needs an older sister," Carol said. "I'm too damn old now."

"Got that right, cranky pants," Amanda said.

The two old friends had been sitting on a step talking about the old days when the two younger women walked in. Then, like many times before, they looked-up at the sky and their eyes went blank.

Chapter Sixteen

Over the next ten days, Gwen and her section were the beneficiaries of personal, intensive training from Carol, Brett, Anne, Dianne, her mother, and her section of Zebras. Even Duncan showed up once or twice.

In addition to their assault rifles, Gwen and her fire team were each issued a new firearm. It was similar to their assault rifles, but incapable of automatic fire. It had a pump under the barrel that loaded the shells and cocked the weapon. It also fired large shells with five 7 mm pellets loaded in each. The magazines held 20 shells. The range was not much more than a blaster's. The hitting power was, however, as Junior put it, awesome. As the pellets left the barrel, they fanned out. At close range, a hit anywhere would be deadly.

They were instructed and tested on how to clear a room. They also learned when, and, just as important, when not, to shoot, and what to look for if someone was hiding a weapon and was prepared to use it.

One morning, the section headed into a tent with desks and was told to sit. Many of them groaned; yet another boring classroom session, they thought.

"Right," Carol said. "We are going to clear up some of the mud for you today. All of your training to this point has been preparation for what you are about to hear.

"Your mission will be to infiltrate, then kill or capture high-value targets. Prisoners are preferred but not necessary. Voice will be providing overwatch for you, at some point. Until she does, you will be on your own."

Carol pulled down a map, rolled-up near the ceiling. It was of a room; a room Gwen knew well.

"These are the Council Chambers of the New Germany ruling cabinet," Carol said. "Your mission is to assault and isolate the room, then capture or kill the people in it. Your discretion as to the last."

"If the Lieutenant may ask?" Gwen said. "I am not comfortable for my troops to be put on a suicide mission, Ma'am. In fact, Ma'am, I must respectfully decline to have my troops or me participate in this mission, Ma'am."

"Even if that meant a court martial, Lieutenant?" Marlene asked, her face expressionless.

"Master Warrant Isabelle," Gwen said. She stood and came to attention. "Even if the Lieutenant is found guilty of mutiny and sentenced to be executed, Master Warrant Isabelle. The Lieutenant would prefer to die with honour than to be sacrificed for no reason. Master Warrant."

"That will not be necessary, Lieutenant," Duncan said. He had been leaning against the back doorpost. He walked forward. He had shaved and obtained a much-needed haircut recently and was now looking more like the father she remembered – other than being armed with an automatic pistol.

"At ease, as you were, Lieutenant," Duncan said.

His blank expression and monotone gave nothing away. Gwen could not figure out if she was in deep shit or not. Sometimes when he pronounced Lieutenant that way, *Lef-ten-ant*, he was making fun of her; other times she was in shit for something.

The Black Shirt Colonel, his aide, one of his majors, and one of his aides were trailing her father.

"Perhaps if more officers followed their officers code, we would not be in the situation we find ourselves in at the moment," Duncan said. He looked directly at the colonel.

"An officer's duty is to refuse any order they feel is unlawful, or that may place their troops in an untenable position," Duncan said. "General, I believe you gave the Lieutenant no other option but to refuse your order. I would have done the same, just a bit more forcefully and probably shooting you the first chance I thought I could get away with it.

"There are times, though, Lieutenant, when we are ordered to do something that may, and most likely will, see ourselves and the troops we command, killed or captured. The General, the Master Warrant, and almost everyone in this room but you and your section, including me, has been placed in that position.

"So, while I agree with the Lieutenant on her position, I believe the Lieutenant should have waited to hear more about the mission before her refusal of the order.

"Is the Lieutenant willing to withdraw her objections until after the mission has been fully explained?"

"Yes, General!" Gwen said after she had come to attention and stomped her right foot into the floor, hard.

"Sorry for the interruption, General," Duncan said. "You may continue with your briefing."

Grabbing one of the empty desks, Duncan dragged it over to the far wall, motioned the colonel and his bunch to join him, and sat down. It was clear he was only there to observe.

"I apologize for not articulating the mission in a more suitable fashion, Lieutenant Kovacks," Carol said. "However, at the beginning of the briefing, I did state that we were going to clarify the situation. In the future, Lieutenant, it would be appropriate for an inexperienced junior officer to wait until said officer has heard the complete briefing and only comment afterward.

"Voice?"

"As stated earlier and as will be explained," Barb said. "Overwatch will not be possible at the time of your initial assault. Once overwatch is established, you will be informed of any counter-assault threats. Initially, you will be on your own. You must secure and fortify your position as best you can until more personnel are in place to assist. Master Warrant Isabelle will be providing you training on how to do so. C-T?"

"Your insertion into the area of operations will be safe and painless. You will be slightly disoriented for a short time, however. The training you receive over the next few days will assist you with that."

"Once you are in your designated positions at the target," Marlene said. "One fire team will secure the room. The other fire team will suppress any opposition in the room itself. You will be on your own for approximately four hours. After four hours' time, another team will clear and secure other portions of the building. We are confident the two teams will be able to coordinate with each other. In any case, help will not arrive for at least two days."

The room stayed silent for a bit, giving Gwen and her section time to think and look at one another.

"The means of transportation is highly classified," CT said, "as will be the methods used to communicate. While efforts will be made to stop the enemy, you should be aware that the enemy also has the same capability, and your planning should incorporate that possibility."

"You should take enough rations to last a week," Carol said. "That includes as much first aid as possible and, if I were on this mission, as much bloody ammo as I could possibly cram on my body. Your opponents will have the same firearms and training as you do. Well, maybe not the training, but close enough."

"The Black Shirt battalion and we Wind Rides are coming to your aid," Duncan said. "I am also hoping for some on-planet assistance. We cannot, however, count on that assistance. Essentially, people, a little over one thousand of us are planning to retake New Germany from the people who took it away from us.

"This is going to be a hard fight, people. Casualties are going to be high. I personally do not expect to live to see the end. But what the hell! Every day is a good day to die. Lieutenant? Stay behind, please. The rest of you are dismissed until after lunch."

"'Why us?' you may be wondering," Marlene said to Gwen after her section left. "My response would be, Why not? Zebra and I conducted a similar operation in that same building. Like you, there were only ten of us."

"Gwen," Duncan said. "C-T, P-G and I will be taking over all communications in the system. We are hoping that, once they see that your mother, you, and I are coming, the people will rally behind us. We can't count on it, though."

Gwen thought for a second and nodded. Then she asked, "Why the delay in support?"

The Wind Riders in the room looked at each other.

"Ok, I'll do it," CT said, after a pregnant pause.

"We know how to transport you," CT said. "We don't know why it works, though. What will happen is, one second you will be standing here, the next you will be in that room."

"Okay, I guess," Gwen said. "If you can do that with us, why not the rest of you? And why the three-day delay?"

"Again," CT said. "We know what happens, but not why."

Because of the distance involved, it would take two days for the rest of the transports to catch up. It was something to do with quantum physics. While the new design of the transport machines was greatly improved, it had its limitations. The one they had was a small, experimental one that had gone unnoticed by the enemy – until, probably, now.

"It can't be that far away if you are only going to be two days behind us," Gwen said.

"It will seem to you almost instantaneous," CT said. "Blink, you are here; blink, you are there. If for example, we were to zap you back one second after you arrived, you would come back here one year after you left. To you, it would have just been seconds."

"While the trip, for you, will seem but seconds," Carol said. "We will have been traveling for three months at super-high speed the whole time, kid. Which is why we will be two days later. It is going to take that long to load up the transports."

"Okay, I guess," Gwen replied. "But again, I have to ask, why us? You guys have a hell of lot more experience at this shit than we do. I can see Mom and Dad coming later, as they are heads of state. But why not the other Zebra and you guys?"

"Again," PG this time said. "We know what happens, not why. The rest of us can't, Gwen. Well, that is not exactly true, we can, but it would take us a year to get there. It was a six-month real-time trip for us to get here, Gwen. Double that for the return, it's a year."

"Oh," Gwen responded. *Shit,* she thought. *If these guys can't explain it, I'm not even going to try to figure it out.*

"Ya," Duncan said. "Gives me a headache whenever I think about it."

"That's because the only time you think about it, you swill beer," CT said.

"Ya, ya, yack it up," Duncan said. "Back to your section, Gwen. They are likely all running like hell away from here. I would if I were them."

They hadn't, though. They were at the table they used for lunch when Gwen walked in.

"Anything we should know?" Junior asked when she plunked her tray of food on the table and sat down.

"Nah," Gwen answered. "Just wanted to raz the rookie. Like normal."

Looking at her watch, Gwen started to shovel her lunch down. Then with a belch, she was finished, collected her tray to toss in the dirty dish spot, jerked her head to the door and, trailed by her section, they all left.

"Listen up," she said, once they had arrived at the training area. "For me, this mission is a go. It is my system, my planet, and my birthright. I have no option. You guys do, all of you, Junior included. This deal is not going to be like what we have been doing here. There will be at least two battalions of combat veterans stationed on that planet and at least two companies of Wind Riders. That's not including around ten thousand or more active reservists. Chances of us being killed? Really fucking good.

"You want to back out? I'll make that happen. No harm, no foul. I would if I were you."

Gwen walked to the other end of the training area to give them time to discuss it. The discussion did not take long.

"Permission to speak freely, Ma'am?" Junior requested, behind her.

Gwen turned to see the nine of them lined up at attention. At her turn, the nine saluted. They all knew that, usually, only be the ranking officer did that. Gwen returned the salute.

"Permission granted, Sergeant," Gwen said softly. She was dreading what she was about to hear. She knew it could be either affirmative or negative.

"The section will be accompanying the Lieutenant, Ma'am," Junior said. "For myself, Ma'am, for what your people have done for mine, Ma'am, I too, have no choice, Ma'am!"

"Nor do we, Ma'am," Christine said. "Your family and you, yourself, have been prepared to sacrifice your lives time after time for us, Ma'am. It is only proper that we return the favour, Ma'am."

"Are you sure?" Gwen asked, blinking rapidly to stop the tears. "All of you are absolutely sure? I am not shitting you guys. I am scared as hell about this one."

"Where the hell would the wet-behind-the-ears Luey be without her henchmen, eh?" Chelsea said.

"Ya," Junior said. "Everyone knows..."

"Only thing better than a rookie looie is no looie at all!" All nine of them belted out.

Gwen didn't know whether to laugh or cry.

"Besides," Junior added. "Look at all the coup I'm gonna count! Woohoo!"

All of them, Gwen included, started to dance around in their high-step coup dance.

"To be young again," Marlene said. She, Carol, Megan, Brett and Amanda had been watching the youngsters from the edge of the tent. They smiled at the dancing and laughing.

"Shit, Mar," Amanda said. "Were we ever young?"

"Hey!" Megan said. "Speak for yourselves, you old farts."

Megan started to gyrate around to a beat only she could hear. Dianne quickly joined Megan. Scott soon showed up and the party started. Marlene even joined in, sweeping the hair back behind her ear. It wasn't long before the rest of Zebra was there.

Seeing something out of the corner of her eye, Christine stopped dancing and looked over at the older people. She shoved Junior in the back, making him stumble.

"What the hell?" Junior said. Then he looked over and shoved Chelsea, who shoved the trooper next to her. Finally, Gwen turned around.

There they were, decked out in combat gear, including rifles. The legends were all dancing to a beat only they could hear. Her mother had her hair swept behind both ears. They were laughing and having a good time.

Scott noticed they were being watched and nudged Marlene. They stopped dancing and formed a line with Marlene at the centre. In step and in line, weapons at the ready, the legends marched forward. Gwen called her section to attention. The legends stopped in front of them and Marlene, a scowl on her face, looked each of the youngsters in the eye.

"You people think this is a fucking party?" she asked. Then she pointed at the scar on her face.

"Does this look like it was fun to get? You jack offs will be lucky just to get something as minor as this where you are going!

"You think this is a party, Lieutenant?"

"No, Master Warrant!" Gwen said.

"Got that goddamned right!" Marlene hollered. More softly she asked, "Can't have a goddamned party without any booze, eh?"

Shandra dug into one of her trouser cargo pockets, as did Brock. Each came out with a bottle of clear fire. Shandra spun the top off hers, took a swig and handed it to Marlene. Marlene took a swig and handed the bottle to Gwen.

"You need to instruct your people better, Lieutenant," Marlene said. "Your section sergeant should speak with mine."

"Aw, come on, Mar," Shandra said. "I ain't telling that rookie all my secrets."

Duncan arrived in a G-Wagon driven by Anne to see, not the training that he had expected, but two groups of armed and dangerous people cavorting around.

"What the hell is going on here!" he belted out. Everyone stopped what they were doing, formed a line and came to attention. Carol saluted.

"Advanced camouflage training, Master Warrant!" Carol said without hesitation. "The troopers require training on blending in with their surroundings, Master Warrant!"

"I see," Duncan said. He began to walk down their rigid line. Marlene still had her hair behind both ears. She also had a smile in her eyes.

"I can see officers being this dumb, Master Warrant," Duncan said nose to nose with Marlene. "You should be better prepared, Master Warrant. I am always prepared, Master Warrant."

Duncan took three steps backward.

"Major!" he yelled.

Immediately music started to blare from the G-Wagon and Anne exited the rear with two flats of 24 beers in her arms.

"If I may, Master Warrant?" Duncan said. He bowed at the waist and extended a hand toward Marlene.

"Why yes, you may, Master Warrant," Marlene said. She curtsied as only a court-trained aristocrat could.

"Jesus!" Carol said. "Dumbest thing I've ever seen. Weapons flapping all over. I mean, really, Mar!"

"You're just jealous," Marlene said. "This hunk is mine, all mine!" Then she grabbed Duncan and planted a big kiss on him.

Now the party was well and truly on.

Chapter Seventeen

M arlene awoke with a start. She was laying on the office couch, a blanket draped haphazardly around her. The last she remembered, she was going over lists, looking for any last-minute items she may have overlooked. The papers she had left in a jumble on the coffee table were now neatly stacked on it.

She didn't bother to look for Duncan. She knew he would not have slept all night. Like herself, he had been repeatedly reviewing his plans, looking for loopholes or overlooked items. Last she had seen him, his fingers were flying over the keyboard of the battered old laptop he was hunched over.

He would be out there somewhere. Marlene sighed, arose, stretched, and made her way to the shower. She chose the best working uniform she had and dressed carefully. Looking in the mirror, she made sure all her ribbons and badges were in place. She carefully positioned her black beret on her head. With a final glance in the mirror, Marlene marched out of the office.

The first rays of sun were breaking over the horizon when she approached the training area. She had expected to see a big turnout for the sendoff – just not that she would be the last one there.

All the Wind Riders and most of the Black Shirt officers were assembled. All were dressed as she was, in their best working uniforms, badges and ribbons in place.

Brock was standing at ease, his feet shoulder-width apart, left hand behind his back, right holding a staff with a furled flag.

Amanda was at his right, standing the same way, a different banner in her right hand.

Megan, her bare sword laying across her right shoulder, stood in front of them. PG, her hair in a tight bun behind her beret, its natural brunette colour today, was on Amanda's left, at ease, her right arm holding her weapon at an angle beside her right foot. Shandra was to the left of Brock, standing like PG.

Duncan made his way to the wide circle of figures on the training ground.

"Holy shit," Marlene exclaimed quietly.

The section must have been up half the night preparing. It must have taken them an hour at least to move all the gear here, Marlene mused. In front of each trooper were three fully loaded packs, each weighing fifty kilos, minimum. Every possible space on combat vests and pants was loaded with magazines, grenades, and anything else they could fit. None had chosen to wear helmets. Berets were placed in whatever fashion the wearer chose: some raked to the left, some to the right, some pushed back on the crowns of their heads.

They all had their sleeves rolled up over their elbows and wore white paint on arms and faces. Gwen had just finished braiding her hair and now tossed it over a shoulder to hang down her back. She had pushed her beret down to come just to the top of her eyebrows.

Junior's braided hair now had an eagle's feather attached to it. In addition to the white paint, each trooper had a personal pattern on their faces. Gwen's was a massive frown.

Duncan made his way around the circle, talking to each trooper after a fast inspection. Now it was Marlene's turn.

The troopers were surprised when she spoke to them. She was talking quietly, not in her normal yelling tone. She sounded like a concerned mother, not a mean and fierce warrior. Her face reflected her tone.

"Ready, my daughter?" she asked Gwen, the last trooper.

"As ready as I can be, Mom," Gwen said.

"Remember, my daughter," Marlene said. "Have your troops surrender if there is no other choice."

"Ya, I know, Mom," Gwen said. "But there is no way those fuckers are taking me prisoner. I'm gonna take as many of the assholes down as I can before they kill me."

"It shouldn't come to that, Gwen," Marlene said.

"No, Mom, you weren't here at the beginning. They are going to kill me, whether I surrender or not. Not many of those jerks are going to live through this if I have my say."

"Clear head, daughter. Clear head," Marlene said. "If your father has drilled one thing into my stupid stubborn head it is this: When we act in anger, we make mistakes. If we make mistakes, we kill our troop mates. Kill the assholes if you have to. Kill them fast and efficiently."

"Ya, listen to the Ice Queen, eh?" Dianne said. "She still is a bonehead from time to time. Give 'em hell for me, eh?"

One by one, all her parents' friends approached and gave her their blessings. One by one, she saw these tough veterans blink away tears. All but the ones by the flags, who stood the way they had been the whole time, not moving a muscle.

The last to approach, as she expected, was her dad.

"What the hell, pop," she said. "If we couldn't take a joke..."

"We should not have joined," Duncan finished for her. He gave a little chuckle. "Hang in there, kid. Your guys look good."

"Thanks, Dad, I'll let them know," Gwen said. She saw the way her dad looked at her, his eyes soft and sad.

"Aw, what the fuck, Dad!" she said.

"Today is a fucking awesome day to die!" she yelled out as loud as she could.

She was answered by loud, long, and shrill shrieks from her team.

Duncan nodded his head and looked at his watch. Gwen took a look at hers and made a circular motion around her head. Duncan turned and started walking to the outside of the circle. He heard Gwen grunt as she shouldered her pack.

"Thirty seconds!" CT yelled out.

"Lock and load!" Gwen ordered.

All ten racked a round into their weapons. Then each trooper faced the direction they had been shown to take. Some went to a knee; others held a length of thick chain.

"Ten seconds!"

Gwen heard a loud noise. She looked to the outside of the ring. Every trooper there had come to attention, saluting. Like the members of Gwen's section, PG and Shandra were now at attention, their rifles held stiffly in front of them in the rifle salute. Megan had swept her sword down and to the side. Brock's flag was unfurled and dropped until it almost touched the ground. It was the Wind Riders' colours. Amanda had brought her flag staff to touch her nose at let-it-fly. She displayed their national colours.

Then they were gone.

Next thing she knew, Gwen stood inside the Federation Council Chamber. She quickly sighted her shotgun on the guard stationed at the door and shot him before he realized what he was looking at. Her immediate task complete, she spun to acquire her secondary target who was already on the ground. The other four guards stationed around the interior of the room were also down.

An explosion, as a grenade went off, followed by more shotgun blasts, told her that the hallways leading to the room were being cleared. The large, heavy doors were slammed shut. The normal bolts that secured them to the doorframes were slammed into place. The rattling of chains on the other side told her the heavy chains were being applied to the panic bars. She and her team were locked inside. They weren't alone, of course.

Most of those in the cabinet room were civilians, except for those at the head table, who were in uniform. Gwen pointed her shotgun at one of those, who was unbuckling the flap of his holster.

"Make my fucking day, asshole!" she roared.

"I order you to stand down immediately," barked the man in the centre, wearing a general's uniform. "Your commanders unlawfully issued you your orders."

"Hey, White Ghost," Junior said. "You give me unlawful orders?" As he spoke, he aimed his shotgun at people brought in front of him, then roughly shoved onto the floor.

"Nope," Gwen replied.

"Weapons on the desk. Now!" Gwen said.

Looking at all the weapons pointed at them, the officers, none of them under the rank of colonel, gently removed pistol belts from their waists and carefully stacked them on the table.

Gwen motioned with her shotgun for the officers to join those on the floor. She waited while zipties were applied to hands behind backs.

"Now sit up!" she ordered.

"I am White Ghost," she said. "You are all, by the order of Grand Duke Kovacks, under arrest. You are charged with mutiny, attempted regicide, and treason. How you conduct yourselves from this point forward will determine if you stand trial, or if I just kill you out-of-hand. If the choice were mine, I'd just shoot all of you assholes. Orders are orders, though."

"Grand Duke Kovacks is still alive?" a woman on the floor asked. "But we were shown proof he, the Grand Duchess, and the Baroness all perished when their transport was destroyed."

"Hey, White Ghost," Christine said. "No wonder you are a ghost and white. You is dead, dead, dead."

Her people laughed as they unloaded packs and distributed boxes of bullets, grenades, field dressings and gas masks around the room. They dragged benches, tables and chairs into positions as barricades or for cover.

"No way you are going to get away with this, young lady," the general said. "In less than an hour a company of armed troops will be here."

"For your sake and theirs," Gwen said. "They better try to negotiate. Or many of them, and you, are going to die. Our orders are very clear. Prisoners are preferred, not required."

"Contact in the hall, L-T," Chelsea said. She was looking at her monitor, which showed what the small camera they had left in front of each door was seeing.

A soldier, not in a combat uniform, was quickly poking his head around the corner and darting back. Encouraged, he came around the corner and, with his pistol ready to fire, made his way down the hall. He rattled the one of the heavy doors, then backed away.

"Good plan, dude," Chelsea said. "You're too cute to blow in half." Her comms unit was patched into the little camera, so the soldier heard her. He ran for all he was worth and dove around the corner to safety.

Their preparations completed for the moment, half Gwen's team relaxed while the others stood guard.

"Do yourselves a favour," the general said. "Give up now. I promise you, as the ruler of this system, that you will be treated as prisoners of war. You are, after all, only following orders."

"Give it up *yourself*, General," Gwen said. "It is going to take your people at least two hours to figure out what is going on and get their shit together. Relax, life is too short as it is."

"Hey hun, how's it going?" Voice came across Gwen's comms unit an hour and a half later.

"Boring as hell, Voice," Gwen said. "Only used one round so far. Thought you said this was going to be a shit show. Saw more action than this my first day on planet."

"Well, things look like they might heat up soon, hun," Barb said. "Company of Provost has cordoned off the area. The building and surrounding buildings are being cleared. Company of PIGs is deploying, and oh ya, looks like a company of Wind Riders is joining in on the fun. C-T almost has full control of the comms. Won't be long now."

"You will be pleased to know, General," Gwen said. "Three companies of your troops are in the process of deploying. Your salvation is in hand." Then she laughed.

A telephone on the desk rang. Gwen walked over and picked it up. "Cabinet office telephone, White Ghost speaking. How may I direct your call?"

Her troops all cracked up hearing that.

"Fucking L-T acting like a clerk," one of her people said.

"If it would not be a problem, miss," a polite voice said. "If I could speak with the person in charge?"

"Well, you could," Gwen said. "But I am not sure they wish to speak with someone who does not identify themselves."

"My name is Major Deschamps, miss," the voice said. "I am the chief negotiator, miss. I would like to resolve this situation peacefully. If I could speak to the person in charge, please."

Gwen held the receiver away from her, but positioned so the major could hear what she said.

"Hey, which of you yahoos is in charge of this shit show?" she said loudly.

"Uh, that would be you, L-T," Junior said.

"Oh yes," Gwen said. "Thank you for reminding me."

"Lieutenant White Ghost, Whiskey Gulf troop, Alpha One Battalion, Wind Riders at your service, Major. What can I do for the major today, sir?"

"What?" The Major said. "Cut the shit, kid."

"No shit here, major." She turned to the room. "Any of you yahoos take a dump in here without telling me?"

Gwen heard some muffled shouting as the major pressed his handset to his chest.

"Who the hell is this?" a new and angry voice bellowed. "There is no Whisky Gulf troop in my Alpha One battalion!"

"Oh my," Gwen said. "*Your* Alpha One battalion."

"Full comms now, White Ghost," Barb said. Gwen tapped her ear.

"Well, whoever the fuck you are," Gwen said, hanging up the phone, "I am sure Ghost is going to be thrilled when he hears some asshole has taken over *his* battalion. Not to worry, you'll be able to explain yourself to him, soon. Now, as I said to the major before you, what can I do for you, Sir?"

"Get this person off our channels!" the Wind Rider yelled.

"How's that working out for you, Sir?" Gwen asked after a few minutes. "Voice? Did you not tell me C-T had everything under control?"

"Why, yes, I did," Barb said in the silky-smooth voice she was famous for. "Voice never lies to her charges, White Ghost.

"Ghost Four. Three tango with one hanging in cover at your pos."

"I would recommend that you call your people back, Sir, before you get them killed," Gwen said.

"Hit the deck!" Chelsea yelled out. A large bang was heard on the other side of the door, followed by another secondary bang.

"Too late," Gwen said. "Any more stupid ideas, Sir? I did warn you."

"You think so, kid? I have enough firepower here to blow you all to kingdom come."

"Well, I am sure your oh-so-grand and glorious leader will be just thrilled to be blown all to hell. Why don't you let a professional do his job, Sir? All you are succeeding in doing is pissing me off.

You really want someone holding a loaded firearm at your glorious leader's head pissed off, Sir?"

"I'll personally blow that kid's head off!"

"Now, now, Colonel," Voice said. "That is no way a flag officer should be talking. Ghost eight, five at your pos. Okay, back off, Eight, they pulled back."

"Got the picture yet, Sir?" Gwen said. "Am I really alone here? Why don't you back off for a bit? Let the major give it a shot, eh? Then you can blame him when the shit hits the fan."

"Hello, Lieutenant. I must say, you are very calm. I don't think I would be in your shoes."

"Well, Sir," Gwen said. "I had very good instructors. I am sure you have heard of Master Warrant Kovacks and Master Warrant Isabelle? Many nights it was difficult to go to sleep because my butt hurt so much."

"What?"

"You thought I was kidding, Major?" Gwen said. "What size do you think Master Sergeant Amanda's boots are, Junior?"

"I dunno, L-T," Junior said. "Size five thousand or so? Hurt like hell, it did."

"Major, we have you thinking now, do we?" Gwen said. "Why don't you run away now like a good major and consult with some higher-up on what you should do next, eh?"

"Good job, kid," Duncan said. "Got them all dazed and confused now."

"C-T says five mikes, hun," Voice said. "Do put on your best party frock now, hear?"

Gwen sat on the table and dangled her legs. She removed her beret and twirled it around her finger.

"One minute," CT said, his voice clearly audible throughout the large chamber. The prisoners looked at each other nervously.

"Thirty seconds, kid," CT said. "Boss says give 'em, hell."

Gwen donned her beret, tugging it down so it almost touched her eyebrows. A hologram of CT sitting behind a computer came alive in the room.

"Ten," CT said.

Gwen stood, placed her feet shoulder width apart, her hands behind her back.

CT put up his right hand, fingers extended and began putting one down per second, then pointed at her.

"We are the cool breeze rustling through the leaves..." she began as her whole section joined in. More voices could be heard in the background.

"I am White Ghost, the bringer of truth and justice. General MacIntosh, you have been tried and found guilty. Prepare to die."

Gwen pulled the automatic pistol she had been holding behind her back and shot the general in the forehead with it.

"The reports of my death were highly exaggerated," Gwen continued, holstering her pistol, "as were the deaths of my father and mother. I am here to reclaim my father's throne and my birthright. Come and get me, traitors. I am waiting for you!"

CT chopped his hand at her and winked out, telling her she was now off the air.

"Four fireteams, kid," Barb said. "Loaded for bear."

"Got 'em, Voice," Chelsea said. She waited, then jammed a finger on Enter on her laptop.

Explosions ripped through the room as the anti-personnel mines at each door went off.

"With the Lieutenant's, permission," came over her comms unit. "If we could retrieve our causalities?"

"Make your day, Major," Gwen said. "More where they came from, Major; don't try a fast one, eh?"

"If I were them," Duncan said. "I'd come at you with C4 on the doors."

"Got it covered, pop," Gwen said. "Give the green L-T some credit, *nyet?*"

"Ghost One," Barb said. "Bravo in twenty."

"Roger, Voice. Bravo in twenty."

"Shit! Down, down!" Chelsea yelled.

The rear doors shuddered and a large hole appeared as a rocket-propelled grenade exploded on them. Immediately, bullets flew through the gaping hole.

One of Gwen's troopers went down, hit at least three times as he sprinted to cover the breach. Another grunted and was flung back and to the right as two rounds hit his right shoulder.

Junior opened up with the squad gun through the hole in the door on full auto. Christine fired a grenade from her launcher through it.

"Gotta give you guys credit," Gwen said once it quieted down again. "An A for effort."

"Jack is dead, Gwen," Christine said. "George should be okay after a bit. Rounds hit him on the armour."

"K," Gwen said.

"Alpha, Bravo," came over her headpiece. "Sit rep."

"Bottled up, Bravo. One KIA, one WIA."

They all heard firing, a lot of it, coming from outside.

"Bravo withdrawing, Alpha."

Gwen could hear the gunshots, lots of them on her comms unit.

"Roger, Bravo withdrawing." she replied.

"Bravo, stairwell two meters to your left. Clear to the second floor."

"Bravo copy."

"Sit rep, Bravo," Barb asked a few minutes later. "Two WIA, copy Bravo."

"Alpha, Bravo one WIA, working on establishing comms, wait one."

"Bravo three, Control," Barb was all business now. "Control, Bravo Three," Gwen heard.

"Alpha One, copy Bravo Three?"

"Control, Alpha One, copy Bravo Three, five by five."

"Bravo Three, copy Alpha One, Control."

"Copy, Bravo Three," Barb said.

"Bravo Three, Alpha One, comms through Alpha Three this free unless you hear from me, copy?"

"Copy Alpha One."

"Control, Alpha One, relay through Alpha Three, copy."

"Alpha One, Control, copy relay through, Alpha Three."

Now Gwen could concentrate on her immediate situation and not worry about the other section.

"You okay, George?" Gwen asked.

"Shit, I'll live, barely," George said. His shoulder was already turning blue and he winced as he put his vest back on.

"Glad to hear it," Gwen said. She patted him on the shoulder.

"Shit, L-T!" George said. "Hit the other shoulder next time, okay?"

Gwen glanced quickly at the sleeping bag-covered body of Jack and looked away again.

No time for that shit, she thought.

"Hang in there, Gwen," Voice said softly. Gwen had not realized she had spoken her thoughts. "Now they have to worry about Bravo, too."

"Anybody we know in Bravo?" Gwen asked.

"I know them," Duncan said. "Tell Junior his dad is okay. Just a minor flesh wound, but his comms unit is toast."

Gwen tapped her earpiece twice.

"Bravo Three, Alpha One. Is Bravo One able to communicate with Alpha Five?"

"Wait one, Alpha One."

"Alpha five, Bravo One, copy."

"Ya got me, go," Junior said.

"Crappy radio discipline Alpha Five. Another reason to kick your ass."

"Pop!" Junior blurted out.

"Bravo One understands Alpha Five has a feather now."

"Bravo One, Alpha One. Bravo One has a feather and ten witnessed coups, Bravo One. Ten!"

"Copy, Alpha One."

"Alpha One, Bravo Four, Alpha Five had better be behaving like a gentleman, Alpha One."

"Who? Alpha Five a gentleman?"

"Ya, Alpha Five works for a living, Bravo Four. He ain't no gentleman."

"All right Alpha, Bravo. Voice is going to become very upset with you. Hold the reunion later, eh? Control to all units. Tango is regrouping. You have some time to get your shit together. Beaucoups bad guys in LAVs on the way."

"I can see Pop being here," Junior said. "But Mom, too?"

"My mom fights," Gwen said. "Why can't yours?"

"I've never seen her with a weapon, let alone in this deep shit."

"From my experience," Gwen said. "Parents don't tell us half the shit they did at our age."

"Listen up, guys," Gwen said. "LAVs on the move. Not much we can do from here. Have to leave them to Bravo. Just the same, LAVs can't get at us here."

"Looks like you guys just became expendable," Gwen said to the ones tied up on the floor.

"What have we got, Control?"

"Looks like first or second years, Alpha One," Barb said. "I doubt they will help you guys out."

"Copy, Control."

"Hey, guys, new plan," Gwen said. "Let the civilians out of here."

"That a good idea, Gwen?" Barb asked. That meant they were on a private secure channel.

"Hoping it buys us some time, Voice."

The zipties were cut from the civilians and the front doors were unshackled. Gwen tapped her ear three times.

"Hey, Major," Gwen said. "I'm letting fifteen of your yahoos free. Do make sure you don't shoot them, eh?"

"Go on," Gwen said. "Get!"

The doors were flung open and the civilians pushed roughly through them before they were slammed shut again and locked.

"Thank you, Lieutenant," the Major said.

"Ah shucks, Major," Gwen said. "They would have just eaten up all our rations. Can't have that now, can we? Ready to give up yet, Major?"

She had pulled out a power bar from her pack and was munching on it now.

"Gotta hand it to you Lieutenant, you have a good sense of humour."

"Why, thank you ever so much for the compliment, Major. Glad you thought that was a joke. Oops, was that an antitank rocket I just heard?"

Gwen heard some cursing before the major cut off his comms.

"Three Tango LAV destroyed, Alpha One."

"Copy, Control, three Tango LAV KIA."

"Right," Gwen said. "Two, Four, Five, on me."

Gwen grabbed an antitank rocket from her pile and the others followed suit.

"We good, Three?"

"Ya, clear to the end of the second hallway. That's all I can see, One."

"Woah up there, Alpha One," Barb said. "What are you doing?"

"Watch and learn, Voice," Gwen said. She nodded at her three teammates and they walked into the main corridor. Two hugged one side, two were on the other.

"Two Tango on your left, ten meters," Barb said. As she watched infrared of the building's interior, she saw the leading trooper on the left side of the hallway swing an antitank weapon across their back and take something off their belt. Stopping briefly at the edge of the door, the figure crouched, then attacked. Staying in the crouch, the figure swung their right hand and the Tango went down, then the Alpha sprang up, perfectly executed a roundhouse turn and swung its right arm as it did so. This time, Barb could see the blood spray from the Tango's head, then the Alpha swiftly turned again and, one hand swinging, hit that Tango in the head as well.

"Tango cleared," Gwen said. And the Alpha fire team moved forward again.

"Two more, next corner," Barb said. This time the leading figure just swung around the corner and attacked.

"Jesus Christ, are you seeing this?" Barb asked.

"Good, isn't she?" Duncan said.

"That's Gwen?" Barb said.

"Holy shit," Amanda said. "And I was trying to teach her?"

While they talked, Gwen took out two more.

"You sleeping over there, Voice?" Gwen asked.

"Sorry, Alpha One," Barb said no hint of astonishment at what she had just witnessed in her calm voice. "Six Tango, twenty meters in front."

Rifles came into hands.

"Entryway clear after that. Two LAVs thirty meters to the front of the door, Alpha."

"Copy."

Suddenly and without warning, the Alpha fire team emerged from the doorway, guns blazing. Six shots, six Tango down. Six more shots, then two antitank rounds flew. They tossed the now empty and useless launchers to the side. Two shooters went to a knee and began firing measured single shots, while the other two went to the ground and laid down cover fire in rapid three-round bursts. As fast as it had started, it was over. The four Alpha ran back down the hallway, shrieking loud war whoops as they sprinted.

"Alpha is clear to the nest," Barb said and she slumped back in her chair.

"Fucking hell," Barb said. Looking around she asked, "What?" Everyone in the room was looking at her. They had never heard Barb say that word before.

"Oh, it's okay for you guys to swear like shit all the time, but not me?"

Duncan patted her on the shoulder.

"You will not be able to do that again, Alpha One."

"Copy, Gulf One. Once was enough for me anyway."

"Control, Bravo One, sit rep."

"Alpha One just cleared six Tango on her own," Barb said. "Alpha One team cleared six Tango at the entrance, two LAV at the blocking position and, I believe, around twenty Tango, including five Tango officers, before withdrawing, Bravo One."

"It is true, then. White Ghost is living up to her name."

"Roger, Bravo One," Duncan said. "White Ghost is better at what she does than Ghost is. Ghost out."

Marlene was looking at the screen and back to Duncan. She was gulping heavily as she did so.

"She does that all the time?" She finally managed to get out.

"Pretty much," Duncan said. "This one was pretty tame. For her. You do the same shit, Mar."

"Not as bloody fast or deadly she doesn't," Barb said.

"Our kids all grow up, Barb," Duncan said. "We teach them, then let them loose."

"Goddamned men," Barb said.

Duncan beat a hasty retreat. He wouldn't win this one.

"Wassup?" Scott asked as Duncan walked into the mess and grabbed the beer the bartender proffered.

CT hit a button and a small hologram of what had just happened played out on the screen.

"Holy shit!" Brett said. Megan didn't say anything, just gulped.

"Ya, no shit," Dianne said. "Who the hell was that in the hallway?"

"Gwen," CT said.

When they looked at Duncan, he shrugged his shoulders.

"Takes after her mom, so she does," Duncan said as he sat down.

"Nah," Dianne said. "Mar likes guns. She's not so good with edged weapons. Not like someone else I know."

"How many of those officers were hers, boss?" Brett asked.

"Three; the other two were Junior's," Duncan said. He took another pull at his beer.

"Boss," CT said as he tapped his ear. "Federation wants to chat."

"What can I do for the Federation today?" Duncan said. "I am afraid it will not be much. I am rather occupied at the moment."

"No," he said after listening for a few seconds. "At this time, it is purely an internal matter. I thank you for your offer of assistance. I believe we have the matter under control, Sir."

"Once again," Duncan said after listening some more, "thank you for the offer of assistance, Sir. I will not hesitate to ask for help, should it be required."

"Good day to you, too, Sir. All the best to your wife and family."

"No biggy," Duncan said to the raised eyebrows at the table. "President offered to help out. Right now, we don't need it. Might need it later. We'll see. Thanks for the beer, Brett. Gotta go."

"Ever the cheapskate, Ghost," Brett said.

"Hey, that's how us rich assholes stay rich," Duncan said as he walked out the door.

"Alpha One, Control."

Junior kicked the bottom of Gwen's foot after the third call.

"Huh? What?" Gwen replied groggily, as she caught the next call.

"Control, Alpha One," she said.

"Wakey wakey, Alpha One. Voice has some customers for Alpha."

"Copy Control." Gwen said fully awake now.

"Company-sized assault, Alpha. Bravo does not think they can get them all. They are coming from all four directions, Alpha. They are Wind Riders this time Alpha, not PIGs."

"Copy, Control."

"Oh, and Alpha. More good news...105s setting up out of your range and, still more good news, heavy armour is en route. Dig in, kid, dig in."

"Shit!" Gwen said.

"Bravo, do what you can, then get the hell to someplace safe."

"Copy, Alpha, it has been an honour to fight with White Ghost and her Ghosts."

"The same, Little Bear," Gwen said. "It is an honour to be allowed to serve with the Cherokee Nation Chief."

"Chief, my ass," Standing Eagle said. "You keep your cute white ass safe, you hear?"

"Not going to happen, Standing Eagle," Gwen said. "My cute white ass is gonna kick the shit out of some Wolf Dogs very, very soon."

"Okay, guys," Gwen said. "Company-sized attack on the way. From all four directions. That's two of us for each door, guys. Get out there and give 'em shit, then get the hell back here, right?"

Gwen had finished her preparations. She removed a rag from one of her packs, wet it down with water from one of her bottles and washed the white paint from her face. Then, she undid her braid and brushed it out, before quickly pulling it together and binding it in a loose ponytail.

"So young," one the rebel colonels said as he watched. "So young."

"Yes," Gwen said. "So young. I turn eighteen next month; did you know that? Right now, my friends and I should be planning what we are going to be doing for our high school graduation. Christine, Chelsea and I should be out shopping for dresses and talking about whether or not we should have sex with our dates for the night.

"Instead, Jack is dead. No parties for him anymore. The rest of us will likely be dead before the day is done. Your people have brought up 105s and tanks. Ya, so instead of going to a party tonight, I will be killing my own people. People I have sworn to protect as their monarch. People not much older than myself.

"I hope you are all proud of yourselves. You took a nice young woman and turned her into one of the most deadly killers you will ever see. You have done that to all of us. Look around you. We are all teenagers. We, and many of those out there, are going to die, you assholes. For what?

"Was my father a tyrant? Was he killing you just for the shit of it? Just because he could?

"I swear to God, before they kill me, I am going to kill each and every one of you."

Gwen bent down and once again made sure her boots were tied tight. Then she went over her combat vest, making sure clips were where they were supposed to be. She pulled back the bolt of her rifle to chamber a round and put it on safe. She repeated the action for her shotgun and pistol. Done, she stood and looked at her eight remaining team members, thinking hard on what to say to them.

What the hell do you tell your friends when they are about to die?

In that moment, Christine made a decision. She stepped forward, went to one knee before Gwen, took her right hand and kissed it.

"My life for your life, Your Highness," she said.

One by one the others came forward and did the same thing. Then they made a line, came to a foot-stomping perfect attention, and gave the hand salute. Gwen returned it just as stiffly.

"Fuck this shit!" Gwen said as she rushed the nearest of them and hugged him. She hugged each of them in turn.

Then the firing started as Bravo began to shoot.

"Right," Gwen said. "Party's on. Junior, no time to count coup this time, eh?"

"Ya, boss," Junior said. "What a hard ass."

"Why thank you for noticing, Sergeant," Gwen said. "A girl has to work hard to look good for all you boys, you know."

"Control, Alpha engaging," Gwen said and the eight of them, in four pairs, melted into the four corridors leading away from the council chamber.

"Alpha, Control. Alpha, I have no way to spot for all of you. This is not part of the plan, Alpha."

"It is now. Clear comms, Control. Bravo, Alpha is engaging, regroup when you can, Bravo."

Gwen took the first Wind Rider in the line with her shotgun, Junior the second with his. Then they went to one knee and took out the rest of the fire team. The covering fire team was just starting to dive for cover when they were hit with the large caliber pellets spraying the hallway. Gwen emptied her clip while Junior switched to his automatic gun, then she flipped it across her back, loaded a grenade into its barrel and fired down the hallway.

They had killed two sections before they reached the main door. Junior loaded a full belt into the squad gun and let it loose on full auto. They caught another section in the open, deploying. Gwen managed to fire two grenades.

"Changing mags!" Junior yelled.

Gwen covered him, shooting three-round shots, while he released the belt from the gun and jammed a twenty-round clip into the bottom of it instead of another belt.

"Clear!" he yelled.

Gwen fired three more rounds, then backed up into the hallway.

"Changing mags!" she yelled. Junior pulled back three steps and went to a knee, firing three-round shots the whole time.

"Clear!" Gwen yelled. She went to a knee. Junior ran behind her.

"Changing mags!" he yelled.

Gwen kept firing.

"Clear!"

They repeated their duet three more times.

"Alpha, Bravo," Barb said. "Tanks inbound, get to cover, my darlings!"

Gwen and Junior didn't even make an attempt to withdraw in order; they turned and ran.

Junior heard Gwen grunt. He turned to see what was going on and was hit hard in the chest – so hard it knocked the wind out of him and blew him off his feet.

Gwen was on the ground firing back the way they had come, firing single shots so fast it sounded like she was on automatic. She rolled to a side, pulled a grenade from her vest, armed it, and tossed it down the hallway. She covered her head as it went off. Then she was on her feet. She grabbed Junior by his epaulets with one hand and began to drag him back, firing her rifle with the other.

Junior felt her stagger and grunt again. Then she went down. He managed to get his weapon forward as his breath returned and he started to fire. Then the hallway exploded in a flash of noise and dust.

"Shitty shot," Junior said. "Missed us." Then he was pulling at Gwen and the two of them stumbled into the council chambers and slammed and locked the big door behind them.

"Fucking tanks can't get at us here," she said.

"Goddamned 105s can, though," Christine commented.

"Knew I should have brought my helmet," Chelsea said. "But oh no, can't mess our hair up, you said. Idiot!"

They were both smiling, though. Now it was time to wait. Curiously, all the explosions seemed to be occurring outside the building. They prepared defences as well as they could. Antipersonnel mines were placed at each of the doors, three layers deep. All the packs were emptied on the floor now. Empty clips were hastily being reloaded from the many boxes of loose bullets from the packs. Many of the bullets fell to the ground as fingers, numb from firing, dropped them.

They caught their breath and waited. Just four of them were in the room now: Junior, Christine, Chelsea and Gwen.

"Have no fear, Voice," a male voice with a German accent said. "The cavalry has arrived."

"About damn time, Zimmerman," Barb said. "You guys been on holiday over there?"

"Now, now, be nice, Voice or no Schnapps for you. Achtung, Links!"

The firing slowed, then stopped.

"I say," a British voice said. "Do make sure not to shoot me, young lady. I have a wonderful bottle of Scotch here and I would like it to stay in my stomach after I drink it."

Five soldiers swiftly entered the room, weapons at the ready and sweeping.

"Clear!" was yelled out a number of times. One of the soldiers dropped his weapon to hang by its strap and dug a bottle with an amber-coloured fluid in it from a cargo pant leg. He spun the top off it and took a deep pull.

"Jolly good party you kids throw, eh?' he said, proffering the bottle to the four figures laying prone on the ground. "Now which of you would be the officer, eh?"

"One of them three," Junior said standing. "I'm the only one who works for a living around here."

"Ach, a man after my own heart then?" he said. "Warrant Farmer at your service."

He held the bottle out to Junior.

"Master Sergeant Little Bear," he said and took a big draft from the bottle then coughed. "Not bad shit."

"Says the baby to the master," Farmer said.

"Okay, Warrant," Gwen said standing. "The one grovelling in the dirt looking for her panties is Ensign Chelsea, that one is Sub-lieutenant Christine. You can call me L-T or Ma'am, take your pick. Hand it over, Junior."

Gwen took a pull, "Vodka is way better. Hey Voice, we all good here?"

"Ya, Alpha One, it's all clear now."

"Good, I need a nap," and she collapsed on the floor.

"Fooking hell!" Farmer yelled. "Get a fooking medic in here stat! White Ghost is hit, I repeat White Ghost is down! Two, make that three, hits. Fooking Hell!"

He ripped Gwen's vest off her and pulled a big knife out of his right boot. He cut her tunic off her, then ripped the first aid pouch off first his, then Junior's, chest.

"Where's that fooking medic!"

Gwen didn't hear anything after that.

Chapter Eighteen

Gwen snapped her eyes open, then rolled to her right and fell off the bed onto the floor, frantically looking about and grabbing at her chest for a nonexistent pistol.

"Easy Gwen, easy!" she heard her mother say. Marlene gently held her still on the floor.

"You are safe," Marlene said. "It's all over, honey. You are safe with me now."

Gwen looked up and into her mother's loving eyes. She was smiling.

"If I let my fierce tiger loose, will she behave?' Marlene asked.

Gwen nodded, then looked down at herself. The hospital gown she was wearing had ridden up on her when she fell, and a clear tube not attached to anything was hanging from her right arm. That arm was bandaged from elbow to wrist. She had trouble getting up, as her left arm didn't seem to want to work. Nor did her legs. In a fright, she looked down and saw she still had both legs and her left arm was in a cast.

"Come on, Miss Prissy," her father said. He gently grabbed her under the armpits and stood her up. He deftly picked her up behind the knees and laid her back on the bed, much like when she was a child. Her mother fussed over her gown and placed a light blanket around her.

A medical team rushed in. An older woman tut-tutted as she surveyed the damage.

"As bad as her damn mother," the older woman, who appeared to be a nurse, said, as the younger one took a new bag of clear fluid, hung it from a post by the bed and attached it to the empty tube hanging from Gwen's arm.

"Worse," Marlene said. "Aren't you retired yet?"

"I was," the older woman said. "I was sitting on my front porch rocking chair telling tall stories to my grandchildren, I was. Then you yahoos showed up and ruined it all, again."

"Out!" she ordered. "Both of you out, before I box your ears!"

"Right, young lady, let's see what damage you did to all my hard work."

With surprisingly strong yet gentle hands, the nurse quickly pulled the gown off Gwen and started probing and poking, watching Gwen's face as she did so.

"Okay, no harm done. Dress her, please, Captain?"

"So, here is your story, Lieutenant," the senior woman said. "You have multiple shrapnel wounds on your right arm and legs. You took one bullet to the left arm, another to the shoulder, and one to your left stomach. You have all your fingers and toes and all the important shit that youngsters like you care about. Just no nooky for you for a while."

Then she cackled. "If you do stupid shit like your mother used to do, you will be here for a long time. You listen to your physical therapist and, more importantly, me, you will out of here in a month. Got it?" The nurse sighed, then added, mostly to herself, "Probably not, just like your mother. Captain, finish up here and find me later, hey?"

In a flurry, she left the room.

"A nurse tells a high-ranking officer what to do?" Gwen asked confused.

"Her?" The captain said. "She's not a nurse, love. She is the best surgeon in the army, Ma'am."

"She'll live," the woman said to Gwen's parents waiting outside. "I just hope she listens better than both of you did, though, or she's going to be here a very long time. It's going to take some time for that stomach wound to heal. The rest, well, normal gung-ho super-trooper-type shit. She might get some cool scars to show off."

"Thanks, Doc," Duncan said. "I really appreciate it."

Marlene hugged her.

"Ah, go on now, the both of you," the doctor urged. They saw her dabbing at her eyes as she hurried away.

"You going to tell her or am I?" Duncan asked.

"I don't know if I can Dunc," Marlene said. Her voice quavered.

Duncan nodded and walked back into the room.

"May we have a moment alone with the lieutenant, Captain?" He asked.

"Yes, Sir," the captain said. "If you need me..."

"Thank you, Captain." Duncan said.

The captain gave them their privacy but was close by. She heard Duncan say something and then Gwen cry out.

"Lieutenant," Duncan had said as he approached Gwen's bed. It had been a signal that it was time to be serious.

"It is my sad duty to inform you that four of your teammates have been killed, and four, including yourself, wounded."

Gwen looked up at her father, her eyes big and pleading. She looked over at her mother and saw tears streaming down her cheeks.

"No! No!" she shrieked. "I have killed them all! What about Bravo team?"

"Five dead, five wounded," Duncan said.

Gwen wailed then. Duncan sat on the bed and held her head. She buried it into his chest.

"Hard for the young ones," the surgeon said to the captain in the hallway. "Tough fight that was. She lost almost half her team. The other half are nearly all wounded. She's the worst. Same with the other team: lost half, the rest wounded. The next time you hear somebody bad-mouthing the Grand Duke, the Baroness, or the Grand Duchess, you remember what you have seen here. That kid's not even eighteen yet, Captain. She has been fighting for her life for the last two years. She and her dad, alone. Go look at the casualty list from that fight at the capitol, Captain. That young girl and her young friends did most of the damage."

"I knew about Jack, happened right at the start," Gwen said. "I figured, when just my fire team made it back, the others were gone. No time to think about it then. Did Little Bear's parents make it out okay?"

"Depends on what you call okay," Duncan said. "None of you guys came out of that building unscathed, kid. But ya, they are okay. Better than you are, that's for sure."

"That's what happens when you forget to duck, White Ghost," Little Bear said as he entered the room. He was in a wheelchair, his right leg in a cast. Standing Eagle, her left arm heavily bandaged, was pushing the chair.

She came over and gave Gwen a soft but long hug.

"Thank you for looking after my son, White Ghost," Standing Eagle said.

"More like the other way around, Ma'am," Gwen said. "Junior dragged me out of the hallway, Ma'am."

"After you pulled him clear, White Ghost," Little Bear said. He held out an eagle's feather. Standing Eagle took it from his hand and wove it into Gwen's hair. Then she touched her right hand to Gwen's chest, then to her own.

"Hey!" Junior said from the doorway. "You got your own parents, White Ghost; hands off mine!" Then he laughed. He, too, touched her chest with his bandaged right hand and touched his own.

"My ungrateful brat!" Little Bear said.

He awkwardly wheeled himself over and made the same gesture the others had.

Gwen looked over at her mother who just shrugged her shoulders.

"By touching your heart," Duncan said, "then their own, they take your spirit into themselves. It is a sign of great respect, Gwen."

Duncan neared the bed and made the same gesture. Like he so often did, his eyes went blank and he quickly left the room. The surgeon hurried after him. She caught him in the stairwell and, before he could go farther, pulled him to her.

"She's so fucking young," he blurted out between sobs.

"And so were you, Duncan," the surgeon said. "So were you."

"Hey, hands off, you floozy." Marlene saw them walking back to Gwen's room with an arm around each other's waist. Marlene hugged the surgeon and kissed her cheek, then went to Duncan's other side and they walked down the hall together. Three old friends, two with arms around the man they both loved.

At least Gwen had company in her misery. She and Little Bear had a long round of physio they had to endure. The bullet had hit him just beneath the knee, almost tearing his leg off. Gwen could at least use both of her legs. The cast was off her arm now, the wounds were no longer weeping in the other places on her body, and her stomach was not hurting as much.

"Oh, to be young again," Little Bear said for maybe the hundredth time.

"Well, if her dumbness there," the surgeon said, "doesn't pay attention, her guts will be spilling out all over the floor and ruining everyone's lunch."

"How do you know my parents?" Gwen asked.

"I did some work on your dad way back when," she replied. "He was not much older than you and just about as dumb. Like him and his bunch, I was shanghaied to this neck of the universe. I was the one who worked on your mom's face. Sorry about the mess I made of it. She's damn lucky she lived through it, though, Gwen; he hit her damn hard. It took me four hours to reattach her face to her skull."

She stopped talking for a minute. Like the other veterans, she suddenly seemed far away, her eyes not in the here-and-now.

"I also did the autopsy on Karen," she said quietly. "I really loved that girl. Just like I love your mom, Gwen. Sometimes this job sucks!"

Gwen watched turn her back and pick up a tissue. She came behind her and gave her a squeeze.

"Goddamn you Kovacks," she said, voice quivering. "Stop making this old broad cry, will you?"

"Hey," Gwen said. "That's what us pains-in-the-ass do."

"Ya, just like that tough broad over there," the surgeon said. Carol had her head down, frantically trying to wipe the tears from her eyes.

"Get your scrawny frozen ass over here," the surgeon said.

"I'm so sorry, Gwen," Carol said. "I tried, Gwen, I tried. They wouldn't let me go with you guys."

"It's all right, Aunty Carol," Gwen said. "I know. Just like I know why you, Megan and Amanda were so hard on us. I tried, Aunty, I tried. Shit happens sometimes though, eh?"

Carol gave her a quick squeeze, then hurried away.

"Worked on her a time or two, too," the surgeon said. "She was about your age the first time. Oh, look there, finally someone I haven't butchered yet."

Barb was walking up, a large plastic container in her hands.

"Good living and better booze and men, Marge," Barb said. "Here Gwen, you must be getting sick of this crappy hospital food."

"Butter tarts!" Gwen said as she lifted the lid and looked inside.

Barb wagged her finger at Marge.

"Hands off the kid's ration; you have your own box on your desk," Barb said. "She behaving?"

"Better than her mom and dad were," the surgeon replied said. "At least she pays attention."

"The gang all said to say hi," Barb said as the doctor hurried away. "They are busy doing what needs doing in their baronies. We'll have all this shit sorted out in a jiffy, Gwen. The people were and still are behind your father, Gwen, and you." She paused, the resumed speaking. "I am so proud of you, Gwen, we all are, not just for what you and your father did on the planet and in the capitol building. For how you acted on your grand tour. That was the true Gwen I knew. Not the spoiled rich kid you could be, but the caring and loving girl I knew you to be. Your grandmother was so proud of you, Gwen. She had a big party planned for you."

Magdalene had died before the attack on their transport. No one had told them, especially Gwen, until after the fast troop transports had left the planet. Gwen had only found out after she had somewhat recovered.

"Were you with her at the end?" Gwen asked.

"No, hun, I wasn't," Barb said. "They told me it was fast. A brain aneurysm or something. She was riding with some of her own people, Gwen. She didn't die alone."

"Gotta go, hun," Barb said suddenly. "Is to dot and Ts to cross and all that."

"Voice?" Gwen said. "Thank you, Voice. We would have really gotten our asses kicked but for you. Your calm voice helped me keep my shit together. Thank you."

"No problem kid, anytime," Barb said, and she ran from the room.

"What the hell did you do to the General, Kovacks?" the doctor asked, returning.

"Nothing," Gwen said. "I just thanked her is all. If she had not been so cool and calm while giving me directions, I would have lost my shit. Honestly, she saved our asses, she did."

"Voice does that, kid," Marge said. She made a mental note to check on Barb.

Marge wandered into the Friday night old-timers' wingding. She had a bottle in each hand.

"What?" the doctor asked as everyone looked at her. "I brought some good shit; not the crap you idiots drink."

"Nah, just surprised the high and mighty Marge got down out of her ivory tower and joined us is all," Marlene said.

"Love you, too, Ice Queen," Marge said. "Whose got a nice comfy chair for my old ass?"

There was no shortage of people standing and offering Marge their chairs. She took one next to Marlene.

"Nice and warm here," Marge said. "What kind of bullshit you idiots bragging about tonight?"

"Not much," Shandra said. "Brock was just regaling us with the latest love of his life."

"Probably show up with a good dose of the clap next week if I know him," Marge said.

"What?" Brock said, "Why...What?"

Everyone laughed. It was not often Brock was rendered speechless. He was the new target for the night. Marge was laughing along with the rest, but she was looking each of them in the eyes, watching. She motioned Shelly to follow and quietly walked to the edge of the firelight.

"Ask Barb to come for a walk with this old broad, eh?" Marge said. "You come along, too."

"Okay, kid, spill it," Marge said. They had walked a long way from the goings on at the bonfire.

"What?" Barb said. "Spill what? It's all good."

"Like hell, kiddo," Marge said. "Stop trying to bullshit a master bullshitter."

Barb crossed her legs and sat down.

"I feel so goddamned helpless sometimes," she finally said. "I can see the shit happening, but I can't do a damn thing to help them. It's different when I have a drone. At least I can help then. This time, all I could do was watch. We were a day off when the shit really hit the fan, Marge.

"Goddamnit," she continued. "That beautiful young kid, Marge. They turned her into one of the deadliest killers I have ever seen. Her dad is not even as cold as she is. No muss, no fuss. She waves a hand and a man dies. Shit!

"I watched her kill six men, six highly trained and skilled men, faster than I just said it. Then she pops five or six more with that rifle of hers. Not to mention the carnage on the last assault. Shit, she's just a baby!"

"That's what they train us to do, Barb," Shelly said. "Duncan did the same thing in Africa, Barb, don't forget that, or what all of you did in Saudi."

"Ya," Barb said. "But none of us were seventeen fucking years old."

"Ya ya," Marge said. "Been there, done that, Barb, so have you, dozens of times. Why now, Barb?"

"She said 'thank you', Marge," Barb said. "She said thank you like I had saved her life or something."

"And you did," Marge said. She squatted and took Barb's face in both her hands.

"Do you know how many times I have heard about you, Barb? As far back as Afghanistan. I would be making my rounds and I would hear them, Barb. How that calm cool voice kept them from losing their shit. You don't even know how many lives you have saved, luv. More, a lot more, than I have. Was that the first time?"

"First time for what?' Barb asked.

"The first time someone said thank you."

Barb nodded her head, then dropped it to her forearms.

"Well, thank you, Barb. Thank you for being there for all these young kids. Thank you for being you, Barb. Thank you for making my job easier, Barb. Thank you for being in my life. Thank you for being my friend."

Then Marge stood and walked away.

Barb felt Shelley's arm go around her.

"Thank you, Barb. Thank you for being there for me, for being like my sister."

Duncan appeared out of nowhere.

"I've got this, Shell. Make sure Marge is okay, eh?"

"Well, Barb," Duncan said. He plopped down beside her. "I'm not the only one who cares enough to say thank you, eh?"

"She's so young, Duncan," Barb said. "They all were."

"Ya, they are," Duncan said. "Just like you and I were once, Barb. She's good, damn good. It's up to us, Barb. We have to make her see her heart. Not to stuff it down. It's never going to be easy for her, never. It's up to us to school her on when, and more importantly when not, to be a cold-hearted killer. She has a lot of good teachers and role models. You are one of them; Carol is another. Gwen sees the tough-as-nails super-trooper cry and she knows we are not killing machines all the time."

"Just most of the time," Gwen said. "Takes a ghost to find a ghost, Pop. You must be getting old. Was easy to find you this time. You okay, Voice?"

"Getting there Gwen, getting there," Barb said.

"Look, Aunty," Gwen said. "When I am on the job, I am on the job. If I am not at the top of my game, my friends die. Or my mom and dad or you, Aunty. That's my job. Your job is to provide me with as much help as you can so I can do my job. Like me, Voice, you are the best at what you do. You keep calm, so we keep calm. You become the smart ass? We know the shit is okay."

Gwen reached over and touched Barb's chest above the heart, then touched her own.

"You are the real warrior, Barb. Not me."

Then Gwen stood and walked away.

"Out of the mouths of babes," Duncan said.

"They grow up so damn fast," Barb said.

Duncan stood and reached down his hand. Barb took it and he helped her up.

"Ya, kids tend to do that," Duncan said.

"Men!" Barb said and she smacked him on the arm just like he knew she would do.

"What the hell do we know," he finished for her.

"Duncan," he said in a high-pitched voice. "You can be such an ass sometimes."

"Jesus," Barb said. She went up on her toes and kissed his cheek.

Chapter Nineteen

Oaken," Duncan said several days later. "Always bloody Oaken."

He tossed the report that CT had given him onto his desk.

"Have your gang dig deeper, C-T," Duncan said. "See how far up the food chain this goes."

"You know," Duncan said to Marlene after CT left, "I really like Tanya. She just can't seem to keep her shit together."

"So, what can we do about it?" Marlene said. "We can't interfere in internal matters unless we are asked to."

"I know," Duncan said. "I'm just a wee bit tired of this Oaken bullshit all the time. I'll figure something out."

He stood and left the room.

"Oh, cousin, what have you gotten yourself into now?' Marlene said softly to herself.

No matter how hard he had tried, the grizzled veteran drill sergeant could not rattle the four new kids. He had to resort to making things up to punish them. They never complained. He never heard them bitch at night like the others would. Their bunks were always properly made for morning inspection. They were never late, or the first, at anything. All their scores were smack dab in the middle of the pack. All the time, just like they had planned it.

It had been that way from the first day of basic. *Well, that's all about to change now*, he thought. Now each candidate would find out if they passed advance infantry training, or failed. Of course, these four were in the same fire team. Nobody, including himself, wanted to split them up.

He really wanted to kick their butts. Especially the tall blonde girl who seemed to be their leader. He and his buddies had taken most of the night to creep in on their position. He was just about ready to pounce when he felt a stick rap him on the shoulder.

"Getting a little too old for this, Sarge?" the blonde girl whispered into his ear. She jumped up and shrieked a high-pitched war cry that went on and on. One by one, three other war cries were shrieking. He knew all members of his team were hit now.

"You brag to your buddies how White Ghost counted coup on you now, Sarge. Have a good night, eh?" And as silently as she had come, she was gone.

"Who the fuck do you think you are, Recruit?" the sergeant yelled. He was going to enjoy this. Now he really could yell at her for something. He was eyeball to eyeball with her. She didn't fall for it. Her eyes were focused above his head.

"Recruit..." she rattled off her regimental number to him as she had been trained to do. Recruits were not allowed to have names, only numbers.

Shit, he thought. *What the hell do I have to do to rattle this kid?*

"Sergeant," he heard behind him. "I think that will be enough for now, Sergeant."

A major in an immaculate Wind Riders uniform was standing there.

"You are dismissed, Recruit," the major said.

"Sir," the recruit belted out, raising her right foot high, stomping it into the ground and saluting.

"They pass?" the major asked, as the four marched smartly off.

"Ya, they passed," the sergeant said. "Not high enough for you guys, though."

"Very well, Sergeant, thank you." Then, as fast she had appeared, the Wind Rider was gone.

The sergeant posted the rankings on the bulletin board. The first surprise was when none of the four even went to check out where they had finished. The second came when they were lined up for his inspection before the parade.

"You shitting me, Recruit?" he hollered at the tall blonde. She, like the other three, were in Wind Rider uniforms. Not only that, she and two others were officers. They displayed qualification badges even he didn't have.

All of them had the crossed rifles on their sleeves that marked them as expert riflemen. The blonde lieutenant and the bronzed sergeant were classified as designated riflemen. They spoke not a word. They stood at parade-rest, their eyes focused above his head.

"A word, Sergeant?"

He looked behind him. A master sergeant in an immaculate Wind Rider uniform stood there. One of the original Wind Riders.

"There a problem here, Sergeant?" the master sergeant asked.

"These recruits entitled to those uniforms, Master Sergeant?" he asked.

"Yes, they are, Sergeant. They have been there and done that. They just had not been through basic or advanced training yet, Sergeant. Now, it's official. If I may, Sergeant?"

The master sergeant walked up to Gwen and saluted.

"Ma'am? If the Lieutenant and her team would follow me, Ma'am?"

"I think not, Master Sergeant," Gwen said. "I believe we are entitled to parade with our class, Master Sergeant."

"Very well, Lieutenant, I will inform the Master Warrant, Ma'am."

"Carry on, Master Sergeant."

"If the Lieutenant would lead us out, Ma'am?" the drill sergeant said sheepishly.

"I believe not, Drill Sergeant," Gwen said. "The Recruit is not the formation leader, Drill Sergeant."

And that is how her troop marched in. Gwen and her three buddies, right in the middle of the formation.

"Ma'am?" The drill sergeant approached the blonde as everyone was meeting up with parents or friends. "Seriously, who the fuck are you, Ma'am?"

"They call me White Ghost, Sergeant," Gwen said. "Thanks for all the help. Learned a lot from you, Sergeant."

"What?"

"I didn't know how the army is supposed to work, Sergeant." Gwen said. "None of us did. We were kind of on our own before, just winging it."

The other two lieutenants and the master sergeant came up and shook his hand. Then they walked off towards the edge of the base.

"Who the hell are those kids?" He asked the veteran Wind Rider master sergeant.

"Remember that shit that went down at the capitol building?" he asked. "That was those kids. See ya, Sarge."

Chapter Twenty

The four of them were left alone in the recruit barracks. The rest of their class had received orders to report to their assigned battle groups. No such orders had been issued for the four young Wind Riders.

The drill instructors and officers were in a quandary. This was not how things were to run in the army. By the end of the day, Gwen was fed up. She dug deep to the bottom of her duffle bag and pulled out the comms unit she had placed there twelve weeks earlier. Putting it in her ear, she tapped it twice.

Control, Whiskey Romeo Alpha One Gulf, Alpha One, copy.

Gwen repeated the call three more times and was about to yank the comms unit out and toss it at the wall.

Unit calling control, repeat.

Control, Whiskey Romeo Alpha One Gulf Alpha One, requesting relay, copy.

Copy Alpha One, wait one.

It was almost ten minutes, not one, before another response came back.

Gulf Alpha One, Charley Tango One, copy.

Tango One, Alpha One, copy

Gwen heard a series of clicks.

Hey Spud, what you still doing in the recruit barracks?

Well, C-T, until someone issues us some kind of orders, we are kind of stuck here. We can't leave and the reg force lifers are going nuts trying to figure this shit out.

Ah yes, those reg force lifers are such tight-ass sticklers for regs. Unlike the rest of us normal folks. Hang in there, Spud. I'll get back ta ya.

Three hours later, they heard vehicles arrive. Although they could not hear the exact words, the tone indicated that someone outside was not happy. The four stood and went over their uniforms, making sure everything was where it was supposed to be.

Another two vehicles showed up. This time they could hear the words.

"You pull that goddamned pistol out of that holster, bud, and I'll shove it so far up your ass, every time you take a shit for the next week, you'll blow a hole in the shitter!"

"Alpha!" another voice yelled. "Get your asses out here. Now!"

The four rushed outside, crashing to a stop in line and at attention. What they saw was a pissed-off Brock and an even more pissed-off Amanda, who was nose-to-nose with a military policeman. The policeman's partner actually had his weapon half drawn when Gwen exploded into motion. Gwen had the man's pistol at the ready and cocked, with her right foot on the policeman's neck, before anyone registered she had moved.

"Sub-lieutenant," Gwen said. "Would you kindly remove that policeman's pistol from him before someone really gets hurt?"

Christine walked up and pulled the other policeman's pistol from his holster, pulled back the slide to arm it, placing the hand holding it across her chest.

"Attention!" Gwen yelled. "All of you assholes! Now!"

There were four master sergeants, two sergeants and two corporals standing in line before her.

"Anybody so much as twitches an eyebrow," Gwen said. "Blow their ass off."

She tossed the pistol to a now grinning Junior and made her way down the rigid at-attention group of veterans, except for the two police corporals. She strode behind them, tugging down the tunic of the fellow she had tossed to the ground, then returned to the front of the line. She moved nose to nose with Amanda.

"What the fuck are you doing threatening violence to one of my police, Master Sergeant? Did I give you permission to threaten my police, Master Sergeant? What? Cat got your tongue, Master Sergeant? Never mind! I don't want to know."

"You Master Sergeant? Why are you here yelling at my soldiers, Master Sergeant?"

She was just slightly taller than Brock. It took effort to keep his eyes above her head. She looked over at the four drill sergeants, one of whom was smirking. In a flash she was in his face.

"You think this is funny, Master Sergeant? Are you laughing at me, Master Sergeant? Did I give you permission to laugh at one of my soldiers, Master Sergeant? Drop and give me twenty, Master Sergeant! Now! Sub-lieutenant, you will shoot the Master Sergeant in the ass if he fucks up or misses count!"

Once the Master Sergeant was standing back in line, Gwen started in on them again.

"Do you know where I received my basic training, people? At the point of a goddamn gun! All four of us did. Not some pussy running-around playing pretend-soldier crap. If we fucked up, we fucking died!

"You two Wind Rider idiots! Stand by your vehicle and you had better be at attention when I look at you! You four drill instructor pussies, get the hell out of my sight!"

Gwen waited until the four drill instructors piled into their vehicle and drove away.

She snapped her fingers at Junior and gestured that he approach, then held her hand out. He placed the pistol in her hand. Gwen deftly dropped the magazine from it, ejected the cartridge in the chamber and replaced it back into the clip. She handed the now empty weapon and clip to the police officer it belonged to. Christine stepped forward without being asked, did the same thing with the pistol in her hand, and handed it back to the policeman Gwen had attacked.

"I apologize for my assault on you, Corporal," Gwen said. "I can't have my soldiers killing each other. Bad for morale. I will commend both of you for having the courage to face down two idiot Wind Rider veterans, though.

"What were your orders, Corporal?"

"To come to the scene where a major disturbance was breaking out, Ma'am," the corporal said. "Once we arrived the two Wind Rider master sergeants were about to assault the four drill sergeants, Ma'am. We felt we had no choice but to stop the altercation, Ma'am."

"Well, perhaps standing back and watching would have been educational for you, Corporal," Gwen said. "I believe it would have been a very short fight. I trust I did not injure the Corporal?"

"Uh, no, Ma'am," the corporal stammered.

"Oh, what the fuck now?" Gwen said. Three vehicles were arriving, two of them police cars with lights flashing.

"Attention on deck!" Junior yelled out as two senior officers emerged from the vehicle in the centre of the two police cars.

As the base commander came up to her little line, Gwen snapped a smart salute.

"Lieutenant Kovacks and party of three! Sir!"

The colonel returned her salute.

"At ease," he said. "What is this disturbance on my base, Lieutenant?"

"Disturbance, Sir?" Gwen said. "I noticed no disturbance, Sir. You two corporals see any disturbance?"

Both men replied in the negative.

"Perhaps the two master sergeants there could tell you something different, Sir. They were here before we were."

"No, Sir," Amanda, the senior of them, said. "No disturbance that we noticed, Sir."

"What are you doing on my base, Master Sergeant?"

"We were ordered to pick up the Lieutenant and her team and transport them to their new barracks, Sir."

"Do you have a copy of those orders, Master Sergeant? I have not been given movement orders for the Lieutenant and her team."

"Sir, yes Sir." Amanda said. "If the Master Sergeant may be permitted, Sir?"

She reached into the vehicle and pulled a sheet of papers out, handing it to the colonel.

"Very well, Master Sergeant," the colonel said, handing the papers back to Amanda.

"You know anything about this, Lieutenant?" the colonel asked Gwen.

"Sir, no sir. We are still waiting our movement and change of post orders, Sir!"

"Well, it would seem you are to report to the Wind Riders camp, Lieutenant," the colonel said. "I am sure the Master Sergeant there will fill you in on the details. And Lieutenant? I have never witnessed as smooth and fast a takedown as you just performed. Good job."

The colonel pointed at the surveillance camera overlooking the street as he walked back to his vehicle.

Gwen walked to Amanda and Brock as the three police cars and the colonel's car left. She held her hand out to Amanda and made the fork it over gesture. Amanda handed her the sheet of paper the colonel had read.

"Very well, Master Sergeant," Gwen said. "Okay, guys! Grab your shit; we have a new home. If the Master Sergeant would be so kind as to retrieve my gear, please?"

Brock jogged to where Gwen had been pointing.

"Ma'am," Amanda said. "You have an eyes-only set of orders, Ma'am." She handed Gwen another sheet of paper.

You and your buddies get your asses home ASAP was handwritten on the paper. It was her mother's handwriting. Gwen chuckled. She looked up and saw Amanda smiling.

"I tell you you could smile Master Sergeant?" Gwen snarled. Amanda wiped the smile from her face and came to attention again.

"Pile the shit in the back, guys," Gwen said as the four troopers arrived with duffle bags on one shoulder.

"Now, my three friends and I will be driving to our new accommodations. You two idiots have a choice to make. Walk or jam in with us."

"Shotgun!" Junior belted out a millisecond before Chelsea did. "Too bad, so sad."

He jumped into the front passenger seat.

"Hey, I'm driving," Gwen said. "You four figure out what is what."

It was a half-hour drive and Gwen's friends saw they were actually going to a house, not a barracks. It was bigger than most houses, there was otherwise nothing outstanding about it. It had a large, landscaped yard, with a medium-sized horse barn and corrals at the back.

Gwen parked next to an older model SUV. No servants came running out of the house.

"You two have time for a beer or do you have to report in?" Gwen asked.

"We're actually off-duty, kid," Brock said. "Nobody else was free so they sent us to rescue the poor lost puppies."

"Come on, guys," Gwen said, grabbing her duffle bag from Brock. "I'll get you all set up. Plenty of room here."

Gwen pointed her friends to a bedroom each, then made her way down to her old room. Tossing her duffle on the bed, she pulled open her closet to find something to change into.

"Shit," she said. Nothing was going to fit now.

Sighing, she dumped the contents of her duffle on the bed and found her PT gear. She carefully hung up her uniform and pulled the faded green T-shirt over her shoulders, leaving the bottom hang over gym shorts. She made her way back down the hall to her friends' bedrooms, leaned against the wall and waited.

Her friends came out wearing jeans and polo shirts. They eyeballed her. Gwen shrugged her shoulders and making the follow me sign, walked down the hall and the stairs to the kitchen. She pulled open the refrigerator and tossed two beers each to her buddies, grabbed two for herself and walked out through the open French doors that led to a huge wraparound deck.

"Been home all of ten minutes and robbing me blind already," Duncan said. Like normal, he was wearing jeans, a denim shirt with the sleeves rolled up over his elbows. His riding boot-clad feet were propped up on the deck railing. His ever-present red ball cap with the white galloping horse was perched on the crown of his head.

"Guinevere!" Marlene said. "What in the hell are you wearing?"

Her mom was dressed like her dad, but she had rolled the bottom of the shirt up to bare her midriff. She was also wearing sneakers and her head was bare, her hair long and loose.

"It was this or my uniform, Mom," Gwen said. She kissed her mother on the cheek. "None of my other stuff will fit anymore."

"This where you live, L-T?" Christine inquired.

"Kind of a dump, eh?" Amanda said.

"It is not!" Marlene said. She tossed a coaster to bounce off of Amanda's head.

"Ya," Brock said. "No servants, no chauffeur, hell, he don't even own a car."

"I will have you know," Duncan said. "I own about ten thousand or so vehicles and the drivers that go with them."

"Well, you could at least buy Mom a new car, Dad," Gwen said.

"Why? She makes more money than I do," Duncan said. "She should be buying me a new car."

"So, what are your plans?" Marlene asked, changing the age-old subject.

"Waiting for orders to deploy," Christine said.

"Oh, for Chrissake, Duncan Kovacks!" Marlene said. "Do I have to do everything?"

"Hey, you put her on your payroll," Duncan said.

Marlene tapped her right ear twice.

"What's Gulf Alpha's status? You stupid shits! They are stuck at the recruit barracks, dummies! Cut some temporary duty papers for all four of them and send them here. We will figure it out for you. Yes here; is that a problem, Major? Now, Major."

"Dumb asses," Marlene said.

"Hey guys," CT came on their comms units. "Don't sweat it. Someone screwed the pooch; I'm working on it. Gulf Alpha is now where they should be. Orders are on their pad units. Up to the CO what happens next."

"Thanks CT," Duncan said. "I keep telling you: delegation, Mar, delegation. All you have succeeded in doing is causing more confusion. I had my people working on it through channels already. So, CT will inform Barb, who will get her people to find out what the heck is going on and fix it. Good?"

"When should we expect to be deployed, Your Highness?" Christine asked.

"First," Duncan said, a sad smile on his face. "When you are in my home as my daughter's guest and I am dressed like this, call me Mr. Kovacks if you must be polite, or Duncan. Now, for some explanations. Your posting orders would have outlined, some, not all of what happens next.

"You must report to the officer in charge of your new unit. That's Marlene for the next little bit, and you have done that. Next, you will be assigned a barracks and move in, and you have done that as well."

"After basic and advanced training, which you have just completed," Marlene said. "You are allowed two weeks paid leave. Which starts now. You do not have to stay in barracks, that is, our home, or on base for this leave period. We do require you to let us know where you are and how to contact you, though."

"Finishing a 180-day tour in a combat situation grants you another two-week leave," Duncan said. "The four of you have completed four of those. Lastly, first-year troopers are allowed two weeks annual leave. You can take all of the leave at once, split it up, take some of the leave, or be credited in cash for the time you do not use."

You could almost smell the wood burning in the young brains as they calculated all the time off they were going to get and the different combinations that came with it.

"No rush," Marlene said. "Take a couple of days to think it over."

"Well, I need to go shopping," Gwen said. "And right now! Come on girls, time you learned how to look like girls."

The three of them hurried off to change. Junior just sat on his deck chair and sipped his beer.

"It's okay if I go home, then?" He asked quietly.

Marlene came over to his chair and crouched down in front of him. She pushed her hair behind her ear and placed her hand on his knee.

"Your parents are expecting you, Junior," she said. "Your little sister misses you terribly."

"May I use your house comms to call home?" Junior said. "I need to get Dad to pay for transport ship fare for me to get home."

Duncan tapped his ear twice.

"Hey," he said. "When is the next transport to the Nations?"

"Add Master Sergeant Little Bear to the manifest if you would? Thank you, Captain."

"Right," Duncan said after tapping his ear again. "You leave on Monday. Regular resupply run. You got lucky; they only run every couple of months to the Nations."

Junior looked from Duncan to Marlene and back again.

"Make sure you show up in uniform, Junior," Marlene said. "You'll have your documents by then. You just show them to the O-D when you get to the ship. They handle it all after that."

"O-D?" Junior asked.

"Officer of the day," Duncan said. "They will be stationed by the entry port."

"Thank you so much!" Junior said. "Your Highness."

"They let some kind of high mucky muck in here when I wasn't looking?" Duncan inquired.

"Sorry, Ghost in the Wind," Junior said, saying the name in Cherokee.

"It's one of the perks of wearing the uniform, kid," Marlene said. She stood and grabbed two more beers, handing one to Junior and keeping the other for herself. "If they have the space, they always take us. Not as convenient as civilian transport, but for sure cheaper. I, we, use them all the time."

"Okay!" Gwen announced her arrival, breezing onto the porch with the other girls in tow. She had a bit of makeup on now. She wore a pair of combat pants rolled up over her calves, combat shirt open to reveal the tops of breasts and rolled up at the bottom to show off her abs. Her hair was loose, long, and combed to the back of her head.

"Off we go to the mall. Wanna come, Junior?"

"Maybe next time," Junior said. "I have to call home."

"Your loss," Gwen said. "Can I borrow your wheels, Mom?"

"No way," Marlene said. "It might be a piece of junk, but it's my piece of junk. All mine. Get your own."

"Phttt," Gwen said sticking her tongue out. She tapped her ear.

"Good afternoon," she said sweetly. "If it would not be too much trouble, could I have the car brought around so my friends and I can go to the mall? Thank you."

"Come girls," she said. She exaggerated her hip swing as she walked away, right hand daintily held in the air. The other girls mimicked her.

The girls' mouths dropped when they saw the size of the car that drove up. An older, veteran master sergeant got out of the front passenger seat and opened the back door for them.

"Lieutenants," he said motioning his hand to the open door.

"Thanks, Sarge," Gwen said. Ducking her head and scrunching sideways, she entered the car. The other girls, not as tall, just crouched a little and walked in.

The sergeant softly closed the door and got back in, he turned to look back at them.

"Where to, Ma'am?" He asked.

"The mall, Sarge," Gwen said. "How's the wife? Hal Junior?"

"Wife keeps bugging me to retire," the Master Sergeant said. "I'd be bored out of my mind. I like this deal. No muss, no fuss. Hal made it to master corporal. How I don't know, dumb ass. Guess the artillery isn't that fussy. How about you, Ma'am? All good?"

"Will be as soon as I get to the mall." Gwen said. She laughed. "Only clothing I have is Army shit."

It was a much faster trip into town than it had been leaving. Magically, every traffic light was green when they reached it. The car stopped at the front entrance. A man and woman dressed in business suits were waiting and came to the car, opening the door. Two security guards were trying to be invisible by the entryway.

"No sense to hang around, Sarge," Gwen said before the mall managers could open the door. "We are going to be a while."

"Hey, cool," Gwen said as she got out of the car. "Like, totally awesome. Glad I entered that contest now, girls? Getting fancy treatment, we are."

The management had been expecting Marlene, or perhaps the Grand Duchess herself, not these...these hicks. Why, the tall one was dressed in a ratty old combat uniform.

Nobody bothered with them after that.

"What was that all about?" Charlene asked.

"Probably had some damn reporters waiting to take pictures of us," Gwen said. "I look a little different from I did when I left, so they lost interest."

The two girls looked around them, eyes big. They had never seen all the wonderful things in the shops they passed, nor the number of shops with their variety of goods. Gwen hustled them right to the food court and ordered a large double cheeseburger, large fries, onion rings and milk shakes for everyone, then dragged them to an empty table.

"Oh God!" She said taking a mouthful of each. "Oh, how I missed you, Mr. Cheeseburger."

"Used to come here after school," she continued. "Almost every day. Good place to hang out and Hunk-watch."

After they finished eating, Gwen led them to one of the larger stores. She left them at it and picked up what she was looking for. The clerk calculating her commission on the major purchase. She was smiling hugely.

"Find anything you like?" Gwen asked her two friends.

"Loads," Christine said. "Only one problem. We ain't been paid yet. Oh ya, we don't even know how much we get paid yet. I don't know if I can even afford this place."

"Grab what you need," Gwen said. "I'll buy. You can pay me back when we get paid. Just don't go all hog-wild. We still have to pack our personal shit to barracks."

As the clerk was tabulating their purchases, Gwen tapped her ear and ordered a cab for them.

"Put it all on this please," Gwen said.

She dug a silver card from a cargo pocket and handed it to the clerk. It was a normal Army card and now the clerk was not so sure about her commissions. It all cleared; however, now she had another problem.

"Just call a delivery service," Gwen said. "Have them send the stuff to this address and to say it's for the lieutenant."

Gwen took her card back, stuffed it back in her cargo pants pocket, thanked the clerk for her time and headed for the door.

"You sure you could afford all that, L-T?" Charlene said.

"Ya, no problem," Gwen said. "Unlike you yahoos, I made sure I got paid."

She didn't tell them she made more in a week, just from the rents from her estates, than they made in a year.

Gwen had the cab driver take them to a car dealership. She made her way over to the used car section, then resisted the sales rep trying to sell her what he thought a young girl would want. She picked up a decent three-year-old pickup with an extended cab.

Once it was verified she was eligible to drive, all the paperwork was completed and off the girls went. The magic that had made all the lights green when they had come into town obviously had run out as they hit more red lights than green ones.

Gwen parked next to her mom's SUV and the girls walked into the house. Gwen pointed at the refrigerator and headed to the pantry, where she picked up some bread and other things. She reached over Chelsea's shoulder to grab lunch meats and beer, and the three of them went out to the deck.

"You guys leave anything in the store for someone else to buy?" Duncan said.

"Barely," Gwen said.

"Any trouble?" Duncan asked.

"Na," Gwen said. "All they saw was three off-planet hicks out on the town."

Marlene picked up her tablet, hit the screen and a hologram of the local news came on.

"After a two-year absence," the commentator said, "The Grand Duchess somehow evaded all security and went on a shopping trip this afternoon."

The shopping clerk was interviewed. She said she was not sure which of the three girls was the Grand Duchess. They were all wearing disguises, looking like off-world visitors. The clerk had only figured it out once she had shipped the goods to the Royal Quarters.

A picture of a much younger Gwen, taken at the same mall before the fateful trip, was shown.

"Ya, you look a lot different now, for sure," Junior said. He had joined them on the deck after a long nap.

Later, as Gwen took her friends to see the sights, they were ignored. They looked and acted like who they were: four young troopers on leave and out for a good time.

The following Monday, Gwen drove them to the spaceport. Each gave Junior a big hug, then watched him report in and be escorted into the transport. They waited until it took off. It was the first time the four would not be together in over a year.

"Okay, kid," Duncan said a week later. "I held it off as long as I could..."

"Your father, as always," Marlene said, "has been shirking his responsibilities."

"All B-S," Duncan said.

"Regimental ball, ladies," Marlene said. "Not to worry, we have a few days. The seamstresses arrive in an hour. So, no, you are not running around today."

"Ah shit!" Gwen said.

"I hate this shit," she and her father said almost at the same time.

"No way I am wearing a fancy gown," Gwen said. "I earned that uniform, Mom."

"I know, luv," Marlene said. "I know. I'm wearing mine, too. It's only for the fancy state functions we have to wear the formal shit, Gwen."

"And," Gwen added, "I am only wearing the full uniform, not the mess dress."

They heard Duncan grumble as he walked off into the house. Marlene laughed.

"He does look oh-so-yummy in that mess dress of his, though," she said.

"Dad hates wearing his general's uniform," Gwen said. "And he has to for a battalion ball."

After much curtseying and to-ing and fro-ing, the seamstresses got to work taking measurements and making suggestions on which colour of gown would suit each girl. Marlene brought out her full uniform.

"All three will look like this," Marlene said. "Just make the uniform. We will handle the badges and other things ourselves."

The final day was frantic. Hair and makeup specialists were all over them. They had spent the morning polishing their buttons and boots, and pinning on all the badging and miniature medals in the right places. Marlene stopped them from pinning the rank stripes.

"Leave that to me, eh?"

The three girls were hustled off to the hair specialists.

They heard a vehicle arrive and a lot of laughing and commenting but were too preoccupied to find out what was going on.

After being released from the specialists' clutches, Gwen went to her bedroom and took her time dressing. She had been to enough of these types of things to know there was a lot of hurry-up-and-wait time. She was just about to call down to find out where her tunic was when her mom entered with it wrapped in a towel. She made Gwen turn around and put it on her, then came to the front to button and straighten it. She already had everything but her own tunic on.

Gwen turned to look at her reflection in the full-length mirror to make sure everything was where it was supposed to be. Instead of the single bar she had been expecting, she saw a double bar.

"Congratulations, Captain," her mother said.

"I don't deserve these," Gwen said. "I'm not old enough or have enough time in yet."

"You are old enough, just," Marlene said. "You have two years credited service, again enough time, just, today in fact. And these, my lovely daughter, these say you earned them."

Marlene gently stroked the medals, especially the wound stripes.

"You are not required to wear the sash tonight, Gwen," Marlene continued. "Nor the sword. You will have to wear the peaked cap, however, instead of the beret. Let's see how that looks, hmm?"

There was a knock at the door. Marlene left Gwen looking in the mirror and adjusting the unfamiliar cap to sit properly on her head.

"What can I do for you, Warrant Little Bear?" Marlene said.

"I was wondering if I could speak with Lieutenant Kovacks, Master Warrant," Junior said. "I am afraid I have gotten the wrong room."

All Junior could see was the back of a female captain adjusting her cap in the mirror.

"Leave the house for ten minutes and they promote all kinds of incompetent idiots while I am gone," Duncan said from behind Junior.

Like Marlene, he was missing his tunic from his otherwise impeccable uniform. Gwen turned around.

"Holy shit!" Junior blurted out. "Ma'am..."

"Oh, come here, you yutz!" Gwen said. She took him by the shoulders and kissed him on both cheeks. "No hugs. Can't mess up this pretty uniform now can we. Looks good though, eh?"

She put a hand on a hip and pirouetted around. Duncan shook his head.

"Get your asses downstairs," he said as he walked away.

"When did you get back?" Gwen asked.

She had taken the cap off and now had it tucked under her left arm. They made their way to the patio.

"A couple of hours ago," Junior said. "Mom and dad were invited and said I should come, so here I are."

"Oh my," Gwen said. "We all got promoted."

Chelsea was now a sub-lieutenant and Christine a lieutenant. Gwen placed her cap beside theirs on the coffee table.

Gwen refused the ride to the club in the limo. The others could not understand it until they arrived and saw the mass of media descend like vultures on the limo as it arrived, most yelling for the Grand Duchess. The four young officers exiting the old pickup and walking into the club went unnoticed.

The tables all had place cards. Gwen followed her friends until they found their table and sighed, as Captain Isabelle was listed to be at that table.

"Thank God," Gwen said. She had been expecting to have to sit at the head table.

Four young Wind Rider male officers were at their table. Gwen didn't know any of them. Introductions were made.

"What unit are you guys with?" A young captain asked.

"Oh," Gwen said. "We're not sure yet. Something in supplies I have been told."

Looking at their uniforms, the others knew these four were not supplies people, but also knew better than to push it.

As the youngest, most junior officer present, Chelsea had been required to give the toast to the Grand Duke. All through the dinner, little hints kept coming from the others at their table.

'Okay guys," Gwen said. "Look, we are here to party. Yes, we have been in the shit. Yes, we are on the same fire team. No, I am not going to talk about it."

Only the young captain had a 180 day in combat medal. The others had not seen combat.

"Hey, Isabelle," Megan said as she approached their table, a full glass in each hand. "Glad to see you could make it. You too, Little Bear. I heard you were off-planet."

"Ya, I went home for a bit," Junior said. "My sister is in this year's basic class. I wanted to see her while she was still just a kid."

"Are your folks here, too?" Megan asked.

"Someplace. I haven't spotted them yet," Junior answered.

"Congratulations on the promotions, ladies," Megan said to the two new lieutenants. "Well deserved and overdue. Catch ya later. I better go before some hussy tries to steal my man."

"You know Major Cochrane?" one of the male lieutenants asked.

"Ya, we've run into each other a time or two," Chelsea said.

Throughout the evening, others of the legendary original Wind Riders stopped by to say hello to them. Finally, as dinner ended and the dance music started, Duncan himself stopped at their table.

"If I may have the pleasure of this dance, Captain?" He asked.

Gwen stood and, putting her arm through his, they made their way to the dance floor.

It was a slow waltz. Right up her father's alley, Gwen knew, as he didn't much like to dance at the best of times.

"Pop," Gwen said. "What's with this annual qualification thing my table mates are talking about?"

"Crap," Duncan said. "One more thing I forgot to tell you. Sorry, Gwen. Too much going on right now and you guys keep falling through the cracks. Ten kilometre run, full combat loads with weapons and ammo. Fire qual right after the run and I do mean right after. Just a formality for you guys, but ya, it needs doing. Friday morning, Spud."

"Okay, no big deal. I'll tell my team to hang around until Friday," Gwen said. "I'm getting a little bored anyway."

"Okay," Duncan said. "I'm taking off right after our dance, Gwen. Ya, ya, no surprise, I know. Once I take off, the other senior officers will, too. Gives the junior officers time to let their hair down, you know? Don't worry about the press. Once they found out the Grand Duchess was not here, they kind of lost interest. Once your mom and I go, they will all go, too.

"I think it would be a good idea if you stayed. Up to you, though," he suggested.

"I'll ask the guys," Gwen said.

The tune ended and Duncan escorted her back to the table. He paused to make a couple of jokes with her table mates. Living up to his nickname, within half an hour, he left, followed by the senior officers. The party really got going after that. Tunics came off, shirts were unbuttoned, and the dance floor was never empty as the DJ switched to the popular dance songs for her age group.

Several hours later, feeling no pain, the four friends staggered out of the officers' club. Gwen presented her chit to have her truck retrieved. Her truck showed up with a G-Wagon trailing it. The Master Sergeant who had driven the limo was behind the wheel of her truck.

"Get in," he said, not leaving the driver's seat. "No way you are driving home in that condition."

"Hey!" Gwen said. "It's my truck, get the hell out. I drive."

"You got a choice kid," the Master Sergeant said. "Get in the damn truck and I drive you home, or you walk."

Gwen got into her fighting stance to take the sergeant on, then fell on her butt. She looked around, then back up to the still-sitting sergeant, now smiling.

"Okay, party pooper," Gwen slurred. "You win."

Her three friends helped her stand and the four of them figured out how to climb into the truck. After that, the sergeant had to put up with the more-than-slightly-tipsy behaviour he had often seen before.

Pulling to a stop in her parking spot, the sergeant unlocked the doors and the four friends poured themselves out of the vehicle and more or less made it into the house. The master sergeant got in the G-Wagon, looked at his buddy, and laughed.

"Been there, done that..."

Chapter Twenty-One

Gwen's pickup was parked beside a number of other private vehicles and official G-Wagons. Several busloads of Wind Rider troopers and even more busloads of troopers from other battle groups soon arrived. All hoped to qualify. The staging area was crowded by the time Gwen and her team checked in. They were each handed a GPS unit and a start time. Their time was just in front of the first of the fireteams from other battle groups trying for the limited empty Wind Rider slots. That meant they were the last of the Wind Riders and had a three-hour wait.

Gwen was laid out on the hood of the pickup, Christine beside her. They were having a snooze. Chelsea was in the truck bed and Junior had fully reclined the front passenger seat. Forty-five minutes before their start time, as programmed, the team's comm units beeped, waking them up. Gwen and Christine got down. Chelsea handed out the packs and other equipment, then got down herself.

They quickly donned combat vests but did not fully close them. Packs were slung on one shoulder, weapons on the other. The four friends walked to the starting grid. They were glad they had not put everything in place ready to go when they arrived.

In typical Army fashion, things were running late. They arrived just in time to watch her mother's Zebra section take off. As usual, the Zebras were at the tail end of the veteran Wind Rider formations. They passed the first of many, still in visual range of the start line. The Captain and his fire team, their table mates from the ball arrived, their gear and weapons ready to go. They would start three places behind Gwen and her team. The captain looked over at them, shook his head and smirked. The four friends ignored them and everyone else around them. They casually began to get ready, tightening up combat vests, making sure packs were well closed.

The team two places ahead of them started and Gwen pulled her pack on, adjusting it to suit her. She placed her assault rifle across the top of it, then jacked a round into the shotgun's chamber and put it on safe. Christine was armed like she was. Junior had the squad gun clipped to his chest, his assault rifle across the pack as Gwen's was. Chelsea had her grenade launcher-mounted assault rifle in hand and the long rifle across her pack.

How they were armed and the layout of their equipment drew more than a few looks and comments from those waiting their turn. Nor were the four of them like the other teams at the start line. They were relaxed, almost too relaxed. As the order was given, the fire team, again unlike everyone else, took the first few steps at a walk, then gradually picked up their pace. Not surprisingly, they were passed by several teams behind them, including the male captain's.

The big difference came at the firing line. Gwen's team actually finished before the captain's. In fact, they had already dumped packs and undone the fronts of the combat vests by the time the other team finished. Another difference was that Gwen's team headed straight for the first bus in line ready to leave, instead of checking for their scores.

Gwen and her team had been told in no uncertain terms they had to join the originals at the start of the customary Friday night Wind Rider party later than evening. It was at the fire range and slightly larger-than-usual.

"You trying to make me look bad, Daughter?" Marlene demanded. It was clear she had already consumed more than a few shots of vodka. "Zebras running that slow. My goodness."

"Not a Zebra, mom," Gwen said nonplussed.

"Got that right," Shandra agreed, also well on her way. "You guys ran like old grannies."

Gwen saluted the both of them with her beer and found a clear space around the bonfire to plop down on.

"Why are we here, Pop?" Gwen asked. The spot she had chosen was next to Duncan.

"I dunno," Duncan said. "I was wondering about that myself."

"Mom's idea, then," Gwen said. "Figures. Thought she was going to rub it into the others, did she?"

"Well..." Duncan said. "You guys did run a little slow."

"You know, I know and she knows, running speed is not everything, Dad," Gwen said. "We train like we deploy. Well almost. Can't give away all our secrets, eh?"

"Picking up the cozy Canuck accent, I hear," Anne said as she sat beside Gwen.

"Like, ya," Gwen said. "Like, these guys don't speak proper 'merican like ya'll. Your German just as bad?" She continued in that language.

"Unlike you," Anne replied in German, "I did not grow up hearing and speaking it every day like you kids do."

"Ah, just jerking your chain, Anne," Gwen said. "Mom's gonna start mixing up her Parisian with Standard pretty soon."

"Got that right," Duncan said and chuckled. "Good thing I'm bilingual."

Marlene came over at that point and, elbowing her way in, sat between Gwen and her father. She very carefully put her beer down to one side, then hugged her daughter, hard.

"Now you are officially one of us," Marlene said in a mixture of French and English. "Nowhere good enough to be a Zebra, but still..."

"Flippen Zebras is all too noisy anyway." Anne said.

"You and your crew get the hell out of here, Gwen," Duncan said. "Go hang out with some kids your own age, eh?"

Gwen laughed, gave her mom a quick squeeze, then she and her team disappeared.

"Christ that team is good," Marlene said, just like that, turning an internal switch.

"All four of them," Duncan said. "All shots in the bull from every weapon. Like she said, Mar, running speed isn't everything. But they can run, my God, they can run. They had to."

"Hey!" The captain from the ball yelled. He waved the four of them over.

There was a group of about twenty troopers their age there.

"How'd you guys do? You took off so fast we couldn't find you after," the captain said.

"We passed," Junior said. He dug in a pants pocket and pulled out a full bottle, took a swig and passed it over.

"Interesting selection of weapons," someone else said.

"We had a choice?" Chelsea said. She shrugged her shoulders. "We just used what we had on our last mission. Had I known we had a choice, Junior could have lugged that damn heavy long gun of his himself."

"Then you would have been stuck lugging the squad gun," Junior said.

"Shit, can't win here," Chelsea said.

Gwen was talking with another female trooper who had a Wind Rider beret on, but a Marauder patch on her shoulder.

"Your captain do that a lot?" a corporal asked Christine.

"What?" Christine said.

"The new kid," the corporal said. "Your captain noticed right away she was kind of like a lost sheep and sat beside her."

"Hadn't noticed," Christine said. "What's her story anyway?"

"She qualified pretty high," the corporal said. "Not a normal thing. Not many from her battle group even try out, let alone pass the qual run."

"What do you expect from an infantry outfit," a sergeant chimed in.

"I thought you were just going to go through the motions, Mary," Gwen said.

"Look who's talking," Mary said, pointing at Gwen's officer's bars.

"Different for me," Gwen said. "Kind of expected. Family tradition and that shit. Also didn't have much of a choice. I kinda got the prima donna act kicked out of me in a hurry."

"Well," Mary said. "Once I got in, I figured I might as well do the best I could. We'll see how this works out. I didn't volunteer for this Wind Rider crap, Gwen. My officers enrolled me. Hell, I only have the one deployment under my belt."

"Me, too," Gwen said. "Shitty as it was. Lost half my team."

"Holy shit," Mary said. "Must have been a hairy one."

"Ya, a little," Gwen said. "We were kind of left out to dry for a bit. It got all straightened out though. Panzer troop came to the rescue; just in time, too. Another story for another time, Mary. How's the rest of the gang doing?"

"Most of them got what they wanted. Supply and services," Mary said. "A couple chose infantry like I did."

Gwen caught Christine's eyes and jerked her head to the left, then stood.

"Time to go, Mare," Gwen said. "Before my folks or one of their buddies find me. So embarrassing all the time. Come on up to the house, Mare, we can catch up some more then, right?"

"Tomorrow okay, Gwen?" Mary said. "I have to report in in the morning. I'll go back to the motel and change, then cab it over."

"Message me the address and time," Gwen said. "I'll pick you up. Check out of the motel, too; we have spare rooms."

As promised, Gwen was parked outside of Mary's motel room. She was sitting on the hood, her back against the windshield, feet extended, ball cap down to her nose, having a snooze. Mary whacked her on the bottom of her sandal-clad feet as she went by.

"Wakey, wakey, Gwenzilla," Mary said as Gwen lifted the ball cap from her nose long enough to look at Mary, give her the finger and place the cap back down again. Five minutes later, a thump in the pickup bed as Mary's duffle hit it told Gwen it was time to leave.

"Pretty low-key for you, Gwen," Mary said as she plopped down in the passenger seat.

"I like it like that," Gwen said. "And you don't say a bloody word about it to anybody, hear? I've got enough trouble staying off the news as it is."

"They've forgotten all about you now anyway," Mary said. "Some other cute rich girl in the Federation that actually likes being on the vids is taking up all their time now."

"Thank God for that," Gwen said.

"So..." Mary started. "Tell me all about that dreamy Junior."

"Really?" Gwen said. "Dreamy? More of a pain in the ass. He's up at the house, too."

"Oh goody," Mary exclaimed. "I haven't had a chance to snare a good fish for a while now."

"Mary!" Marlene said the moment they arrived. She rushed up, gave Mary a big hug and kissed her on the cheek. "We haven't seen you for ages!"

"Ah, come on, Mar," Duncan said. "We were kinda busy for a while. Hey Mary. Grab your usual room."

"What you up to, Pop?" Gwen asked, pointing to the laptop and two tablets on the kitchen table in front of Duncan.

"Trying to match up a new fire team and another section for you, Gwen," Duncan said.

"Okay," Gwen said. "Put Mary as one of my second fire team members, Pop."

"She doesn't have the training yet, Gwen," Duncan said. "She just qualified on Friday and only had the one deployment before that."

"Check out what she did on that deployment, Dad," Gwen said. "I did. I also checked out her score from Friday. She goes on my section, Pop. I'm not gonna argue about it."

"You're a little female heavy as it is, Gwen," Duncan said.

"Ya, so?" Gwen said. "Christine and Chelsea are both going to be fire team leaders. Christine will be the other section leader, Junior the other fire team leader. Other than Mary, I don't care who, what gender or what rank they are."

Mary came downstairs, Gwen nodded her head at the refrigerator and Mary made her way over and pulled out two vodka coolers.

"Ah, crap!" Mary said. She pulled out her comms unit and read what she found there. "Gotta report to some unit called Gulf Tango on Monday. You know anything about them, Gwen?"

"Who me?" Gwen said. "Not likely. Not to worry Mare, I'm still on leave, but I'll get you there on time on Monday."

"Asshole," she mouthed to her father as she followed Mary onto the deck.

"Love you too, Gwen," Duncan said.

It didn't take long for Mary to fit in with the others. She was their age and, once they found out she had gone to school with Gwen, Gwen had little peace and few opportunities for comebacks as Mary disclosed all the stupid things she had done in her youth.

Mary descended the stairs Monday morning, in her uniform, to see the other three were also in their uniforms.

"Leave got cancelled," Junior said. "Typical Army."

"Ya," Duncan said from the kitchen table. "Somebody ought to complain to the boss."

Mary was quiet and nervous as they drove together in Gwen's pickup to the Wind Rider base.

"You'll be fine," Gwen said, as they stopped at the enlisted gate. "I'm sure you will fit right in with your new team."

"Hope so," Mary said, and she was gone.

There were seven other people waiting where Mary had been told to report. She saluted the captain there and then went to the far end of the line where the other enlisted were. Of the seven, two were officers, the captain and a lieutenant. Then there were two master sergeants, two sergeants and a master corporal. Mary was the only private.

The master corporal, one sergeant and both master sergeants were female.

Five more people walked up. They were walking in a relaxed manner but in step. The group comprised a male warrant officer, and four females: a master sergeant, a sub-lieutenant, a lieutenant and a captain.

"Good morning," Gwen called, getting their attention. "Welcome to Gulf Tango. I am commander and section one leader Captain Gwen. Next to me is Warrant Little Bear, fire team two leader. Next to him is section two leader Lieutenant Christine and fire team four leader sub-lieutenant Chelsea. Master Sergeant Amanda will oversee your training for the next week. Your leaders have other tasks to perform the rest of this week."

"During the next week," Amanda said, "I will be evaluating you and determining what positions you will occupy in your fire teams. Gulf Tango does not recognize regular Army protocol as far as assignments are concerned. You will be placed where the commander of this platoon feels you are most suited; no consideration for rank, experience or time in service will be considered. Only your performance over the next week."

"You have until 08:00 to request a transfer if you do not wish to serve under these conditions," Gwen added. "We have plenty of suitable candidates to replace you if you choose to do so. If you survive the next five days and are still here, your asses are mine, all mine. Carry on, Master Sergeant."

Gwen and the gang stayed for the first five minutes as Amanda started her chew-their-asses out routine, then slid quietly away.

"Okay, what have we got, Master Sergeant?" Gwen asked the next Monday morning. The twelve were still present and were just heading out for their morning run.

"Like you," Amanda said. "I figured the captain would be an issue. He kind of was the first day and a half. Then he saw he wasn't as much of a hotshot as he thought he was. Also like you figured, the private is outstanding. Still a little dumb, though. The rest? All very able, Ma'am."

"Very well, Master Sergeant," Gwen said. "Can't have a mere private with us, eh? Bad for morale. I'll handle that one. What's on tap after the run today, Amanda?"

"One-on-one unarmed combat, Gwen," Amanda said. "You wanna handle that one?"

"Na," Gwen said. "I think Charlene should, don't you?"

Charlene was the shortest and slightest of them.

"Oh, goody," Charlene said. "Fun time for Charlene for once."

When the twelve sweaty team members arrived at the unarmed combat area, they saw the four team leaders lounging with the Master Sergeant.

"Right!" Amanda said. "Today is one-on-one unarmed combat trials. Team four leader has agreed to assess you. Team leader?"

Charlene walked into the square of hard-packed earth and beckoned the largest of the male troopers to her.

"Come on!" she teased as she easily sidestepped the man, slapping him hard on the butt as he went past her. "You can do better than that. My granny fights better than you."

She went through all twelve of them in quick succession; the only one who demonstrated any proficiency was the captain.

"Enough of this shit!" Gwen said. She stood and pulled her beret down to just above her eyebrows and walked into the square, motioning Christine to leave.

"Come on, all of you now!" Gwen said motioning them to come at her.

"Attack! Now! All of you!"

The confused troopers made a rough circle around her trying to figure out if she was serious or not.

"Fuck this!" Gwen said, launching herself at the nearest trooper. All twelve were down and clutching some part of their bodies in seconds.

"You people better get with the program or I can goddamned guarantee all twelve of you will be dead on our first deployment!"

"Master Sergeant?" Gwen said, bowing and extending a hand, inviting Amanda into the ring.

In motions so fast at times their arms were blurring, the women attacked each other. Amanda lasted longer than the first time she had faced Gwen, but not much.

"Better, Master Sergeant," Gwen said, reaching down to help Amanda up. "There is hope for you yet.

"Little Bear! Chelsea. Show them how real Gulf Tango train!"

They entered the square. Each held an axe in one hand and a long, nasty combat knife in the other. They circled, relaxed, for a moment and then, almost simultaneously, attacked each other. It was fast and it was hard. Neither held anything back. Then Junior tripped on something and went down. Chelsea pounced on him and slapped him on the shoulder with the side of her hand axe. Then she raised both hands in the air and shrieked long and loud.

"Okay," Junior said, picking himself up. "Ya got me. I'm still two ahead of you, though."

"Nya nya," Chelsea said prancing around Junior. "I got you, I got you."

"Okay, Master Sergeant," Gwen said. "You have permission to show them why this is necessary. I am late for my hair and nails appointment. Come, girls."

Amanda called the twelve over and activated an infrared hologram. Junior brushed dirt from his uniform. Two figures, one behind the other, were making their way down a hallway. At the first corner, the first figure crouched down, then exploded around the corner in a fury and cut down two figures standing there. They did the same thing twice more, then the first figure fired a grenade from a rocket launcher and continued firing while advancing. The second figure started firing what turned out to be a squad rifle. Neither weapon was on full-automatic. They fired short, timed shots. The one with the squad gun pulled back and changed magazines while the first sped up the rate of fire, then ran back behind the one with the squad gun and changed magazines. This pattern was repeated several times and the figure with the assault rifle stumbled on two separate occasions. The one with the squad gun went down. The first one started to drag the squad gun operator back with one hand while firing with the other. The dragged one clapped a hand on the first one's leg and stood, backed up a few steps and turned, just as the first one went down. Then the dragger became the draggee. Amanda cut it off.

"That's why," Amanda said. "What you just witnessed was White Ghost and Gulf Five on the last assault at the Capitol building. Eight went in, four came out alive. They killed one hundred troops, more than half Wind Riders. On their own. For a day and a half. This is what Gulf Tango does, people. Get with the program or, I can assure you, White Ghost will kill you if you get in her way.

"See ya Junior, I have a spa appointment."

"Ya, leave it to the junior male noncomm," Junior said. "Questions, people?"

"You the one with the hatchet, Warrant?" The female master sergeant asked.

"Na, I had the squad gun. White Ghost had the hatchet."

"Oh, Charlene then," the captain said. Junior did not contradict him.

Junior said, "This was a nasty fight, but we have been in worse. No fancy pictures of that shit though. Seriously, you guys don't pick it up, you are really going to die. What we do? No time to piss around. You fuck up, you die, that simple. Mission comes first. Only reason White Ghost dragged me back was we were pulling back anyway. Otherwise, she would have left me there and I her. That it? Now, I gotta get ready for a hot date tonight."

The four of them, especially Junior, were quietly sitting on the deck, slowly sipping their beer. That's how Mary found them. She had intended on giving Gwen a blast for not telling her she was the leader of Gulf Tango, but changed her mind when she saw their moods. She quietly took a chair at the far end of the table and sipped her vodka cooler. Marlene walked in, ready to make a comment, but also stopped when she saw what was going on, especially with Junior.

"You okay, hun?" Marlene asked as she crouched down beside him.

"Huh...Ya, I guess," Junior said. "Fuck, that was close, Gwen. Have you seen that footage? Shit, was way worse than I remembered."

"No," Gwen said softly. "And I don't want to ever see it. Bad enough I see it at night."

"Where were you that day, Gwen?" Mary asked.

Gwen looked over at her, her eyes starting to well up.

"Right in the fucking front," she said quietly. "Maybe if I hadn't been, four of my people would still be alive."

"And maybe all of you would have died if you were not," Marlene said. "How do you think we felt, watching that in real time? It should have been us in there, Gwen, not you, and we all know it."

"Ah, you guys are too damn old for this shit," Gwen said. Her moment had passed.

"I'll show you too old, young lady!" Marlene said jumping up. Gwen put both palms forward.

"Woah up there, super Zebra," Gwen said. "I surrender."

"Moving on," Gwen said. "We cannot have a private on Gulf Tango, Master Warrant. Unacceptable."

"Not up to me, Captain," Marlene said. "You are not Zebra. I'll pass it up the chain, Captain."

"Thanks, Mom," Gwen said. "I'd do it myself, but don't know how."

"Early days daughter, early days. Who wants pizza?"

Gwen, her mom, and Junior went into the kitchen.

"That was very impressive, Chelsea," Mary said. "Is that why they call you White Ghost?"

"Me? White Ghost? Not even in my wildest dreams! I'm not even close to what she can do." She stood and went to the kitchen.

"Nope," Christine said not waiting to be asked. "I was there, just someplace else. White Ghost will reveal herself when she thinks the time is right, Mary."

The training picked up after the first day. The team leaders had joined them. They never rubbed it in, but they toyed with the recruits often. They demonstrated a technique or watched the recruits attempt it, usually in slow motion.

"*Tango One Four, Control. Bravo your two at four.*

The comms came alive as Tango One Four blew into her mike twice to acknowledge.

"Shit," Barb said. "Gwen has trained these guys well for only two weeks of training. I can hardly spot them and I know where they are supposed to be."

The team's task was to eliminate an enemy listening post. Almost before Barb spotted a target, it was gone.

Control, Tango One One, Echo eliminated, RTB.

"*No fair Tango One One, Voice is bored. Voice has toys Voice want to play with, too.*

Voice snoozes, Voice looses. Tango One One clear.

The dejected Wind Rider team drove into camp. Shortly after that, sixteen troopers in camo walked into camp and dumped their gear in their tents.

"We waiting for the rest of your company before we start the debrief?" The captain in charge of the defeated Wind Rider company asked.

"Nope," Gwen said.

"Okay, people," Megan said. "Captain, the reason we are not waiting for the rest of her company is because there is no rest of her company. Those sixteen guys just kicked the crap out of you."

Barb stood and turned on a hologram. The Wind Rider positions were clearly marked by infrared.

"Something seems to be missing from this picture," Barb said. "Wait for it."

In quick succession, the infrared showed weapons firing at every Wind Rider position. Quick, without warning. Then nothing.

"If it is any consolation," Megan said. "You are not the first Wind Riders to be taken out by Gulf Tango."

Another hologram came alive. This time it was during the day and very grainy. A GW2 was clearly visible with four troopers around it. Then a single figure erupted out of the ground. Within seconds, three troopers were down before a second figure came out of the ground and entered the fight. In less than two minutes all four troopers were down. The hologram blinked out.

"Those four Wind Riders died for real," Megan said. "Two Gulf Tango took them out with nothing more than hand axes and knives. They did better later, much better, once they had firearms. Firearms the Wind Riders donated to their cause.

"Like you," Barb said. "We want to know how White Ghost can keep her people hidden even from infrared detection. So far, White Ghost is living up to her name and not only not revealing who she is, but how she does it. I was overwatch for them on this mission and knew their positions. But even I had a hard time spotting them and usually couldn't see them for long."

"We have been relying on our technology for far too long," Megan said. "White Ghost was forced to operate with none of that for a long time. She is used to making do only with what God gave her: her nose, her ears, her eyes. She has trained her people to do the same and, I can tell you firsthand, her people are nowhere near as good as she is."

"Captain," Barb said. "Your task is to begin training your people to see, hear, and smell. Once your company can do that, they will, in turn, teach other Wind Rider companies the same."

"Don't feel bad, Captain," Junior said. "We did the same thing to Zebra last week."

"I don't know about you guys," Gwen said during the Friday night gathering at the firing range. "But this training shit is beginning to bug me."

The more they worked together, the closer the sixteen of them had become.

"I have a ton of leave left," Gwen said. "If they don't need us for an op, I'm gonna take some."

The others nodded in agreement.

"Hey," one of the team leaders from the defeated Wind Riders said. "We keep hearing about this White Ghost. When we going to meet her?"

"Dunno," Gwen said. "Never been introduced to her myself."

"White Ghost does what White Ghost does," Junior said. "When she wants to talk to you, she will. You might not like it though."

"Ya," Chelsea said. "Not many people survive it when she reveals herself."

"Speaking of meeting White Ghost," Mary said on the trip back to Gwen's house. "Can I at least meet her?"

"Like I said, Mary," Gwen said. "I've never been introduced to her."

"She'll show up when she shows up, Mary," Junior said. "Don't push it."

Chapter Twenty-Two

Their mission was to establish surveillance on the sprawling complex. One of leading crime organizations had finally gone too far. Generally, the Federation looked the other way. They knew who all the groups were and that they would operate anyway, so as long as things were low key, the Federation had a hands-off policy. In fact, the crime groups had their own system of governance that roughly parallel the Federation's, and they kept things under control.

This time, one organization had become greedy. Bad blood was boiling over with the other crime groups and this particular group had begun killing civilians. The Federation had asked New Germany to look into a solution. This was it.

Gulf Tango had been in position for two weeks now. It had taken three weeks to get into place. Rations were running low. They would have to be resupplied or withdrawn soon.

At last, headquarters had received enough intel and the operation would begin today. In an hour, to be exact.

Tango One, Control.

The mission had a high enough profile that Barb was running overwatch.

60 mike, Tango. All green.

Gwen blew into her mike twice. Mary pulled the bolt back on her long gun enough to place a round in the chamber without taking one from the magazine, flipped it on safe again, and continued scanning the area with her scope. Gwen was scanning with her binoculars and Mary's spotter was doing the same with his spotting scope. Their squad gunner was confirming his initial belt was free. The other three teams were scattered around the grounds performing similar quiet preparations. Nothing was changing. The target was still in the building, meeting with his leadership. All the guards had been pinpointed. This should not be a big deal.

Ten mikes, Tango One.

The spotter concentrated on Mary's first targets, getting wind direction and distances down pat. Gwen kept scanning the grounds.

"Something doesn't feel right," she whispered. She couldn't put her finger on it. Everything looked the same as it had for the last two weeks, but something was off.

Five mikes, Tango.

Gwen was scanning as fast as she could.

One mike, Tango.

Gwen could hear the transports in the distance. She jacked a round into her chamber and placed a grenade in the launcher under the barrel. The noise grew into a roar as the transports came into view and hovered to a stop.

Break off, break off!! Gwen yelled into her comms unit and fired her grenade at a portal that had slid open.

Gulf Tango, multiple bogeys in bunkers!

High-caliber automatic machine guns began to go off along with high-powered blasters. The grounds were lit like daylight now from high-powered lasers firing from the bunkers and the grenades and tracer rounds going off all around. The assaulters were sitting ducks and one of the transports blew up in a massive fireball.

Voice, where are the fucking drones! We need them now!

Get the fuck out of my way, Tango! Charley, White Ghost is on the way!

Gwen stood and, firing as she ran, made her way toward the ambush site. She took out two bunkers with her grenade launcher. Figure after figure was going down in front of her as Mary picked them off with her long gun. When her launcher had no more grenades and her rifle was out of ammo, she pulled out her pistol and emptied two clips as she rushed the house. Then it was hatchet time. She saw four figures drop before she got close. Game on.

She stopped when only the boss was left alive and she had him up on his tip toes, her left hand around his neck.

"You fucked with the wrong people this time, asshole," she said softly. The man was scared out of his wits. "Who tipped you off, asshole?"

The man looked at the aberration holding him up. Her arm was dripping blood from her elbow and running down her face. He blurted out a name.

"Compliments of White Ghost," she said and hit him right between the eyes, burying the blade of her hatchet to the handle. She needed both hands to remove it from his skull.

Sit rep, Voice.

Almost out of ordinance, White Ghost. Time to go, hun.

How many left, Voice?

Twenty, maybe twenty-five.

Ghost Team, White Ghost. Nobody leaves here with any turkeys left alive, copy?

Gwen slapped her hatchet into her belt, pulled another clip for her assault rifle and slammed it home. That's when she noticed her squad gunner was beside her. Like her, he was covered in blood.

"All good, Tony?" She asked.

"Five by five, White Ghost," Tony said. He had just slammed a clip into his squad gun.

Gwen ran out of the building, acquiring targets and firing as she ran. So was Tony.

Any Charley, White Ghost.

White Ghost, Charley, Five Six.

Sit rep, Five Six?

Fucked if I know, White Ghost. I got two effective here.

Okay Five Six, take a deep breath, it's under control now.

They heard three shots from Christine's position.

Thought you said it was under control, White Ghost.

Didn't say it was over, Five Six, just under control.

Tony pulled the trigger on a moaning enemy as he walked by.

Ghost Two and Four, get a sit rep on Charley. Control, got a fix on Five Six?

White Ghost, Control. Five Six is ten meters to your nine.

Ghost One, Two, got me?

Copy.

Advance on my pos, Ghost Two and Three. We clear, Voice?

Copy, no traffic incoming or outgoing, Ghost One One.

Extract with medic ASAP. One transport KIA.

Copy, Ghost One One. Wait one.

Gwen went to a knee beside a prone trooper. He still had his rifle training around the grounds. There were a lot of shell casings around him and his teammates.

"How's it going, Five Six?" Gwen asked. Tony was on one knee two meters away, scanning with his squad gun. Seconds later Mary and her spotter slid in. The long gun was across Mary's back.

"See what you can do for these guys, Mary, Walter." Gwen said.

"Just a flesh wound, Sergeant," Gwen said to Five Six as she slapped a bandage on the man's thigh. Good job here, Sergeant."

Medivac in twenty mikes, relief in five, White Ghost.

Copy, Voice. Resistance finished, repeat, resistance finished.

Copy White Ghost, resistance over.

"Changing mags," Gwen said. She replaced the magazine in her rifle with a full one and placed the half-empty one in an empty pouch. She did the same with her pistol.

"Clear," she said taking up her rifle to scan the area.

"Changing mags," Tony said. He also announced *Clear* when he was done.

Satisfied, Gwen lowered her rifle barrel but kept her hands near the trigger.

"You really, White Ghost?" Five Six asked, looking up at her.

"That's what they tell me from time to time," Gwen said. "Why, wanna take me out on a date?"

"Nnnoo...Uh, I mean..."

"It's okay, Sarge," Gwen said. "I don't bite on the first date, much." Then she laughed.

Sound off, Ghost Team.

Her people all reported in. No casualties.

Extract five mikes, Ghost One One.

They could hear the transports coming in the distance, low and fast.

The transports came roaring in. Dust flew everywhere and troops poured out almost before the loading ramps were fully open.

Gwen grabbed Five Six under the shoulders and helped him stand. She and the other Ghost Team members each helped a trooper to a transport.

"See ya when I see ya, Five Six," Gwen said. Then she joined her people and they all piled into the next transport. It could hold thirty troopers. It took off with just them in it.

"Well, that was fun," Christine said. She tossed a water bottle at Gwen who deftly caught it and took a deep pull. "Always a good time when I get all fancied up and get to dance."

Gwen looked down at her right hand.

"Shit!" she exclaimed.

The interior of the transport was instantly quiet.

"I think I broke a goddamn nail!" She looked around at their faces. "What? A girl has to look her best around all these super females in this team."

Then Junior looked down at his blood-stained hand and blew on the nails.

Gwen looked at them all, then stood, raised both hands over her head and screeched. Junior was right behind her as were Christine and Chelsea. They began to dance around in a circle screeching their war cry. The rest of the team quickly joined them.

The pilots looked behind them as the screeching turned into laughing, the dancing became joyous and finally the blood-stained kids fell to the floor, laughing their heads off.

Megan was waiting for them when they landed; it was her half-battalion that had executed the assault.

"How bad was it?" Gwen asked as they walked off the pad and toward the group of tents that made up the forward operating post.

"Seventy percent casualties," Megan said.

"Sorry, Megan," Gwen said. "We didn't see those bunkers. Honest."

"You weren't the only ones, Gwen," Megan said.

She stopped Gwen before they entered the tent for the after-action debrief.

"Thank you, White Ghost," Megan said. "You saved a lot of my people out there."

"Just part of the job, Megan, no biggy." Then Gwen walked into the tent, the rest of her team following her.

"What a fucking cluster fuck!" the colonel exploded. "Can someone explain to me why and how a highly trained and qualified recon team could not spot those bunkers? Who and where are those fuckers?"

"Colonel!" Gwen stood, stomped a foot into the ground and came to attention. Her team following her. "Captain Isabelle and Gulf Tango, Sir!"

The glare on the colonel's face softened as he took in the bloodstained bare arms and uniforms of the team members. He swallowed twice.

"Colonel, Brigadier General Cochrane, Colonel!" Barb came to a foot stomping attention beside Gwen.

"Shit," the colonel said. "I guess I can add my name to the list as well. At ease. Sit the fuck down."

Gwen and Barb continued to stand, giving a blow-by-blow account of what they had observed and the actions they had taken. The medical officer walked in then. Like Gwen's team, he had blood up to his elbows.

"The ones coming in are stabilized," the medical major said. "Sounds like we have about twenty dead, another fifty or so wounded."

An aide entered and handed the colonel a sheet of paper.

"Shit!" The colonel said. "Okay, the follow-up team is being augmented by a full battalion. They'll handle the cleanup and do the investigation. Dismissed. Captain Isabelle? General Cochrane, good job out there today, people."

"Thank you, Colonel," Barb said, she came to attention and saluted. So did Gwen, who nudged Junior, who saluted with the rest of the team.

They made their way outside, just in time to see body bag-laden stretchers carried from a transport. Megan was standing in front of the line of stretchers as they moved toward the waiting ambulances. She was at attention and saluting.

Gwen came up beside her and assumed parade-rest. The rest of her team, including Barb, stood beside them. They saluted each of the fallen and the wounded as they returned. Afterward, their little line stayed, behind Megan. Finally, Megan shook her head and turned around. She had not noticed they were there.

"Officer on Deck!" Gwen shouted out.

The sixteen of them came to attention and saluted Megan.

"Thank you, Ghost Team," Megan said softly after she had returned their salutes. "You saved a lot of my people today."

The team had only enough time to shower and change uniforms, then they were hurried to a fast transport and on their way to Mountain View, the barracks planet. They slept for the whole two days it took to get there.

Duncan greeted them when they exited the transport. He returned their salutes and pointed to a bus. After they all got on, he motioned the driver to leave, then climbed in and shut the door.

"Good job out there, guys," Duncan said. "Nothing any of you did caused this disaster. Nothing. We, the whole Army, are damn proud of what Ghost Team and White Ghost did out there. Now, take the next few days off. Go clubbing or whatever. Then we ship you back to New Germany for a while. Good?

As they pulled up to their stop, Gwen approached her father. "Captain?" he said. "A moment of your time?"

Duncan opened the door and climbed out of the bus followed by Gwen. Duncan motioned for the driver to get back in the bus. He took his daughter's right hand and looked at her nails. She hadn't been able to get all the blood off them yet.

"Tough one, eh?" he said dropping her hand.

"Not so bad for us, Pop," Gwen said. "Kinda situation normal for us. But those bunkers caught me. I knew something was wrong but couldn't figure out what. I tried to call it off, Pop, honest."

"Ya, I read the transcripts, Gwen," Duncan said. "Was too late by then. You got us some good intel just the same. Ghost says thank you. Tell your team that, eh? Now get the hell out of here for a while."

They had cleaned up themselves and their weapons, stacked the weapons away and put on green base uniforms. They headed for the all-ranks club. They pulled two tables together at the back. They were quiet for a while, taking in their surroundings. Gwen saw Mary looking at her.

"Not now, not here," Gwen said. Then she made a joke at Tony's expense and the ice was broken.

They made it back to New Germany in time for the Friday night bonfire at the firing range. Gwen took her platoon right to the fire the originals sat around. She had her people stand there until all the originals stopped what they were doing and looked at them.

"Voice?" Gwen said, motioning Barb to join them.

"This is Ghost Team," Gwen said. "Most of you have heard about us and know our names. Now you know the faces that go along with the names. You piss with one of them, you piss with me."

She put her head down for a second and took a deep breath. She moved a few steps in front of her team and turned to face them.

"All these people have known me my whole life," Gwen said. "I trust them all with my life."

"In case you are too dense to have figured it out yet, I am White Ghost," Gwen said, then she repeated the name in Cherokee.

"Junior's father called me that the first time he met me." Gwen continued. "My mother says that is what my name means in an old Home World language called Gaelic. I don't like White Ghost much as a person. But sometimes she is necessary, like the other day. End of story."

Gwen took her beer and walked into the darkness.

"Fucking Ghosts," Carol said. "Her and her old man. They will fight for us, they will put themselves in the deepest shit you could ever imagine for us. They never ask a damn thing from us they are not willing to do themselves and more. They pull our asses out of the fire, time after time. They console us when we are down and yes, they kick our asses for us when we need it. Not once, not once has Ghost ever asked any of us to help him. He takes our hurt, our pain to himself and keeps his own to himself. She is just like him.

"I will die for both of them."

Carol sat down and almost finished the bottle of vodka she had in her hand.

"Everyone here will, guys," PG said. Today, except for her dark clothing, she appeared almost normal, not her garish normal. "Her mom will do all that too, just a little differently. Was in a situation just like yours one time. Lost most of my people. Ice Queen calmed me down and did her job. She was firing that goddamn big gun of hers so fast it sounded like a semi-auto. When it was over, she had one round left. One. Out of fifty, she had one round left. Her right palm and cheek were blistered from the heat of the barrel. The stock was smoking. On the way back she apologized to all of us. Then she went and sat by herself. She didn't know we knew she was crying."

"Now you guys know why everyone loves them," Barb said quietly.

"Do you know she apologized to me," Megan said. "It wasn't your fault guys, nor hers, but she apologized for not doing her job correctly."

Megan buried her head in her hands and started to softly cry.

"Welcome, brothers and sisters," Amanda said, coming up and handing a bottle to Tony.

"Welcome to your new family. A family forged in blood. All of us have stories like the ones you have just heard. Stories about when one of the Kovacks family has helped us."

She grinned an evil grin then.

"You wanna hear mine?" She said. "Well, I'm gonna have to be a whole lot drunker, kiddies, and I never get that drunk."

Welcomed into the club, the newcomers sat down or were pulled down by someone in the large circle around the bonfire. Jabs and jokes flew. Sometimes it went silent as a memory was triggered.

Christine quietly stood. Mary saw it and Christine motioned her to follow. They found Gwen sitting at a picnic table that overlooked the shooting range. She had her head down, feet dangling, and arms braced on the table on each side of her.

"Hey Cap," Christine said as they approached. She handed Gwen a beer. "All good, Cap?"

"Ya Chris," Gwen said. "All good. You guys?"

"They're telling tall tales back there," Christine said.

"I used to think that," Gwen said. "They might be joking around, but I'm pretty sure most of that shit really happened."

Christine sat down beside Gwen and gave her a quick squeeze.

"Just like we joke about horrors we've faced," Christine said.

"I've never heard you guys talk about stuff," Mary said.

"You weren't there, Mare," Christine said. "We probably will now that you have seen it firsthand. We screw up all the time. Nobody notices, though, most times. Duncan does, but he laughs along with us. We've seen him screw up more than once, too."

"Why? Gwen?" Mary asked. "Why didn't you tell me?"

Gwen sighed.

"Like I said, I don't like White Ghost much, Mare," Gwen said. "Not the name; it's just a name. I'm saying I don't like who I am when I am White Ghost. And I wasn't lying, Mare, I really have not been formally introduced to White Ghost."

"I don't much like Ghost either," Duncan said walking up on them. He produced a flat of beer. "I have learned to live with him, though. It's not who we are Gwen, it's who we have to be from time to time."

"Just like Spooky there, or you, Viper," Duncan said. "What, you didn't think you had nicknames? Ask Viper how she got hers and why she is a Ghost Team and not a private in a ground pounder unit. Only my friends or my enemies call me Ghost. The same with White Ghost. The right to know that name or to call us that has to be earned."

Then, like his name, he was gone.

"Gwen and her dad did a lot of shit on my planet," Christine said. "On their own. I was the first one they picked up."

"Ya, stuck-up know-it-all spoiled brat you were," Gwen said. Christine hit her on the shoulder.

"Just like another whiney bubble-headed blonde I knew in school," Mary said.

"I was not!" Gwen said.

"Like hell you weren't," Mary replied. Mockingly, she continued, "I'm only going to do my five-year minimum, then become a hairdresser. Why do we all have to be in the army anyway? My parents are such assholes."

"Well, you got me there," Gwen said. "But you were coming right along with me. Look at us dummies now, eh?"

The three of them returned to the old-timers' fire with their arms around each other.

"Hey!" Gwen yelled out. "Some asshole done drank my beer!"

And all was good in everyone's world then.

Also by R.P. Wollbaum

Baren und Adler
Baren und Adler

Bears and Eagles
Bears and Eagles
Eagles Claw
Eagle's Talon
As Eagles Swarm
Bears Maul
Desert Eagle
Eagle's Nest

Wind Riders
Oaken
Wind Riders Zebra
White Ghost

Standalone

Cal's Quest Part 1
Joss Lynn

Watch for more at www.bearsandeagles.com.